Snowmen, Elves and Nutcrackers

Three Christmas Plays

by Bob May

Baker's Plays
7611 Sunset Blvd.
Los Angeles, CA 90042
BAKERSPLAYS.COM

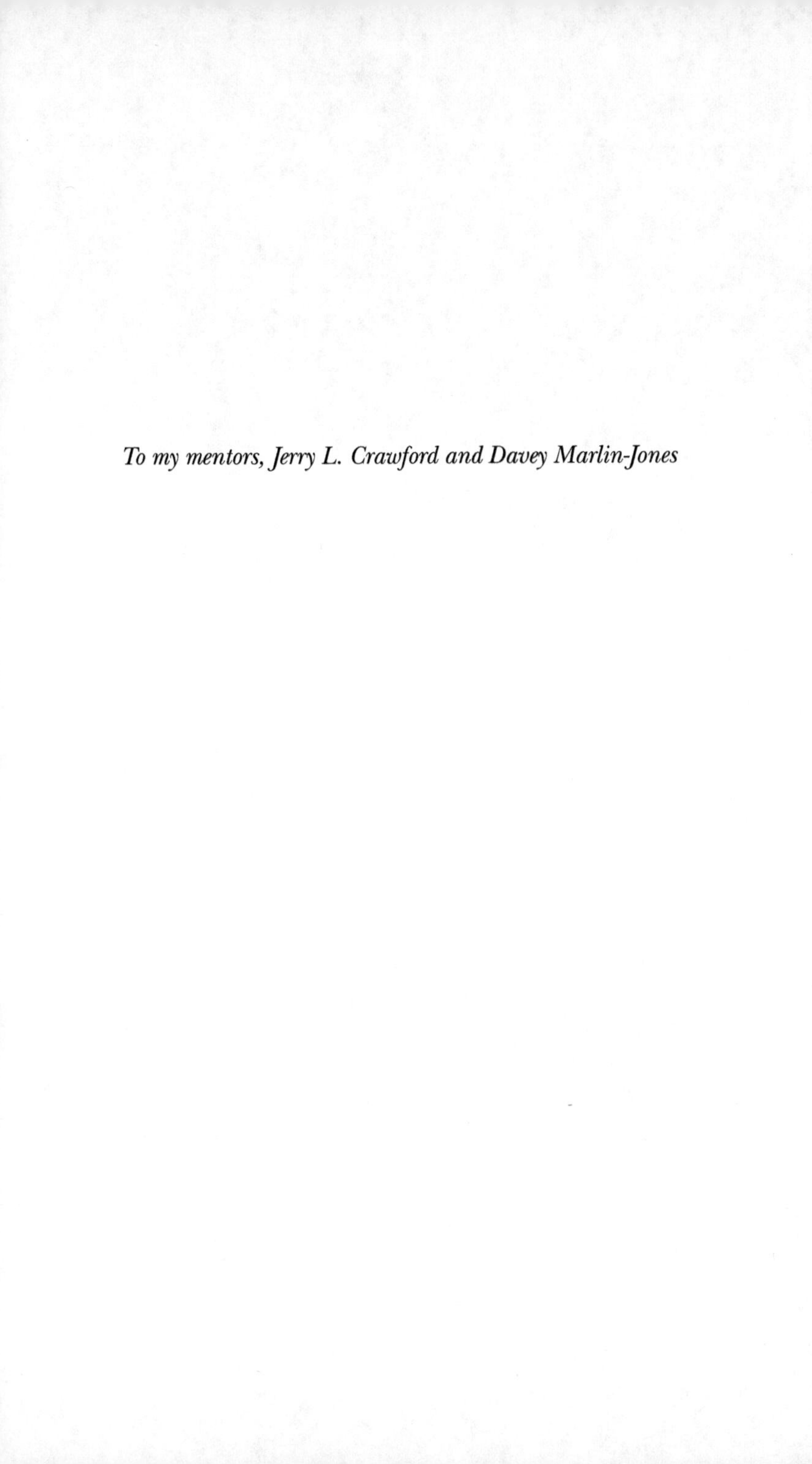

To my mentors, Jerry L. Crawford and Davey Marlin-Jones

ELSON, THE FIRST CHRISTMAS ELF

A Play in One Act

CAST OF CHARACTERS

(In Speaking Order)

SANTA CLAUS

MRS. CLAUS

ELLIOT

ELSON

EFFIE

ELERD

ELDA (A GIRL)

EZAR

EWA

ELDER ELF

ELF GRANDE

A FAIRY

ELMER

ELOWEZE

EUGENE OR EUNICE

PUCK

The premiere of **ELSON, *THE CHRISTMAS ELF*** was presented by Children's Theatre To Go, Inc. at the at Reynolds Performance Hall in Conway, Arkansas, on December 13, 2007, under the direction of Bob May, with set design by Joe Meils and costume design by Nikki Webster. The cast was as follows:

SANTA CLAUS . . . . Brent Wood

MRS. CLAUS . . . . Llewellyn Webster

ELLIOT . . . . Ben A. Scheuter

ELSON . . . . Jacob Webb

EFFIE . . . . Jace Motley

ELERD . . . . Kevin Glover

ELDA . . . . Mollie Mae Henager

EZAR . . . . Wendy Miers

EWA . . . . Jeni Fuller

ELDER ELF . . . . Katie Oslica

ELF GRANDE . . . . Dahren White

A FAIRY . . . . Maddie Moss

ELMER . . . . Ian Turpin

ELOWEZE . . . . Caitlin Straw

EUNICE . . . . Katie Barber

PUCK . . . . Abby Shourd

SYNOPSIS OF SCENES

SCENE ONE: Santa's home, North Pole. The day after Christmas.

SCENE TWO: Deep in the Elfin Forest. Afternoon. February.

SCENE THREE: Santa's home, North Pole. February.

SCENE FOUR: The office of the Elder Elf. Later that afternoon.

SCENE FIVE: Santa's home, North Pole. Late afternoon.

SCENE SIX: Elf Grande's home. Early evening and various scenes from the past.

SCENE SEVEN: Outside Elliot's home. Not long after.

SCENE EIGHT: Santa's home, North Pole. Not long after.

SCENE NINE: Elf Grande's home. Not long after.

SCENE TEN: Santa's home, North Pole. Midnight.

SCENE ELEVEN: Elf Grande's home. Midnight.

SCENE ELEVEN-B: Control central. April 1. Fools Day.

SCENE TWELVE: The office of the Elder Elf. Just after midnight. April 1st.

SCENE THIRTEEN: Santa's home, North Pole. The next morning.

SCENE FOURTEEN: Elf Grande's home. The nest morning.

SCENE FIFTEEN: Control Central and the Railway Station. July 4th.

SCENE SIXTEEN: Santa's home, North Pole. July 4th.

SCENE SEVENTEEN: The middle of the nowhere. Just after Thanksgiving.

SCENE EIGHTEEN: Santa's home, North Pole. Christmas Eve.

SCENE NINETEEN: Santa's home, North Pole. The day after Christmas.

SET DEMANDS

The show can be done very simply by dividing the stage into three areas: up center-stage, downstage right, and downstage left. Lighting can separate the areas. There can be cross over.

Up center is the Santa area. In this area are two stools and a workbench with snow scene painted on the front of it,

Downstage right and downstage left become the other locales needed. All can be done with these minimal set pieces.

There is a forest drop which flies in and out in front of the Santa area. This is an optional drop.

Other set pieces include six tree stumps, one desk-like piece of furniture, one machine panel, and one "Rail Way Station" sign.

The use of the objects is noted in the script stage directions.

SCENE ONE

(AT RISE: **MRS. CLAUS** *is discovered in the toy workshop at their North Pole home.* **SANTA** *enters.)*

SANTA. *(Not very enthusiastically.)* Ho, ho, ho.

MRS. CLAUS. Welcome home, my dear. I bet you are exhausted.

(She kisses his cheek.)

SANTA. Yes, delivering all the toys on Christmas is always a very long and tiring undertaking.

MRS. CLAUS. How was the flight?

SANTA. The reindeer were spectacular. No problems. And the weather was on our side too; Rudolph never had to turn his shiny red nose on.

MRS. CLAUS. I do worry about you when the weather is bad. Would you like me to fix you something to eat?

SANTA. Oh, my goodness, no. I've eaten enough cookies and drank enough milk to last me for quite awhile. No, Mrs. Claus, I just want to get some sleep.

MRS. CLAUS. I bet you do. We must start building toys for next Christmas as soon as you wake up.

SANTA. Yes, I know, this job is never ending.

MRS. CLAUS. Is my jolly husband complaining?

SANTA. Heavens no. I love making the toys that make the good children of the world happy just as much as you do.

MRS. CLAUS. But?

SANTA. But as the population of the world grows, so does our job. You and I just can't keep up with the demand.

MRS. CLAUS. It sounds to me like you're complaining.

SANTA. So, maybe I am complaining a little. No, a lot! I don't know how much longer we can keep this up? Maybe we should just call it quits?

MRS. CLAUS. Call it quits? What would the world be without

Santa Claus at Christmas? You won't think that way after a good night's sleep.

SANTA. When was the last time either of us got a good night's sleep?

MRS. CLAUS. Maybe we just need some helpers in the toy workshop.

SANTA. You might be right, but who are we going to get that would want to live at the top of the world in all this cold and snow?

MRS. CLAUS. People who live in Alaska or Canada are use to this kind of climate. Maybe we can recruit some of them?

SANTA. They must be toy makers.

MRS. CLAUS. I've heard Minnesotans love to play games and are very winter-tough.

SANTA. You know, I really don't think humans are who we're looking for. They're not cut out for the kind of work we do. If we're going to recruit some help, I think we need some fantasy figures

MRS. CLAUS. You mean like dwarfs or trolls?

SANTA. Maybe dwarfs, but definitely not any trolls. Let me get some sleep and dream on it.

MRS. CLAUS. I'm sorry, yes my dear, you do need to get some sleep. I'll feed the reindeer.

SANTA. They're probably not hungry. They ate more than their share of carrots tonight.

MRS. CLAUS. Christmas sure is fattening for everyone. Look at you and how much weight you've put on.

SANTA. If I retire, I'll have plenty of time to work it off.

MRS. CLAUS. I'm not worried. I'll love you no matter what you look like.

(She embraces **SANTA.***)*

Sleep well.

SANTA. Good night, my love.

(He kisses **MRS. CLAUS.***)*

MRS. CLAUS. What about elves?

SANTA. What?

(He yawns.)

MRS. CLAUS. Elves, as some toy workshop helpers.

SANTA. Elves might work. Or even fairies.

MRS. CLAUS. I'll get the word out to all dwarfs, elves, and fairies that we need helpers here at the North Pole.

SANTA. You go ahead and do that.

(He yawns.)

MRS. CLAUS. The reindeer can fly to the seven corners of the world spreading the word...that we need help.

SANTA. Let them get some sleep first.

MRS. CLAUS. Of course, I will. Meanwhile, I'll get the shop ready for work. Good night.

SANTA. You're a wonderful wife. Thank you and good night.

MRS. CLAUS. Hey, Santa?

SANTA. Yes, Mrs. Claus.

MRS. CLAUS. Please don't quit.

(The LIGHTS fade to black.)

SCENE TWO

*(**AT RISE:** **ELSON** and **ELLIOT** are discovered deep in the Elfin forest. **ELSON** is writing notes on a piece of paper. Two tree stumps downstage right.)*

ELLIOT. Elson, the work whistle ending our day is about to sound; are you almost finished?

ELSON. If you'd stop talking to me, I would be. Shhh!

(Pause.)

ELLIOT. You know…you're lucky I'm your best friend.

ELSON. You're not just my best friend; you're my blood brother.

ELLIOT. Yeah, only a blood brother would put up with the way you've been acting since you talked to that flying reindeer.

ELSON. I know, Elliot, buddy. Thanks. It wasn't just any flying reindeer. It was Rudolph.

ELLIOT. The red-nosed Reindeer?

ELSON. Yes, and these notes are the final part my presentation to the Elder Elf. Shhh.

(Pause.)

ELLIOT. And your meeting with the Elder Elf is as soon we get off work?

ELSON. Please.

(Pause as he wraps things up.)

Okay, there…I'm finished.

ELLIOT. I'm sorry, I'm just nervous for you. Do you really think the Elder Elf is going to give you his blessing to go to the North Pole?

ELSON. Why not? Elves are magical and hard working. Santa Claus needs help and I want to be the first elf there to help him. I can't plant trees for the rest of my life.

ELLIOT. But that's what elves do.

ELSON. There has to be more to life than deciding whether I should plant an oak, hickory, or pine tree. He has to give us his blessing.

ELLIOT. Us? I don't want to go with you.

ELSON. Why not? I need a companion. You know the Elfin lore.

ELLIOT. I have my own dreams.

ELSON. I know…the elf-ball league. Yes, your ticket out is your height. Mine is…I'm good at making things. Don't you like the way I put rubber balls in the heals of your shoes?

ELLIOT. They do make me jump higher.

ELSON. And what about the new elf-ball games I programed into your elf-toy.

ELLIOT. Nerdy Elson sure is good at making things, especially electronics. You know, some think Santa Claus is a myth.

ELSON. You don't believe that.

ELLIOT. I believe there's a reason no elf has ever left this colony.

ELSON. Oh yes, the Evil Elfin Spirit, Excy.

ELLIOT. You know if you leave the Evil Elfin Spirit will devour you.

ELSON. Devour you? What does that mean? Talk about myths. Have you ever seen Excy?

ELLIOT. No. But, I've never seen Santa Claus either.

ELSON. I think the Evil Elfin Spirit is a myth the Elder Elf uses to keep all us worker elves under control. The Elder Elf needs to join the real world.

ELLIOT. What if Excy's not a myth?

ELSON. If we get the Elder's blessing we won't have to worry about Excy.

ELLIOT. Are you sure?

>   (*With a LIGHT flash and a SOUND thunder clap* **EFFIE** *enters disguised as the Evil Elfin Spirit Excy.*)

EFFIE. WHAT IS GOING ON HERE?

> (**ELLIOT** *screams.*)

ELSON. Who are you? And what do you want?

EFFIE. You don't recognize me?

ELSON. No.

EFFIE. It is I...the Evil Elfin Spirit Excy.

> (*SOUND: Thunderclap.*)

ELLIOT. I told you so.

EFFIE. How dare you think you can leave this colony. Aren't you happy with your worker elf existence?

ELLIOT. Yes sir, it was Elson's idea to leave.

EFFIE. Worker elves are not supposed to question their existence.

> (*SOUND: Thunderclap.*)

> They have done the same thing for thousands of years.

> (*SOUND: Thunderclap.*)

ELSON. I want to break that tradition.

EFFIE. To work for this Santa Claus?

ELSON. Yes, Santa Claus brings happiness to all the children around the world. And he's asking for our help.

EFFIE. Silence.

> (*SOUND: Thunderclap.*)

> You know the punishment for any elf that leaves the colony?

ELLIOT. Please don't devour us...him. He hasn't left the colony yet, and I never planned to.

EFFIE. Get on your knees before me.

ELSON. What gives you the right to stop me?

ELLIOT. Elson, watch your mouth.

EFFIE. Do you dare question the Elfin Spirit Excy?

ELSON. Yes.

ELLIOT. No.

(He falls to his knees.)

EFFIE. I said get on your knees.

(SOUND: Another thunderclap.)

ELLIOT. Come on, Elson. Get on your knees.

*(He pulls **ELSON** to his knees too.)*

EFFIE. That's how it should be. The two of you on your knees before me.

(He begins to laugh.)

ELSON. What are you laughing at? This isn't humorous.

EFFIE. *(Laughing.)* Sure it is. Hey, losers, it's me.

(He reveals himself, laughing.)

Ha, ha, I sure had you both fooled.

(Shouts offstage.)

Come on in, my friends.

*(**ELERD** and **ELDA** enter laughing. They carry a thunder sheet made of a strip of tin.)*

EFFIE *(Continued.)* *(In his Excy voice.)* It is I...the evil Elfin Spirit Excy.

*(**ELERD** and **ELDA** shake the thunder sheet. **EFFIE**, **ELERD**, and **ELDA** laugh. **ELSON** starts for **EFFIE**.)*

ELSON. Ohhh...

*(**ELLIOT** holds **ELSON** back.)*

ELLIOT. Hold on, Elson. Effie, you are so jealous.

EFFIE. Jealous of what? Nerdy Elson and his Santa Claus elf-helper dreams?

ELERD & ELDA. Yeah.

ELLIOT. Effie, as an elf-orphan, like Elson, you should support one another.

ELSON. He's always been envious that I have my Elf Grande.

EFFIE. Envious? I'm the son of the Elder Elf.

ELERD & ELDA. Yeah.

ELSON. The adopted son of the Elder Elf. He's not your real family.

ELLIOT. That's right, Elf Grande is blood family to Elson.

EFFIE. What do you know, Elliot, about family? Being adopted is better than having the loser parents…that you have.

ELERD & ELDA. Yeah.

> (*SOUND: The work whistle ending the night's work goes off.*)

EFFIE. The work whistle just sounded. It's time to go home.

ELERD & ELDA. Yeah.

EFFIE. Hey Elerd…

ELERD. Yeah?

EFFIE. …and Elda…

ELDA. Yeah?

EFFIE. …say "goodbye and good luck" to the loser and the dreamer.

ELERD & ELDA. Yeah.

ELSON. Please get out of our way.

> (**EFFIE, ELERD,** *and* **ELDA** *start mocking* **ELSON** *and* **ELLIOT.**)

EFFIE. Are we blocking his way?

ELERD & ELDA. No.

> (**EFFIE, ELERD,** *and* **ELDA** *laugh. A beam of LIGHT flashes before them.*)

ELLIOT. What was that?

> (**EFFIE, ELERD,** *and* **ELDA** *continue to bully and laugh.* **EZAR** *enters. His commanding voice stops the ruckus.*)

EZAR. What is going on here?

EFFIE. What's it to you?

ELERD & ELDA. Yeah.

EFFIE. And who are you?

ELERD & ELDA. Yeah.

EZAR. To answer both your questions in reverse order. I guess I'm sort of a peacekeeper and I just don't like to see this sort of bullying going on. I suggest the three of you back off and get out of here.

EFFIE. Come on, Elerd and Elda, this freako-elf belongs with these two odd balls.

(**EFFIE, ELERD**, *and* **ELDA** *start to exit.*)

Oh and, Elson, say "hi," to my daddy at your big blessing interview.

(**EFFIE. ELERD**, *and* **ELDA** *exit laughing.*)

ELSON. Thank you.

EZAR. You're welcome.

ELSON. Does the peace maker have a –

EZAR. A name? Yes it's —

ELSON. Ezar.

EZAR. That is correct.

ELLIOT. Are the two of you reading each other's minds?

EZAR. It seems that way.

ELSON. You're not anyone I know from this colony?

EZAR. No, just racing through.

ELLIOT. Racing through at just the right time. Thanks.

ELSON. You're racing a fairy named Puck around the world.

EZAR. Right you are.

ELLIOT. How can you do this?

ELSON. Where are you from?

EZAR. Here, there, and everywhere.

ELLIOT. A traveling elf?

EZAR. Yes, but I'm actually only half elf. My mother was…

ELSON. …a giantess.

ELLIOT. You're doing it again.

EZAR. Yes, we are. In all my travels I've only met a few others that have the power.

ELLIOT. Power? Mind reading isn't normal.

ELSON. Do the Elder Elves of your colony let you travel?

EZAR. This travel ban is unique to your colony.

ELLIOT. Aren't you afraid of the evil Elfin Spirit Excy?

ELSON. Isn't the Evil Elfin Spirit Excy just a myth?

EZAR. Now I wouldn't say that. And I wouldn't call him "evil" either.

ELSON. In your travels have you ever been to the North Pole?

EZAR. My race with Puck began and will end at the North Pole.

ELSON. So Santa Claus does exist?

EZAR. He does in my world, and I hear he and Mrs. Claus are looking for some help.

ELSON. I want to be his first Elf helper.

EZAR. Then go for it. Look, I have to run. That Puck is a fast little fairy.

ELSON. You come into our lives in a flash, save us, and now you're gone.

EZAR. Maybe I'll see you at the North Pole. Meanwhile, you can contact me through elf-talk.

ELSON. Elf-talk?

EZAR. It's a long distance version of what our minds have already been doing. Bye now.

(He exits.)

ELLIOT. Elf-talk? How long have you known you could do it? Can you read my thoughts?

ELSON. Forget it. It'll never happen again. Did you hear him? Santa Claus needs our help.

ELLIOT. Right now you need help getting to the Elder if you are going to make it on time. Do you want me to go with you?

ELSON. No, you go home. I'll stop by later.

ELLIOT. Good luck, Elson, the first Christmas Elf. It has a good ring to it.

*(**ELSON** and **ELLIOT** hug as the LIGHTS fade to black.)*

SCENE THREE

(AT RISE: SANTA *and* MRS. CLAUS *are discovered at their North Pole home. It's February. They are making toys.)*

MRS. CLAUS. It's been several days since the reindeer delivered the help wanted news to the seven corners. Dwarves, fairies, and elves all got the news. I don't understand why we haven't gotten any responses.

SANTA. I told you it takes a special type of being to do what we do. I knew it wasn't humans. Well, obviously it's not fantasy figures either.

MRS. CLAUS. Give it a little more time. Christmas is ten months away.

SANTA. This demand for video games keeps increasing. What do I know about electronics?

MRS. CLAUS. I'm learning how to make video games on line. I'll handle that part.

SANTA. The verve I once had for this entire Christmas thing is fading.

(The LIGHTS fade to black.)

SCENE FOUR

(AT RISE: **ELSON** *is discovered in the outer office of the* **ELDER ELF**. **EWA** *greets him. Two tree stumps and a deck looking object downstage left.)*

EWA. Hello.

(They fall instantly in love. They audibly breathe in as they look to the audience and then sigh as they look back to one another.)

EWA *(continued)* May you help me? I mean…may I help you?

ELSON. I'm…a…a…looking for…a…a…the…Elder Elf's office?

EWA. You found it, but the Elder Elf only sees Elves by appointment.

ELSON. I have one.

EWA. Oh, then you must be, Elson?

ELSON. Am I?

EWA. I've been expecting you.

ELSON. You have, who are you?

EWA. Ewa.

(They audibly breathe in as they look to the audience and then sigh as they look back to one another.)

EWA *(continue)* I mean the Elder Elf has been expecting you. Please have a seat. I'll tell the Elder that you are here.

*(***EWA** *starts to exit, stops, and forgets where she is going.)*

Oh goodness, where am I going?

ELSON. It doesn't matter.

EWA. Oh, yes. Appointment! I'll be right back. I think it is wonderful that you want to help Santa Claus.

(They audibly breathe in as they look to the audience and then sigh as they look back to one another. **EWA** *exits.)*

ELSON. Oh, rest my beating heart.

*(The **ELDER ELF** and **EWA** enter. The **ELDER ELF** greets **ELSON** with a big warm hug.)*

ELDER. Elson, it's good to see you.

ELSON. Thank you, Elder.

ELDER. Your Elf Grande and I go back along way. What's on your mind? Sit down.

ELSON. After you, sir.

*(They both sit. **EWA** stands in the background. **ELSON** pulls out his notes.)*

First, let me say thank you for seeing me. It's an honor to be here before you.

ELDER. That's not what you've said to your coworkers about me.

*(**ELSON** doesn't know what to say.)*

ELSON. Ah, excuse me?

ELDER. Just this morning didn't you said to Elliot, "the Elder Elf needs to join the real world."

ELSON. Well, I…

ELDER. I am in the real world. It seems like you are the one in the fantasy. Elves are born to work for mankind.

ELSON. And I still want to do that. Only instead of helping mankind by planting trees, I want to help Santa Claus by building toys for children.

ELDER. What about the Elfin Spirit Excy?

ELSON. If you give me your blessing, I won't have to worry about him.

ELDER. Don't you mean, worry about the myth? What makes you better than any other worker elf in this colony?

ELSON. I never said I was better than anyone.

ELDER. Who is going to finance this expedition? Are you going to go by yourself?

ELSON. Well I…

ELDER. Blessing denied.

ELSON. What?

ELDER. I couldn't live with myself if I let you leave the safety of the colony.

(**ELSON** *runs from the office.*)

EWA. Elson.

(*She runs after him as the LIGHTS fade to black.*)

SCENE FIVE

(AT RISE: **SANTA** *and* **MRS. CLAUS** *are discovered at their North Pole home. They are still making toys.)*

MRS. CLAUS. Did you get the mail yet?

SANTA. What for? You know the beginning of the year is always a very slow time for children to send Christmas letters.

MRS. CLAUS. I was hoping maybe we get a resume or two in the mail of some helpers.

SANTA. It's looking like no one is interested in helping us.

(The LIGHTS fade to black.)

SCENE SIX

(AT RISE: **ELF GRANDE** *is discovered in his abode, reading a newspaper.* **ELSON** *enters. Four tree stumps arranged as sofa, coffee table, and chair DR.)*

ELF GRANDE. Where have you been? The work whistle sounded hours ago. Putting in a little overtime?

ELSON. No, Elliot and I were talking. Time just got away from us.

ELF GRANDE. I take it that your meeting with the Elder Elf didn't go too well.

ELSON. I'm sorry I embarrassed you.

ELF GRANDE. You know this urge to do something different with your life runs in the family. I wanted to explore, and so did your mom and dad.

ELSON. Why haven't you ever told me this?

ELF GRANDE. I've been waiting to see if you felt the same way. Now that I know you do…I'll support your expedition to the North Pole.

ELSON. What? You would go against the Elder Elf?

ELF GRANDE. Yes, it's time we stopped hiding our past. You know, once upon a time even the Elder felt just like you.

ELSON. I don't think the Elder and I have anything in common.

ELF GRANDE. Yes, as a youth he longed to travel.

(The **ELDER** *– looking younger – and a* **FAIRY** *are discovered in a LIGHT special downstage left with two tree stumps.)*

ELDER. I have been everywhere in the Elfin Wood. I want to go farther.

FAIRY. The key to going anywhere farther is in the city.

ELDER. Really? Please show me.

FAIRY. I'll lead you to the edge of the Elfin Wood, but after that you are on your own.

ELF GRANDE. And that's just what the fairy did.

ELDER. Which way now?

FAIRY. See that light in the distance?

ELDER. The city is full of lights.

FAIRY. The one with the magical glow by the railway station.

ELDER. I see it.

FAIRY. You can catch a ride to where you want to go there on the Freedom Express.

ELDER. Won't you please come with me?

FAIRY. The city is no place for a fairy or an elf. Good-bye and good luck.

(She exits.)

ELF GRANDE. The Elder stared at the magical glow for hours and then decided to go on by himself.

ELSON. Was he successful?

ELF GRANDE. Working his way through the Elfin Wood and maneuvering in the city was as different as night and day.

*(The **ELDER** moves down center-stage. SOUND: Lots of car noises, honking of horns, city life. The **ELDER** runs downstage left to upstage left to center-stage as **GRANDE** says the next line.)*

ELF GRANDE *(continued)* So he ran back to the colony to enlist the help of some others.

ELDER. Grande, I need your help.

*(**ELF GRANDE** moves to the **ELDER**.)*

ELF GRANDE. *(To **ELDER**.)* Help…

ELDER. I found a way out of the Elfin Wood, but it's in the city. I tried to get there, but the city almost devoured me.

*(**ELF GRANDE** puts his arm around the **ELDER** and they move downstage right.)*

ELF GRANDE. You know it's Elfin lore that you never travel alone; you must always go with two companions. And even then the Elfin Spirit Excy might not let you go anywhere.

ELDER. Will you come with me?

ELF GRANDE. I'll be one of your two…just as I know you'd be one of my two.

ELSON. Who was the other one?

ELF GRANDE. Elmer and Eloweze.

(**ELMER** *and* **ELOWEZE** *enter.*)

ELMER. Your search for explorer companions is over.

ELSON. Effie's mama and papa, but you only needed one more.

ELOWEZE. Elmer doesn't go anywhere without me. Tell Grande to stay behind.

ELDER. I guess this adventure will have three companions. Let's go.

ELSON. Obviously you didn't make it to the Freedom Express.

(**GRANDE** *moves to* **ELSON** *downstage right.*)

ELF GRANDE. No, we didn't even make it out of the Elfin Wood. We ran into a terrible February winter storm. The wind was howling. The temperature dropped like a heavy weight. Snow fell upon us in blankets.

(*A storm hits the four elves, complete with SOUND and LIGHTS.* **GRANDE** *moves to them downstage left.*)

ELF GRANDE (*continued*) Maybe we should turn back? We need to find some shelter.

ELMER. No, once we get to the city, we can seek shelter.

ELOWEZE. Yes, let's keep going; what's a little snow to an Elf?

(*A beam of LIGHT flashes in front of them.*)

ELDER. What was that?

ELMER. It's Excy showing us the way. Come on.

ELF GRANDE. I really think we should seek shelter and stay put until this storm is over.

ELOWEZE. You can stay put if you want.

ELMER. Come on, Elder, let's go.

ELDER. I think I'll stay with Grande.

ELOWEZE. Forget them, Elmer. We'll be famous when we are the first to find the Freedom Express.

(ELMER *and* ELOWEZE *exit.* ELF GRANDE *walks to* ELSON. *LIGHTS fade on the other scene.*)

ELF GRANDE. And that's when Effie's parents were lost.

ELSON. So the story of them working through a winter storm trying to protect trees is not true?

ELF GRANDE. No. The Elder swore the Elfin Spirit Excy got them because we had four in our party and not three.

ELSON. What do you think?

ELF GRANDE. I don't know. There was that flash of light that passed before us right before they left.

ELSON. How did you and the Elder survive?

ELF GRANDE. We huddled together for warmth.

(ELF GRANDE *moves back to the* ELDER.)

ELF GRANDE *(con't)* Hold me, my friend.

(ELF GRANDE *huddles next to the* ELDER.)

ELDER. We're not going to make it.

ELF GRANDE. We'll be fine.

(*SOUND: the wind howls. The snow falls.* EZAR *enter.*)

EZAR. You look like you need some help.

ELSON. That's Ezar, he's the elf that helped me today.

EZAR. Come, my little elves, I'll get you back to your colony.

(EZAR *helps* ELDER *and* ELF GRANDE *up.* GRANDE *walks to* ELSON *as the LIGHTS fade on the others.*)

ELSON. Ezar saved you?

ELF GRANGE. He didn't tell us his name. I'm not sure he was even there. We were delirious, and some how we made it home.

ELSON. Ezar is real. I met him.

ELF GRANGE. In any case…I think the Elder felt very guilty

about losing Effie's parents and that's why he adopted him.

(**ELDER** *enters in LIGHT special downstage left.*)

ELDER. We will never talk of this failed expedition.

(**GRANDE** *looks to* **ELDER.**)

ELF GRANDE. Why?

ELDER. Leaving the colony is just too dangerous. We don't need to lose any more elfin lives to the Evil Spirit.

ELF GRANDE. No Evil Spirit did anything. Elmer and Eloweze were lost in the winter storm.

ELDER. As Elder, I forbid any travel.

(*The LIGHTS fade on the* **ELDER.**)

ELF GRANDE. That's when the rivalry between the Elder and me began. Do you have a team?

ELSON. I don't need anyone.

ELF GRANDE. You must believe the Elfin lore. Do you have two friends that want to go with you?

ELSON. Effie has turned everyone against me.

ELF GRANDE. What about Elliot?

(**ELSON** *runs from the house as the LIGHTS fade to black.*)

SCENE SEVEN

(AT RISE: **ELSON** *is discovered at the front door of* **ELLIOT***'s home downstage left.)*

ELSON. Elliot. ELLIOT! Are you home?

*(***ELLIOT*** enters.)*

ELLIOT. I'm here, I'm here. I heard what the Elder Elf said. I'm sorry.

ELSON. You did. Who told you?

ELLIOT. Well a…

ELSON. It doesn't matter. My Elf Grande will support my going to the North Pole. But I need two companions. It's Elfin lore. Please be one of them.

ELLIOT. But what about my elf-ball career?

ELSON. You can always do that later. Come on, Blood Brother.

*(***EFFIE*** enters with a* **SANTA** *hat on.* **ELERD** *and* **ELDA** *enter behind him wearing reindeer antlers.)*

EFFIE. Ho, ho, ho. Merry Christmas. Please Elliot, you must join Elson's stupid adventure.

ELERD & ELDA. Yeah.

ELSON. Effie.

EFFIE. The children of the world need him at the North Pole.

ELERD & ELDA. Yeah.

ELSON. Why do you make fun of me because I want to help Santa Claus?

EFFIE. You only have one friend in this colony, and he's about to say, "no" to your expedition.

ELERD & ELDA. Yeah.

ELLIOT. You're wrong, Effie, I say, "yes." I'll go with you Elson.

EFFIE. Ha!!! Good luck finding another elf in the colony that will support you.

ELERD & ELDA. Yeah.

    (**EFFIE, ELERD,** *and* **ELDA** *exit laughing.*)

ELSON. Thanks, Elliot. You better tell your parents of your plan.

ELLIOT. My parents won't even know I'm gone.

ELSON. At least leave them a note.

ELLIOT. I'll call them from your Grande's house.

    (*The LIGHTS fade to black.*)

SCENE EIGHT

(AT RISE: **SANTA** *and* **MRS. CLAUS** *are discovered at their North Pole home. They are still making toys.)*

SANTA. Do you ever think about having friends?

MRS. CLAUS. Aren't you my friend?

SANTA. Other than me.

MRS. CLAUS. The reindeer are my friends.

SANTA. When was the last time you were in Florida?

MRS. CLAUS. My dear, I've never been to Florida.

SANTA. Let's go now.

MRS. CLAUS. We can't go now. We have too many toys to make.

SANTA. Come on, I can harness up the reindeer, and we can fly to Florida, and go to Disney World.

MRS. CLAUS. Stop talking nonsense.

SANTA. It's important to have friends in time of need.

(The LIGHTS fade to black.)

SCENE NINE

(AT RISE: **ELSON**, **ELLIOT**, *and* **ELF GRANDE** *are discovered in* **GRANDE***'s home downstage right.)*

ELF GRANDE. Elliot is only one companion.

ELSON. I know, but he's my only friend.

ELF GRANDE. You need another companion.

ELSON. You can be the third.

ELF GRANDE. Oh, I wish I could, the traveling urge has never left me, but I'm too old.

ELLIOT. Then who can do it?

ELSON. Ezar.

ELF GRANDE. Don't be silly. Even if Ezar is real; how could you ever find him?

ELSON. Elf-talk.

ELF GRANDE. Where did you hear about elf-talk?

ELSON. Ezar told me I could contact him that way.

ELLIOT. Why do you sound so concerned?

ELF GRANDE. Elf-talk was used by the ancient elves. It's a mind reading message that is sent by harnessing the wind. Not many Elves could do it.

ELLIOT. You and Ezar were doing some kind of mind reading.

ELSON. So how do I do this elf-talk?

ELF GRANDE. You must hold in your right hand an acorn from an oak tree over fifty years old; and in your left, a green pine cone from a young jack pine tree.

ELSON. Neither of us were holding those items when Ezar and I did the mind talking this morning.

ELF GRANDE. Elf-talk is used when two mind talkers are not together. It's a long distance communication.

ELLIOT. Let's go outside and find what we need.

ELF GRANDE. I have what we need right here.

(**ELF GRANDE** *gets the acorn and pinecone.)*

ELSON. Why do you have these things?

ELF GRANDE. There was a time when I tried it. So did your parents.

ELSON. Were you successful?

ELF GRANDE. It only works for a chosen few.

(He gives the acorn and pinecone to **ELSON.***)*

ELSON. What now?

ELF GRANGE. You ask the Elfin Spirit Excy to carry your message on the wind to the person you wish to contact.

ELSON. Great Spirit Excy, please sent a message for me.

(SOUND: The wind begins to howl.)

ELLIOT. I don't think this is such a good idea.

ELF GRANDE. Continue.

ELSON. Please send my message to Ezar...ask him...if he would join my team to travel to the North Pole?

(SOUND: The wind screams. **ELSON** *is knocked over. The wind SOUND stops.)*

ELLIOT. Are you alright?

ELSON. I'm fine. When will we get an answer?

ELF GRANDE. It's supposed to work instantaneously. Did you receive any messages?

ELSON. Maybe. The wind was so loud. I'm not sure.

ELLIOT. Well, so much for elf-talk.

ELSON. Elliot and I can go just go on this expedition. We don't need a third elf.

ELF GRANDE. I insist that there are three of you.

ELSON. And by doing so you have put an end to me ever helping Santa Claus.

*(***EWA** *knocks on the door and enters.)*

EWA. I want to help Santa Claus too, and I'd like to join your expedition to the North Pole.

ELSON. Ewa.

EWA. Elson.

(They both sigh and do a take to the audience.)

ELF GRANDE. Hello, Ewa.

ELLIOT. Who's Ewa?

ELSON. How do you know Ewa?

ELF GRANDE. I organized a second expedition to try to get to the Freedom Express.

EWA. My father and your parents, Elson, joined forces and attempted to make the journey the Elder's party failed to do.

(**ELDER ELF** *appears in a LIGHT special downstage left.*)

ELDER. So, Grande, you have gone against my wishes and attempted to find the Freedom Express?

(**GRANDE** *turns to the* **ELDER.**)

ELF GRANDE. We should be able to leave this colony if we want.

ELDER. And look what happens when we do.

(*The LIGHTS fade on the* **ELDER.**)

ELSON. So my parents didn't die protesting the extinction of the forest for the building of another Wal-Mart?

ELF GRANDE. That was the Elder's way of covering up another failed expedition.

ELSON. So what really happen?

ELF GRANDE. No one knows for sure. A distorted elf-talk was picked up...

EWA. (*She picks up the acorn and pinecone on the table.*) Are you trying to see if Elf-talk really works?

ELSON. Who sent it? So my parents did know elf-talk?

ELF GRANDE. Both of them?

ELSON. Who received it?

ELF GRANDE. It happened so long ago it doesn't matter. Elf talk seems to have died along with your parents.

ELSON. What did the message say?

ELF GRANDE. It contained something about seeing a flash of light at the railway platform. And we never heard from them again.

ELLIOT. But there were only three of them. It couldn't have been Excy.

ELF GRANDE. Who said anything about Excy? It's late. Let's all get some sleep. Elliot, you can sleep in Elson's room. Ewa, you get the guest room. There's something I have to share with the three of you before you leave.

ELSON. What?

ELF GRANDE. It can wait until morning.

(The LIGHTS fade to black.)

SCENE TEN

(AT RISE: **SANTA** *and* **MRS. CLAUS** *are discovered at their North Pole home. They are still making toys.)*

MRS. CLAUS. Maybe we should get some sleep?

SANTA. I can't believe you're suggesting sleep with all the toys we have to make.

(SOUND: The clock begins to strike twelve.)

MRS. CLAUS. It's midnight.

SANTA. Do me a favor and let me sleep-in in the morning.

MRS. CLAUS. If that's what you want to do.

(The LIGHTS fade to black.)

SCENE ELEVEN

(The clock continues to strike into the next scene. **AT RISE:** *The scene is* **GRANDE**'s *home DR. The stage is empty. The clock continues to toll as* **EWA** *sneaks into the room. She moves to the table and picks up the acorn and pinecone.)*

EWA. *(In a whisper.)* Oh, Great Spirit Excy…

(SOUND: The wind begins to howl.)

Send my message to…

*(***ELF GRANDE*** enters.)*

ELF GRANDE. Can't you sleep, Ewa?

(The wind SOUND stops.)

EWA. Oh! You startled me.

ELF GRANDE. What are you doing?

EWA. Yes, I couldn't sleep.

ELF GRANDE. And these?

(As he points to the acorn and pinecone.)

EWA. Oh? And I've always wanted to try Elf-talk.

ELF GRANDE. Who would you elf-talk with?

EWA. No one.

ELF GRANDE. Did it work?

EWA. Of course not…not with me!

*(***EWA*** laughs. **ELSON** and **ELLIOT** enter.)*

ELSON. It seems no one can sleep.

ELF GRANDE. And sleep is one thing you will need before you begin this quest.

ELSON. Sleep is not going to happen, Grande, please show us what you were going to show us in the morning.

ELF GRANDE. Alright.

(He pulls a hand held device from his pocket.)

This is a locale jumper.

ELSON. A what?

ELF GRANDE. A location jumper. It can be used to travel from one place to another instantly.

ELLIOT. Elf-talk and locale jumping. This is all sounding like a science fiction novel.

ELSON. That locale jumper is what you were saving for the morning?

ELF GRANDE. Only part of it. Let's use the locale jumper, and I'll show you what I mean. Hold hands. Come on Elliot.

(All do so.)

Locale jumper… take us to Elf Control Central.

(The LIGHTS flash as they all spin to downstage left into a room full of scientific equipment. SOUND accompanies this. LIGHTS on all the equipment flash. **ELSON,** **ELLIOT,** *and* **EWA** *are in awe.)*

SCENE ELEVEN – B

ELF GRANDE *(Continued.)* Welcome to Control Central. I have been preparing for this moment since your parents were lost.

*(***EUGENE*** enters.)*

EUGENE. Why did you used the locale jumper to get here?

ELF GRANDE. This is Eugene, my assistant. I wanted to show them how it worked.

EUGENE. You know we lose days every time it is used.

(Frantically typing on a keyboard.)

By using it we jumped a head…

(A discovery.)

…a month and a half. The date is now April first.

ELLIOT. Ha, ha, April fools.

EUGENE. Do I look like I'm joking?

ELF GRANDE. *(To* **ELSON.***)* A small problem we are working on.

EUGENE. The locale jumper is only supposed to be used in emergencies.

(To **ELSON** *and the others as he shakes their hands.)*

Hi. I'm so excited that an expedition will finally get underway and we can use all this electronic equipment.

ELF GRANDE. With this equipment…we can track your every move and no one will ever be lost again.

EUGENE. …and the three of you will be the first elves to become Santa's helpers.

ELSON. Wow, and I thought I was good at making electronic things.

ELF GRANDE. Here. Take this radio. We can always be in communication.

(He hands **ELSON** *a radio.)*

Now that you know you'll be protected on this journey, I think we should go back home and get some sleep.

ELLIOT. Use the locale jumper to get us back.

ELF GRANDE. Another technical glitch. The locale jumper is only good for one jump per day. We're working on fixing that.

EUGENE. And remember every time you use it more months will be lost. It's just for emergencies.

EWA. Yeah, we wouldn't want to move too far into the future. That wouldn't help Santa.

ELLIOT. So are we stuck here until tomorrow?

ELF GRANDE. No, we're just directly under my house. Go out that door and take the stairs up to a good night's sleep. Eugene will show you the way.

EWA. I'm impressed.

ELLIOT. Science fiction is alive and well and living in the Elfin Wood.

(**EUGENE, ELSON, ELLIOT,** *and* **EWA** *start to exit.*)

ELF GRANDE. Elson, a word.

ELSON. You two go ahead.

(**EUGENE, ELLIOT** *and* **EWA** *exit.*)

ELF GRANDE. I wouldn't trust Ewa.

ELSON. Why do you say that?

ELF GRANDE. I caught her trying to use elf-talk with someone.

ELSON. Who?

ELF GRANDE. I don't know.

(*The LIGHTS fade to black.*)

SCENE TWELVE

(AT RISE: The **ELDER** *and* **EFFIE** *are discovered in the outer office of the* **ELDER ELF***. The only major change – two tree stumps and desk move in DL as machine panel moves out.)*

ELDER. It's past midnight, and I want to go to bed.

EFFIE. So do I.

ELDER. What have you discovered?

EFFIE. What is Elf-talk?

ELDER. Is this an April Fools joke?

EFFIE. No.

ELDER. Elf talk is just hocus-pocus. It's all in the past. It doesn't work. Tell me what you've found out.

EFFIE. Elf Grande plans to send Elson, Elliot, and your secretary off tomorrow morning.

ELDER. Are you sure Ewa is one of the three?

EFFIE. Yes, so much for loyalty.

ELDER. Where are your two loyal friends?

EFFIE. *(Shouting.)* Elerd and Elda.

(**ELERD** *and* **ELDA** *enter.)*

ELERD & ELDA. Yeah.

ELDER. Since Grande continues to challenge my wishes, the three of you must stop Elson and his companions from making it to the North Pole.

EFFIE. Won't the evil Spirit Excy do that for us?

ELERD & ELDA. Yeah.

ELDER. Just in case he doesn't. You must stop them. Better yet…why don't you be the first elf to the North Pole to help Santa.

EFFIE. Let the geek go. Besides I don't really want to be a Santa helper.

ELERD & ELDA. Yeah.

ELDER. Then I guess it's time I tell you the truth about your parents demise. It was because of Elf Grande's negligence. He left them in a blizzard as he ran home for shelter.

EFFIE. I knew there was a reason I didn't like Elson. How can we beat him?

ELDER. You need to get to the Freedom Express. It will take you to the North Pole.

EFFIE. Can't we please get some sleep first?

ELERD & ELDA. Yeah.

ELDER. No time, not if you want to get through the Elfin Wood and to the train station before Elson does. I have someone who has infiltrated their team and will keep me posted of their progress.

EFFIE. Ewa?

ELERD & ELDA. Yeah.

ELDER. Who it is…is not important. And this might help.

(He produces a small spray bottle.)

EFFIE. What's that?

ELDER. A sleeping spray.

EFFIE. Oh, please, spray it on me.

(He falls to his knees.)

ELERD & ELDA. Yeah.

(They fall to their knees.)

ELDER. It's time to avenge the perishing of your parents and show Elf Grande who the Elder Elf of this colony is.

*(**ELDER** holds the spay bottle high in one hand as the LIGHTS fade to black.)*

SCENE THIRTEEN

(AT RISE: **MRS. CLAUS** *is discovered at the North Pole home. She is drinking coffee.* **SANTA** *enters.)*

SANTA. Mrs. Claus…

MRS. CLAUS. Good morning, sleepyhead.

SANTA. …why did you let me over-sleep?

MRS. CLAUS. I only did what you asked me to do.

SANTA. Did I sleep for a month? The calendar is now reading April.

MRS. CLAUS. It seems something is happening with our time.

SANTA. The older we get the faster time passes. It just means we only have eight months before Christmas. I better go feed the reindeer.

MRS. CLAUS. I fed them.

SANTA. I hope a lot since they haven't been feed for a month.

(The LIGHTS fade to black.)

SCENE FOURTEEN

(AT RISE: **ELSON, ELLIOT, EWA,** *and* **ELF GRANDE** *are discovered in* **GRANDE**'s *house DR.)*

ELF GRANDE. Good morning, my North Pole travelers. Are you ready to enter the city and catch the Freedom Express?

ELSON. Why can't we just use the locale-jumping device to get us all the way to the North Pole?

ELF GRANDE. Another thing we are working on. It doesn't work that way. Minor jumps only. We can use it to get you to the city, but that's about as far as it works. Eugene and I are working on making it work on long distance jumping. So don't change the adjustments just yet.

ELLIOT. Aren't we going to mess up time again if we use this thing?

ELF GRANDE. I'd rather mess up time and lose a month or two than risk running into Effie and his gang.

ELSON. Go for it, Grande. Send us away.

ELF GRANDE. No, you do it. You'll be the one who might have to use it later.

ELSON. What do I say?

EWA. Oh, come on. The three of us need to hold hands.

ELF GRANDE. She's right.

(They do so.)

EWA. Now, say where you want to go?

ELF GRANDE. Just a second.

(He speaks into a radio.)

Eugene, do you have them on the radar screen?

*(**EUGENE** is discovered at Control Central.)*

EUGENE. I got 'em.

ELF GRANDE. As Ewa said, say where you what to go.

ELSON. Locale jumper…take us to the city. The railway station and the Freedom Express.

(SOUND begins.)

ELF GRANDE. Good luck.

*(The LIGHTS fade to black. **GRANDE** moves to downstage left.)*

SCENE FIFTEEN

(AT RISE: **ELF GRANDE** *and* **EUGENE** *are discovered at Control Central downstage left.)*

ELF GRANDE. *(Into a radio.)* Did you make it? Hello, Elson. Hello, Elson!

EUGENE. Is something wrong?

ELF GRANDE. I thought you said you had them on the radar screen?

EUGENE. They were there…now they are lost.

ELF GRANDE. Find them.

*(***EUGENE*** frantically works on the equipment. The LIGHTS fade up on* **ELSON**, **ELLIOT**, *and* **EWA** *at the railway station DR.* **GRANDE** *and* **EUGENE** *are still at Control Central.)*

ELSON. Hello?

ELF GRANDE. Elson!

ELSON. I can hear you.

ELF GRANDE. Me too. I hear you too.

ELSON. We made it. How much of the year did we lose?

EUGENE. *(Typing and discovering.)* The month is now…July. To be exact – July Fourth.

ELF GRANDE. That's a good sign. July Fourth is Independence Day.

ELSON. Yes, our independence from the Elf colony. And we still have five months before Christmas.

ELF GRANDE. Get on that Freedom Express, and you shouldn't have to use the locale jumper anymore.

ELSON. I think we should rename the Freedom Express… the North Pole Express.

ELF GRANDE. I like it. Now get on that train. Over and out.

ELSON. Out.

(The LIGHT fades on **GRANDE** *and* **EUGENE.***)*

EWA. It seems odd catching a North Pole Express in July.

ELSON. Which platform do we take to catch the train?

ELLIOT. Nine and three quarters.

(ELSON *and* EWA *look at him and grown.*)

ELLIOT *(Continued)* Ask someone.

EWA. Odd too…that there's no one around to ask?

ELSON. Yes, this place should be bustling with excitement especially on a holiday like the Fourth of July.

(EFFIE, ELERD, *and* ELDA *enter.*)

EFFIE. Yes it should, but I think we scared everyone off.

ELERD & ELDA. Yeah.

ELSON. Effie, what are you doing here?

EFFIE. We're going to beat you to the North Pole and become Santa's first helpers.

ELERD & ELDA. Yeah.

ELSON. This doesn't have to be a competition. We can all go together. I'm sure Santa could use all our help. Let's shake on it.

(*He holds out his hand for* EFFIE *to shake.*)

EFFIE. That would mean six elves traveling together.

ELSON. I know.

EFFIE. And Excy doesn't like more than three.

ELSON. We'll be alright.

EFFIE. And besides…it seems that all the tickets for the North Pole Express are taken.

ELSON. What?

(EFFIE *sprays the sleeping spray in* ELSON, EWA, *and* ELLIOT*'s face. The three fall down.* EFFIE *laughs as he,* ELERD, *and* ELDA *exit. SOUND: Train taking off.* PUCK *enters on the run.*)

PUCK. Here in a flash. Which way is the Freedom Express?

(*Sees the elves.*)

Hmmm. Elves in the city. And under some sort of sleeping potion spell.

(She casts a spell.)

Elves sleeping means trouble.
Wake up, on the double.

(She flicks her hands. A spell SOUND is heard. **ELSON,**
EWA, *and* **ELLIOT** *begin to stir.)*

ELSON. Oh, I'm so dizzy.

PUCK. That will go away in a bit.

*(***EWA*** *is startled. She let's out a scream.)*

ELSON. Who are you?

PUCK. A fairy in a hurry…who just woke you up.

ELLIOT. What did he spray on us?

EWA. The Elder has been working on a sleeping spray. I
guess it works.

PUCK. Primitive, but effective. Why are you elves in the
city?

ELSON. We're trying to catch a train.

PUCK. Me too. I gotta beat Ezar.

ELSON. Are you the fairy Ezar is racing around the world?

PUCK. Puck's the name. Being fast is my game.

ELSON. Who's winning?

PUCK. If I can catch the Freedom Express, I will be.

EWA. The Freedom Express has been renamed the North
Pole Express.

PUCK. The North Pole is where this race ends. Where do I
catch it?

ELSON. The train's already left the station.

PUCK. And I bet Ezar is aboard.

EWA. Why not use some fairy magic to get to the North
Pole?

PUCK. No magic allowed on this race.

ELLIOT. Hey, the train can't have gotten very far. Use the
locale jumper to get us all aboard it.

ELSON. We can't use the locale jumper, remember it can
only be used once a day and we used it to get here.

PUCK. Let me see your jumping device.

(**ELSON** *hands it to* **PUCK.**)

PUCK (*Continued.*) I think if I make these minor altera-tions...you can use this thing as often as you want.

ELSON. My Elf Grande said not to make any adjustments.

(**PUCK** *pushes some buttons on the gadget. A magic SOUND is heard.*)

PUCK. Done. It can now be used many times in one day.

ELLIOT. Come on, Elson get us to the train before it gets too far away.

EWA. We must all join hands.

(*They do so.*)

ELSON. Locale jumper...get us aboard the North Pole Express.

(*SOUND: Wind begins. LIGHTS flash and then fade to black.*)

SCENE SIXTEEN

(AT RISE: SANTA and MRS. CLAUS are discovered at their North Pole home. They are just finishing their coffee.)

MRS. CLAUS. I guess it's time to get to work.

SANTA. You know sometimes when I'm flying around the world delivering the toys, I wish that time would skip ahead and I could be done in the blink of an eye.

(The SOUND of the wind picks up, LIGHTS flash.)

MRS. CLAUS. What's happening?

SANTA. I don't know, I have a feeling we are about to lose some more months.

(The LIGHTS fade to black.)

SCENE SEVENTEEN

(AT RISE: **ELSON, ELLIOT, EWA,** *and* **PUCK** *are discovered DR in the middle of nowhere. The SOUND from previous two scenes stops.)*

EWA. I thought we used the locale jumper to get aboard the North Pole Express?

ELLIOT. We did.

EWA. So, why are we standing in the middle of nowhere? Where's the train?

PUCK. We made it. The North Pole Express is headed right towards us.

(A beam of LIGHT flashes in front of them. The loud SOUND of the train coming at them is heard.)

ELSON. We must have over jumped it.

EWA. How are we going to get on board?

ELLIOT. I think we should be asking, how are we going to get out of its way?

ELSON. Look out.

(They all jump out of the way. SOUND: The train screeches to a halt.)

ELSON *(Continued)* Why is it stopping?

PUCK. I hope so we can get on it.

*(***ELF GRANDE** *and* **EUGENE** *are discovered in a LIGHT special DL.)*

ELF GRANDE. Elson, are you there?

ELSON. *(Talks into the radio.)* Roger.

ELF GRANDE. How were you able to use the locale jumper twice in one day?

ELSON. Puck made some adjustments to it.

ELF GRANDE. That's good news.

EUGENE. The bad news is…by using it again…you have jumped ahead in time four months.

ELSON. What?

ELF GRANDE. It's now the end of November, just after Thanksgiving.

ELSON. Thanksgiving!

EUGENE. If you continue to use the jumper, you'll push your way right past Christmas and then you won't be of any use to Santa.

(*It begins to snow.*)

EWA. Look it's snowing.

PUCK. That's not good news.

(**EUGENE** *hands* **ELF GRANDE** *a piece of paper.*)

EUGENE. Don't forget this.

ELF GRANDE. Eugene has just handed me a weather forecast, and there is a blizzard headed in your direction. You need to find some shelter.

ELSON. 10 – 4.

ELF GRANDE. Out.

(*The LIGHT fades on* **GRANDE** *and* **EUGENE.**)

PUCK. I'm sorry I messed up your locale jumper.

ELSON. My Grande says you actually made some improvements to it.

EWA. This snow is really falling hard.

ELSON. The train has stopped…let's board it and seek the shelter we need.

PUCK. Excellent idea.

(**PUCK** *and* **ELVES** *exit. LIGHTS come up on* **SANTA** *and* **MRS. CLAUS** *in their area up center-stage.*)

SANTA. What do you mean Thanksgiving is over? How did this happen?

MRS. CLAUS. There has to be a logical explanation to why we keep losing months.

SANTA. There's no way we can get all the toys made by Christmas. And look it's snowing.

MRS. CLAUS. You know, I'm beginning to agree with you. Maybe we should just quit this Christmas toy making and move to Florida. We didn't get any responses to the "help wanted" plea.

SANTA. I told you it takes a special kind of being to want to do what we do.

MRS. CLAUS. Do you still want to go to Florida?

SANTA. Right now we better batten down the hatches and make sure the reindeer are safe. This storm has all the makings of a bad one.

(The LIGHTS fade on **SANTA** *and the* **MRS.** **PUCK,** **ELSON, ELLIOT,** *and* **EWA** *enter downstage right.)*

ELLIOT. I just saw the train. Where did it go?

PUCK. This blizzard is hiding everything from us.

ELSON. We really need to find some shelter.

ELLIOT. This is sounding all too familiar.

EWA. There's nothing around to shelter us.

ELSON. Then we need to hold one another and form our own shelter.

ELLIOT. You know, this is Excy's doing.

(They huddle together.)

ELSON. That's enough, Elliot.

(A faint cry for "HELP," is heard.)

PUCK. Did you hear that?

EWA. What?

PUCK. There's someone crying for help.

VOICE. Help us.

ELLIOT. I heard it.

VOICE. Help.

ELSON. So did I.

EWA. They're not that far away.

PUCK. We must save them.

ELSON. I'll go find them.

ELLIOT. No, the snow is falling too hard. You'll never find your way back. We must stick together for warmth.

ELSON. We must hold hands.

ELLIOT. You're not going to use the locale jumper again?

ELSON. No, hold hands and we'll make a chain with our arms and stretch as far as we can go. I'll be at the end and hopefully I can find who ever is crying for help.

(They form a chain that almost stretches offstage.)

VOICE. Help.

ELSON. I'm almost there. Ewa, do you have anything we can use to stretch us farther?

*(**EWA** takes off a costume piece making the chain longer. **ELSON** is now offstage.)*

ELSON *(Continued)* I got them. Pull us back in.

*(The three pull. **EWA**, who has **ELSON**'s hand, slips and all three fall. **ELSON** is not there.)*

EWA. Elson?

(Pause.)

I lost him.

ELLIOT. What?

EWA. We were all pulling so hard…he slipped.

ELLIOT. You let go of his hand?

EWA. Not on purpose.

PUCK. Elliot, what are you suggesting?

ELLIOT. She use to worked for the Elder Elf.

PUCK. Traitor!

*(**ELSON** enters with **EFFIE** in tow.)*

ELSON. Help me.

PUCK. Are you alright?

EWA. I swear, Elson, you slipped.

ELLIOT. It's Effie. You should have left him out there.

EFFIE. My friends. You must rescue them.

ELSON. Effie, what happened to the train?

EFFIE. I don't know. It stopped and then disappeared. And we were stuck in this blizzard. What about my friends?

PUCK. This storm is getting worse. We can't risk another rescue.

ELSON. Puck is right. Come on, Effie, we must all huddle together.

EFFIE. But my friends!

ELSON. I'm sorry, Effie. Come on, Elliot.

(The five of them huddle together. A beam of LIGHT flashes before them. After a beat **EXCY** *enters with* **ELERD & ELDA.** *)*

EXCY. Are you looking for these two?

EFFIE. Yes, thank you. Are you two alright?

ELERD & ELDA. Yeah.

EFFIE. Who are you?

EXCY. You don't recognize me?

*(***EXCY*** *waves his hand – SOUND: a thunder\clap is heard.)*

ELSON. Only the evil spirit Excy could make it thunder in the middle of a snowstorm.

EXCY. That's right. But I am not the evil Spirit Excy…I am the great Spirit Excy.

(All the elves and **PUCK** *fall to their knees.)*

ELLIOT. Please don't devour us.

EXCY. You know what happens to any elf that leaves the colony.

PUCK. They were only trying to help Santa Claus.

EXCY. Silence, fairy.

*(***EZAR*** *enters.)*

EZAR. What is going on here?

EXCY. Another elf…just in time to be devoured by the great Spirit Excy.

EZAR. I don't think so.

EXCY. How dare you defy me.

EZAR. The great Spirit Excy doesn't devour elves.

EXCY. He has…I mean I have done so for centuries.

EZAR. You made that silly rumor up to cover your own faults.

EXCY. I'll show you rumor.

(He waves his arms and a spell SOUND is heard. **EZAR** *is knocked down.)*

EZAR. You've gained some magical powers over the years, Elder Elf.

ELSON. Elder Elf?

EFFIE. Father?

*(***ELDER*** *takes off a hood or something that reveals who he is.)*

ELDER. Yes, that's right. The Elder Elf, your father. I'm here because, Effie, I knew you would fail in this quest, so someone had to stop Elson. Join me now and we will get to the North Pole before Elson and his losers.

EFFIE. No, I'd rather stay with Elson.

(The **ELDER** *groans as he pushes* **EFFIE** *towards* **ELSON**.*)*

ELSON. It looks like we are all united against you, Elder.

ELDER. I wouldn't be so sure.

EFFIE. He has a spy within your team.

ELSON. Ewa?

EWA. It's not me.

ELSON. Grande told me about the elf-talk.

EWA. I was only trying to see if it was my dad who sent the message. It's not me.

EZAR. You're bluffing; you don't have anyone on your side.

ELDER. I'm not bluffing, it's Elliot.

ELSON. Blood brother?

ELLIOT. I'm sorry Elson. He told me he'd get me on a team in the elf-ball league.

ELDER. Elerd and Elda are loyal to me too.

ELERD. That is correct.

ELDA. We are forever in your service.

EFFIE. They can actually speak.

(*There is a beat as no one says anything and then* **ELF GRANDE** *and* **EUGENE** *appear at Control Central DL.*)

ELF GRANDE. (*In his radio.*) Elson, are you there?

ELSON. (*In his radio.*) Here.

ELF GRANDE. Are you alright? I know how to help you.

ELSON. I hope so because we really need some help right now.

ELF GRANDE. Our instruments are showing you have company.

ELSON. That is correct.

ELDER. Elliot, get the radio from Elson.

ELLIOT. Give it to me, brother.

(**ELSON** *hands the radio to* **ELLIOT.**)

ELDER. Let me have it.

(**ELLIOT** *hands the* **ELDER** *the radio.*)

Give it up, Grande. I have finally defeated you.

ELF GRANDE. Elder, what are you doing?

(**ELDER** *tosses the radio back to* **ELLIOT.**)

ELDER. Now smash it.

(**ELLIOT** *does so. The LIGHT on* **GRANDE** *and* **EUGENE** *fades.*)

ELDER (*Continued.*) Elerd, you know how to get to the train?

ELERD. Follow me.

ELDER. Next stop…the North Pole.

(**ELDER, ELLIOT, ELERD,** *and* **ELDA** *exit.*)

ELSON. So, I guess there really isn't an evil Spirit Excy.

EZAR. Yes, there is an Excy, and he will deal with those evil ones at the right time. Right now we need some help and your Grande said he could do that. You need to get back in contact with him.

ELSON. Ewa, I'm sorry I doubted you.

EWA. Forget it.

> *(They sigh at one another.)*

EFFIE. I'm sorry, Elson, that I've always been mean to you.

PUCK. I think we need to cut all the hugging and apologies and get in touch with your Grande.

ELSON. How? The radio is broken.

EZAR. Use elf-talk.

ELSON. It doesn't work. I tried to contact you with it.

EZAR. Try it again.

ELSON. I don't have an acorn or a pinecone.

EZAR. I bet you can do it without.

EWA. Elson, we have to do something.

EFFIE. Yeah.

EZAR. Just open your mind.

ELSON. Elf Grande…can you hear me?

> *(Nothing happens.)*

There, you see, it doesn't work.

EZAR. You didn't believe.

ELSON. Because it doesn't work.

EWA. Try it for me.

> *(They sigh at one another.)*

ELSON. Elf Grande, can you hear me?

> *(SOUND: The wind begins to howl. **ELF GRANGE** and **EUGENE** appear in a LIGHT special downstage left.)*

ELF GRANDE. Elson, I'm glad to see you've finally conquered elf-talk.

ELSON. You said you could save us…how?

ELF GRANDE. Use the locale jumper.

ELSON. We've already used it two times today and lost seven months.

ELF GRANDE. Eugene tells me that if you —

EUGENE. …program a date…it won't go past it.

ELSON. Are you sure? I would hate to jump past this Christmas.

ELF GRANDE. He's pretty sure.

ELSON. Pretty sure?

EZAR. Do you have a better alternative? There's no shelter. This storm is not letting up. And we must save Christmas.

ELSON. Are we close enough to the North Pole?

PUCK. With the adjustments I made earlier long distance is no longer a problem. We can jump anywhere.

EUGENE. Puck is right.

ELSON. Alright.

EWA. Come on, join hands.

(They do so.)

ELSON. Locale jumper…get us to the North Pole… and make it before Christmas Eve.

(SOUND: The wind begins to howl louder as the LIGHTS fade to black.)

SCENE EIGHTEEN

(*AT RISE:* *The wind is still howling.* **SANTA** *and* **MRS. CLAUS** *are discovered at the North Pole home.*)

SANTA. What do you mean it's Christmas eve? I can't do it.

MRS. CLAUS. The reindeer are harnessed and ready to fly.

SANTA. No. Christmas is over.

(**ELSON, EWA, EFFIE, PUCK,** *and* **EZAR** *enter.*)

EZAR. Hold on, Santa. Reinforcements are here.

SANTA. I should have known the great Spirit Excy had something to do with this mess.

ELSON. Did he just call you the Great Spirit Excy?

EZAR. It is I.

(*SOUND: A thunderclap.*)

These Elves are here to help you.

SANTA. It's too late, Excy. Whatever you have done…the toys are not made…and I can't get around the world in so little time…I quit.

EZAR. Elson can help you.

SANTA. Who's Elson?

EZAR. The first Christmas Elf.

MRS. CLAUS. Deep down in my heart, I knew someone would come.

ELSON. How can I help?

EZAR. You have the locale jumper. Use it to help Santa around the world.

ELSON. But if we use it again, the time will jump right past Christmas.

EZAR. Puck solved using the device more than once in a day and made it so it can be use on long distance.

PUCK. You need to fix it so we don't lose any time.

ELSON. I'm not sure how?

EWA. I thought you were good with electronics.

EFFIE. Yeah.

ELSON. I am.

SANTA. I should have left hours ago if I'm going to make it around the world.

EZAR. Elson, have you even looked at the workings of the device?

ELSON. My Grande said not to mess the settings.

EZAR. Do you want to save Christmas?

> (*SOUND: A train pulls in and stops.* **ELDER**, **ELLIOT**, **ELERD**, *and* **ELDA** *enter.*)

ELDER. He might want to think he can save Christmas, but we don't intend to let him change anything on that device. Get it.

> (*There is a chase through the audience that ends back on stage with the bad guys holding* **ELSON**.)

MRS. CLAUS. Now, you elves must stop all this.

ELDER. Give me the locale jumper.

ELSON. Never.

ELDER. Take it from him, Elliot.

> (**ELLIOT** *takes the device.*)

EZAR. Alright. I've had enough.

> (*He casts a spell.*)

Good elves…bad ones…who is who?
I tried to leave that decision up to you.
With my powers as the Elfin Spirit Excy…
I command the bad become stiff as trees.

> (*He flicks his wrist. A spell SOUND is heard. The bad guys freeze in tree-like positions.* **ELSON** *takes the jumping device from* **ELLIOT** *and runs to the good guys.*)

Effie, spray them with the sleeping spray.

> (**EFFIE** *does so. The bad guys fall to the ground.*)

EZAR (*Continued.*) Now, Elson, reprogram the locale jumper so this Christmas can happen.

ELSON. I'm not sure that I can.

EWA. You must try.

(**ELSON** *and* **EWA** *look at each other and sigh.* **ELSON** *looks at the device.*)

ELSON. Oh, I see.

(*He pushes some buttons on the device. SOUND accompanies this.*)

There. Santa should be able to locale jump all over the world in plenty of time to save this Christmas.

SANTA. Without losing any time?

ELSON. In and out of each house in a flash.

SANTA. What about the toys?

EZAR. With a little fairy magic from Puck...all toys have been made and loaded in your sleigh.

(**PUCK** *runs and jumps into* **EZAR**'s *arms.*)

PUCK. Ta da!

(*She smiles.*)

SANTA. I hope this device works.

ELSON. I'll go with you to make sure it does. And with my Grande's control central looking after us we'll be safe too.

(**GRANDE** *and* **EUGENE** *are discovered in a LIGHT special downstage left at Control Central.*)

ELF GRANDE. That's right, Santa. We'll track your every move from control central.

EUGENE. It's an honor, Mr. Claus.

(*The LIGHTS fade to black. A map of the world is flown in and then with the spot light or a laser beam the sleigh moves around the world as SOUND: "Here Comes Santa Claus" is heard.*)

SCENE NINETEEN

*(AT RISE: **MRS. CLAUS** and **EWA** are discovered in the Toy Workshop. **SANTA** and **ELSON** enter.)*

SANTA. Ho, ho, ho.

MRS. CLAUS. Welcome home, my dear.

(She kisses his cheek.)

And you too, Elson. I bet you're both exhausted.

SANTA. Actually we're not, my dear. Elson's locale jumper worked to perfection. We made it to every stop all over the world and it feels like we never left.

ELSON. Except for all the cookies we ate. My tummy is not feeling too well.

MRS. CLAUS. Come here, Elson dear, I have something for that. It's called a hug.

SANTA. I think this elf helper relationship is going to work out just fine.

MRS. CLAUS. So Santa is not going to quit?

SANTA. And let all the good children down? Never.

*(**GRANDE** and **EUGENE** are discovered in a LIGHT special DL at Control Central.)*

ELF GRANDE. Congratulations Elson and Santa. Eugene has programmed the locale jumper so it can move our entire Elf colony to the North Pole. All the elves will be dedicated to helping you build and deliver all the toys for every Christmas. And as soon as Elson pushes the "Okay," button on the locale jumper…elves will always be known as the official Santa's helpers.

ELSON. What about the Elder and the others?

ELF GRANDE. The sleeping spay has turned them into happy elves.

MRS. CLAUS. Push that button, Elson.

SANTA. Your fellow elves can't get here fast enough.

ELSON. Let me ask my elf partner.

EWA. Push that button, Elson.

ELSON. Let's push it together.

> (**ELSON** *and* **EWA** *push a button on the locale jumper. A SOUND is heard and then all enter with a cheer and celebrate to music and dance.*)

SANTA. *(To the audience.)* Ho, ho, ho, Merry Christmas.

> *(The LIGHTS fade to black.)*

THE END

PROP LIST

Two cups of coffee – Santa and Mrs. Claus

Wood mallet – Santa

Paper and pen – Elson

Thunder sheet – Elda

Toys on Santa's workbench

Tools on the workbench

Newspaper – Grande

Pinecone – Grande

Acorn – Grande

Locale jumper – Grande

Three radios – Grande, Grande gives Elson one, Eugene

Spray bottle – Elder

Piece of paper – weather report – Eugene

CRYSTAL AND THE CHRISTMAS SNOWMAN

CAST OF CHARACTERS

(In speaking order)

JOSH, ten years old

JESSICA, eleven years old

LAUREN, twelve years old

STAN, THE WEATHERMAN

FATHER

MOTHER

CRYSTAL, THE SNOW ANGEL

FOSTER, THE CHRISTMAS SNOWMAN

SANTA CLAUS

The premiere of ***CRYSTAL AND THE CHRISTMAS SNOWMAN*** was presented by Children's Theatre To Go, Inc. at the at Reynolds Performance Hall in Conway, Arkansas, on December 14, 2005, under the direction of Bob May, with set design by Joe Meils and costume design by Nikki Webster, under the stage management of Andi Schultes. The cast was as follows:

JOSH . . . . Col Schott

JESSICA . . . . Madelyn Wilhite

LAUREN . . . . Katie Oslica

STAN, THE WEATHER MAN . . . . Chad Bradford

FATHER . . . . Patsy L. Paul

MOTHER . . . . Erin Lewter

CRYSTAL, THE SNOW ANGEL . . . . Erin Lewter

FOSTER, THE CHRISTMAS SNOWMAN . . . . Patsy L. Paul

SANTA CLAUS . . . . Connie Oslica

Special thanks to my sister/editor –

Vicki May-York

SYNOPSIS OF SCENES

SCENE ONE: Jessica's bedroom, around 10 PM, Christmas Eve.
SCENE TWO: Outside, Christmas morning.
SCENE THREE: Still outside, immediately following.
SCENE FOUR: Jessica's bedroom, Christmas morning

SCENE ONE

(AT RISE: JESSICA *and* LAUREN *are discovered in* JESSICA*'s bedroom. Both are in bed.* JOSH *runs into the room. He turns on the light as he enters.)*

JOSH. Hey, sisters. Finally. It's going to snow. I've been waiting all winter for this.

JESSICA. Josh, please get out of my bedroom.

JOSH. The first thing I want to do is build a snowman. Jessica, will you help me?

JESSICA. I promise. Now will you please get out of here.

LAUREN. Listen to your sister and leave. I want to go to sleep.

JOSH. Remember the snowman Dad helped us build last year? I want to build one better than that.

JESSICA. Daddy is the best snowman builder in the whole wide world.

JOSH. We can build one better without him.

LAUREN. It's not going to snow.

JOSH. Stan said there's a one hundred percent chance.

JESSICA. Let's not fight. Goodnight, Josh.

JOSH. Alright, goodnight.

*(*JOSH *exits.)*

LAUREN. It's about time. Jessica, please turn the light off.

JESSICA. No problem.

(She turns the light out and then moves to the window.)

I can see when the snow begins to fall better with the light off.

LAUREN. At last.

(After a beat a flash of LIGHT flutters around the room ala Tinker Bell in Peter Pan.)

JESSICA. Did you see it?

LAUREN. I don't want to talk.

JESSICA. It was a snow angel begging to be made.

LAUREN. What are you babbling about?

JESSICA. A snow angel. You've never made a snow angel?

LAUREN. There's not much snow in Florida.

JESSICA. It works best in freshly fallen snow.

(JESSICA *turns the light on and then pulls* LAUREN *from the bed.*)

Come on, get up. I'll show you how to make one.

LAUREN. I don't want to do this.

JESSICA. You lie down in the snow…go on…lie down.

LAUREN. There's no snow.

JESSICA. Here, we'll pretend these clothes are snow.

(*She throws clothes on the floor.*)

Lay down.

(*She makes* LAUREN *lie down on top of them.*)

And now you whip your arms up and down and your and legs back and forth to create what looks like an angel. Go on, move those limbs.

(JESSICA *makes* LAUREN *do the moves.*)

Your arms make the wings. And the legs make the skirt.

(LAUREN *gets up.*)

LAUREN. It's a gown. Angels don't wear skirts.

JESSICA. Do you see the wings and gown?

LAUREN. No. It looks like a pile of dirty clothes swished around all over the floor.

JESSICA. Well, it looks better in the snow of course. The ice crystals in the snow shimmer and make the angel look magical. And once you create one…that angel looks after you the rest of the day. Just like our mama.

LAUREN. She's not my mother.

JESSICA. She could be if you'd let her.

LAUREN. I have a mother, just not a father. Look, I really

want to go to sleep.

(**LAUREN** *climbs back into her bed.*)

JESSICA. How can you sleep on Christmas Eve? Aren't you excited? Santa Claus will soon be here. I hope I get my new sled. If I do, you can have the first ride on it. What did you ask for?

LAUREN. Santa Claus has never been very kind to me.

JESSICA. You know, Lauren, this year you're sharing Christmas with your daddy – my step-daddy – but I don't think of him as a step anything. He's my daddy now and if you'd stop feeling sorry for yourself, you'd find a father and another mother that love you. And meanwhile you might just have a good time too.

LAUREN. Please turn the light out. Remember, I'm older than you.

JESSICA. And this is my bedroom. Oh, whatever.

(**JESSICA** *turns the light off and then goes and sits by the window.*)

LAUREN. I've never seen snow. Do you really think it will snow tonight?

JESSICA. Stan, the TV Weatherman, promised it would.

LAUREN. My mother says, "Weathermen are never right with their predictions and should never be trusted."

JESSICA. Stan's just a weatherman, not a villain.

LAUREN. I still don't trust weathermen.

JESSICA. What time is it?

LAUREN. What?

JESSICA. It's just after ten o'clock. I bet we can hear Stan's latest forecast.

(**JESSICA** *turns on a TV. It's a box that* **STAN** *can stick his head in and look like he's on TV. In the original production, a small TV was hollowed out, a hole was cut into the bottom, and* **STAN** *slipped his head inside the TV. He then sat behind a table so it looked like the TV was sitting on the table.*)

LAUREN. Jessica, it's time to go to sleep.

JESSICA. Shhh, listen.

STAN. Stan, the Weatherman, here. You want a White Christmas? You got it. I promise that by tomorrow morning there will be at least six inches of perfect snow for creating wonderful snow angels and snowmen.

JESSICA. You'll get to experience your first snow.

STAN. I can't promise that for all the kids across the country. It seems our state is receiving special treatment. In Florida, they are experiencing record high temperatures. So, my weather survey question tonight is… would you rather have a White Christmas or a snow-free Christmas? You can vote by going to our web site –

*(***LAUREN*** gets out of bed and turns off the TV.)*

JESSICA. I vote for a White Christmas.

LAUREN. I vote for a snow-free Christmas.

*(***LAUREN*** gets back into bed.)*

JESSICA. You know, the first snow of the year is supposed to be magical.

*(***FATHER*** and ***MOTHER*** enter and turn on the light as they do. ***FATHER*** wears a top hat and tails and ***MOTHER*** wears a gown with a boa, and a big bonnet.)*

FATHER. And since the first snow is on Christmas day, it will have double the magic.

JESSICA. Hey, Daddy. You look great.

*(***JESSICA*** runs to him and gives him a hug.)*

FATHER. A Christmas snow can make people do things they wouldn't normally do.

MOTHER. It can make enemies become friends.

FATHER. Or let children know that having more than one mother is alright.

LAUREN. Why are you both dressed so weird?

FATHER. *(Almost angry.)* We told you at dinner.

LAUREN. *(She didn't forget.)* I forgot.

MOTHER. *(Stopping the fight.)* It's a Christmas tradition that your daddy and I dress up for Santa's arrival.

FATHER. And you are beautiful, my dear.

(He bows.)

MOTHER. You look very nice too, Foster, darling.

(She curtsies.)

(FATHER kisses MOTHER's hand.)

JESSICA. Mama, please let me wear your bonnet.

(MOTHER hands bonnet and boa to JESSICA, who puts them on.)

JESSICA *(con't)* Do I look like you?

MOTHER. A spittin' image.

(They point a finger at each other, wink, and do a clicking sound to each other.)

FATHER. Lauren, would you like to wear my top hat and tails? They're magical.

LAUREN. No, thank you.

FATHER. I'll leave them here in case you change your mind.

(FATHER takes off his hat and coat and puts them on LAUREN's bed.)

MOTHER. Lauren, did you remember to send Santa a letter?

LAUREN. Letters to Santa are stupid.

FATHER. Santa doesn't need to get a letter; he knows what you want.

LAUREN. Jessica had just turned the light out, and I was about to go to sleep.

(JOSH runs in.)

JOSH. Hey, everybody, it's snowing. It's beginning to snow. Big, wet flakes, perfect for building a snowman. Look out the window, it's snowing, just like Stan the

Weatherman said it would.

JESSICA. He's right; it's snowing. This Christmas is going to be so special.

JOSH. Come on, let's go outside and build a snowman.

(**JOSH** *and* **JESSICA** *run towards door.*)

FATHER. Hold on there, you two.

JOSH. But, papa, I've been waiting since last year to make another snowman.

MOTHER. Josh, daddy's right. The snow will be there in the morning.

FATHER. Besides, weren't you all waiting for Santa Claus to come.

JOSH & JESSICA. Yes.

MOTHER. I think while we've been talking, he's been here and gone.

JOSH. What? I didn't hear him.

JESSICA. You're kidding. Did I get my sled?

JOSH. I hope I got the new game cube discs.

MOTHER. Run downstairs and look. I'll race you and beat you down.

(**JOSH** *and* **JESSICA** *run from the room, laughing.* **MOTHER** *is right behind them, laughing too.*)

FATHER. Lauren, I'm sure Santa left some gifts for you. Didn't you want a cell phone?

LAUREN. I miss my mother.

FATHER. And she misses you. Remember, we're going to call her in the morning. Maybe you can use your new cell phone?

LAUREN. Sure.

FATHER. Let's go downstairs.

LAUREN. I don't want to disturb your new family.

FATHER. You know, Lauren, the miles between us may be great and our hours together few, but you'll always be a part of me and I a part of you.

(**FATHER** *kisses her on the top of the head and exits.*)

LAUREN. TURN OUT THE LIGHT!!!

(*She gets out of bed, turns out the light, and then gets back into bed.*)

LAUREN (*Continued*) First snow…magical snow? Yeah, right! If it's so magical…please grant me my Christmas wish and fly me back home to my mother.

(**LAUREN** *buries her head in her pillow and begins to cry. After a beat or two* **CRYSTAL** *enters. Her garb is a hodgepodge of different styles, colors, and outfits. But it still reflects the look of an angel, crystals reflecting off the light. The same actress that plays* **MOTHER** *plays* **CRYSTAL.**)

CRYSTAL. You want to get home. I'm here to help you.

LAUREN. Who are you?

CRYSTAL. You don't recognize me?

LAUREN. I've never seen you before.

CRYSTAL. You created me.

LAUREN. Created you?

CRYSTAL. You laid on the floor and moved your arms and legs back and forth and created me. I'm your Snow Angel.

LAUREN. My stepsister made me do that.

CRYSTAL. Why do you call her your stepsister? Isn't a sister a sister? Anyway, I'm your snow angel for the day. And I'm here to make sure your wishes come true. The name's Crystal.

LAUREN. Because of the ice crystals shimmering in the light.

CRYSTAL. That's right.

LAUREN. You have the wrong person. My wishes never come true.

(**CRYSTAL** *checks a letter.*)

CRYSTAL. It says right here. Lauren. Isn't that you?

LAUREN. Did my father put you up to this?

CRYSTAL. Nope, Santa sent me. He got your letter. See.

(**CRYSTAL** *shows* **LAUREN** *the letter.*)

LAUREN. Hey, how did you get that? I didn't mail it.

CRYSTAL. Santa knows what you want and he said, if your Christmas wish is to go back to your mother's, he'd personally fly you there in his sleigh once he finishes delivering all the toys.

LAUREN. This can't be real. I must be dreaming. You don't even look like a snow angel.

CRYSTAL. I guess I'm dressed so strangely because you created me in a pile of clothes and not in some soft snow.

LAUREN. So how long is it going to take Santa to get here?

CRYSTAL. That depends on the weather.

LAUREN. *(Sarcastic.)* Why don't we turn on the TV and ask Stan the Weatherman?

(*She turns on the TV and* **STAN** *appears in the TV.*)

STAN. Do you think you're living in a world that is not real? Does it all seem like a dream? Maybe the forecast of your life has changed? If you have a question, ask Stan, the Weatherman.

LAUREN. Stan, help me. Is she a real snow angel?

STAN. She doesn't look anything like a snow angel to me.

(**STAN** *comes to life up. The TV stays attached to his head. He wears a tacky/nerdy suit. Music accompanies his transformation – ten seconds or so of Stravinsky's Firebird, "Kastchei Awakens."*)

LAUREN. *(During the transformation.)* Holy Christmas.

STAN. *(Once the transformation is complete.)* I wouldn't trust anyone dressed like that?

CRYSTAL. Who believes the weatherman? Especially one trapped inside a TV, looking very evil.

LAUREN. I don't know who I should believe?

STAN. Why don't we let the children in TV land decide.

CRYSTAL. That's fine with me. Go ahead and call for a vote.

LAUREN. What are you two talking about?

CRYSTAL. All your friends are here to help you decide who to trust. See them.

(**CRYSTAL** *does a gesture and the house lights come up. A spell SOUND should accompany the gesture.* **LAUREN** *sees the audience.*)

LAUREN. Now I know I am dreaming. I don't have that many friends.

CRYSTAL. Believe it; they are your friends. Go on, ask them to voice their opinion on who to trust.

LAUREN. Those of you who think I should trust Stan yell now.

CHILDREN. Boo.

LAUREN. Is the Snow Angel my friend?

CHILDREN. YES!!!

CRYSTAL. The children have spoken. Stan, the Weatherman, you are the villain of this piece.

STAN. I don't like it when my predictions aren't correct. It really irritates me. So, Lauren, you want to go home to your mama in Florida?

CRYSTAL. And Santa will get her there.

STAN. Not if I have anything to do with it. The weather is my friend, and it will help me spoil this Christmas Day and that flight home will never happen. You haven't seen the last of me.

(**STAN** *exits with a villainous laugh.*)

LAUREN. He can't really spoil me from getting home, can he?

CRYSTAL. We don't have time for him to spoil anything, especially this day.

LAUREN. You mean night. I need some sleep before my ride home.

CRYSTAL. No, he was right on that prediction. Christmas Day is upon us, and it's time to have fun. But, you're not dressed to go out in the cold. I know.

(She grabs **FATHER***'s top hat and coat from the bed as it rolls off.)*

Here, put this on. It'll keep you warm.

(She helps **LAUREN** *put the coat and hat on.)*

Remember, your father said it was magical. Come on, let's go outside and enjoy the snow.

*(***CRYSTAL*** *claps her hands, a magic SOUND is heard. The scene shifts to outdoors.)*

SCENE TWO

(The scene is now a snow covered yard with the house in the back ground. There is a section of a wall right of center. **JESSICA & JOSH** *run in and join* **LAUREN** *and* **CRYSTAL.** **JESSICA** *carries a sled.)*

JESSICA. Lauren, look what Santa brought me. Who's your friend?

CRYSTAL. The name's Crystal. I'm the snow angel you helped her create in the pile of clothes.

JESSICA. That explains the strange outfit.

LAUREN. She's here to help me get back to my mother.

JOSH. Why would you want to leave all this snow?

JESSICA. Daddy's coat and hat look good on you.

LAUREN. I wish I could return the compliment.

JOSH. Are you girls finished talking about fashion? Can we get to some serious snowman building?

JESSICA. First, let's ride my new sled.

JOSH. Jessica, you promised.

CRYSTAL. Josh is right, let's make a snowman.

JOSH. Yeah, a big one, something daddy will be proud of.

LAUREN. You sure like to create things around here.

JOSH. We need to roll a big base.

*(***CRYSTAL***'s cell phone rings.)*

CRYSTAL. Excuse me. I better get this… on my new cell phone. It could be about your ride. Hello…

(She exits.)

JESSICA. A snow angel is just like your mama. You're going to love her.

LAUREN. I will if she grants me my wish.

JOSH. Stop yapping and start rolling.

*(The three begin to build a snowman as the LIGHTS fade. ***STAN*** enters in a LIGHT special.)*

STAN. There are several dilemmas one faces in creating a snowman…should the man of snow have a base and how big should the base be? Or should he have legs? The base can't be too big if the snow is wet or the other sections of the body will be too big to lift up to create the body and head. Go ahead, make your stupid snowman. I don't think he'll be able to bring this family any closer. Those smiles will soon turn to frowns.

(The LIGHTS cross fade from **STAN** *to* **CRYSTAL***. She talks on her cell phone in a LIGHT special as* **FOSTER** *gets into place.)*

CRYSTAL. That's right, Santa, she's building a snowman with her stepbrother and sister. Sorry, brother and sister. But, we have a problem with a weatherman. That's right, his name is Stan. Poor ratings have driven him to do more than that. Do you think you can get here any sooner? Oh and one more thing, can you pick up some angel gowns? Very funny, no, not a skirt, a gown.

(The LIGHT special fades.)

SCENE THREE

(AT RISE: JESSICA, JOSH, and LAUREN are discovered standing next to a perfect looking snowman, FOSTER. The same actor that plays FATHER plays FOSTER. The snowman should have his back to the audience, so they can't see his face.)

JOSH. This is the best snowman I've ever seen.

JESSICA. Yeah, I don't think we've ever build one this good.

JOSH. Thanks for helping, Lauren. What do you think?

LAUREN. It's alright.

(CRYSTAL runs in.)

CRYSTAL. Lauren, you ride home is on his way.

(To ALL.)

Whoa, what a perfect looking snowman. And he's kinda cute too.

(She blows kiss to FOSTER.)

JOSH. He's so real; we need to give him a name.

JESSICA. Frosty the Snowman.

JOSH. No, that's a stupid name. Let's name him after dad since he taught us how to build snowmen.

LAUREN. Foster, the Snowman?

JOSH &JESSICA. Yes.

LAUREN. Do you both really like my dad that much?

JOSH. He's my only dad.

JESSICA. He loves you, Lauren.

CRYSTAL. Foster needs a face.

JESSICA. Yes, he does; here's a button for his nose.

(JESSICA pulls a button off her coat and puts it on FOSTER's face. In the original production the snowman head had a carrot for a nose, so "button" was changed to "carrot. Jessica justified having the carrot in her pocket by saying she was going to feed it to one of Santa's reindeer.)

JOSH. And two game cube discs for his eyes.

(**JOSH** *pulls two game cube discs from his coat pocket and puts them on* **FOSTER***'s face.*)

LAUREN. All the snowmen I've ever seen are usually smoking corncob pipes. He can be a smoking snowman.

CRYSTAL. Nah, no one should ever smoke, especially a man made out of snow. Heat is their enemy.

LAUREN. He's not real…this is not real…so it won't hurt him.

CRYSTAL. He's real to us.

JESSICA & JOSH. Yeah.

LAUREN. If he's so real, why can't he move?

CRYSTAL. All he needs to move like a real man is a special magical hat.

JOSH. Try my baseball cap.

CRYSTAL. Yeah.

(**JOSH** *puts his hat on* **FOSTER**. *All anticipate something happening. Nothing happens.*)

JESSICA. A baseball cap is not a hat; it's a cap. Try mama's bonnet.

LAUREN. No, nothing from her.

CRYSTAL. Go ahead, try it.

(**JESSICA** *puts bonnet on* **FOSTER**. *All anticipate something happening. Nothing happens.*)

JOSH. Lauren's right, a bonnet is no more a hat than my baseball cap.

CRYSTAL. I kind of like it. Do you mind if I wear it?

JESSICA. Go ahead. It's my mama's.

(**CRYSTAL** *puts bonnet on.*)

CRYSTAL. How do I look? Anything like a mother?

JESSICA. A spittin' image.

(*They point a finger at each other, wink, and do a clicking sound to each other.*)

JOSH. Now what do we do?

CRYSTAL. Try your daddy's top hat. It's special because it's the one hat that is a part of all three of you.

JOSH. She's right. Put it on him, Lauren.

LAUREN. Like this top hat is really going to make a man made of snow come to life.

CRYSTAL. What have you got to lose?

LAUREN. Will it get me home any faster?

CRYSTAL. That and a lot more.

> (**LAUREN** *puts the top hat on* **FOSTER**. *All anticipate something happening. Nothing does. All sit with their back to* **FOSTER**. *After a beat or two he slowly begins to move, one limb at a time. "Magic Spell Begins," (time on the CD - 2:08 - 2:55) from The Nutcracker works here. He moves in behind the four and says his line.*)

FOSTER. *(As though saying, "Ho, ho, ho.")* Snow, snow, snow! Merry Christmas.

> (*All four turn and jump to their feet as* **FOSTER** *does a short dance. "Magic Spell Begins," (time on the CD - 2:59 - 3:13) from The Nutcracker works for the dance.*)

JOSH. Foster is alive.

FOSTER. Yes, I am.

JESSICA. Daddy's hat made him come to life.

LAUREN. Is this a Christmas trick set up by dad?

CRYSTAL. Stop doubting everything and enjoy your time here with your brother and sister.

FOSTER. Hey, who got the new sled for Christmas?

JESSICA. I did.

FOSTER. Let's give it a try.

JESSICA. I promised Lauren that she could have the first ride.

LAUREN. That's alright. If he wants to ride it, he can.

FOSTER. Why don't we all ride it together?

JESSICA. It's not big enough for all of us.

FOSTER. I can make it big enough. Come on, everybody, get on.

(The five scramble to center stage and sit with legs around the person in front. **JESSICA** *is in the front,* **FOSTER** *is in the rear.)*

FOSTER *(con't)* Here we go.

(They ride down an imaginary hill. This is created with LIGHTS. ALL laugh and talk as they ride down.)

JOSH. This is the best ride I've ever had.

JESSICA. It's because the first snow is at Christmas.

FOSTER. We're just like an Olympic bobsled team. And a team is just like a family.

CRYSTAL. Josh, I think those game cube discs for eyes have gone to his brain.

(The ride comes to an end.)

JESSICA. That was fantastic.

JOSH. Let's do it again.

FOSTER. What does Lauren want to do?

LAUREN. Crystal knows what I want to do.

CRYSTAL. I don't understand the delay; Santa said he was on his way. I'll give him a call.

(She moves downstage right to talk on phone.)

FOSTER. Meanwhile, come on let's take another ride, and this time Lauren can steer us down the hill.

LAUREN. I've never steered a sled before.

FOSTER. We'll all be there to show you how. Come on, let's do it again.

(The four scramble to get on sled. **LAUREN** *is in front this time.)*

JOSH. Foster, you're the greatest.

FOSTER. You're not so bad yourself, kid. We're all glad you're here, Lauren.

LAUREN. Thanks.

FOSTER. Are we ready?

KIDS. Yes.

FOSTER. Steer us down the hill, Lauren. Our lives are in your hands. Here we go.

(The four laugh as they begin to ride the sleigh.)

JESSICA. Now, do you believe that the first snow of the season is magical?

LAUREN. Maybe it is.

FOSTER. Lauren, you steer like a champion.

*(The four laugh. **STAN** enters downstage left.)*

STAN. Freeze frame.

(He clicks a TV remote control and the four freeze. A SOUND effect should accompany this. Referring to the frozen four.)

What a cute picture.

CRYSTAL. Go away, Stan, and let these kids enjoy this Christmas Day.

(She gestures, a SOUND effect is heard, and the four begin to move and shout happily.)

JOSH. Can you make it go faster?

FOSTER. If that's what you all want.

KIDS. Yes!!!

(They begin to go faster with an, "Ahhh.")

STAN. Channel change.

(He clicks the TV remote control again and the four freeze. A SOUND effect should accompany this.)

CRYSTAL. Let Lauren, discover love for her family.

STAN. Boo hoo. Cry me a river. I'm not here to have fun. It's my job to spoil this Christmas for all of you.

CRYSTAL. You know what's nice about television? I can change the channel if I don't like what I'm hearing.

(She gestures, a SOUND effect is heard, and the four begin to move and shout once again.)

FOSTER. Is this fast enough?

THREE KIDS. Yes.

STAN. Lauren seems to be making the channel choices here, not you.

(He clicks the TV remote control again and the four freeze. A SOUND effect should accompany this.)

CRYSTAL. Stan, did you ever play in the snow?

STAN. I've played in lots of snow, sleet, ice, freezing rain, frozen precipitation. And I discovered they all have one thing in common…it's all just frozen water. Let me remind you that both you and the snowman are made up of nothing but frozen water.

CRYSTAL. Stop twisting weather facts. What is your forecast?

STAN. You'll find out soon enough; but meanwhile I think I'll make their ride a little rougher than they wished for. You see that they're about to come to the bottom of the hill and…

*(**STAN** nods his TV head and the four begin to yell and move. A different SOUND effect is heard.)*

… aren't they going a bit too fast?

CRYSTAL. No, Stan, don't do that.

STAN. Opps, I think they're about to have an accident.

*(He nods again and the four yell. There is a crashing SOUND. The kids tumble around, the LIGHTS flicker, and when all comes to an end, the three kids lay about the stage and do not move. **FOSTER**'s legs and body can be seen laying about the stage too.)*

CRYSTAL. What have you done?

STAN. My forecasts are updated on the eight's. Tootle loo.

*(**STAN** exits.)*

CRYSTAL. Is everyone alright?

(No one answers.)

Oh, no.

(She runs to **JOSH**.*)*

Josh, Josh, are you all right?

(There is a moment before **JOSH** *jumps up.)*

JOSH. I'm fine.

CRYSTAL. What about Jessica?

*(***CRYSTAL** *and* **JOSH** *run to* **JESSICA**.*)*

CRYSTAL *(Continued.)* Jessica?

(There is a moment before **JESSICA** *jumps up.)*

JESSICA. I'm fine too.

CRYSTAL. How about Lauren?

(The three run to **LAUREN**.*)*

JESSICA. Sister?

JOSH. Are you hurt?

(There is a moment before **LAUREN** *jumps up.)*

LAUREN. That was fantastic.

CRYSTAL. Does that mean you're finally having a good time?

LAUREN. It's not a bad way to pass the time…

(Not as enthusiastic.)

…until Santa gets me home.

CRYSTAL. Where's Foster?

*(***FOSTER**'s *head talks from the top of the wall.)*

FOSTER. Over there, and over there, but the talking part is over here.

(They all run to the head on top of the wall.)

JOSH. Does it hurt?

FOSTER. Can't feel a thing.

(All laugh.)

CRYSTAL. We have to put him back together.

FOSTER. I'd like that.

JESSICA. But how?

LAUREN. The same way we built him. One section at a time.

JOSH. Here try this.

(He puts a cut out of the body of Sponge Bob Squarepants under the head of **FOSTER,** *on the wall.)*

FOSTER. I live under the sea.

(All laugh.)

FOSTER *(con't)* No that won't work.

JESSICA. How about this?

(JESSICA *puts a cut out of the body of Donald Duck below the head of* **FOSTER. FOSTER** *sneezes as Donald Duck. All laugh.)*

FOSTER. That's not me.

JOSH. I like this.

(JOSH *puts a cut out of a Star Wars figure under* **FOS- TER***'s head.* **FOSTER** *talks as the figure. All laugh. The cut outs that the kids put under* **FOSTER** *can change with each production. Have fun with it.)*

FOSTER. I'm a snowman.

LAUREN. Get those parts over there.

(JESSICA & JOSH *pick up the parts of* **FOSTER** *and meet* **LAUREN** *behind the wall.* **LAUREN** *comes from behind the wall with a snowman cut out and puts it under the head of* **FOSTER.***)*

FOSTER. That's me.

(The LIGHTS fade on that scene as all laugh. **STAN** *enters in a LIGHT special to give time for* **FOSTER** *to get it together.)*

STAN. I guess they've just brought new meaning to the family that plays together, stays together. Let them play. For those of you who know your weather… today's weather trivia question is: What always follows a cold snap? The answer will be revealed during my next forecast.

(**CRYSTAL** *is discovered in a another LIGHT special. She is talking on her cell phone.*)

CRYSTAL. Santa, can you hear me?

STAN. Oh, by the way. Santa's reindeers are experiencing some delay in the heat and the humidity that the southern part of the world is throwing their way.

CRYSTAL. But you promised Lauren you'd get her home. How long do you think it will take you? Hello… can you hear me? Hello. Yes, I can hear you now. Good. Well, get here as soon as you can.

STAN. My forecast maps are showing he won't get here before my big surprise does.

CRYSTAL. Get out of here.

STAN. Enjoy things while you can.

(**STAN** *exits. The LIGHTS come up to reveal ALL around* **FOSTER**. **CRYSTAL** *moves to the group and flirts with* **FOSTER**. *He returns it.*)

CRYSTAL. For a man made of snow you sure are looking pretty solid once again.

FOSTER. That bonnet frames the face of the most beautiful snow angel I've ever seen.

(*They blow kisses to one another.*)

LAUREN. (*To* **CRYSTAL**) So, where is my ride home?

CRYSTAL. He's on his way.

JOSH. What can we do now?

FOSTER. Let's play tag.

JESSICA. That would be fun.

FOSTER. Snowmen are usually stuck in one spot, but now that I'm alive and mobile tag is the perfect game for me to take advantage of my freedom.

JOSH. Not it.

JESSICA. Me neither.

FOSTER. I'll be it.

(*They all run around, laughing, and playing tag.*)

FOSTER. Lauren, you're it now.

*(****FOSTER**** tags ****LAUREN****.)*

LAUREN. Josh, you are about to be it.

(The game of tag moves into the audience. It moves back on stage.)

FOSTER. I'm beat. I need to rest.

CRYSTAL. A rest is a good idea.

LAUREN. Don't stop now.

JOSH. I'm hot.

JESSICA. Me too.

FOSTER. Yes, all this running around has gotten me very hot; and the warmer a man made of snow gets, the shorter his life expectancy becomes. I need to cool down.

*(****STAN**** enters.)*

STAN. And the answer to today's weather trivia question is… surprise! A warm front. Yes, the predicted warm front I've been waiting for has finally arrived. Say goodbye to all this snow…and to any snowmen or snow angels too. For all you sun lovers…

(He sits in a lawn chair and holds a sun reflector under his chin/face.)

…I promise the temperature is on the rise.

LAUREN. You can't do this. Why does everyone leave me after I get fond of them?

STAN. The present temp is approaching thirty-three. And I believe that is above freezing. Not a good thing for anyone made of snow.

FOSTER. He's right if the temperature continues to rise, I don't have much life left.

*(****FOSTER**** falls down.)*

JESSICA. We can put you in mom and dad's freezer.

JOSH. He's too big. He won't fit.

CRYSTAL. We need to get him to the North Pole.

(**CRYSTAL** *falls down.*)

JOSH. What's wrong with her?

JESSICA. She needs to get to the North Pole too. Remember she's a snow angel.

JOSH. But how can we get them there?

STAN. Don't worry about them. This happens every year. Snowmen melt and the images of snow angels disappear too.

LAUREN. He's right…you can create another snowmen and angel next year. I just want to go home.

JOSH. We gotta save Foster and Crystal because they are real.

JESSICA. And they've become real because they're family.

STAN. I'm tired of your step-brother and sister getting in my way.

(**CRYSTAL** *manages to get to her feet.*)

CRYSTAL. They are her brother and sister.

STAN. And you too, you mothering Snow Angel. Let me just wipe the three of you from the weather map with a sudden winter tornado.

(*A strong wind is heard. SOUND: Use wind tubes to create this effect.* **JESSICA**, **JOSH**, *and* **CRYSTAL** *spin off stage.*)

LAUREN. Where are they?

STAN. Who really needs them? You don't!

FOSTER. I will save them.

(**FOSTER** *fights to stand.*)

STAN. And today's high, Mr. Man-Made-of-Snow, is now at forty degrees. And by my villainous math that is well above the freezing mark; so your existence is not long in this winter.

(**FOSTER** *falls down.*)

LAUREN. (*Runs to him.*) Are you alright?

FOSTER. Snowmen are only seasonal.

LAUREN. What are we going to do?

FOSTER. You know, Lauren, the miles between us may be great and our hours together few, but you'll always be a part of me and I a part of you.

LAUREN. What did you say?

STAN. Sunshine and sixty-nine. I think he was saying, "good-bye."

FOSTER. Remember Christmas is about creating family… with those who love you.

LAUREN. If I go downstairs, will it save Jessica and Josh from Stan the Weatherman?

FOSTER. Only if you mean it. Good bye.

LAUREN. You can't melt now. I love you.

(LAUREN *holds* FOSTER *to stop him from melting.*)

STAN. He'll soon be a puddle of water that we'll need to mop up.

(SANTA*'s sleigh is heard landing.*)

STAN *(con't)* Your ride is here, Miss Lauren.

LAUREN. I won't let you hurt my father.

(SANTA *enters.*)

SANTA. Ho, ho, ho. Merry Christmas. Is there a Lauren here ready for a ride back to Florida?

LAUREN. Yes, I'm Lauren, but I've changed my mind.

(*She continues to hold* FOSTER.)

SANTA. You've changed your Christmas wish?

LAUREN. I give up my ride. You must use your sleigh to get Foster to the North Pole.

STAN. What do you think you're doing?

SANTA. This wish was not in your letter.

LAUREN. I thought you were supposed to know what children wished for without a letter.

STAN. She's not thinking straight right now.

SANTA. Are you sure you want to transfer your wish to this Snowman?

LAUREN. I'm positive.

SANTA. Alright, my sleigh's over here.

STAN. It's too late for him.

LAUREN. Can you help me? He's a little weak.

(SANTA *runs to help get* FOSTER *to his feet.*)

FOSTER. Crystal…don't forget…Crystal.

SANTA. Has something happened to Crystal?

FOSTER. She…the kids…lost in evil weather map.

STAN. And you'll never find them.

SANTA. A weatherman doesn't have any real power. He's actually a slave to the weather. Release them, Stan.

(SANTA *shakes his sleigh bells and* JESSICA, JOSH, CRYS-TAL *enter. The two kids hold a very weak* CRYSTAL.)

STAN. I'm sorry to report that the heat has gotten to the mother.

LAUREN. She's not my mother.

JESSICA. Hasn't she shown you the same love as your mother.

FOSTER. Put her in…Santa's sleigh.

(JESSICA & JOSH *begin to move* CRYSTAL *towards the sleigh.*)

STAN. Hold on, they can't do that?

JESSICA. Why not?

SANTA. He's right. This is Lauren's wish. She has to give the okay.

(*ALL look to* LAUREN.)

FOSTER. Help her, Lauren. This…Christmas…she…made it special.

JESSICA. I'll give you my new sled.

STAN. This forecast is not looking too positive.

SANTA. It's looking very positive…Lauren is on the verge of creating a real family.

LAUREN. Put them both into Santa's sleigh.

(CRYSTAL *and* FOSTER *move to* LAUREN.)

CRYSTAL. Thank you.

FOSTER. We promise to…

CRYSTAL. …be there…

FOSTER. …for you…

STAN. Oh, please.

CRYSTAL. …every Christmas snow…

FOSTER & CRYSTAL. …and always.

> (**SANTA** *moves to* **CRYSTAL** *and* **FOSTER**, *takes them by the arms, and leads them off stage.*)

SANTA. I better get these two to the North Pole if they are going to keep those promises.

ALL. Good-bye. We love you.

> (**SANTA***'s sleigh is heard taking off.*)

STAN. Bah humbug…My forecast for this New Year is cold… extra cold weather.

JESSICA. We have each other to stay warm.

> (*The three stand arm in arm.*)

LAUREN. Yes, get out of here, Stan.

STAN. Enjoy your family creation.

> (**STAN** *exits. The three children cheer victoriously.*)

JESSICA. You just gave up your Christmas wish.

LAUREN. It comes with a price.

JESSICA. What's that?

LAUREN. Didn't you promise me your sled?

JOSH. You did, Jessica.

JESSICA. I'll play you a game of tag for it.

LAUREN. Alright. And I'm not it.

JESSICA. Me either.

LAUREN. Josh, you're it.

JOSH. What?

> (**JOSH** *chases* **JESSICA** *and* **LAUREN** *around the stage as the set shifts back to the bedroom.* **LAUREN** *climbs into the bed.* **JESSICA & JOSH** *exit. The LIGHTS flicker and*

a SOUND effect of **SANTA***'s bells is heard.)*

SCENE FOUR

*(**AT RISE:** **LAUREN** is sleeping in her bed.* **JESSICA** *&* **JOSH** *enter and move to* **LAUREN** *on the bed.)*

JOSH. Wake up, Lauren.

JESSICA. Sister, it's Christmas morning. Wake up.

LAUREN. What? I'm awake.

(She yawns.)

I've been awake all night. You've both been with me, fighting off Stan, the Weatherman.

*(**LAUREN** moves to the TV and turns it on.* **STAN** *and the TV are back in the normal place in the bedroom.)*

STAN. Good morning snow lovers. Stan, the Weatherman here to report about a weather related human interest story...A snow angel and snowman this family built together has united them on this special Christmas day.

*(**MOTHER** and **FATHER** enter. They are dressed in their bonnet and top hat.)*

MOTHER. Merry Christmas, Lauren.

LAUREN. Thanks, mom.

*(**LAUREN** embraces* **MOTHER.** *)*

And Merry Christmas to you too. I love your outfit.

FATHER. Lauren, there's a call from Florida on a new cell phone that Santa left for you.

*(**LAUREN** embraces her* **FATHER.** *)*

LAUREN. Thank you, Daddy, for everything you do for me. I love you.

(On phone.)

Hello, Mother. Merry Christmas to you too. Yes, I'm

having a wonderful time. Okay, I will. Bye. Oh, Mom, I'll see you soon.

JOSH. Let's go outside and build a snowman.

JESSICA. No, let's ride my new sled.

LAUREN. We have all day to do both…and lots more.

(The LIGHTS fade to black as ALL embrace and "We Wish You a Merry Christmas" is heard.)

THE END

A DIFFERENT KIND OF NUTCRACKER

An Alternative to the Ballet in One Act

**suggested by
E. T. A. Hoffmann's tale**
The Nutcracker and the Mouse King

CAST OF CHARACTERS

(In order of appearance)

FATHER
MOTHER
MARIE
FRITZ
GODFATHER HOFFMANN
MICE
MOUSE KING
NUTCRACKER
SOLDIERS
KING
QUEEN
MADAME MOUSERINK
COURT ASTROLOGER
NURSEMAID ONE
NURSEMAID TWO
PEARLIPLATE
BROTHER
A GYPSY
SUGAR PLUM FAIRIES
LADY SUGAR PLUM

The mice become citizens of the court, along with the soldiers, and sugar
plum fairies in the crowd scenes.

A DIFFERENT KIND OF NUTCRACKER had its beginnings with a two-act adaptation of the Hoffmann story being read at the University of Nevada, Las Vegas, in October 1993. That adaptation was produced by the Up North Family Theatre in Brainerd, MN, under the direction of Kay Churchill in December 1993. Rewrites were completed on a three-act adaptation in June 1999 with a reading at the University of Arkansas at Little Rock.

The premiere of the one-act adaptation of *A DIFFERENT KIND OF NUTCRACKER* was presented by Children's Theatre To Go, Inc. at the at Reynolds Performance Hall in Conway, Arkansas, on December 13, 2006, under the direction of Bob May, with set design by Bob May and costume design by Nikki Webster. The cast was as follows.

FATHER	Brent Wood
MOTHER	Karen Owings
MARIE	Katie Oslica
FRITZ	Jace Motley
GODFATHER HOFFMANN	David Keith
MICE	Jeni Fuller
	Ellie Halloran
	Miranda Moore
	Abby Shourd
	Austin Smith
	Kiana Smith
MOUSE KING	Col Schott
NUTCRACKER	Ben A. Scheuter
SOLDIERS	Dylan Barber
	Jay Barber
	Marshall Bellando
	Alex Brewington
	Nicholas Carter
	Keith Clement
	Ian Turpin
	Jacob Webb
KING	Brent Wood
QUEEN	Karen Owings
MADAME MOUSERINK	Caitlin Straw
COURT ASTROLOGER	Patsy L. Paul
GUARDS	Dylan Barber

Jacob Webb

NURSEMAID ONE. . . . . Shelbi Smith

NURSEMAID TWO . . . . .Jeni Fuller

PEARLIPLATE . . . . Katie Barber

BROTHER. . . . . .Connie Oslica

A GYPSY . . . . Mollie Mae Henager

SUGAR PLUM FAIRIES. . . . . .Miki Brewington

Ashtyn Pendley

Sarah Pendley

Rebecca Robinson

Shelbi Smith

LADY SUGAR PLUM. . . . . .Sarah Pendley

Special thanks to my sister/editor –

Vicki May-York

SYNOPSIS OF SCENES

SCENE ONE: The Stahlbaum family drawing room, just before midnight on Christmas Eve.

SCENE TWO: Marie's bedroom, Christmas morning and various places in the story.

SCENE THREE: The Stahlbaum family drawing room, Christmas eve, one year later.

SCENE ONE

*(The scene is the Stahlbaum family drawing room just before midnight on Christmas Eve. A Christmas tree is the central focus. There is a grandfather clock and a glass case on the set. **AT RISE:** The stage is empty. After a beat, a carol is heard from off stage sung by **MOTHER**, **FATHER**, **FRITZ**, and **MARIE**.)*

ALL FOUR.

> O CHRISTMAS TREE, O CHRISTMAS TREE
> O TREE OF GREEN UNCHANGING

*(**MOTHER** enters; she has her hands over **MARIE**'s eyes and is leading her into the room. **FATHER** has his hands over **FRITZ**'s eyes and leads him into the room. **FRITZ** wears a wooden sword.)*

ALL FOUR *(Continued)*

> O CHRISTMAS TREE, O CHRISTMAS TREE
> O TREE OF GREEN UNCHANGING
> A SYMBOL OF THE LORD OF LOVE
> WHOM GOD TO MAN SENT FROM ABOVE
> O CHRISTMAS TREE, O CHRISTMAS TREE
> YOU SET MY HEART A SINGING

(The carol comes to an end, and the parents remove their hands from the children's eyes.)

FATHER. Merry Christmas, my children.

MOTHER. May the magic of the day bless us in all that we do.

MARIE. Oh, Mother, the tree is so beautiful.

MOTHER. Thank you, Marie. There's a present under it for you.

FATHER. And one for Fritz too. Go ahead, open them.

MARIE. Shouldn't we wait for Godfather Hoffmann before we open any gifts?

MOTHER. Oh, he sent word and said he was running late and to start without him. He might not even make it tonight; and if that is the case, he'd see us in the morning. So, go ahead and open your gift.

FATHER. Fritz, why the long face?

FRITZ. I agree with Marie; we should wait for Godfather.

FATHER. You're afraid we didn't get you what you want.

FRITZ. No, that's not it.

MOTHER. Godfather's gifts are always so unique. He's the best inventor…toy maker…in all of Germany.

FRITZ. In the whole wide world.

MARIE. Father, why don't you open my gift to you.

FATHER. You know it's tradition that only children open gifts on Christmas eve. Here, Fritz, open yours. You might be surprised.

*(**FRITZ** opens the present and finds several toy-Calvary-men atop their horses.)*

MOTHER. Just what you wanted. Calvary men and their horses. When they join your foot soldiers…you should have a regiment.

FRITZ. Yes, thank you, now all I need is a chestnut brown stick horse to be a real commander. But I understand if you couldn't get one.

MARIE. It's Christmas time, Brother, and miracles are known to happen.

*(**MARIE** gets a gift from under the tree and gives it to **FRITZ**. From the shape of it…it looks like a stick horse. **FRITZ** smiles.)*

FRITZ. I knew Godfather wouldn't let us down.

*(**FRITZ** begins to rip the paper off and indeed finds a stick horse.)*

MOTHER. That's not from Godfather Hoffmann. It's from Marie.

FRITZ. Oh.

(The stick horse is very crudely constructed.)

Thank you.

MARIE. I know it's not a chestnut brown stick horse.

FATHER. Marie, open your gift.

MARIE. Alright.

> (**MARIE** *opens the gift and finds a doll, but not the one she wanted.*)

FRITZ. That's not the one she wanted.

MARIE. It doesn't mater.

FATHER. I'm sorry I lost my job, and this Christmas can't be better.

MOTHER. Enough of this. Please stop. This is not what Christmas is all about.

MARIE. I love my doll. It looks as sleepy as we all are. I'm going to make a nice bed for it under our beautiful Christmas tree.

> (*There is silence as she makes the bed.* **HOFFMANN** *bursts into the room with a sack thrown over his shoulder, ala Santa Claus.*)

HOFFMANN. Ho, ho, ho, Merry Christmas. I beg your forgiveness for being late.

MOTHER. Godfather, I'm so glad you made it tonight. You're just what we needed at this moment.

HOFFMANN. Cheer up everyone. The new year is going to be a special one. Here, Fritz, is this what you've been waiting for.

> (**HOFFMANN** *pulls a chestnut brown stick horse out of his bag.*)

FRITZ. Oh, Godfather, he's magnificent.

> (*He mounts the stick horse.*)

Bugler…sound the charge.

> (*He vocally trumpets, "Charge," and gallops out of the room.*)

Thank you.

HOFFMANN. And how are you, Marie, my princess?

MARIE. Oh stop, Godfather. I'm never going to marry a prince.

HOFFMANN. Perhaps this silk dress will encourage one to ask you.

(HOFFMANN *pulls a white silk dress from his bag.*)

MARIE. It's beautiful.

MOTHER. Oh, Ernst, it's too much.

FATHER. There's not a Prince in the world that could resist you now.

MARIE. I wish you all would stop about me and a Prince.

(FRITZ *enters.*)

FRITZ. Warning, the enemy approaches. But, I promise to protect everyone.

HOFFMANN. Oh, I have one more gift for you, Marie.

FRITZ. Why does she get two gifts?

HOFFMANN. Because she's a girl, and I need someone who will take special care of this gift.

(*He pulls out the* NUTCRACKER.)

MARIE. He looks lonely. What kind of doll is this?

HOFFMANN. He's not a doll. He's a nutcracker. And a mighty soldier.

FRITZ. A soldier? Don't make me laugh. Let's see how strong he is. Can he crack a walnut?

(FRITZ *tries to crack a walnut, but instead breaks the* NUTCRACKER*'s jaw.*)

Ha, the nut broke his jaw. He'll never make a soldier in my regimen.

MARIE. He would never dream of being one of your stupid soldiers.

(FRITZ *gallops off.*)

MARIE *(Continued.)* That must hurt. Here, this will help.

(*She pulls a yellow ribbon from her hair and ties the* NUTCRACKER*'s jaw shut.*)

He needs rest. I can put him in the bed I made for my doll.

(She puts him in the bed under the tree.)

HOFFMANN. I believe the Nutcracker is in good hands. I have to run. I have a few more stops, and it's so late. Merry Christmas. Ho, ho, ho!

*(***FRITZ*** enters.)*

FRITZ. Warning! The enemy approaches! Take cover!

FATHER. Alright, everyone it's time for bed.

FRITZ. Oh, Father, not yet. Can my new horse and I conquer the enemy before the bugler sounds taps?

FATHER. I'm going to see Godfather out and lock up. When I return, I expect to find this room empty.

*(***HOFFMANN*** and ***FATHER*** exit as all ad lib "goodbye, thank you, and Merry Christmas.")*

FRITZ. Mother, may my horse sleep in my room?

MOTHER. Only if you go right now.

FRITZ. First, I have to put my Calvary men in the glass toy case with my foot soldiers.

MARIE. No, he can't do that. The glass toy case is for Godfather's special toys.

FRITZ. You don't expect them to sleep out here with him.

(He gestures to the **NUTCRACKER.***)*

MARIE. There's nothing wrong with the Nutcracker. Mother, don't let him do this.

MOTHER. One night won't hurt, dear!

MARIE. Fine, go ahead and do it. My Nutcracker would rather be alone.

*(***FRITZ*** takes his Calvary men to the glass case. He has trouble opening the latch.)*

MOTHER. What's wrong?

FRITZ. There's something wrong with the latch. I got it. Foot soldiers meet your comrades in arms.

(He shuts the case door and speaks to **MOTHER** *as he mounts his horse.)*

Mother, would you like a ride to your bedroom?

MOTHER. I beg your pardon. Why would I want that…when my horse is faster than yours.

FRITZ. What are you talking about?

(**MOTHER** *grabs the stick horse* **MARIE** *made.*)

MOTHER. I'll bet this beautiful horse can beat yours to your bedroom.

FRITZ. No way.

(**FRITZ** *takes off and so does* **MOTHER**. *They both exit.*)

MOTHER. *(As she exits.)* Coming, Marie?

MARIE. *(Calling to them.)* I'll wait for father!

(**FRITZ** *and* **MOTHER** *can be heard laughing and having a good time.* **MARIE** *smiles. There is a silence. Then we hear the* **MOUSE KING** *'s voice.*)

MOUSE KING. Where are you? I'll find you! You can't hide from me forever!

(**MARIE** *is startled. She looks around.*)

MARIE. Father, is that you?

(*She moves slowly. The mood should be spooky. She goes to the* **NUTCRACKER**.)

Are you alright? How are you feeling? I'm sorry Fritz hurt you. He can be so rough.

(*Pause as she fawns over the* **NUTCRACKER**. *Set the mood of peace. Then* **FATHER** *bursts into the room…he's only playing!*)

FATHER. Boo!!!

(**MARIE** *screams.*)

FATHER *(Continued.)* It's only me, Marie.

MARIE. Oh, daddy, you frightened the life out of me.

FATHER. I'm sorry; it's almost midnight; let's go to bed.

MARIE. Let me just look after the Nutcracker. Make sure he's comfortable. I'll be right along.

FATHER. Alright, but don't stay up too late.

(*FATHER moves to go.* **MOTHER** *enters. She carries* **MARIE**'s *stick horse.*)

MOTHER. Marie, you're staying up?

MARIE. Just to tuck in the Nutcracker.

(**MOTHER** *gives the stick horse to* **MARIE.**)

MOTHER. Your horse beat Fritz's horse to his bedroom.

MARIE. I'm sure it was the rider, but thank you.

MOTHER. Merry Christmas, darling.

(*She kisses* **MARIE.**)

(**FATHER** *and* **MOTHER** *exit.* **MARIE** *sets the stick horse beside the* **NUTCRACKER.**)

MARIE. Here's a gift for you on this Christmas eve. I know you'll appreciate him more than Fritz did. This horse will serve you well. I promise.

(*She tucks the* **NUTCRACKER** *into his make– shift bed.*)

There, are you warm and comfy?

(*SOUND: The grandfather clock begins to strike midnight. This startles* **MARIE.** *She lets out a tiny scream. She talks to the* **NUTCRACKER** *as the clock strikes.*)

It's only the clock striking midnight! Announcing the arrival of Christmas Day. The birth of our savior. Good night, my new friend. Sleep well.

(*She stands to go to her bedroom.*)

(*On the eighth chime of the clock the room is filled with the SOUND of hissing.* **MARIE** *looks frightened, trapped. She doesn't know where to go. The hissing builds to a peak as the grand– father clock strikes midnight. On the last strike... all goes silent.* **MARIE** *looks around. Nothing happens. Just as she relaxes – an army of* **MICE** *emerge from every corner and crevice of the room. Hissing once again fills the room. It grows in intensity as the* **MICE** *surround* **MARIE.** *SOUND: a fanfare is heard. Two* **MICE** *hold* **MARIE.** *The others scatter to make way* *for the* **MOUSE KING**'s *entrance.)*

MOUSE KING. Where is he? You must tell me!

MARIE. *(Crying for help.)* Father!

(The **MOUSE KING** *barks a command to the* **MICE**.*)*

MOUSE KING. Surround her! She'll tell us! Advance!

(The **MICE** *surround* **MARIE**.*)*

MOUSE KING *(Continued.)* I asked you a question, young lady; and I expect an answer. Where is he?

MARIE. Please don't hurt me. I don't know what you're talking about.

(The **NUTCRACKER** *rises from the bed* **MARIE** *made for him. When the actor takes over for the doll, it should look like he grew from the bed. SOUND/music accompanies this. All the* **MICE** *scatter to take up defensive positions. The* **MOUSE KING** *grabs* **MARIE**. *The* **NUTCRACKER** *wears the yellow ribbon around jaw.)*

NUTCRACKER. Mouse King, here I am. Leave the girl alone.

MOUSE KING. So, you're not hiding behind the skirts of this young girl.

NUTCRACKER. Leave the girl out of this.

MOUSE KING. You can have her.

*(**MOUSE KING** pushes* **MARIE** *to the* **NUTCRACKER**. *The* **NUTCRACKER** *puts* **MARIE** *behind him to protect her.)*

NUTCRACKER. Can't we give this conflict a rest for a few days until this special holiday is over?

MOUSE KING. This holiday means nothing to me. I demand to know why you continue to run from me?

NUTCRACKER. You have it all twisted. It is you who avoid me!

MOUSE KING. Not true. I only want to put an end to this.

NUTCRACKER. Vengeance is mine! It was your mother who cursed me.

MOUSE KING. You make me laugh.

(He pulls his sword out.)

I fight for my mother's honor!

NUTCRACKER. I have forgiven your mother. Can't we move on?

MOUSE KING. How can you? Look at yourself. Your jaw.

NUTCRACKER. Leave this girl alone. She has nothing to do with the us.

MOUSE KING. What about the prophecy?

NUTCRACKER. I believe the prophecy can come true without violence.

MOUSE KING. Again, you make me laugh.

NUTCRACKER. Please just leave me alone!

MOUSE KING. That will never happen. I also fight in the memory of my relatives!

*(The **MOUSE KING** puts his sword at the **NUTCRACKER**'s throat. The **NUTCRACKER** is without a weapon. Pause, as it looks like the **MOUSE KING** has won. The **MICE** cheer the **MOUSE KING** in his victory. The **NUTCRACKER** leaps for the stick horse. He gets it and uses it as a sword. A sword/stick fight between the **NUTCRACKER** and the **MOUSE KING** begins. The **NUTCRACKER** eventually pins the **MOUSE KING** to the floor. The **MOUSE KING** cries for help.)*

MOUSE KING. Help me! Attack, my mice! Remember your relatives!

*(The **MICE** attack the **NUTCRACKER**.)*

MARIE. Stop this! This isn't fair! Help! Father! Fritz!

*(The **NUTCRACKER** cries out to **MARIE**.)*

NUTCRACKER. Release my men! The glass toy cabinet! Let my men out.

*(The fight builds. **MARIE** finally understands what she must do. She tries the door to the cabinet. It's jammed.)*

MARIE. The lock is jammed.

*(**MARIE** frantically tries to open the door. Nothing doing...the door will not open. She breaks the glass on

the door to the toy cabinet. In doing so, she cuts her wrist. The SOUND of glass shattering is heard.)

Oh!!!

(FRITZ's Calvary and soldiers enter. A battle ensues… it climaxes when it looks like the MOUSE KING has the NUTCRACKER trapped. MARIE cries out as she takes off her shoe and runs over to the MOUSE KING and starts beating him with it.)

MARIE *(Continued.)* NO!!! Please, stop this fighting!

(The MOUSE KING gets off the NUTCRACKER. He calls out.)

MOUSE KING. Ow! What is going on? Retreat! All mice retreat!

(The MICE scamper to behind the MOUSE KING. The SOLDIERS to behind the NUTCRACKER.)

MOUSE KING *(con't)* This isn't over, Nutcracker. I'll get you.

(The MOUSE KING and MICE exit. The NUTCRACKER talks to his troops.)

NUTCRACKER. Secure the perimeters.

(The SOLDIERS exit at the four corners of the stage.)

NUTCRACKER *(Continued.)* Thank you miss. That was a very brave thing you did. You saved my life.

(MARIE is beginning to feel the effects of "loss of blood.")

MARIE. You're just like Fritz. And I thought you were different. Godfather has made you so real. Are you real? Or is this just a dream?

NUTCRACKER. I promise you the Mouse King will not bother you again.

(From offstage we hear FATHER call.)

FATHER. Marie, are you coming to bed?

NUTCRACKER. Are you alright? You've been hurt. Let me look. That's a nasty cut.

MARIE. I'm fine. This is not real. It's all just a dream. I

better just go to bed.

NUTCRACKER. Relax, my princess.

(**MARIE** *passes out. The* **NUTCRACKER** *catches her in his arms as the LIGHTS fade to black.*)

SCENE TWO

(*AT RISE:* **MARIE** *is discovered in her bedroom, laying in her bed asleep.* **MOTHER** *and* **FATHER** *enter.*)

MOTHER. She's still sleeping.

FATHER. That was a bad cut.

MOTHER. Seven stitches worth.

FATHER. The doctor did say the sedative he gave her would make her sleep.

(**MARIE** *wakes up.*)

MARIE. I'm awake. Is the Nutcracker alright?

MOTHER. Relax, darling.

MARIE. There was a battle. Mice. There were mice everywhere. The Nutcracker fought them off.

FATHER. You're just tired, my dear.

MARIE. No, please listen to me. It's true.

(**FRITZ** *storms into the room.*)

FRITZ. What did you do to my soldiers?

MARIE. Yes, Fritz, your soldiers helped the Nutcracker fight off the mice and the Mouse King.

FRITZ. Don't listen to this story. She was trying to get into the glass toy case cause she didn't want my Calvary men in it. The latch wasn't working and the glass broke, cutting her.

MARIE. No, Fritz, believe me. You should be proud. Where is the Nutcracker?

FRITZ. Godfather took him early this morning.

MOTHER. Come on, we need to let Marie rest.

(**HOFFMANN** *enters.*)

HOFFMANN. Merry Christmas.

MARIE. What have you done with my Nutcracker? Fritz said you took him.

HOFFMANN. Only to fix his broken jaw.

MARIE. Then he's safe?

HOFFMANN. Yes.

MARIE. I was so worried.

FATHER. Godfather, maybe you can calm Marie down.

HOFFMANN. Leave us. I'll try.

FATHER. Come, Fritz.

(**FATHER, MOTHER,** *and* **FRITZ** *exit.*)

HOFFMANN (*Continued.*) The Nutcracker told me you saved his life last night. Thank you.

(**MARIE***'s attitude changes when* **HOFFMANN** *says this.*)

MARIE. What? Then you believe my story?

HOFFMANN. Yes, I believe you.

MARIE. Is the Mouse King real?

HOFFMANN. The Mouse King is very real and can be very pushy.

MARIE. Why are the Nutcracker and the Mouse King enemies?

HOFFMANN. It's a long story.

MARIE. And what is this prophecy they both speak of?

HOFFMANN. To understand it completely, you must travel back with me in years before either the Nutcracker or Mouse King was even born.

MARIE. I must know.

HOFFMANN. It was in Nuremberg. There was a King and Queen…

(*As* **HOFFMANN** *tells his story all the scenes come to life in the bedroom, around the bed as* **HOFFMANN** *and* **MARIE** *watch.* **QUEEN** *and* **KING** *enter and play scene down left.*)

HOFFMANN (*Continued*) …who had always been told by the court doctors they would never have an heir.

QUEEN. Is there nothing we can do to have a child?

KING. I will consult the court astrologer.

(**KING** *exits.*)

HOFFMANN. The Queen of the castle mice, Madame Mouse-rink...

(**MOUSERINK** *enters and plays scene down right.*)

HOFFMANN *(Continued)* ...had magical powers and she paid the Queen a visit.

MOUSERINK. Are you ready to accept my assistance, my fellow Queen.

(**QUEEN** *moves to* **MOUSERINK.**)

QUEEN. I just can't believe that a rat can help me.

MOUSERINK. I'm not a rat; I'm a mouse. A magical mouse.

QUEEN. I want a baby.

MOUSERINK. And I want food and security for my mice subjects.

QUEEN. I'd gladly give you that if you can help me with a child.

MOUSERINK. You can never tell anyone of our arrangement.

QUEEN. Don't worry...if I told anyone, they would only think I was crazy.

MOUSERINK. If you do...the child will die instantly.

(**QUEEN** *and* **MOUSERINK** *exit down right.*)

MARIE. Did the Queen get pregnant?

(**HOFFMANN** *gestures to the* **KING** *and* **COURT ASTROL-OGER** *as they enter and play scene down left.*)

KING. Court Astrologer, will my wife ever have a child?

COURT ASTROLOGER. There's an inventor who lives here in Nuremberg making some very realistic toys. The talk of the town is he can do anything. His name is Hoffmann.

MARIE. Godfather, is he talking about you?

KING. What do toys and a toy maker have to do with the Queen having a child.

COURT ASTROLOGER. Well, he's more than just a toy maker. He's sort of a magician too.

KING. I don't want magic! I want predictions. Will my wife have a child soon?

COURT ASTROLOGER. I don't know!

KING. Why do I put up with you?

(QUEEN *enters down right and moves to* KING.)

QUEEN. Are you barking at the help again, dear?

COURT ASTROLOGER. May I go, sire?

(*The* KING *nods and the* COURT ASTROLOGER *scampers off.*)

KING. He's a fool. I don't know why I keep him in our employ.

QUEEN. Maybe I can cheer you up, my big-bad-King!

KING. Just seeing your face does that, my cuddly-Queen!

QUEEN. While you've been seeking answers from Astrologers…I've been dealing with Doctors.

KING. Oh, my dear, are you sick?

QUEEN. Do you believe in miracles?

KING. (*Very hopeful.*) What? No! It can't be. It's not possible?

QUEEN. (*With a smile.*) Hi, Daddy!

KING. Come, we must prepare for the birth.

QUEEN. It's nine months away.

KING. You can never start too early.

(*The* KING *and* QUEEN *exit down left.*)

MARIE. I don't understand how this connects with the Mouse King and the Nutcracker?

(*The* MOUSE KING *appears up left and moves to bed.*)

MOUSE KING. Yes, why bore her with all these past details.

HOFFMANN. She needs to know the past; so she'll understand how she fits into the puzzle.

MOUSE KING. I will put an end to things long before you can finish the story. Tell the Nutcracker to stop hiding behind you and this girl.

(MOUSE KING *exits up left.*)

MARIE. What do you mean, how I fit into the puzzle?

HOFFMANN. You will understand soon.

MARIE. Did the Queen have her baby?

HOFFMANN. Yes, the Queen gave birth.

(KING *and* QUEEN *enter with baby in hand and play scene down left.* COURT ASTROLOGER *enters behind them.*)

KING. Behold citizens of Germany. The Queen has given birth to a beautiful baby girl.

HOFFMANN. The Queen never told anyone about her arrangement with Madame Mouserink. All through her pregnancy, she furnished cheese to the Mouse Queen and her castle mice. They all grew strong and healthy, and their population grew. It was the King who got worried because of all the mice.

KING. We seem to have a problem with rats…maybe I should call an exterminator. We can't have rats in the castle with a baby.

QUEEN. They're not rats, dear, they're mice…and they're really harmless. Please don't do anything rash.

KING. What's the name of that inventor?

COURT ASTROLOGER. Hoffmann. His name is, Herr Hoffmann.

(*The* KING *speaks to* HOFFMANN.)

KING. Thank you for coming, Inventor Hoffmann.

MARIE. Godfather, I think he's talking to you.

(HOFFMANN *and* MARIE *move to the* KING.)

HOFFMANN. Your Majesty.

(HOFFMANN *bows,* MARIE *curtsies.*)

KING. Welcome, Herr Hoffmann. You've quite a reputation, sir. My Court Astrologer can't stop talking about you. He says you can do just about anything.

HOFFMANN. I'm humbled…and your servant. How may I serve you, my King?

KING. Mice. They infest the castle. I want you to get rid of them.

HOFFMANN. It sounds like you need the Pied Piper…not me.

KING. Do you mock your King?

HOFFMANN. Not at all. I'll do my best to serve you, Sire.

QUEEN. This really isn't necessary, my King. I beg you. Don't do this. It will only cause problems.

KING. The future of this country depends on you, Mr. Inventor. I'll give you two days.

(To the **QUEEN.***)*

Come dear.

(The **KING, QUEEN,** *and the* **COURT ASTROLOGER** *exit down left.)*

MARIE. What did you do?

HOFFMANN. With only two days…I could have panicked. And I almost did, but instead I put all my skills as a toy maker to use.

(As **HOFFMANN** *tells the following, it is acted out by several mice.)*

HOFFMAN. *(Continued)* Since the mice had grown quite fond of the Queen's cheese, I had hundreds of small oblong boxes built. They were placed throughout the castle. From a wire inside each box, a piece of cheese dangled temptingly. When the mice ate the cheese, they pulled on the wire which was connected to the door of the box. The door slammed shut…trapping them inside the cage. Mouse after mouse was caught… until finally all the mice in the palace were behind bars. Then they were all destroyed!

(The **KING, QUEEN, COURT ASTROLOGER,** *and two* **GUARDS** *enter and play scene down left.)*

KING. Congratulations, Inventor.

*(***HOFFMANN** *and* **MARIE** *join the* **KING.***)*

COURT ASTROLOGER. Don't forget, Sire, it was I who recommended him.

QUEEN. *(Scared.)* You're positive you caught all the mice in the palace? What about Madame Mouserink? Are you sure she's gone?

COURT ASTROLOGER. My Queen, it is as the Inventor says. I see it in the stars. The palace is free of mice.

KING. You'll be handsomely rewarded, sir. But, first do me the honor by saying you'll help us name the new Princess.

(**HOFFMANN** *looks at the baby.*)

HOFFMANN. Pearliplate…because of her beautiful smile… which will soon be filled with the most beautiful pearly white teeth this kingdom has ever seen.

COURT ASTROLOGER. Hail to the Princess Pearliplate.

MARIE. Godfather… this is so exciting!

KING. Bless the Princess Pearliplate.

(*Madame* **MOUSERINK** *explodes onto the scene from down right.*)

MOUSERINK. Blessings? Ha! If you're going to pass out blessings…how about a blessing for all of the mice that you have destroyed?

QUEEN. I knew it. I knew she wasn't captured. I knew she lived.

MOUSERINK. Yes, I live, and you betrayed me. Revenge is mine.

QUEEN. I'll give you whatever you want, but please don't hurt my baby.

MOUSERINK. Your words are a waste of your lying breathe. My ears don't hear them.

KING. Inventor, what is the meaning of this?

MOUSERINK. It means that some two-bit inventor can't out smart the mighty Madame Mouserink.

KING. Guards…get rid of this…this thing!

(*Two* **GUARDS** *move toward* **MOUSERINK.**)

MOUSERINK. Don't come near me you fools…you idiots!

> *(She throws up her hands stopping the guards in mid-step. A spell SOUND is heard. She moves to the **QUEEN**.)*

> I want satisfaction…and I swear on the souls of my subjects that I will get it!

> *(**MOUSERINK** looks at the baby in the **QUEEN**'s arms.)*

> She is so beautiful! And what a gorgeous smile!

QUEEN. No. Don't do anything. Get away from my baby.

MOUSERINK. My dear Queen, I trusted you. What a fool I was. Now, I warn you…don't leave the Princess alone. Ever. I have a very special spell I've cooked up just for her.

> *(**MOUSERINK** laughs villainously and with a wave of her hand and a flash of smoke…she is gone. A spell SOUND is heard.)*

KING. Guards, after her.

> *(The **GUARDS** break their freeze and exit after **MOUSERINK**. The **KING** speaks to the **QUEEN**.)*

KING *(Continued.)* Do you know this creature?

QUEEN. I know she is very powerful, and we better take heed to her threat. The princess must be guarded all the time. If we are not with her…the princess must have a nursemaid at her side twenty-four hours a day! No, not one, but two strong nursemaids with her at all times! With big, healthy tom cats at each one of their sides.

COURT ASTROLOGER. This Madame Mouserink is a phony, your majesty. Please, believe me. There is nothing to worry about.

KING. Shut up, you imbecile. Hoffmann…you've certainly made a complete joke of my daughter's celebration! Nothing better happen to the princess.

> *(The **KING** and **HOFFMANN** hold a look for a moment. Then the **KING**, **QUEEN**, and **COURT ASTROLOGER** exit down left.)*

MARIE. Godfather, what is going on. Is this real?

HOFFMANN. Very real.

MARIE. Continue.

HOFFMANN. The Queen interviewed hundreds of nurse-maids to protect the Princess Pearliplate. Six of the best were hired. Those six would take turns…two at a time…guarding the Princess. The King offered a handsome reward for the biggest Tom cats in the land! The country had never seen so many cats in one place. Within a day, the Princess was protected.

MARIE. She must have been safe.

HOFFMANN. Three months time past! Hide nor hair was seen of Madame Mouserink…or any other mouse for that matter. The nursemaids and their cats began to relax on the job.

(**NURSEMAIDS ONE** *and* **TWO**, *with cats on their laps, are discovered down right, sleeping. The baby crib is down left. SOUND: A clock tolls.*)

ONE. I hate this midnight shift.

TWO. I'm sorry, did you say something?

ONE. No!

(*Pause. They both doze.*)

TWO. This midnight shift is boring.

ONE. What?

TWO. Nothing!

(*They both doze. SOUND: The baby cries.*)

ONE. Oh great…it's going to be a restless night.

(*She moves to the crib.*)

TWO. You know, I don't think this Mouserink even exists.

ONE. Or for that matter, any mice in this castle either.

TWO. There's no need for both of us to stay awake.

ONE. It's our shift, but hey, you're right. I'll flip you for it! Call it!

(**ONE** *takes out a coin and flips it.*)

TWO. Heads.

MARIE. Madame Mouserink is just waiting for something like this, isn't she?

HOFFMANN. She's a very smart Queen.

ONE. Tails! Sorry. Good night!

(**ONE** *sits in her chair and falls asleep. Pause.* **TWO** *looks at the Princess in her crib, and moves back to her chair.* **MOUSERINK** *enters. She sneaks up behind* **TWO**, *waves her hands over* **TWO**, *a spell SOUND is heard, and* **TWO** *falls instantly asleep.* **MOUSERINK** *moves to the crib.*)

MARIE. What about the cats?

HOFFMANN. Earlier that day Mouserink had put something in their food to make them sleep!

MOUSERINK. *(As she stands over the crib.)* Hello, Princess Pearliplate. Oh, such a lovely smile.

(She waves her hands over the crib as she chants.)

Your smile is your best feature
I'll just emphasize that, my dear.
Smiling will always be in your future.
Extend that smile from ear to ear.

(She stops waving her hands and a spell SOUND is heard.)

There! That should do it!

(**ONE** *wakes up and sees what is happening.*)

ONE. Oh, my goodness! Sound the alarm! There's a rat by the princess!

(**MOUSERINK** *moves to* **ONE**.)

MOUSERINK. I'm not a rat, you fool! I'm a Queen!

(She pushes **ONE** *into her chair.)*

Tell your Queen…justice has been served!

(**MOUSERINK** *scurries away.*)

ONE. Wake up! Wake up! She's been here!

TWO. What?

ONE. The mouse Queen was here! She was standing over the Princess' crib!

TWO. Is the princess alright?

(*They run to the crib and look in.*)

ONE. Oh my…..she looks awful.

TWO. Grotesque is a better word.

ONE. Is she alive?

TWO. No, I think the princess is dead.

(**ONE** *and* **TWO** *carry the crib off down left. Chairs are struck down right.*)

MARIE. The Nutcracker is revenging the death of the princess. That's why he is fighting the Mouse King.

(*The* **KING** *enters down left, shouting.*)

KING. Get me the Inventor. I want Hoffmann here…right away.

(**HOFFMANN** *and* **MARIE** *move to the* **KING.**)

HOFFMANN. You called for me, your majesty.

KING. My daughter looks like a monster. Have you seen what that Rat did to her beautiful smile?

HOFFMANN. I'm sorry.

KING. That's all you have to say, "I'm sorry." It's because of you this has happened. This spell must be broken.

HOFFMANN. I promise to find the cure.

KING. I'll have your head if you don't.

(*The* **KING** *exits down left.*)

MARIE. You mean the Princess was alive?

HOFFMANN. Madame Mouserink didn't kill her…she just turned her into a freak. Made her smile from ear to ear.

MARIE. How did you break the spell?

HOFFMANN. It was like looking for the needle in the haystack. I had no idea where to even start.

(The **COURT ASTROLOGER** *enters down right and moves center.)*

COURT ASTROLOGER. May I offer my services?

MARIE. Oh, goodness, Godfather, not him. He's a fool.

COURT ASTROLOGER. What a perceptive young girl. It does seem like I am the Court Jester as of late.

HOFFMANN. Why do you want to help me?

COURT ASTROLOGER. I must win the King's favor once again.

HOFFMANN. Solve the riddle yourself… and tell the King. Why involve me?

COURT ASTROLOGER. He won't listen to me anymore.

MARIE. I wouldn't trust him.

HOFFMANN. I'm at a dead end at the moment. And besides, what have I got to lose, except my head.

COURT ASTROLOGER. Oh, thank you, Herr Hoffmann. I know we can help one another.

HOFFMANN. Do you have the answer?

COURT ASTROLOGER. First we must consult the stars.

(The **COURT ASTROLOGER** *claps his hands and the LIGHTING shifts. Stars fill the bedroom. Use mirror ball.)*

MARIE. My goodness, how did you do that?

(The **COURT ASTROLOGER** *is all business now. He looks at the stars.)*

COURT ASTROLOGER. Ah…It's a very good night to read the heavens.

MARIE. Look! I just saw a shooting star. Did you see it?

COURT ASTROLOGER. That's a fantastic sign. Inventor, when were you born?

HOFFMANN. The year?

COURT ASTROLOGER. No, month and day.

HOFFMANN. Tenth of January.

COURT ASTROLOGER. Marie?

MARIE. This is silly.

COURT ASTROLOGER. Birthday!!!

MARIE. January twenty-first.

COURT ASTROLOGER. Excellent. Hoffmann is a Capricorn, the goat. And Marie, Aquarius, the water bearer. Earth and air are represented. When was the Princess born?

MARIE. How is this going to help?

COURT ASTROLOGER. Please. Believe.

HOFFMANN. March second.

COURT ASTROLOGER. Ah, she's a Pisces. It's all falling in to place. Three signs that are neighbors… all in sequence on the astrological calendar. And with a Pisces, that means earth and air are joined by water.

(**MARIE** *sees something in the sky. Mirror ball begins to spin.*)

MARIE. Look! The stars are moving!

COURT ASTROLOGER. They are aligning. Capricorn, January tenth –

HOFFMANN. My birthday.

COURT ASTROLOGER. Aquarius…January twenty-first.

MARIE. Mine.

COURT ASTROLOGER. And the Princess is Pisces…March second. Three signs in a row. Earth, air, and water are all represented.

(The LIGHTS flash.)

MARIE. What's happening?

COURT ASTROLOGER. The heavens know that I complete the cycle

(SOUND of thunder is heard.)

HOFFMANN. Can you put that into toy maker language?

COURT ASTROLOGER. I was born March 31…I'm an Aries… the next sign in line with all of you. And Aries is a fire sign.

*(SOUND: A clap of thunder is heard. **MARIE** clings to*

HOFFMANN.*)*

MARIE. *(Scared.)* Godfather.

(The LIGHTING changes.)

COURT ASTROLOGER. Witness the heavens open…as we four…earth, air, water, and fire…unite in this quest for truth!

(He pulls out three white candles.)

We must each light one of these white candles. The Princess being a Pisces and the color for Pisces is white. White stands for purity, truth, and sincerity. I'll light the first.

(He lights the candle.)

This candle I light to represent the Princess Pearliplate. It burns as does her spirit.

(To **HOFFMANN.** *)*

Inventor, you light the second.

(As **HOFFMANN** *lights the candle.*

These are the symbols of truth.

(To **MARIE.** *)*

Marie, please light the last one.

(As **MARIE** *lights the candle.)*

They are joined with the spirit of Princess Pearliplate and to us show all truth.

(The SOUND of thunder is heard.)

Tell us truth! How do we break the spell Madame Mouserink has cast upon our Princess?

(More SOUND: thunder is heard.)

COURT ASTROLOGER *(Continued)* Tell us!!!

(LIGHTS and SOUND: thunder.)

I demand to know!!!

(A flash of lightning strikes the **COURT ASTROLOGER.**

(*A deafening SOUND of thunder echoes throughout the theatre. The* **COURT ASTROLOGER** *is thrown back. He falls to the floor.* **HOFFMANN** *and* **MARIE** *run to him. The LIGHTING returns to normal.*)

HOFFMANN. Are you alright?

(*The* **COURT ASTROLOGER** *does not move.*)

MARIE. He's dead. What is happening? Too many people are getting hurt in this story. Who is this Mouse King? Is he Madame Mouserink's husband? Godfather, please end this mystery.

(*The* **MOUSE KING** *enters down right.*)

MOUSE KING. I'm not Mouserink's husband. I am her son.

(*The* **NUTCRACKER** *enters down left.*)

NUTCRACKER. Leave this room at once.

MOUSE KING. I was wondering what had happened to you. It's been awhile since I've seen you.

NUTCRACKER. Hoffmann has repaired my jaw and tended to my wounds.

MOUSE KING. Good. I don't want to defeat someone not at full strength.

(**MOUSE KING** *exits down right.*)

NUTCRACKER. Come back here.

(*HE runs after the* **MOUSE KING** *and exits.*)

MARIE. Godfather, what about the Court Astrologer?

HOFFMANN. Don't worry, my Marie, the Court Astrologer is not dead. He's only stunned!

(*The* **COURT ASTROLOGER** *begins to stir. He's groggy.*)

COURT ASTROLOGER. I have discovered the answer.

MARIE. Please, tell us.

COURT ASTROLOGER. (*Blows out the candles as he speaks.*) To break the spell cast on the Princess Pearliplate…she must eat the sweet kernel of the krackatuk!

HOFFMANN. She must eat what?

COURT ASTROLOGER. The nut krackatuk!

MARIE. That should be easy.

COURT ASTROLOGER. Here comes the hard part. This nut must be cracked in the presence of the Princess by the teeth of a young man whose beard has never felt a razor and who has always worn boots.

MARIE. This is getting very complicated.

COURT ASTROLOGER. There's more. Then the nut must be offered…no presented…to the Princess by the young man with his eyes closed. He must then take seven steps backward without stumbling.

HOFFMANN. And that will break the spell on the princess?

COURT ASTROLOGER. That's what the stars told me. Do that and the princess' smile will return to normal.

(The **COURT ASTROLOGER** *and* **HOFFMANN** *share a look, both sit. The excitement is gone from both their faces.)*

MARIE. Why all this gloom and doom? All we have to do is find this nut…krackatuk.

HOFFMANN. Easier said than done. You see, my dear, the krackatuk is a very rare nut. The Court Astrologer and I searched for it for fifteen years.

COURT ASTROLOGER. Always keeping an eye out for a young man wearing boots…whose face had never seen a razor. I consulted the stars frantically.

HOFFMANN. We traveled the world crisscrossing it from pole to pole and side to side.

MARIE. Did you find the nut?

(The **KING** *and two* **GUARDS** *enter and play scene down left.)*

KING. Welcome back…my world travelers. I have believed in you for fifteen years.

*(***HOFFMANN, MARIE,** *and* **COURT ASTROLOGER** *move to the* **KING.***)*

HOFFMANN. Is the Princess healthy, your Majesty?

KING. She is as physically fit as one of my best knights.

HOFFMANN. And after fifteen years…she must be a beauty.

KING. Yes, she is very beautiful. But, a beauty still under the curse.

(He turns to a guard.)

Get my daughter.

GUARD. Yes, Sire.

(He exits.)

KING. *(To* **HOFFMANN.***)* I've told her for all these years…not to worry, that you would find a cure. You can deliver the good news to her face.

(Princess **PEARLIPLATE** *and a* **GUARD** *enter. She is a girl of fifteen. She is a perfectly beautiful young girl, except for her smile which spans from ear to ear. She is very hopeful.)*

PEARLIPLATE. Yes, father, are they finally back? Is the quest over? Have you found the krackatuk?

HOFFMANN. No, my princess. I'm sorry to say…that we have not.

KING. What?

COURT ASTROLOGER. Hold on, everyone! I'm getting some weird vibes. I think we're really close.

KING. Guards…take that babbling idiot away!

*(***GUARDS** *move to the* **COURT ASTROLOGER** *and hold him. The* **KING** *barks again.)*

KING *(Continued)* Arrest the Inventor too!

*(***GUARDS** *seizes* **HOFFMANN.***)*

MARIE. You can't do this. He's done nothing wrong. He just spend fifteen years of his life searching.

KING. There's nothing more to be said. Five years…fifteen years…or fifty. Promises were made. Now, if I were you young lady…I'd hold your tongue. That is, if you don't want to join them.

PEARLIPLATE. Father, please let her speak.

MARIE. Doesn't a condemned man usually get a last request?

KING. I'm really losing my patience.

PEARLIPLATE. She's right. Grant him a last request.

KING. Only for you, my daughter. Alright, Inventor, what do you want to do?

HOFFMANN. I'd like to see my brother?

KING. You have one day.

> (*The* **KING**, **PEARLIPLATE**, *and* **GUARDS** *exit down left.* **BROTHER** *enters down right.*)

BROTHER. Ernst, is that really you? How long has it been?

> (**HOFFMANN**, **MARIE**, *and* **COURT ASTROLOGER** *move to* **BROTHER**.)

HOFFMANN. Yes, brother. It's really me.

> (**HOFFMANN** *and* **BROTHER** *embrace.*)

BROTHER. What a wonderful Christmas surprise. It's been a long time!

HOFFMANN. Fifteen years.

COURT ASTROLOGER. Actually, it's only been fourteen years…ten months and –

HOFFMANN. Let me introduce my fellow traveling companions…the Court Astrologer!

BROTHER. Happy holidays!

COURT ASTROLOGER. I've had much more pleasant ones.

HOFFMANN. And my Goddaughter, Marie.

BROTHER. How long can you stay?

HOFFMANN. The King has only given us one day.

BROTHER. And then you must return to his prison?

COURT ASTROLOGER. I say we make a run for it. Travel the world again. We have the advantage of knowing it now. We don't owe this King anything. He'll never catch us.

BROTHER. What was it you failed to find?

HOFFMANN. Enough about me! What's new in your life?

BROTHER. I'm a father.

HOFFMANN. Congratulations. A boy or a girl?

BROTHER. He's a young man now. He just turned fourteen.

HOFFMANN. You mean to tell me; I'm an uncle.

COURT ASTROLOGER. Excuse me, what is your son's birthday?

(The **BROTHER** *gives* **HOFFMANN** *a look.)*

HOFFMANN. Humor him, please.

BROTHER. December fifth.

COURT ASTROLOGER. Excellent! Just as I was hoping.

(Beat.)

Excuse me. I must be alone!

(The **COURT ASTROLOGER** *exits.)*

HOFFMANN. What's his name?

BROTHER. Nathaniel Ernst.

HOFFMANN. I'm honored that you've named your son after me!

BROTHER. Thank you, but stop all this small talk. Why do you refuse to talk about your quest?

HOFFMANN. It's just too crazy. We should be talking about my will.

BROTHER. Nothing is too crazy if my brother is to be executed tomorrow. Maybe we can stop this.

HOFFMANN. Okay. We were looking for a krackatuk. Nobody's ever heard of –

BROTHER. Krackatuk...the nut.

HOFFMANN. You mean you've actually heard of it?

BROTHER. Not only have I heard of it...I own one.

HOFFMANN. Are you serious? This is hardly a time to jest.

BROTHER. I bought it...the day Nathaniel was born. I was returning home from the hospital...happy and proud to be a papa. It was a very dark and over cast day.

(The LIGHTS begin to reflect this day.)

A big blizzard was on its way. I was hoping to get home before it hit, so I took the short cut through the north end.

HOFFMANN. That's a bad section of town to be caught in at any time.

BROTHER. I was stopped by a very tiny creature.

(**GYPSY** *enters down left.*)

BROTHER (*Continued*) A Gypsy woman.

GYPSY. Merry Christmas to you, sir.

(**BROTHER** *moves to* **GYPSY.**)

BROTHER. And a happy holiday to you too.

GYPSY. What's your hurry? Slow down and enjoy the holiday spirit.

BROTHER. Beg pardon, miss. The storm. I must get home.

GYPSY. You're in such a hurry. Please buy some of my hot roasted nuts?

BROTHER. Thank you, but I must get home… before the blizzard –

GYPSY. My children need help. And now that you're a new father…I'm sure you understand.

BROTHER. Excuse me, do I know you?

GYPSY. Nathaniel, is a fine name for a first born son!

BROTHER. What do you want? You, Gypsies, scare me.

GYPSY. You don't really want any roasted nuts. I got something special for you. It's a krackatuk.

BROTHER. I must make it home before the blizzard hits.

GYPSY. The blizzard isn't going to hit here.

BROTHER. Don't be silly; look at the sky.

GYPSY. In celebration of Nathaniel's birth…you can have this special nut for only fifty marcs.

BROTHER. Don't be absurd. I don't need a nut.

GYPSY. You drive a tough bargain. Because it's almost Christmas…you can have this magical nut for only forty marcs. And I promise to leave you alone. Please think of my children.

(Just to get on his way **BROTHER** *pulls out a five marc note.)*

BROTHER. All I have is a five. Take it or leave it.

GYPSY. Sold.

(She grabs the money.)

One day this nut is going to save the life of a love one. My children thank you. I thank you. Merry Christmas.

(She flicks the nut to him and exits laughing. **BROTHER** *moves to* **HOFFMANN.** *)*

HOFFMANN. May I see it?

(BROTHER *moves to* **HOFFMANN** *and hands the nut to him.)*

BROTHER. And the bizarre thing is the blizzard never came that night. From that day on, the nut became my lucky charm. I really believe it has helped me…no…I know it's the reason I am the man I am today and so successful. And, if you need it. It's yours. I hope it treats you as well.

HOFFMANN. This is indeed a krackatuk. It says so right here.

(HOFFMANN *shows* **BROTHER** *writing on the nut.)*

BROTHER. You can you read that?

HOFFMANN. In my travels, I learned many languages.

(From offstage right **NATHANIEL** *calls.)*

NATHANIEL. Father, I'm home!

BROTHER. Oh, good. It's Nathaniel. You get to meet him.

(NATHANIEL *enters down right. The same actor that plays the* **NUTCRACKER** *plays* **NATHANIEL.** *He is a handsome young, fourteen year old boy, smartly dressed, and wearing boots.)*

BROTHER *(Continued)* Nathaniel, I have a surprise for you. This is your Uncle Ernst.

MARIE. Hey, it's the Nutcracker.

BROTHER. And his Goddaughter, Marie.

HOFFMANN. Yes, my nephew is the Nutcracker.

MARIE. But why did he become a nutcracker?

NATHANIEL. Father has told me so much about you and your toys…that I think I already know you.

(The **COURT ASTROLOGER** *bursts into the room.)*

COURT ASTROLOGER. *(To* **HOFFMANN**.*)* I got the answer! Your nephew's a Sagittarius. The sign that proceeds yours, Marie's, the princess', and mine! He is the boy we're looking for to break the spell.

MARIE. We're way ahead of you. Look. He wears boots, and I don't think his face has ever seen a razor.

COURT ASTROLOGER. Now all we need is the krackatuk.

*(***HOFFMANN** *tosses the nut to the* **COURT ASTROL-OGER**.*)*

COURT ASTROLOGER *(Continued)* We sure do make a pretty good team. Let's go find the King!

*(***BROTHER, NATHANIEL, COURT ASTROLOGER** *exit. The* **MOUSE KING** *enters.)*

MOUSE KING. This is my favorite part. Marie, you're about to find out why the Nutcracker is my mortal enemy. Go ahead Old Man, talk away.

*(***MOUSE KING** *exits.)*

MARIE. He doesn't scare me.

HOFFMANN. Come on then, or we're going to miss out on the festivities!

*(***MARIE** *embraces* **HOFFMANN**. *The bedroom becomes the grand ballroom of the* **KING***'s palace. The room is soon filled with lords and ladies of the kingdom.* **BROTHER** *enters and moves to* **HOFFMANN**. *Trumpets SOUND. The* **COURT ASTROLOGER** *enters and moves to a throne.)*

COURT ASTROLOGER. Attention! Attention! Ladies and Gentleman of the Kingdom! This day will be celebrated in history forever. The curse on the Princess Pearliplate will finally be broken this Christmas Day.

(The crowd cheers.)

We searched the world for the answer to the riddle. When all along the answer was right here in Nuremberg. Please kneel in honor of your royal family.

*(The crowd goes to its knees. The **KING**, **QUEEN**, and **PEARLIPLATE** enter. **PEARLIPLATE** sits in the throne, flanked by her parents.)*

COURT ASTROLOGER *(Continued)* And now enter Nathaniel Ernst...nephew to Inventor Hoffmann.

*(As **NATHANIEL** enters to applause and cheers, **MARIE** talks to **HOFFMANN**.)*

MARIE. If this nut is so hard to find...I bet it's going to be harder to crack. Remember, he broke his jaw on the walnut Fritz gave him.

HOFFMANN. Faith...my Marie...have faith!

*(**NATHANIEL** stands before **PEARLIPLATE**. He bows. The **COURT ASTROLOGER** moves to **NATHANIEL** and places a blindfold over the boy's eyes.)*

COURT ASTROLOGER. Can you see?

NATHANIEL. I saw a beautiful princess...but no longer.

COURT ASTROLOGER. He says he can no longer see. Do you have the krackatuk?

*(**NATHANIEL** holds the nut high.)*

Then, please, Nathaniel Ernest Hoffmann, break the curse on the princess.

*(**NATHANIEL** puts the nut into his mouth. He works at cracking the nut. After a struggle...he succeeds in breaking the nut open. SOUND: the cracking of a nut.)*

COURT ASTROLOGER *(Continued.)* He has cracked the nut.

(The crowd cheers.)

Now, present it to the princess.

(**NATHANIEL** *moves forward and feeds the nut to* **PEARL-IPLATE**. *Instantly her ear to ear grin disappears. The crowd cheers.*)

COURT ASTROLOGER *(Continued)* Quiet. Please, quiet. The cure is only half way complete.

(The crowd falls quiet.)

COURT ASTROLOGER *(Continued)* Nathaniel faces a curse himself. He must walk seven steps backwards…without stumbling.

(**NATHANIEL** *begins to step backwards. On his first step the* **COURT ASTROLOGER** *announces.*)

COURT ASTROLOGER *(con't)* One!

(**NATHANIEL** *takes another step.*)

Two!!

(*As* **NATHANIEL** *takes the remaining steps the* **COURT ASTROLOGER** *encourages the crowd and the kids in the audience to count with him.*)

ALL. Three!!! Four!!!! Five!!!!! Six!!!!!!

(Just as **NATHANIEL** *is about to take the seventh step…* **MADAME MOUSERINK** *scurries on. She trips* **NATHAN-IEL**. *He falls…never completing the seventh step. All cower in fear.)*

MOUSERINK. How can you celebrate…when we have suffered for all these years and so many of my kinsmen have been killed?

(To **NATHANIEL**.*)*

So, you cracked the nut? And cured the princess? A curse be on you now. You will be a nutcracker now and forever. A different kind of nutcracker.

(**MOUSERINK** *gestures towards* **NATHANIEL**, *a spell SOUND is heard, she exits.*)

KING. Guards…seize that villain!!!

(**GUARDS** *exit after* **MOUSERINK**. **NATHANIEL** *doesn't* *move.)*

PEARLIPLATE. Is the boy alright?

*(**BROTHER** and **HOFFMANN** run to **NATHANIEL**.)*

BROTHER. Nathaniel, son, are you alright?

*(**NATHANIEL** sits up. He has the jaw of the **NUT-CRACKER**. **PEARLIPLATE** screams.)*

PEARLIPLATE. He has the jaw of a Nutcracker.

BROTHER. Brother, what have you done to my son?

PEARLIPLATE. Father, I'm scared!

KING. Come, my dear.

*(The **KING** ushers **PEARLIPLATE** off. ALL but the **COURT ASTROLOGER, HOFFMANN, MARIE, BROTHER,** and **NUTCRACKER** exit.)*

BROTHER. I curse the day you returned from your quest. I never want to see you again.

*(**BROTHER** takes **NATHANIEL**/ **NUTCRACKER** by the arm and they exit. **HOFFMANN** looks at the **COURT ASTROLOGER**.)*

COURT ASTROLOGER. We found the cure for the princess. We'll find a cure for the boy. We will.

*(**HOFFMANN** runs after his **BROTHER** and exits.)*

COURT ASTROLOGER *(Continued.)* I promise you…I'll find one.

*(The **COURT ASTROLOGER** exits after **HOFFMANN**. **MARIE** is alone.)*

MARIE. Godfather, why have you left me alone? Hello?

*(**NUTCRACKER** enters.)*

NUTCRACKER. So now you know how I got this way.

MARIE. Did the Court Astrologer find the cure?

NUTCRACKER. Yes, the prophesy has two parts. First, I must defeat the Mouse King.

MARIE. What's the second part?

NUTCRACKER. Let's not worry about the prophesy.

MARIE. It must be awful to deal with it.

NUTCRACKER. Yes, and it's gone on for far too many years. It sometimes get to me too. When that happens, I usually escape by going to Toyland.

MARIE. Godfather has talked about Toyland.

NUTCRACKER. So you've been there?

MARIE. We can't go there. It's not real.

NUTCRACKER. Haven't you learned by now that anything is possibly when dealing with the man you call Godfather. Come, we need to go to Toyland. It will take our minds off our troubles. You'll love it. Especially at Christmas time.

(**MARIE**'s *bedroom becomes Toyland.* **SOLDIERS, SUGAR PLUM FARIES,** *and others enter dancing and playing.* **MARIE** *laughs with amazement and joy.*)

MARIE. What? Oh, this can't be real.

NUTCRACKER. This has been my escape since…well, since this entire mess began.

MARIE. Who are they?

NUTCRACKER. Sugar Plum Fairies. I can always depend on them and Toyland to cheer me up.

LADY SUGARPLUM. Everyone! Hail! The prince has returned.

(*All cheer. A short ceremony unfolds as the* **SOLDIERS** *salute and the* **SUGAR PLUM FARIES** *curtsey to the* **NUTCRACKER.**)

MARIE. Are you a prince? Are you really a real prince?

NUTCRACKER. It's just a title. Something Godfather gave me in this world that has made me a man. This world I love.

MARIE. Let's stay here. I never want to go back to the real world.

(*The* **MOUSE KING** *enters.*)

MOUSE KING. HA!!!

(ALL Toyland subjects scream and cower.)

MOUSE KING *(Continued.)* So now you understand the prophesy and why the Nutcracker and I are enemies. He must defeat me to look normal again.

*(The **MOUSE KING** draws his sword. All the subjects of Toyland panic.)*

NUTCRACKER. Don't worry, Marie. Stand behind me. I'll protect you.

MARIE. What will you fight him with? Come on. Run.

*(**MARIE** pulls the **NUTCRACKER** into the audience and a chase begins as the **MOUSE KING** follows them. During the chase the set is shifted to the drawing room. When they get back on stage **FRITZ** enters, riding the stick horse that **MARIE** gave him for Christmas. **SOLDIERS** enter behind **FRITZ**.)*

FRITZ. Leave this house at once…or suffer the consequences.

NUTCRACKER. Thank you, Fritz. But, I must be the one to do this.

MOUSE KING. I respect your dignity. But, what are you going to fight me with?

NUTCRACKER. Fritz, may I borrow your sword?

FRITZ. I can take care of him.

NUTCRACKER. Fritz, it must be me. The prophecy.

*(**FRITZ** hurls his sword to the **NUTCRACKER**. The **MOUSE KING** and the **NUTCRACKER** square off. They begin to fight. The fight goes back and forth, each looking like they will win. Finally the **NUTCRACKER** slays the **MOUSE KING**. There is a cheer from the **SOLDIERS**.)*

NUTCRACKER *(Continued.)* Remove this thing.

*(All **SOLDIERS** exit carrying the **MOUSE KING** with them.)*

MARIE. My, Nutcracker, are you hurt?

NUTCRACKER. Thank you, Marie, no I'm fine. And thank

you too, Fritz.

(He tosses the sword back to **FRITZ**.*)*

You're a splendid soldier.

*(***MOUSERINK*** *bursts onto the scene.)*

MOUSERINK. Nutcracker.

*(***NUTCRACKER*** *turns to her.)*

What have you done to my son?

NUTCRACKER. The prophecy has been fulfilled.

MOUSERINK. *(She waves her hands as she advances on the* **NUTCRACKER**.*)*

Only half the prophecy has taken place.

Look at your jaw and look at your face.

As long as I live and breathe the air,

The second part will never happen, I swear.

*(***MOUSERINK*** *waves her hands, a spell SOUND is heard. The* **NUTCRACKER** *cries out in pain and falls.* **MOUSERINK** *runs off.)*

FRITZ. I will end her evil ways.

*(***FRITZ*** *runs after* **MOUSERINK**. **MARIE** *runs to the fallen* **NUTCRACKER**.*)*

MARIE. Oh, no, please, you can't be dead. Please don't be dead. I love you.

(SOUND: An eruption begins to rumble. **MARIE** *looks up, scared.* **MOTHER, FATHER, HOFFMANN,** *and* **COURT ASTROLOGER** *enter.)*

FATHER. Godfather…what is the meaning of this?

HOFFMANN. *(To the* **COURT ASTROLOGER**.*)* Do you want to say it? You've earned the right to make the announcement.

COURT ASTROLOGER. Thank you, friend.

(Announcing.)

The second part of the prophecy has been fulfilled! The curse on the Nutcracker has finally been broken!

HOFFMANN. It's because Marie said... "she loved the Nut-cracker"...in spite of his deformity.

(**NUTCRACKER** *stands and he looks like* **NATHANIEL**.)

MARIE. My Prince, are you safe?

NUTCRACKER. Yes, Marie, please relax.

MARIE. But what about Madame Mouserink?

(**FRITZ** *enters sheathing his sword.*)

FRITZ. She won't bother us ever again.

NUTCRACKER. Marie, will you honor me by becoming my bride?

MARIE. Godfather, was this your plan all along?

GODFATHER. It depends on your answer.

MARIE. *(To* NUTCRACKER.*)* I am yours now and forever.

COURT ASTROLOGER. Let it be known...that on next Christmas eve...

HOFFMANN. ...Prince Nathaniel Ernst Hoffmann will make Marie Elizabeth Stahlbaum a princess.

(*The LIGHTS fade to black.*)

SCENE THREE

*(The scene the drawing room. Christmas Eve, one year later. A Christmas tree is still the central focus. **AT RISE:** The room is filled with the guests of the wedding. A processional begins. **HOFFMANN** and the **ASTROLOGER** lead the way. Then comes **NATHANIEL**, and his father, **BROTHER**. **FRITZ** enters with **MOTHER** on his arm. **MARIE** should then enter with **FATHER**. **MARIE** wears the white silk dress that **HOFFMANN** gave her at the beginning of the play. A pretty wedding tableau is formed. The **COURT ASTROLOGER** will marry them.)*

COURT ASTROLOGER. On this Christmas Eve…and one year since the prophecy was fulfilled…I am honored to unite these children in marriage.

(Pause.)

Do you Nathaniel…take Marie…to be your wife and princess?

NATHANIEL. I do.

COURT ASTROLOGER. Do you Marie…take Nathaniel…to be you husband and prince?

MARIE. I do.

COURT ASTROLOGER. By the powers vested in me…I now pronounce you husband and wife…prince and princess. You may kiss the bride.

*(**NATHANIEL** kisses **MARIE**. There is a cheer from the crowd.)*

COURT ASTROLOGER *(Continued.)* Let the festivities in celebration of this union begin.

*(MUSIC is heard as the celebrations begins. All dance as **HOFFMANN** and the **COURT ASTROLOGER** work their way through the party to down stage. They look at the audience and talk to them.)*

HOFFMANN. Merry Christmas.

COURT ASTROLOGER. And Happy Hanukkah too.

(They join in on the party and dancing as the LIGHTS fade to black.)

THE END

Christmas By The Book
And Other Plays
By Sandra Cowsill

Flexible casts range from 11-18, plus extras
This is one of the best Christmas collections we've seen. Each one-act play in this excellent collection provides a clear-cut application of the message of Christmas to contemporary problems in society, presented with humor and sympathy. Contains: *Christmas by the Book*; a stuffy hotel manager insists that her staff runs Christmas "by the book," until an eccentric bunch shows her she's been reading the wrong book. *The Spirit of Christmas*; a dysfunctional family learns that even the emotional wounds handed down from generation to generation can be healed. *Tapestry*; examines the source of a love that reaches beyond emotion, as friends seek to help a woman who has announced her impending divorce. Within each storyline is a re-enactment of the scriptural account of Christ's birth, as told in Luke 2.

Please visit our website
bakersplays.com
for complete descriptions and
licensing information

Contents

Editor's note

Mahatma Gandhi is not just a name on the world stage but a symbol of peace and non-violence. His philosophy is not a new philosophy with which the Indian society or the world has come to know for the first time but the eternal values, thoughts, traditions of Indian culture which come from Vedas, Upanishads and Smritis etc. Gandhi adopted the same in his life, behaviour and conduct and showed the world that sacrifice, non-violence, non-accumulation, truth etc. can be adopted in practical life, public life and even in politics.

He changed the direction of history through his work and principles and created a new history. The way he forced the British to leave India by following the path of Satyagraha, peace and non-violence, no other example of this can be seen in world history. That is why the United Nations has also declared to celebrate Gandhi Jayanti as 'World Non-violence Day' from the year 2007.

He was a man of principles and strong beliefs and he always preached what he himself followed. For him, there was no contradiction between theory and practice, and neither did he differentiate between public and private life.

That is why Steve Jobs (co-founder of Apple) proved Gandhi's relevance by saying, "I choose Mohandas Gandhi as the man of the century because he showed us the way out of the destructive side of human nature. Gandhi showed that we can implement change and justice through moral aggression rather than physical aggression. Our species never needed this knowledge so much before."

The ideology and philosophy given by Mahatma Gandhi are as relevant and exemplary today as they were before. What is the utility of the ideology and philosophy of such a great man in Indian politics, this is a small effort to present through the book titled "Gandhi: Ideology, Philosophy and Indian politics". The main objective of publishing the present book "Gandhi: Ideology, Philosophy and Indian politics" is to make the thoughts of that great man reach the society so that all materialistic problems can be solved and the dream of a beautiful, well-organized world can be fulfilled by molding the whole world in the thoughts of Gandhi.

This book comprises of thirty-one precious papers contributed by subject experts and intellectuals which have been written by experts of specific fields on politics, religion, education, truth, non-violence, satyagraha, swaraj, trusteeship, women empowerment etc. The ideas and facts presented in the research article are of the author. I have only compiled and edited them. I am grateful to all the scholars, with whose cooperation this research-article collection is being published in this form. Your cooperation is my strength.

But it cannot be claimed that the presented book is completely flawless and faultless. Yes, it can definitely be said that an attempt has been made to present it in an authentic form as far as possible. If this book is able to generate even a little curiosity in the readers about Gandhi's thoughts, then I will consider my efforts worthwhile.

Before concluding, I would like to once again appreciate and thank all the intellectuals who have submitted their research papers for this book. Thanks to our family members and colleagues for their support and valuable suggestions who have always supported us and without their encouragement and inspiration this work would not have been possible. Thanks to all those who have helped directly or indirectly in this great effort.

I express my gratitude to Pustak Bhartiya, Canada for giving invaluable suggestions to publish the book in this form.

Dr. Pratima Gupta
Assistant Professor,
DAV PG College Varanasi

ii

Role and Relevance of Gandhian Political Philosophy in the Contemporary Global Scenario

Dr. Santosh Kumar
Associate Professor
School of Humanities and Social Sciences
BBD University, Lucknow
Email: Skumars.official@gmail.com

Abstract

The ideas of Mahatma Gandhi have been fascinating all irrespective of their political or cultural boundaries in the world. His thoughts are neither confined within a political entity nor is limited to his times. His philosophy has a vital element of continuity. In fact, his thoughts are evolutionary however the fundamental principle of his ideas remains unchanged even though passing through different ages. Humanity is the core principle of his belief. In the contemporary times, his thoughts are scrutinized from the perspective of their relevance. The ongoing 21st century is high time to examine the role and relevance of his thoughts. The question is raised on the role and relevance of Gandhian philosophy whether it is political, economic or social. Scholars confront the criticism of Gandhian philosophy of non-violence in dealing with the existing conflicts. Apart from his thoughts on politics, his ideas on economy also generates interest in the backdrop of globalization, privatization and liberalization. The critics believe that the thoughts of Mahatma Gandhi might have been appreciated in his times. But the ongoing political and economic landscape is different. In the changed scenario, Gandhian philosophy is questioned. Critics may have their opinion about the thoughts of Mahatma Gandhi and his relevance in the contemporary circumstances. In spite of this, the nature of problems humans is confronted with are not very different from those of colonial period when Mahatma Gandhi experimented with tools of non-violence and truth. The present chapter attempts to explore the role and relevance of Gandhian philosophy in the contemporary global political and economic backdrop.

Keywords: Philosophy, Evolutionary, Perspective, Globalization, Colonial Period, Non-violence.

Introduction

Antonio Guterres, Secretary General of the United Nations Organisation says that Mahatma Gandhi was "one of the giants of the 20th century." He also thinks that Mahatma Gandhi was "global icon of peace and an advocate for the most vulnerable." In the opinion of Guterres, the United Nations is based on the cardinal principle of Gandhiji. This was he who brought different factions together and paved the way for India's freedom from colonialism. Mahatma was far beyond his core identity as a political leader.

He believed on freedom, equality and justice for all irrespective of any man-made boundary. The UN has set an agenda for 2030 which is sustainable development. This is not beyond the scope of Gandhian philosophy. What Mahatma Gandhi had said is not limited within India. This does not mind the political boundaries. If someone says that Mahatma Gandhi was relevant in his days only, that is not the truth. His ideas ranging from environment to equality in society are very relevant in the current scenario as well (UN, 2019)

On the 70th birthday of Mahatma Gandhi, Albert Einstein had said that "generations to come, it may well be, will scarce believe that such a man as this one ever in flesh and blood walked upon this Earth." No doubt, his thoughts inspired millions of people during and after his times. He led the struggle for freedom against the colonial rule in India with his most effective tools of non- violence and truth. It is also very important to know that Mahatma Gandhi alone was experimenting with his tools based on high level of morality. Many like Nelson Madela and Martin Luthar King followed his ways of movement. They also became successful in their respective ventures. In his famous autobiography, My Experiments with the Truth, Mahatma Gandhi mentions how he experimented truth. This was his life long process of observing himself following the great ideals of humanity. When one looks around himself, he can easily understand that the tools of Mahatma Gandhi are the very base of existence of human civilization. In today's world of globalization, nothing is confined within a country or a particular territory. The issues are now more comprehensive and are equally important for all irrespective of their own land. The issues like global warming and climate change, terrorism, immorality, human trafficking etc. are impacting the whole world. Gandhi ji had firm faith that by cultivating these ideals, one can achieve the ultimate goal of humanity. That is why Mahtam Gandhi becomes more relevant in the present scenario. During his active years, Mahatma Gandhi was not focusing within his own country. He would think from the humanitarian point of view. During second World War and earlier, the use of violence made him sympathetic to the affected people. He criticized Hitlar for using excessive violence against the innocent Jews of his country. He did not like Stalin as well due to his political methods and tools. His extreme behavior left Gandhi ji with never forgotten impression. This shows that he was worried for all the humanity. This also proves that his thoughts were universal (Dhulekar, 2021)

Satya and Ahinsa set the base of Gandhian thought through which other ideas of Mahatma Gandhi manifest. Non possession or aparigraha is one of them. Non possession or aparigraha, non-stealing or Astey, Sarvodaya, Elementary education, prohibition of untouchability, khadi etc. are some of the core ideas of Mahatma Gandhi. One finds him advocating for great human values which are also found enshrined in the ideology of Mahatma Gandhi. His cardinal principles are not the consequences of either his life experiences or his political farmwork rather theses were based on the wider perspective of his dharma. His thoughts are the outcomes of his pragmatic application of truth. He denies on several occasions to have drawn his ideas from the abstract theories mentioned in the books. He himself says that he learnt through his own experiments. This approach affected the political philosophy that was also evolved in this philosophical backdrop. He describes the human life to achieve self -realisation having eliminated all evils on the way to this destination. Whether it has been his social reforms or political campaign for the welfare of society, he remained intact with his principles based on satya and Ahinsa or truth and non-violence (Ghoshal,1968).

Political philosophy is one of the most significant contributions of Mahatma Gandhi not only to India but also to the world. A peaceful and judicial political order is the core objective of Gandhian political philosophy. But this is not the politics alone that weaves the base of a political life. It incorporates various other facets like ethics or dharma, artha or the democratic politics based on egalitarian prosperity. It also includes kama or pleasure and moksha or spiritual transcendence. What makes Gandhian political philosophy original is that in rest of the ideas the aforementioned facets are excluded from the core philosophy of politics. Gandhiji did not agree with this view. He amends this discrepancy by incorporating these elements in his philosophy of politics. This inculcation of Mahatma Gandhi in his thoughts makes his ideas original and relevant. Politics is considered as a part of artha which mingles both violence and different interests. On the other side, the elements like moksha, kama and dharma etc. are from the sphere of non-violence. Generally, these two facets are interpreted separately by the scholars in the world. Gandhiji goes beyond this approach. He brings both of these facets together. At one place Mahatma Gandhi says that without dharma there can be no politics. Gandhiji believes that non-violence is the basic principle of human civilization. Gandhiji also signifies the importance of ends as well means simultaneously. It simply means that in the absence of right path to achieve right ends, the state cannot be justified. One of the most important aspects of Gandhian philosophy is that he finds the non-violence to be compatible with the state that is known for the use of conceive power. Here the rights of the citizens should be emphasized with their duties. This would establish the legitimacy of the state. In this backdrop, it is clear that Mahatma Gandhi emphasizes on a welfare state which is ethically based on core values of humanity not confined within the territory but equally applicable to all parts of the world. This tells explicitly that his philosophy is based on the confluence and coordination rather than coercive and confrontation. Mahatma Gandhi not only mentioned these ideas philosophically but he used them politically. His political initiatives against the British colonialism were incorporating these ideals. He experimented with satyagraha and used this pacific tool against the colonialism in India effectively. This was not confined within political arena. He also experimented with the same tools in the social transformations (Parel, 2016)

International Political Economy and Gandhian Philosophy

After the fall of the USSR, the tendency of world political economy is inclining to capitalism. In fact, capitalism is the latest ongoing trend in the global economy. This has resulted into the concentration of wealth in few countries. The global south is comparatively facing severe economic difficulties. This structure of existing global economy is not compatible to the economic thoughts of Mahatma Gandhi. Gandhiji was against the concentration of wealth in any form and he would believe that the welfare of all is the key to durable peace and harmony.

On November, 13, 1924, Mahatma Gandhi expresses his views in his newspaper Young India on modern economy. He does not find industrialization suitable for holistic growth and development. He does not like the machines to be used for productions in place of human hands. He says that humans are capable to produce anything and the use of machines would result into the concentration of wealth in few hands. Through machines, the capitalists would control the resources of production and distribution in the world. This monopoly is against the basic principles of justice. In this way Mahatma Gandhi encourages the role of humans in entire process of progress. He upholds the ideals of trusteeship which means that the rich must use the money for the welfare of the people and certainly not for the purpose of concertinaing the wealth in their hands.

The thoughts of Mahatma Gandhi on economy can be understood from his views expressed in his own newspaper. Gandhi ji had drawn the picture of a modern independent India. He had dreamt of an India that is free from conflict between the have and have nots. He was of the opinion that concentration of wealth is not in the wider interest of the people. Instead, he believed that there should be judicious distribution of wealth. He wanted to develop India as a self-sufficient economy in itself. He was against exploitation of both human and natural resources. He was also thinking that all the communities would live together in peace and harmony. He was of the opinion that a society without gender equality can not progress anywhere in the world. He further says that there would be no conflict between the countries. All would live with harmony and this relationship would be based on the mutual co-existence (Gandhi ji, Young India, 10th September, 1930)

Today the word development is used comprehensively. Progress for Mahatma Gandhi was more suitable because this enshrines ethical and judicious growth of a society. He also found this word as having universality. Mahatma Gandhi believed that only material achievements are not enough for human beings. The development should also inculcate moral progress. He believed on non- violence and truth as the based of economic development as well (Karmakar, Asim et al, 2023). Mahatma Gandhi used the word progress in place of development. Mahatma Gandhi believed on the ideas of humanity. He was very particular on the egalitarian social order. Gandhiji dreamt an economic order which is based on welfare of all and mutual cooperation and certainly not on the basis of competition. He was against the exploitation of weaker people. He was of the opinion that the labor has a dignity in itself. That is why it is should be respected. He is sure that without economic justice, political freedom is meaningless. His theory of trusteeship is based on the idea that the wealth should not be concentrated. Instead, it should be used for the common cause that is the welfare of all. In the current global political scenario, it can be understood that the tendency of concentration of wealth has increased manifold. The rise of neo liberal state and the policies of laissez-faire have resulted into the concentration of wealth both at the national and international levels. This trend is rising worldwide and free flow of capital stands against the basic principles of Mahatma Gandhi (Bhatt, 2023).

Political Philosophy of Mahatma Gandhi

Bhikhu Parekh has contributed many publications like Critical Assessments of Jerremy Bentham, Crisis and Change in Contemporary India, The Decolonization of Imagination and Gandhi's Political Philosophy. His seminal work on Mahatma Gandhi throws light on the role and relevance of Gandhian political philosophy in the modern world. Generally, the western tradition of thought manifests human being isolated from rest of others. Gandhiji on the other hand is known for the universalization of existence of humans. This Cosmo centric view of man is actually the Indian tradition. The versatile existence of different elements depends on one another. This ranges from material to human who are governed by some certain universal laws. This existence is not possible in the absence of friendliness. In fact, harmony is the base of human relationship. This is in favor of the world that all humans live together with peace and harmony. It means that peace and harmony is the core principles of Gandhian political philosophy.

Gandhiji's views on Satyagraha and non- violence have always been the center of attractions in the world. In the backdrop of anarchic character of world political structure as the realists define, the Gandhian political philosophy provides another way which is more constructive. A number of scholars have analyzed Gandhian political philosophy in the context of contemporary global political scenario. J. Bundurant in the Conquest of Violance 1965, D. Dalton on Mahatma Gandhi: Non -Violent Power in Action, 1993 etc. are the efforts to establish that Mahatma Gandhi is equally important in different parts of the world particularly the places where humanity suffers. The thoughts of Mahatma Gandhi were not shaped within the bracket of his native land. Instead, he was impressed by the ideas of thinkers from different parts of the world. There is no doubt that he was an epitome of Indian civilization. He was open to all thoughts emanating from the fertility of truth and non-violence. In fact, the political philosophy of Mahatma Gandhi got the shape from varied approaches from across the world. He learnt from east as well as from the west to develop his own way of thinking. This makes him ideals universal (Swan, 1985)

There are approximately four hundred biographies on

different aspects of life of Mahatma Gandhi. Gandhiji is not an idea in fact a thought which incorporates versatile thoughts in it. Sometimes it is complementary while on the other it is contradictory. At the same time exists both realism and utopian facet in his thoughts. His ideas are equally important wherever are oppressed and destitutes in the world. Pt. Nehru writes about him, "To write about Mahatma Gandhi, it is essential to be like him." It is said that the Sun never sets in the British Empire. However, the same empire could not remain standing against Mahatma Gandhi in India. His main concerns were discrimination among the people on the basis of caste, creed, religion, region, sex etc. He was restless on the exploitation of humans by humans. He had firm faith on non-violence, truth and satyagraha. All these aforementioned vices are still existing in the world. This proves that Gandhian political philosophy still is relevant in dealing with these core issues directly associated with humanity. This is an open secret that politics has declined significantly. Ethical values are also deteriorating. In this backdrop, Gandhian philosophy paves the way for remedy (Pandey,1998).

Conclusion

A. L. Basham calls Mahatma Gandhi an epitome of Hindu Civilization. Some of the important facets of this civilization are peace, mutual coexistence and brotherhood. Since ancient times, the idea of vasudhaiva kutumbkam has been practiced in India. From Vedic Age to the current times, this ideal has been the core principle of India as a nation. Mahatma Gandhi incorporated of these basic ideals in his thoughts. Some experts believe that what Mahatma Gandhi cultivated on the soil of politics was the rejuvenation of the old values of India. He did not introduce anything novice in the field of politics. Instead, he recultivated the same. In today's world, materialism is dominating the policies of powerful countries. Besides, there has been an unprecedented rise in violence. Both state and non-state actors have been using violence to achieve their goals. Amidst all these developments, the importance of Gandhian political philosophy increases. Gandhian thoughts are global by nature. That is why they have equal value irrespective of political territories. At this time, there are two major devastative wars going on in the world. The Israel- Palestine conflict is far from peaceful settlement. This is spreading in other areas as well. If the war is escalated, this would be so difficult to restore peace and normalcy in the Middle- East. On the other side, the Russia - Ukraine war is at the threshold of horrifying situation. Both these armed conflicts are having the potential to escalate to the level of nuclear confrontation. Mahatma Gandhi believed that violence can never solve an issue instead gives birth to another violence. It is better to negotiate for the purpose of reaching logical conclusions. Besides, when someone looks at the current state of affairs in the world, he or she can easily conclude that human values practiced by Mahatma Gandhi are forever. They are not limited to his times only. However, in the changed political and economic scenario, there is a decline of his preached values in India as well as in the world, it does not mean that his political philosophy is meaningless. Gandhian idea of Sarvodaya believed that there should be upliftment of all universally. Today, there has been sharp rise of the gap between the have and have nots in the world. Without universal rise of the people, it is absurd to dream for durable peace. Mahatma Gandhi always advocated durable peace and harmony among the nations of the world.

References:
1. Ghosal, A. K. (1968): A Glimpse of the Political Philosophy of Mahatma Gandhi and its Relevance to the Present Age. The Indian Journal of Political Science, 29(3), 294-303. http://www.jstor.org/stable/41854285
2. Dhuelekar, Prerna (2021): Relevance of Gandhi in 21st Century, Times of India, retrieved from https://timesofindia.indiatimes.com/readersblog/justmorea live/relevance-of-gandhi-in-the-twenty-first-century-37972/ on 22-08-2024
3. United Nations (2019): retrieved from https://www.un.org/sg/en/content/sg/statement/2019-09-24/secretary-generals-remarks-the-event-leadership-matters-relevance-of-mahatma-gandhi-the-contemporary-world-delivered on 21-08-2024.
4. Parel, A. J. (2016): Pax Gandhiana: The Political Philosophy of Mahatma Gandhi, New York: Oxford University Press, p. 8-15
5. Pandey, Janardan (1998): Gandhi and 21st Century, Concept Publishing Company, New Delhi, p. 69-75
6. Bhatt, Purnima Mehta (2023): "An Examination of Gandhian Economic and Political Thought and Its Relevance to the Empowerment of Women," Monsoon: South Asian Studies Association Journal: Vol. 2: Iss. 1, Article 7. Available at: https://digitalcommons.lmu.edu/monsoon-sasa-journal/vol2/iss1/7
7. Karmakar, A. K., Asim, K., Sebak, K.J. (2023): How relevant is Gandhian political economy for Today's India. Retrieved from https://mpra.ub.uni-muenchen. de/ 119582 /1/MPRA_ paper119582.pdf on 25-08-2024.
8. Swan, M. Gandhi (1985): The South African Experience, Johannesburg: Ravan.
9. Gandhi, M. K. (1947): India of My Dreams, The Navjeevan Trust, Chaps. I-VI.

Mahatma Gandhi's Political Philosophy and Its Relevance in Contemporary India

Dr. Avijeet Kumar Biswas
Research Officer, School of Internal Security
Defence and Strategic Studies, Rashtriya Raksha University
Lavad-Dahegam, Gandhinagar, Gujarat
Email: akb2201@gmail.com

Dr. Man Norbu
Guest Faculty, Department of Political Science
Rajiv Gandhi University, Rono Hills, Doimukh, Itanagar
Arunachal Pradesh
Email: mannorbu12@gmail.com

Abstract

Mohandas Karam Chand Gandhi, popularly known as Mahatma Gandhi, was a towering political leader and a social reformer of the 20th Century, a great thinker whose political thought influenced India long after his death. Gandhi's philosophy, which is based on the principles of truth, non-violence, and self-reliance, played a key role in inspiring millions of Indians during India's independent movement. However, his ideas did not cease to be relevant post-1947, rather they offer a moral and ethical foundation for addressing several issues faced by contemporary India. This paper explores the fundamental principles of Gandhi's political philosophy and evaluates their applicability to contemporary India. It examines how these concepts have been incorporated into India's democratic procedures, governance and socioeconomic policies to demonstrate that Gandhi's ideas are still vital for directing the country's development. The paper also addresses the difficulties of putting Gandhi's ideas into practice in the modern, globally interconnected world, where the pressures of modernisation frequently clash with the principles of self-reliance and simplicity that Gandhi advocated.

Keywords: Mahatma Gandhi, India, Political Philosophy, Truth, Non-violence, Self-reliance, Environmental Sustainability.

Introduction

Mahatma Gandhi continues to inspire people even after his passing more than seventy-five years ago, particularly those who wish to explore alternative ideological traditions. His writings on a variety of subjects are many and unambiguous, which makes it easier for researchers to decipher his philosophical underpinnings. His account is not just clear and straightforward but it is as significant as it did during the largest national movement of the 20th century which he spearheaded along with other nationalist leaders of the time. Gandhi wrote frequently on topics of contemporary relevance in leading newspapers of the time such as Harijan, Indian Opinion and Young India. Although his works may not seem relevant today if approached superficially, they often addressed issues which were pertinent to Indians of the period. He used metaphors and homilies to remind the general public about their strengths and their rich cultural heritage. In this manner, he engaged Indians in non-violent resistance against communal disharmony, untouchability and British imperialism. It must be noted that Gandhi was an inspired teacher rather than a systematic thinker who shared his sincere realisations and innermost feelings. In the first section of this paper, the core tenets of Mahatma Gandhi's political philosophy are explored in their historical context. In the second section, the authors attempt to throw light on Gandhi's influence on contemporary Indian governance and in the final section the contemporary challenges that hamper the realisation of Gandhian philosophy are put forward.

Core Political Principles of Mahatma Gandhi

Gandhi's political philosophy developed during India's independence struggle, which was characterised by the revolt against exploitation and oppression by British colonialism. His approach was founded on several fundamental and interconnected principles namely *Satya* (truth), *Ahinsa* (non-violence) and *Swaraj* (self-rule). According to Indian philosophy, the human personality is trichotomic, consisting of the body, mind and pure consciousness. Great sages of India have indulged in deep contemplation of the inner self for millennia. The vast exploration during the Vedic era resulted in the revelation of the Vedas and the sages discovering *Brahman*, "the supreme, indivisible and boundless universal consciousness" (Patil, 2018). It emerges that this consciousness is the "Universal Ultimate Truth," upon which all actions and experiences are predicated. The pure consciousness also referred to as the *Atman* in the individual is an accurate representation of the universal consciousness. There are three facets to the *Atman*: *Sat* which stands for truth and existence, *Chit* stands for consciousness or knowledge and *Ananda* stands for bliss. Mahatma Gandhi began experimenting with truth at a very young age. He started using truth as a weapon to combat injustice and atrocities in society as he was convinced that truth is a power in and of itself.

Gandhi was a prominent proponent of *Ahinsa* in his political philosophy. The concept of *Ahinsa* was conceived and practised across India and was not an original contribution of Gandhi. However, it was he who took it beyond the individual level to other levels such as institutional, political, economic and domestic. His interpretation of *Ahinsa* went much beyond simply abstaining from physical violence. It also meant avoiding harm by words or deeds. In addition, he saw *Ahinsa* as a realistic alternative, while acknowledging the importance that modern society bestows upon the violent resolution of conflict. Gandhi felt his message of non-violence would have been ignored if India could use the sword to defeat the British (Jayakar,1958). Gandhi did, however, advocate violence over cowardice. He wrote (1920), "I would risk violence a thousand times than risk the emasculation of a whole race" (p. 3).

Mahatma Gandhi defined *Swaraj* as Self-rule. It implies that everyone in the society is granted freedom and all have access to the basic amenities of life, not just a select few. It places a strong emphasis on justice for everyone while rejecting majoritarian rule. Gandhi's perception of *Swaraj* was substantive to include the right of every person to govern their own life without causing harm to others and not merely political freedom from British rule. *Swaraj* meant government by many, not the consolidation of power in the hands of a select few (Azadi Ka Amrit Mahotsav, 2023). Gandhi advocated for the decentralisation of economic and political power, which he argued could only be accomplished by starting from the bottom up rather than the other way around to empower individuals and communities.

Closely related to the principle of *Swaraj* is *Swadeshi* which means love for all things that are native to one's own country. Gandhi applied the concept of *Swadeshi* to religion, economy and politics. When applied to the context of religion, Swadeshi would mean following one's hereditary religion. In the economic context, *Swadeshi* would mean to limit one's consumption to goods produced by one's native industries and support them in whichever way deemed necessary, particularly those that have the potential to grow. *Swadeshi* in the economy also referred to the boycott of imported commodities. In politics, *Swadeshi* refers to traditional Indian political institutions over Western institutions. Gandhi advocated the establishment of village panchayats and *Ganarajya*. In the field of education too, Gandhi propagated the adoption of an indigenous and traditional scheme over the English system of education (Ghosal, 2018). Gandhi advocated for Swadeshi in multiple domains to encourage people to imbibe courage, self-reliance, and self-confidence in their mindset.

Mahatma Gandhi's Influence on Post-Independent India

India's democratic institutions and political culture have been significantly influenced by Mahatma Gandhi's principles. His focus on inclusion and non-violence helped the nation shape its commitment towards secularism and pluralism, which are fundamental components of India's democratic framework. Gandhi's teaching of non-violence had a lasting impact on India's political process. New Delhi has institutionalised non-violence as a means for resolving conflicts, which has affected how it manages social movements, internal conflicts and even foreign policy. India has consistently focused on dialogue and negotiation over force and coercion, creating a political environment that is favourable to democratic governance. For instance, India has demonstrated its adherence to Gandhi's principles by prioritising dialogue and negotiation over armed action when dealing with separatist movements in various Indian states (Nanda, 2002). Similarly, in keeping with Gandhi's idea of a pluralistic society, the Indian government has frequently engaged in interfaith discussions and encouraged peaceful coexistence as a means of combating communal violence. Following his untimely death in 1948, it was Jawaharlal Nehru that carried forward Gandhi's legacy. Nehru stated that "the policies and philosophy which we seek to implement are the policies and philosophy taught to us by Gandhiji" (Datta Ray, 2015). Even in contemporary Indian politics, Gandhian principles are perceived as goals that are to be achieved.

The inclusivity of *Swaraj* finds expression in the current government's approach to governance, *sabka sath, sabka vikas, sabka vishwaas*, which translates to participation, development and trust for all. Through several schemes, past and current Indian governments have strived to achieve inclusion and remove discrimination of all kinds. The 73rd and 74th amendments of the Indian constitution gave more power to local self-governments which took India closer to Gandhi's dream of achieving decentralisation (Anjum, n.d.) and grassroots democracy. India's approach to governance especially in the areas of accountability and transparency has been guided by Gandhi's emphasis on truth. His legacy of advancing governmental transparency is reflected in the enactment of the Right to Information (RTI) Act in 2005. By enabling individuals to acquire information from public bodies, the RTI Act improves accountability and transparency in the way government operates (Weber, 2004).

India's economic policies have been moulded by Gandhi's idea of self-reliance, especially in the years following independence. Gandhi's theories greatly impacted India's economic policy in the early decades of its independence, emphasising self-sufficiency, rural development, and small-scale industries (Brown, 1989). Gandhi's idea of an economy that balanced development with social justice was partially reflected in the adoption of the mixed economy model, which blended aspects of socialism with market mechanisms. However, some of Gandhi's economic ideas were abandoned with the adoption of the liberal economic model in the 1990s. There has been tremendous economic development as a result of the move towards a more market-oriented economy and greater integration into the global economy, but at the same time, Gandhi's emphasis on local economies and self-reliance has also come under scrutiny for being outdated in the current context (Kapila, 2010). Notwithstanding these developments, Gandhi's principles continue to impact modern economic policies; the 'Make in India' project, for instance, is a manifestation of Gandhi's vision to encourage indigenous manufacturing and lower reliance on imports. Similarly, Gandhi's call for simplicity and conscientious use of natural resources aligns with initiatives to advance sustainable development and tackle environmental issues (Nanda, 2002).

Gandhi's adherence to social justice and inclusivity continues to be relevant in today's India, especially in light of the continuous struggle for the rights of marginalised groups. He was a fervent supporter of the Dalit and movements for the rights of Dalits and other marginalised communities continue to be inspired by his conviction to end the practice of untouchability and foster social peace (Parel, 1997). Gandhi's idea of an inclusive society, in which members of various castes, religions, and communities live in harmony with one another, is especially relevant given the escalating sectarian unrest and identity-based politics in India. His focus on the values of truth, non-violence, and respect for one another offers a moral framework for dealing with these issues and fostering societal cohesiveness (Bhikhu, 2002).

Gandhi's emphasis on sustainability and simplicity provides insightful guidance for tackling India's current environmental problems. Gandhi's appeal for a harmonious coexistence of humans and the environment is especially pertinent in light of contemporary problems like pollution, deforestation and climate change (Weber, 2004). His antipathy to industrialisation and support of village-based economies underscores the need for sustainable development models that put community well-being and environmental preservation ahead of unbridled economic expansion. Gandhi's effect on contemporary environmental policy is apparent in India's enthusiastic participation in international environmental agreements, such as the Paris Agreement, and in New Delhi's initiatives to promote sustainable practices and renewable energy. While India tries to strike a balance between its development objectives and the requirement to safeguard its natural resources, the conflict between environmental sustainability and economic development poses a serious challenge (Kapila, 2010).

Challenges in Adopting Gandhi's Philosophy in Contemporary India

The contradiction between the demands of modernisation and Gandhi's traditional values makes implementing his principles in modern-day India a great challenge. Gandhi spoke against materialism and industrialisation and was in favour of a return to more basic, environmentally friendly lifestyles. But these concepts might occasionally appear out of sync with the demands of economic progress and the goals of a growing middle class in a society that is modernising and globalising at a rapid pace (Brown, 1989). The difficulty lies in figuring out how to apply Gandhi's principles in the current context when raising living standards and tackling social challenges are frequently equated with economic expansion and technological innovation. Gandhi's philosophy must be carefully considered in light of current reality to achieve the difficult task of balancing modernisation with the need to maintain cultural and ethical values (Nanda, 2002).

The applicability of Gandhi's philosophy in present-day India is further challenged by globalisation. His emphasis on local economies and self-sufficiency appears at odds with the realities of a world that is becoming more linked and reliant on foreign trade and investment. Mahatma's ideas of economic self-sufficiency must be reconciled with the opportunities and challenges brought about by globalisation (Weber, 2004). While India has benefited economically from globalisation, it has also resulted in rising inequality, social unrest and environmental degradation. Gandhi's concepts provide insightful guidance on how to tackle these issues, especially when it comes to advancing equitable and sustainable development. However, putting these concepts into practice in a globalised economy calls for innovative solutions that would strike a balance between the requirements of global integration and the values of sustainability and self-reliance (Kapila, 2010).

Finally, there is the difficulty of striking a balance between Gandhi's idealism and the pragmatism required to deal with the intricate problems of modern governance. His philosophy is often viewed as utopian, especially in light of his focus on moral rectitude and non-violence in politics. There is a conflict between the necessity for practical answers to real-world issues and the pursuit of Gandhi's principles in a society where power politics and realpolitik frequently dominate (Iyer, 2000). Finding practical and efficient ways to implement Gandhi's philosophy without sacrificing the fundamental principles he stood for is a challenge that we face. This necessitates a thorough understanding of his philosophy as well as a readiness to adapt his concepts in light of the changing conditions and difficulties of modern-day India (Bhikhu, 2002).

Conclusion

The political philosophy of Mahatma Gandhi continues to be relevant in modern-day India since it provides a moral and ethical framework for dealing with the various issues that the country faces. His concepts of truth, nonviolence, and self-reliance had a significant impact on India's democratic processes, political system, and socioeconomic policies. Gandhi's principles also offer insightful perspectives for dealing with modern problems like environmental degradation and social injustice. However, the implementation of Gandhi's principles in contemporary India is not an easy task. The contradiction between modernisation and traditional values, globalisation and the idealism-pragmatism debate pose major barriers to the full realisation of Gandhi's vision.

Nevertheless, India continues to draw inspiration and guidance from Gandhi's enduring legacy as it negotiates the challenges of the twenty-first century. The applicability of Gandhi's philosophy will likely depend on how well India adjusts to new circumstances. India can strive towards the goal of creating a just, sustainable, and inclusive society that aligns with Mahatma Gandhi's vision for his beloved country by creatively and suitably incorporating his principles into contemporary reality.

References:
1. Anjum, S. (n.d.): Relevance of Gandhi in the 21st Century.
2. https://sageuniversity.edu.in/blogs/relevance-of-gandhi-in-the-21st century#:~:text=Gandhi's%2 0philosophy%20can% 20be%20used,terrorism%2C%20political%20and%20administrative%20corruption.
3. Azadi Ka Amrit Mahotsav, (2023, January), Definitions of Swaraj (Essay by Mahatma Gandhi).
4. https://amritmahotsav.nic.in/district-reopsitory-detail.htm?10758#:~:text=Gandhi%20viewed%20Swaraj%20for%20the,power%20of%20a%20handful%20few.
5. Bhikhu, P. (2002): Gandhi's Political Philosophy: A Critical Examination, Palgrave Macmillan.
6. Brown, J. M. (1989): Gandhi: Prisoner of Hope, Yale University Press.
7. Dasgupta, I. (2020): Gandhi and New India, National Institution for Transforming India (NITI Aayog).
8. https://www.niti.gov.in/sites/default/files/2020-01/GANDHI_AND_NEW_INDIA.pdf.
9. Datta Ray, D. K. (2015): India's Gandhian Foreign Policy, In F. Godement (Ed.), What Does India Think (pp. 28-32). European Council on Foreign Relations.
10. Gandhi, M. K. (1920): Crusade Against Non-Co-Operation, Young India, 2(31), 3.
11. https://www.gandhiheritageportal.org/journals-by-gandhiji/ young-india

12. Ghosal, D. (2018): Philosophical Foundation of Mahatma Gandhi's Social and Political Thought: An Appraisal, Heritage, V. 14-19.
13. https://www.bethunecollege.ac.in/heritagejournal/journals/heritageJournalVolV2018/articles2018/Heritage2018-14-19-MahatmaGandhi.pdf
14. Iyer, R. N. (2000): The Moral and Political Thought of Mahatma Gandhi, Oxford University Press.
15. Jayakar, M. R. (1958): The Story of My Life, Asia Publishing House.
16. Kapila, S. (2010): An Intellectual History for India, Cambridge University Press.
17. Nanda, B. R. (2002): Mahatma Gandhi: A Biography, Oxford University Press.
18. Parel, A. J. (Ed.). (1997): Gandhi: 'Hind Swaraj' and Other Writings, Cambridge University Press.
19. Patil, R. K. (2018): International Peace in the Light of Indian Philosophy, International Journal on World Peace, XXXV(4),9-12.
20. https://callisto.ggsrv.com/imgsrv/FastPDF/UBER1/RangeFetch=contentSet=UBER1=prefix=PI-0BEC-2018DEC00SPI=startPage=7=suffix==npages=28=dl=INTERNATIONAL_PEACE_IN_THE_LIG=PDF.pdf?dl=INTERNATIONAL_PEACE_IN_THE_LIG.PDF
21. Weber, T. (2004): Gandhi as Disciple and Mentor, Cambridge University Press.

Assaying the Effect of Gandhian Philosophy on Indian Fiction

Dr. Amit Y. Kapoor
Head, Department of English
Shree Jayendrapuri Arts & Science College
Bharuch (Gujarat)
Email: amitkapoorjpc@gmail.com

Abstract

Mohandas Karamchand Gandhi, popularly referred to as Mahatma Gandhi, rose to prominence as the head of the nationalist movement opposing British rule in India. Mahatma Gandhi created the Gandhian doctrine, which emerged in India during the late nineteenth and early twentieth centuries amid a historically volatile atmosphere. A combination of social, religious, and political concepts that Mahatma Gandhi himself formed between 1893 and 1914, both while he was living in South Africa and later during the Indian independence movement, is known as the Gandhian Philosophy. Gandhian philosophy is simple and complex, old, and modern, and political, moral, and religious all at the same time. Although Gandhiji was exposed to many Western influences, it has its roots in ancient Indian culture, which harnesses global moral and religious concepts. Gandhi's main concerns are ethics as the first philosophy and the development of moral character and conduct. God and the spiritual or religious component are its key ideas. Gandhiji believed that human nature is inherently moral. Every single person is thought to be capable of both reform and highly moral development. The majority of the Indian fictional experiments had a substructure based on the Gandhian ethos. From metropolis to village, there was a constant contrast between opulence and simplicity. There has been a noticeable shift in the writing style aside from the theme selection. It became more straightforward and uncomplicated, devoid of any emotional or sentimental embellishments. The impact of the Gandhian ideology on Indian novelists, particularly those from Bengal, Tamil Nadu, and Punjab, is extensively explored by the researcher in this work. These novels include Satinath Bhaduri's *Dhorai Charit Manas,* Bhabani Bhattacharya's *So Many Hungers,* R. K. Narayan's *Waiting for Mahatma* and Nayantara Sehgal's *Storm in Chandigarh.*

Keywords: Mahatma Gandhi, Philosophy, Satyagraha, Ahinsa, Swadeshi, Indian fiction

Introduction

Indian lawyer, politician, social activist and writer Mohandas Karamchand Gandhi, popularly referred to as Mahatma Gandhi, rose to prominence as the head of the nationalist movement opposing British rule in India. He became known as the *Father of the Nation* as a result. Gandhi's distinct ideology has earned him respect on a global scale. Gandhi was regarded by millions of his fellow Indians as the *Mahatma* or *Great Soul.* During his lifetime, his fame grew globally and it continued to grow after his passing. Many were affected by his philosophy of Truth and Nonviolence, which Martin Luther and Nelson Mandela both embraced for their own struggles. These days, Mahatma Gandhi's name is among the most widely known worldwide.

Gandhian Philosophy: An Overview

Mahatma Gandhi created the Gandhian doctrine, which emerged in India during the late nineteenth and early twentieth centuries amid a historically volatile atmosphere. India was ruled by the British Empire in an oppressive manner at that time. This led to economic exploitation, political subjugation and racial discrimination throughout the nation. The Indian subcontinent was rife with nationalist fever after revolutionaries like Dadabhai Naoroji, Bal Gangadhar Tilak and Bipin Chandra Pal started advocating for self-governance and independence. Gandhi's early encounters with racial discrimination against Indians in South Africa served as the impetus for the development of his philosophy of Non-violent Resistance and Civil Disobedience. Gandhi created the concept of *Satyagraha* or *Truth Force*, during his time living in this harsh environment of oppressive colonial rule and growing Indian nationalism. He also organised demonstrations emphasising the effectiveness of peaceful resistance, such as the Salt March. World events, particularly the two world wars had a major impact on the course of the Indian independence movement. India finally gained its independence in 1947 but the Partition that followed came with its own special set of challenges. Movements for civil rights, social justice and peaceful transformation are still fuelled by the historical crucible in which Gandhi honed his principles of nonviolence, *Truth* and *Social Justice*.

A combination of social, religious and political concepts that Mahatma Gandhi himself formed between 1893 and 1914 both while he was living in South Africa and later during the Indian independence movement is known as the Gandhian Philosophy. Through decades, Gandhi's experiences, experiments and vision eventually shaped his philosophy as it exists now. Gandhian philosophy is simple and complex, old and modern and political, moral and religious all at the same time. Although Gandhiji was exposed to many Western influences, it has its roots in ancient Indian culture which harnesses global moral and religious concepts. There are multiple levels of philosophy: moral, political, economic, social, individual and collective as well as spiritual or religious. Gandhi's main concerns are ethics as the first philosophy and the development of moral character and conduct. This is distinct from both traditional Indian philosophy and the history of Western philosophy. God and the spiritual or religious component are its key ideas. Gandhiji believed that human nature is inherently moral.

Every single person is thought to be capable of both reform and highly moral development. These concepts were formed by Gandhiji with influence from a variety of sources, including *The Bible*, Jainism, Buddhism, Gopal Krishna Gokhale, Tolstoy and John Ruskin. Mahatma Gandhi was greatly influenced by the book *The Kingdom of God is within you* by Leo Tolstoy. John Ruskin's work *Unto this Last* was interpreted by Gandhiji as *Sarvodaya*. Later Gandhians expanded on these concepts, most notably Vinoba Bhave and Jayaprakash Narayan in India and Martin Luther King Jr. and others outside of India.

The Major tenets of Gandhian Philosophy

Based on the ideas and teachings of Mahatma Gandhi, the Gandhian worldview includes a broad spectrum of morals and convictions. Major tenets of Gandhian ideology include the following:

➤ *Ahinsa (Non-Violence)*: The cornerstone of Gandhian thought is perhaps *Ahinsa* or *Non-Violence*. Gandhi was a strong proponent of using non-violence to fight injustice and oppression. He stressed compassion and refraining from injuring any living thing in his practice of non-violence in word, deed and thought.

➤ *Constructive Work:* Gandhi believed in combining activism with *Constructive Work*. He urged people and groups to get involved in worthwhile endeavours that would benefit society as a whole and improve their own financial situation. Gandhi understood that the Satyagraha campaign could not succeed unless all villagers were intoxicated in order for it to become a revolution in and of itself. He believed that the advancement of this change is greatly aided by women and students. People would be immediately impacted by Gandhi's program as he awakened their dormant strength. Gandhi believed that if he were to get power and pass legislation, he would surely start with a prohibition bill.

➤ *Equality and Unity:* Gandhi was a fervent supporter of social and religious harmony. He devoted his life to bridging the divides between various caste and religious groups in order to advance *Equality* and *Unity* for all.

➢ ***Fearlessness:*** Gandhi espoused the virtue of *Fearlessness*. In his opinion, people should not be scared to defend their beliefs and ideals in the face of criticism or persecution.

➢ ***Sarvodaya (Welfare of All):*** *Sarvodaya* is a phrase that signifies *Progress of All* or *Universal Uplift.* The phrase was originally used by Gandhiji to refer to his translation of *Unto This Last,* a political economy tract by John Ruskin. The philosophy of Gandhi placed a strong emphasis on promoting the *Wellbeing of All* people but particularly the weak and oppressed. He supported the abolition of social injustices and the development of a just society that would help the most vulnerable.

➢ ***Satyagraha (Truthfulness):*** *Satyagraha* and *Nonviolence,* which translate to *Truth Force* or *Soul Force,* go hand in hand. Speaking the truth at all costs is crucial and Gandhiji saw it as the main tenet of his *Satyagraha Movement.*

➢ ***Swadeshi (Self-Reliance):*** Gandhi campaigned for *Self-Sufficiency* and *Self-Reliance* at both the individual and the national levels. He supported the utilisation of local resources and the restoration of traditional handicrafts to reduce dependence on foreign items.

➢ ***Swachhata (Cleanliness):*** Gandhi placed a strong emphasis on the moral and practical value of *Swachhata (Cleanliness).* He thought that for both individual and societal well-being, a clean environment and a clean heart were necessary.

➢ ***Swaraj (Decentralization of Power):*** Decentralised political and economic systems were something Gandhi supported. In his view a just and equitable society required community-based, decision-making and local self-governance. Decentralised governance or decentralised politics required the presence of village swaraj. The ideal system of government is *Swaraj*. It can only be established by sharing authority among the people rather than by a small number of persons in positions of power. Gandhiji envisioned a perfect political system in which each person is their own monarch and governs themselves so as never to impede others.

➢ ***Simple Living:*** Gandhi himself led a *Modest* and *Austere Lifestyle*, which he believed to be necessary for both societal and individual well-being. He promoted living in tune with nature and reducing material wants.

➢ ***Trusteeship:*** Gandhiji introduced the socio-economic theory of *Trusteeship*. It offers a way for the wealthy to serve as trustees of trusts that looked out for the wellbeing of the populace as a whole. This idea is a reflection of Gandhiji's spiritual growth, which he attained in part through his intense study of *The Bhagavad Gita* and the writings of the Occult as well as his intimate engagement with them.

Global movements for social justice, peace, and civil rights are still motivated by these Gandhian ideas. Gandhi's life and teachings offer a timeless illustration of how a single person's dedication to social justice, truth, and nonviolence may result in a significant improvement in society.

The Effect of Gandhian philosophy in Indian fiction

The ideology, teachings and principles of Mahatma Gandhi have been a major source of inspiration and encouragement for many Indian writers who have worked on social issues of the society. His deep structural thoughts on nearly all of the problems prevalent in society, including social evils, inequality, standard of living, etc. have made his teachings a distinct field of literature in and of themselves. Indian literature and Indian fiction in particular, owes a great deal to Gandhi. Since it is hard for one writer to cover every one of these connected topics in his works, some well-known Indian writers have attempted to include these lessons in their books.

The majority of the Indian fictional experiments had a substructure based on the Gandhian ethos. From metropolis to village there was a constant contrast between opulence and simplicity. There has been a noticeable shift in the writing style aside from the theme selection. It became more straightforward and uncomplicated, devoid of any emotional or sentimental embellishments. In actuality Gandhi's influence was so great that a lot of writers incorporated his political, spiritual, and religious views into their works. Most of the fictional writers were fired with the nationalistic ideology and were Gandhian by one way or other.

The impact of the Gandhian ideology on Indian novelists, particularly those from Bengal, Tamil Nadu and Punjab is extensively explored by the researcher in this work. These novels include Satinath Bhaduri's *Dhorai Charit Manas,* Bhabani Bhattacharya's *So Many Hungers,* R. K. Narayan's *Waiting for Mahatma* and Nayantara Sehgal's *Storm in Chandigarh.*

➢ **Satinath Bhaduri's *Dhorai Charit Manas:*** *Dhorai Charit Manas* is an epic Bengali novel written by Satinath Bhaduri. The title is taken from the *Ramcharitmanas,* an old Hindu epic. Too little of the style adheres to the pattern. The story of Dhorai, a Tatma from the impoverished Purnia suburb of Bihar is told in the novel. Dhorai's father passes away while he is still a toddler. He is left in the custody of an ignorant sannyasi after his mother marries Babu Lal. The sannyasi Bouka Bawa raises him with the nurturing of a father. He is hoping he will follow him. Dhorai is not prepared to lead a mendicant's existence. He begins working on building roads and is married to Ramia. Bouka Bawa leaves Dhorai's life behind. The book takes place over the course of almost thirty years and covers some of the most volatile moments in the history of the liberation movement, particularly the Dandi March for Salt Satyagraha, which led to Gandhi's ascent to prominence as a mass leader. Since Gandhi is an embodiment of Ram, Gandhiji came to represent both patriotism and naturally, optimism for socioeconomic change specifically, the desire of bringing in Ram-Rajya, the reign of Ram.

➢ **Bhabani Bhattacharya's *So Many Hungers:*** Bhabani Bhattacharya's novel, *So Many Hungers* centres on the 1942 Quit India Movement. The book sheds insight on the social climate of the day in addition to the war for independence. Beneath the struggle for independence, it addresses pressing concerns of sex, politics, poverty and love. In the book, the terrible and devasting 1942 Bengal famine and its aftermath are discussed. The novel is divided into two halves, each telling a separate story that the author ultimately skilfully connects. Gandhi as the man and Gandhi as the vision clash in the story. Gandhi is portrayed by the main character Rahul as the man and by his grandfather Desesh Basu (Devta) as the vision. Rahul is the main character in the first section, and Kajoli is in charge of the second. The aftermath of the 1942 great famine is shown in the story convincingly. Following the famine, Bengal experienced extreme poverty and the author has attempted to highlight the dire circumstances surrounding Kajoli's attempt to become a prostitute.

➢ **R. K. Narayan's *Waiting for Mahatma:*** A key discovery in Narayan's *Waiting for the Mahatma* is the protagonist Sriram's transformation from a young, naive person to an activist impacted by Gandhi's ideas. The impact of Ahinsa and satyagraha on Sriram's political involvement and personal life is depicted in the novel. Gandhi's constant emphasis on self-purification and self-sacrifice serves as a model for Sriram and other characters in the story. The way that the tenets of *Satyagraha* such as taking vows of *Truth, Non-Violence* and *Non-Possession* are shown emphasises how profoundly transformational they are for people. Gandhi's practical philosophy is also clarified by the book, which highlights the value of routine actions like walking, conversing and spinning in the effort to create a democratic and independent society. Gandhi's attempts to oppose caste prejudice are depicted in the representation, even though they were constrained by the laws of his era. Gandhi's earthly life and interactions with children are shown in the story through comedy, which counterbalances his holy persona with humane traits.

➤ **Nayantara Sahgal's *Storm in Chandigarh:*** In her book *Storm in Chandigarh*, Nayantara Sahgal tries to offer a nonviolent response to the violence that has broken out in Punjab. She violently expresses her disdain at the crazed violence that has broken out in the recently split states of Punjab and Haryana around the Chandigarh problem. She believes that the best way to ensure that society prospers and peace reigns is through nonviolence. Thus, in *Storm in Chandigarh*, Nayantara Sahgal expresses her commitment to Gandhian principles. Through the storylines of Inder-Saroj, Jit-Mara, and Vishal-Leela, the novel deftly juxtaposes two worlds: the interpersonal realm of politics and the personal world of man-woman relationships. Sahgal describes the senior Home Minister as the final living representative of the Gandhian era, implementing his programs to maintain political relevance in the face of changing political circumstances. The book also addresses topics like poverty, extramarital affairs, and human incompatibility brought on by misunderstandings. The novel touches with the existential nature of life on Earth.

Relevance of Gandhi in the contemporary context

Since *Truth* and *Nonviolence* are the cornerstones of Gandhiji's philosophy, they are applicable to all people and are regarded as universal. Mahatma Gandhi's lessons are relevant now more than ever as people look for answers to the unchecked consumerism, pervasive violence, and avaricious greed. Mahatma Gandhi's influence is evident in the numerous oppressed societies around the world where his method of mobilising people has been successfully implemented by leaders such as Martin Luther King in the United States, Nelson Mandela in South Africa, and Aung San Suu Kyi in Myanmar.

Conclusion

Gandhi has had a profound influence on Indian writing. His larger-than-life ideals, charisma, ability to draw big crowds, and ultimately his committed work and ideology have completely changed the landscape for writers of literature in India. Through his life and ideals, Mahatma Gandhi has had a lasting impact both in India and elsewhere. Because he has modelled behaviour for others to imitate, authors cannot ignore his effect. He is what all ages need. World literature should be influenced by his life and philosophy. The nations of the globe must adhere to and follow Gandhian philosophy if progress and peace are to be achieved.

References:
1. Diwakar, R. R. (1976): Gandhian Philosophy and Social Evolution, Kolkata, Gandhi Darshan Samiti.
2. Krishnamurthi, Y. G. (1949): Gandhi for Millions, Patna, Pustak Bhandar.
3. Mathur, J. S. (1999): Gandhian Philosophy: Its Relevance Today, New Delhi, Decent Books.
4. Prasad, A. N. (2011): The Champion of Indian Fiction in English, Jaipur, Sunrise Publishers.
5. Raghavan, Iyer. (1983): The Moral and Political Thought of Mahatma Gandhi, London, Oxford University Press.
6. Shahane, V. A. and Cowasjee, Saroj (1981): Modern Indian Fiction, New Delhi, Vikas Publishing.
7. Verma, M. M. (1990): Gandhi's Technique of Mass Mobilization, New Delhi, R. K. Gupta & Company.

Arrival of Mahatma Gandhi in Indian Politics and his Ideology

Dr. Pratima Gupta
Assistant Professor
Department of Political Science
DAV PG College, Varanasi
Email: pratimag81@gmail.com

Abstract

Mahatma Gandhi played a very important role in changing the ideology, direction and nature of the Indian National Movement. After his arrival in Indian politics, a new phase of struggle began. Mobilizing the people against the British was now the main objective of this movement. Gandhiji dominated the national movement from the beginning till independence. Under this research paper, we will mention the struggle started by Gandhiji in India and along with it Gandhiji's political activities in India. This was a period in which Gandhiji was trying to understand the economic, social and political reality of India. In this era, Gandhiji used new methods of struggle. In this research paper, we will also discuss his ideology and see how he gave a practical form to his ideology in politics.

Keywords: Arrival, Indian Politics, Ideology, Movement

Introduction

Mohandas Karamchand Gandhi, popularly known as Mahatma Gandhi, was born on 2 October, 1869 in Porbandar (Kathiawar, Gujarat) in a traditional Hindu family. In 1881, Gandhi went to England to get education, passed matriculation in London and qualified to become a lawyer. In 1891, Gandhi returned to India and started practicing law in the High Court of Bombay. When he did not get success as a lawyer, he went to Rajkot and started writing petitions.

In 1893, Gandhi went to Durban in South Africa in connection with the case of the Indian firm Dada Abdulla & Co. Although Gandhi went there for only one year, he stayed there till 1914. In South Africa, Gandhi fought against racial discrimination. Due to the racial discrimination policy of the government there, the Indian community did not have any human rights which were necessary to live a civilized life.

The arrival of Mahatma Gandhi in Indian politics in 1915 was a turning point in the freedom struggle. Gandhi's philosophy of non-violence and Satyagraha revolutionised the way Indian people fought for freedom.

Objectives

➤ To know the causes of Champaran and Kheda movement.
➤ To understand the work done by Gandhiji for the farmers.
➤ To know the role of Gandhiji during the strike of workers of Ahmedabad.
➤ To make Gandhian ideology relevant to the challenges of Indian politics.

Arrival of Gandhiji in Indian politics

Before Gandhi's arrival, the Indian National Congress (INC) was a largely ineffective organisation. The INC was founded in 1885, but it was unable to achieve any significant progress in its campaign for Indian independence.

Gopal Krishna Gokhale, a senior leader of the Indian National Congress, invited Gandhi to join India's struggle for independence against British rule. Gandhi came to India in 1915 and made Gopal Krishna Gokhale his political guru in India. Gokhale wanted Gandhi to join 'the Servants of Indian Society' but Gandhi could not become a member of it due to strong opposition from some members of the society. Gokhale took a promise from Gandhi at that time that he would not express any opinion on political issues in India for a year. Following the promise, Gandhi spent most of his time in 1915 and 1916 touring various places in India. He visited every village in the country to prepare the strategy for the freedom struggle. The benefit of all these visits was that Gandhi gained a lot of information about Indians and their situation.

Gandhiji's active entry into Indian politics took place during 1917-18 which was related to three local problems. These problems were the struggle of farmers in Champaran and Kheda and the struggle of workers in Ahmedabad. Here Gandhi used the technique of Satyagraha and ultimately through these local struggles he emerged as the leader of the whole of India.

Champaran Movement

Mahatma Gandhi started the Satyagraha movement in India with the Champaran movement of Bihar (year 1917). It was through this movement that Gandhiji entered Indian politics and this movement gave a mass leader like Gandhi to the Indian freedom struggle.

The case of Champaran's indigo planters was going on since the 19th century. Under the Tinkathiya system, farmers were required to cultivate indigo on 3/20th of their land. But when chemical colours were discovered, cultivation of indigo became unnecessary. But to exploit the farmers, the British increased the rates of rent and illegal taxes in lieu of freeing them from the indigo contract. To get rid of this exploitation, Champaran's agitator Rajkumar Shukla decided to call Gandhiji to Champaran in 1917. The British government constituted a commission to investigate the Champaran case, in which Gandhiji was also given membership. Gandhiji had statements of eight hundred farmers, on the basis of which Gandhiji talked about ending the Tinkathiya system and compensation for the illegal recovery made from the farmers. The planters agreed to return 25 percent of the illegal recovery and within 10 years they left Champaran too. Thus, Champaran Satyagraha brought Gandhi among the people and by knowing the demands and problems of the people, he worked to put forward the people's side strongly before the

British government. Apart from this, Gandhi's strategy of Satyagraha and peaceful protest also brought Gandhi closer to the people. As a result, Gandhi became established as a mass leader in the national movement.

Kheda Movement

Kheda Satyagraha took place in Kheda district of Gujarat. This Satyagraha was organized by Mahatma Gandhi for the second time in favor of farmers. The main objective of this movement was to support the farmers. This movement was started by Mahatma Gandhi for the farmer-Patidar community of Kheda. The farmer-Patidar community of Kheda refused to pay 25% tax after the entire crop was destroyed due to famine and flood. According to the land tax rules, if the crop in any year is 25% less than the normal level, then in such a situation the farmers were to get complete exemption in land tax. Two lawyers of Mumbai, Mr. V.J. Patel and G.K. Parikh investigated in this regard and came to the conclusion that a large part of the production had been destroyed. Despite the drought, the officials of the Bombay Government were not ready to accept that the yield had decreased. Therefore, they were not ready to give exemption to the farmers. Farmers were constantly pressured to pay the rent. The government believed that this demand was not made by the farmers but was instigated by outsiders who were associated with the Home Rule League and Gujarat Sabha. Gandhiji himself was the president of this Gujarat Sabha.

The British government has warned the farmers that if they do not pay 25% tax, their land will be confiscated and they will not be able to grow crops. Gandhiji requested the citizens of Kheda district not to pay unnecessary taxes and started Satyagraha by holding a meeting in Nadiad on 22 March 1918. Gandhiji visited many villages to boost the morale of the farmers and remove the fear of the government from their hearts. Indulal Yagnik, Vitthalbhai Patel, Anasuya

Sarabhai and Mohanlal Pandey etc. played a major role in this movement. When the government issued an order here that the rent will be collected only from those farmers who can pay it and poor farmers will not be forced to do so, then Gandhiji announced the end of Satyagraha.

Ahmedabad Movement

After the success of Champaran movement in 1917 and Kheda movement in 1918, Gandhiji's second successful movement was the leadership of Ahmedabad mill workers' strike of 1918. Cotton textile mill workers went on strike for 21 days. In 1917, due to the spread of plague disease in Ahmedabad, mill workers were given plague bonus. In 1918, the mill owners announced the abolition of bonus, which was opposed by the mill workers. Gandhiji intervened in this matter and asked the mill workers to go on a peaceful, non-violent strike and demand 35% bonus, but the workers were demanding 50% allowance. Gandhiji decided to go on a hunger strike in support of the workers. Seeing the strike, the mill owners agreed to give 20% allowance. With Gandhiji's support, the enthusiasm of the workers increased and the movement became more active. Ambalal Sarabhai's sister Anusuiya Ben supported Gandhiji in this movement and also published a daily newspaper. The mill owners were forced to agree to a compromise with the workers. The entire matter was handed over to a tribunal. After considering the entire matter, the tribunal announced to give 35% allowance to the workers, which ended the strike. This was Gandhiji's second successful movement in India. In this movement, Gandhiji went on a hunger strike for the first time.

The Khilafat Movement

The Khilafat Movement of 1920 was a worldwide movement. Its main reason was the British reducing the dominance of the Turkish Caliph. This caused anger against the British among Muslims all over the world. In India, the Khilafat movement was led by the 'All India Muslim

Conference'. Gandhiji was the main spokesperson of this movement. He returned the honors and medals given by the British, due to which Gandhiji became the main leader of the people of all communities of India.

The Rowlatt Act

To suppress the voice of freedom rising in the country, the British introduced the Rowlatt Act in 1919. The Rowlatt Act is also known as the Black Law. This law gave the Viceroy the right to control the press, arrest any politician at any time as well as arrest anyone without a warrant. It was opposed across the country under the leadership of Mahatma Gandhi.

Non-cooperation movement

Gandhiji believed that the British were able to establish their power in India with the cooperation of Indians. If every Indian does non-cooperation with the British, they will leave the country.

The Non-Cooperation Movement was launched in 1920 under the leadership of Mahatma Gandhi and the Indian National Congress. This movement gave a new direction to the Indian Independence Movement. Gandhiji believed that it is impossible to get proper justice from the British hands, so he planned to withdraw the nation's cooperation from the British government and thus the Non-Cooperation Movement was started.

Civil disobedience movement

In 1930, Gandhiji started the Civil Disobedience Movement. It meant breaking the government laws without violence, which Gandhiji started by violating the Salt Law. That is why it is also called Salt Satyagraha.

Through this movement, Gandhiji diverted the attention of the Indian people towards achieving the independence of the country. On 12 March, 1930, Mahatma Gandhi took out a 24-day march from Sabarmati Ashram in Ahmedabad to Dandi village.

Dalit Movement

In protest against the untouchability prevailing in the country, Mahatma Gandhi started the anti-untouchability movement on 8 May 1933. This movement spread across the country in such a way that untouchability was eradicated to a great extent. Whereas Gandhiji founded 'the All India Anti-Untouchability League' on 30 September 1932.

Quit India Movement

Gandhiji's Quit India Movement played a very important role in getting independence for India. Mahatma Gandhi started the Quit India Movement against the British in August 1942, due to this movement the British were forced to leave India.

In this movement, Gandhiji gave the slogan of 'Do or Die' due to which the people of India became very angry towards the British. Due to this movement, the foundation of the country's independence was laid and the British Government decided to free India.

Ideology of Mahatma Gandhi

Mahatma Gandhi's personal experiences in life contributed the most to the development of his ideology. His initial ideology was particularly influenced by the traditions of 'Vaishnavism' and 'Jainism'. Gandhiji was also influenced by the 'Bhagwat Geeta'. Apart from this, Jesus' 'Sermon on the Mount', the writings of Tolstoy, Thoreau and Ruskin also influenced his thinking.

Truth

Truth means honesty, justice and fairness. Gandhi said that truth is not only the relative truth of our concept but also the absolute truth, the eternal principle, which is God. Truth is the only foundation on which any strong society can stand. Truth should not be only in words but also in actions. The path of truth is full of thorns, but it is the right path. Gandhi believed that where there is truth, there is God and morality is its basis.

Non violence

Gandhi's goal was attainment of truth and non-violence was the means for him. He considered non-violence to be the greatest power of life, which keeps life free from violence. According to him, without non-violence, the dream of finding truth and attaining God is incomplete. According to Gandhi, violence is not a weapon of cowardice, but a powerful symbol of a person's strength. Non-violence is not the shield of a coward, but the highest quality of a brave person. Having negative thoughts about any person is violence.

Ahinsa has two different meanings. In the narrow sense, it means not harming others or oneself by body or mind. In the positive and broad sense, it means boundless love and charity. He says, "In its negative form, [ahinsa] means not harming any living being by body or mind. Therefore, I cannot injure any wrongdoer or bear any ill-will towards him and thereby cause him mental suffering. In its positive form, ahinsa means the greatest love, the greatest charity. If I am a follower of ahinsa, I must love my enemy or stranger as I love my wrongdoing father or son. This active ahinsa essentially involves truth and fearlessness".

Satyagraha

Satyagraha is a modern political philosophy propounded by Mahatma Gandhi in his struggles against British rule. The idea of Satyagraha emphasizes the power of truth and the search for truth. Its simple meaning was that for true objectives, there is no need to use any kind of physical force against the unjust. The objective is to be achieved by awakening the consciousness of the unjust only on the strength of non-violence, without resorting to the feeling of vengeance or aggression. Non-violence is the basic mantra of Satyagraha. Satyagraha is to force the oppressor or the unjust to accept the truth on the strength of non-violence.

Sarvodaya

Mahatma Gandhi started the Sarvodaya movement. The word 'Sarvodaya' meant 'progress for all' and it aimed to develop society through non-violence and peaceful cooperation.

Sarvodaya is a book by English writer Ruskin, translated into Gujarati by Gandhiji, titled Unto This Last. 'Unto This Last' means - even this last one. Sarvodaya means - rise of all, development of all.

Swaraj

For Gandhi, Swaraj meant self-rule of the people and hence he clarified that for him Swaraj meant freedom for the citizens and in its fullest sense, Swaraj is much more than independence.

Swaraj does not only mean independence from foreign rule at the political level, but it also contains the idea of cultural and moral independence. It emphasizes mutual cooperation and harmony in nation building. Swaraj means self-restraint, village rule, and decentralization of power. To promote Swaraj, Gandhi advised the people to be self-reliant, adopt indigenous products and become self-sufficient.

Trusteeship

According to Mahatma Gandhi's trusteeship principle, a person who accumulates more wealth than his needs has the right to use the property only for fulfilling his needs, the remaining wealth should be managed by him as a trustee and spent on social welfare. Mahatma Gandhi believed that the capacity of all people is not the same, some people have more earning capacity while some have less, so those who have more earning capacity should earn more but after fulfilling their needs, the remaining amount should be spent on the welfare of the society.

Swadeshi

According to Gandhiji- "Swadeshi means the feeling that we

have of using the products made in our vicinity. It prohibits the use of products from outside. Swadeshi is a religion, a duty that binds us within the limits of ancestral religion. If there is any flaw in it, then it should be corrected. In the field of politics, it is only about using swadeshi institutions and removing the flaws in them and then using them. In the economic field, it is about using only those products that are made in the vicinity, and improving and using the products made in the neighbourhood."

Religion

Gandhiji believed that religion is the only thing that connects a person to God. It not only establishes a mutual relationship between God and a person, but also binds people together. Religion does not separate people from each other but establishes unity among them.

According to Mahatma Gandhi, God has no religion. The person who understands the pain and suffering of others is the real religious person. Mahatma Gandhi believed in equality of all religions. His religion was based on truth and non-violence. For Gandhiji, truth was his God. According to him, non-violence is the best means to attain God.

Major Contributions of Mahatma Gandhi in Indian Politics

1. He introduced the concept of non-violence as a tool of political protest.
2. He organised mass movements to fight for the rights of the Indian people.
3. He helped unite various religious and social groups in India.
4. He inspired the Indian people to believe in themselves and their ability to achieve independence.
5. Gandhi's arrival in Indian politics was a turning point in the freedom struggle. He helped transform the Congress into a mass movement and he gave the Indian people the inspiration and means they needed to achieve

independence. Gandhi's legacy continues to inspire people around the world who are fighting for social justice and freedom.

Conclusion

In this research paper we have seen how Gandhiji entered Indian politics and the era of mass movement began. Initially, Gandhiji raised local problems and through these he emerged as a national leader. There have been differences among scholars regarding the significance of Gandhiji's ideology, but the truth is that his ideology widely influenced the national movement and gave it a definite direction.

References:
1. Pruthi, R. K. & Chaturvedi, Archana (2009): Perspectives on Gandhian Thoughts, Commonwealth Publishers Pvt. Ltd., New Delhi.
2. Iyer, R. N. (1973): The Moral and Political Thought of Mahatma Gandhi, Oxford University Press.
3. Gupta, P. K. (2014): Mahatma Gandhi 's Strategy and Indian Politics, Swastik Publications, New Delhi.
4. Gandhi, M. K. (1942): Constructive Programme: Its Meaning and Place, Navajivan Publishing House.
5. Meena, Hemraj & Fernandez, Preeti (2013): Gandhi: A Socio-Political Contribution to Indian Politics, Aadi Publications, Jaipur.
6. Kumarappa, J. C. (1949): Economy of permanence: A quest for a social order based on non-violence, Navajivan Publishing House.
7. Gupta, P. K. (2015): Mahatma Gandhi and His Struggle for Satyagraha, Swastik Publications, New Delhi.
8. Nanda, B. R. (2002): Mahatma Gandhi: A Biography, Oxford University Press.
9. Kurtz, L. R. (2008): Gandhi and his

legacies, Encyclopedia of Violence, Peace & Conflict.
10. Gandhi, M. K. (1927): The Story of My Experiments with Truth, Navajivan Publishing House.
11. Parekh, B. (1989): Gandhi's Political Philosophy: A Critical Examination, University of Notre Dame Press.
12. Dalton, Dennis (1998): Non-violence in Action: Gandhi's power, Oxford University Press, Delhi.
13. Guha, Ramachandra (2014): Gandhi Before India, Penguin India.
14. Tendulkar, D. G. (1951): Life of Mohandas Karamchand Gandhi, in 8 vols, Bombay.
15. Gandhi, M. K. (1958): Satyagraha (Non-Violent Resistance), Ahmedabad.

Appraising Mahatma Gandhi's Philosophy and Indian Democracy

Dr. Yadavendra Dubey
Assistant Professor
Department of Political Science
Gram Bharti College Ramgarh, Kaimur, Bihar
Email: yadavendra4@gmail.com

Abstract

India has a democratic system of governance. Since India is a large nation, it requires appropriate and efficient governance. The democracy envisioned by Mahatma Gandhi which is surrounded by non-violence does not yet exist in any country in the world. In the framework of Indian democracy, his ideal stateless democracy would be a federation of satyagrahi village communities that operate on the principles of voluntary collaboration and respectful, peaceful coexistence. There is a lot of inequality and centralization in modern democracies. According to Gandhi's theory of self-rule, swaraj is a true democracy in which each person understands that they are the true rulers of their own lives and that their power lies within them.

While he supported India's independence, he thought that Satyagraha was the best way to get it. In addition, he thought that Indians ought to take part in nonviolent protests against untouchability, British imperialism, and intergroup strife. He came to see that social ills like untouchability and discord between communities were the main contributors to India's suffering. He was always destined for self-rule i.e. swaraj is the real form of democracy.

Keywords: Satyagraha, Non-violence, Untouchability, Swaraj, Democracy

Introduction

One of the most influential and captivating Indian leaders who battled for his country's independence was Mahatma Gandhi, also called the "Father of the Nation." He was a realistic combatant who focused on issues; today, his life seems to be the stuff of legends or philosophy. Hence, Mahatma Gandhi was among our greatest philosophers if philosophy is wisdom. He was a revolutionary who led a powerful movement against British imperialism but never permitted the movement to be accompanied by hatred, malice, or resentment against Englishmen. He was dedicated to overthrowing all forms of tyranny and social injustice but never harboured malice towards anyone. In the traditional meaning of the word, he was not an intellectual, he wasn't an academic philosopher who presented his ideas in an exacting, formal, and dry way. Finding contradictions and inconsistencies in some of his comments would not be difficult. In his commitment to the truth, he was utterly consistent. Like the ancient sages, he was a sincere seeker of truth who experimented throughout his life to uncover the truth and apply it to the real-world issues that faced humanity. He was also a spiritual explorer and scientist. He established and pursued satyagraha, a method, another strategy for eradicating oppression and injustice is satyagraha. The alternative is to establish a social structure that may eliminate all forms of exploitation and eliminate the necessity for force or Satyagraha. Like that Social order necessitates a democratically chosen global government. Socialist economy, national state, and power decentralisation force governments to do justice.

Mahatma Gandhi's essence of philosophy

Mahatma Gandhi was of firm opinion that the global government would institute the rule of law among states and scientifically utilise global resources for the good of humanity as a whole. It could deal with any act of aggression or a stubborn nation by using some force. Since force is always needed to enforce the law, no one can argue against its use. The police will be maintained by the democratic state to suppress anti-social groups and handle the internal affairs of the people. Naturally, using force to defend the rule of law by a duly elected, civic-minded authority is perfectly acceptable. He was a decentralist who favoured the decentralization of all political and economic power so that people would truly feel free and not be subject to a centralized authority. Gandhiji promoted village autonomy, a loose union of communities to meet common needs, and each village should be essentially autonomous and self-governing through panchayats. As a spiritualist, he advocated for moral restraint, self-control, and persuasion rather than legislation as a means of bringing about societal change. Capitalism was not Gandhi Ji's cup of tea. He detested its greed, emphasis on self-interest, and exploitation of the underprivileged.

Mahatma Gandhi was utterly opposed to both the current economic structure and the growing materialistic tendency. He opposed the contemporary trend towards extravagant living and the variety of desires, as well as the persistent expansion of large industrial combines' operations and the displacement of small producers by ever-increasing mechanisation of production. He supported self-help, physical labour, self-sufficiency, cottage and small-scale industry production, and simple and honourable living. He advocated for universal employment and the provision of necessities for a healthy lifestyle, including clothing, food, and housing. While he did not object to the use of machinery, he did desire it to serve man rather than to subjugate him.

Gandhiji was not an individualist in the traditional sense of the word—a guy driven by self-interest, striving for self-aggrandizement and granting society the minimal authority to control his behaviour. He was a supporter of individualism in the moral and spiritual sense, understanding it as the idea that man is an end in himself by nature and that he needs freedom to grow morally and enrich communal life while remaining good and constantly well-aware which is constrained by Dharma. He is oblivious to the concept of service because capitalism's fundamental motivation is profit. One of the main factors contributing to war's growing devastation is the desire for power.

Democracy, capitalism, and war preparations are incompatible. Since the latter demand an extreme level of centralized, absolute control, it is understandable why the majority of "civilized" States now meekly acquiesce to the despotism of various types of tyrants. In the modern State, nationalization of conscience and intellectual regimentation are quickly becoming commonplace aspects of daily existence. This unquestioning adoration of violence and riches cannot continue indefinitely without the human race descending back into barbarism.

Gandhi developed the ideology of Satyagraha based on his understanding of satya with Ahinsa as the means, and sarvodaya, or non-violent socialism, as the common goal, thanks to his understanding of Ahinsa. When self-reliance is properly interpreted and lived, it serves as a vital tool for nonviolent social change. "As long as and to the extent that it is an aid to one's self-respect and spiritual discipline, self-reliance is a necessary ideal." It is not an aim in and of itself since individuals who undergo moral and spiritual renewal and grow more responsible become the quickeners, capable of igniting a fresh impulse in the murky recesses of social life. Gandhi's political vision revolved around the ideal of Ramarajya, even if he lacked a comprehensive plan for societal reform. He was adamant that Ahinsa would eventually become a worldwide standard of civilization. This belief, along with his belief in the enchanted force of millions of people working towards a similar goal, gave him a distinct, if innate, sense of intuition.

Sarvodaya is based on the sharing of authority and a strong belief that social virtue should take precedence over individual interests. Harmony must take precedence over rivalry. This change in social and political outlook needs to be viewed as a revolutionary endeavour that will ultimately benefit all of humanity, a spiritual necessity in a civilized world, for it to be effective direction. Sarvodaya was founded on the division of powers and the conviction that the good of society should come before personal gain. Rivalry has to give way to harmony. For this shift in social and political perspectives to be successful, it must be seen as a revolutionary undertaking that would eventually benefit all of humanity a spiritual requirement in a civilized world. Since society is a macrocosm of the individual seeker, it must learn to reject everything that is in opposition to the idea of shared responsibility.

Gandhi was extremely concerned about the pervasive tendency of State authority to turn into active violence, but he was also worried about the possibility that people might lose their souls and reject their humanity by renunciating personal moral accountability in favour of the Leviathan. Individual consciences bear the primary responsibility for ensuring the well-being of all people. It is a perilous misconception to believe that any part of this responsibility can be abdicated on behalf of the legal system, the social compact, tacit consent, or the rule of law. Furthermore, no moral agent can ever unquestioningly accept the majority of laws, proclamations, and policies made by any political organisation, regardless of the rationale.

Mahatma Gandhi's ideas on democracy

Non-violence

As it is today, no country in the world possesses the democracy that Mahatma Gandhi envisioned—a democracy completely surrounded by non-violence. In his imagination, democracy exists without any form of punishment, and even the "State" as an organisation is rendered obsolete. This is due to Mahatma Gandhi's belief that the state is a symbol of concentrated, planned violence. As non-violence is connected with the human soul, man can be non-violent whereas in opposition to it, "… a State is a soul-less machine. On this accord, it is impossible to get rid of violence. Its very existence depends upon violence." According to Mahatma Gandhi's philosophy, nonviolence should be accepted as an inherent aspect of existence, and modern societies must function based on this principle.

Stateless democracy

In Gandhi's vision, there would be no states and a federation of satyagrahi village communities that would cooperate freely and live in dignity and harmony with one another. It is not conceivable for there to be no state, as Mahatma Gandhi cherished, either now or in the near future. Even so, it is the responsibility of the individuals residing in state organisations to cultivate a nonviolent character that is ingrained in them and to progressively raise it to a sufficient degree. In addition, the democratic system ought to promote the growth of nonviolence on a personal, social, communal, and national level. It is impossible to eliminate the culture of dread that permeates our environment, the decline in life's values, and the problems that have emerged visibly without creating it.

Decentralization and equality

However, there is a lot of inequity and centralization in today's democracy. There is equality and decentralization in a stateless democracy. Breadwinners and non-professionals ought to represent the ideal in society. Every person has the greatest freedom to dedicate themselves to serving society to the best of their abilities in a stateless democracy.

Economy of the Village

Once more, Gandhiji supported decentralized production while advocating for highly centralized production. The goal was to prevent power from being concentrated in the hands of a small group of wealthy individuals, not to completely eliminate machines as such. He wanted to revitalize the rural economy to eradicate poverty. The focus was on individual, varied, intensive, small-scale farming, as well as an economy centered around cattle.

Swaraj

Gandhian concept of Self Rule means Swaraj is a real democracy, where people's power rests in the individuals and each one realizes that he or she is the real master of one's self. Thus, people are sovereign in a democracy but in a parliamentary democracy, the party system has a vital role to play. However, Gandhi was highly critical of the parliamentary democracy and in his monumental book "Hind Swaraj" (Self Rule or Home Rule, he called the British Parliament a "sterile woman and a prostitute" (Hind Swaraj-Ch-V, p.12), though for him "good government is no substitute for self-government." (Tendulkar, DG, Mahatma, Vol.II, p.24) Gandhi saw the national swaraj, or battle for freedom, from the larger viewpoint of the ideal swaraj. He hardly cared about independence in and of itself. He felt that India could only actively promote global interdependence and international cooperation through national self-rule.

 Gandhi believed that genuine swaraj could only come from the individual and village levels, so he could not place a high value on political freedom alone. Similar to the ongoing process of self-purification that characterizes individual swaraj, national swaraj also necessitates national self-purification. This includes the eradication of economic exploitation, the removal of social abuses, the transcendence of religious differences, the beginning of spiritual rebirth, the radical reconstruction of internal structures, and the comprehensive reform of an entire social system. Gandhi pointed out the shortcomings that Indians themselves would need to overcome in order to achieve true swaraj, even as he denounced imperial rule.

Form of Democracy

Although Gandhi's remarks regarding parliamentary democracy are contradictory, he nevertheless states that "disciplined, enlightened democracy is the finest thing in the world" as he delves deeply into the principles of democracy. At the same time, he also cautions people against wholesale copying of the Western Model of democracy, where there are only nominal democracies. However, he has the highest regard for Democracy and he calls it "a great institution" Again conscious people say, "It is liable to be greatly abused." Even today, all over the world, democracy is a widely accepted principle of the system of governance and there is no alternative to democracy.

Future of Democracy in India

It is therefore abundantly clear that the Gandhian concept of democracy, which must be applied at the local level, the party system's foundational principles rather than partisan lines, the elimination of defection, and the observance of recalling dissident representatives, represents the only hope for the future. The current democratic system of government needs to be cleansed of its flaws and shortcomings. To keep democracy safe, people's authority must be acknowledged; otherwise, if democracy is exploited or misused, people's future is doomed.

Conclusion

Mahatma Gandhi was a man of action and a leader with significant influence over men rather than a meticulous philosopher. Mahatma Gandhi, like Buddha and Socrates, emphasised only a few fundamental principles and did not methodically discuss the fundamental philosophical tenets as well as the sociological, political, and theories' economic ramifications from a sophisticated intellectual perspective. Still, he had undoubtedly made clear several essential concepts for the revitalisation of the human race and the rebuilding of politics and society, and in this regard, he could be recognised as a political, social, economic, and moral philosopher. His magnificence was revealed in his commanding personality, his moral leadership in politics, his innate intuition, and his teachings on nonviolence and the truth. He was a prolific writer of strength and power as well. Nearly every social, educational, cultural, political, and economic issue facing the modern world was addressed in his books. Gandhi voiced a number of ideas that are extremely pertinent to the current era, despite not being a system-builder in the traditional academic sense.

References:
1. Goswami, K. P. (1971): Mahatma Gandhi: A Chronology, Publications Division, Government of India, Entry for 9 July 1914.
2. Malhotra, S. L. (2001): Lawyer to Mahatma: Life, Work and Transformation of M. K. Gandhi, Deep & Deep Publications, p. 5, ISBN 978-81-7629-293-1.
3. Jain, Jagdish Chandra (1987): Gandhi, the Forgotten Mahatma, Mittal Publications, pp. 76–77, ISBN 978-81-7099-037-6.
4. Kamath, M. V. (2010): 'Gandhi: A Spiritual Journey', Indus Source Books, Mumbai, pp.142 – 182.
5. Gupta, P. K. (2015): 'Mahatma Gandhi and His Struggle for Satyagraha', Swastik Publications, New Delhi, pp. 1 – 12.
6. Das, Shyamal (2014): 'Gandhi in Contemporary World Order', ABD Publishers, Jaipur, p.176.
7. Pruthi, R. K. & Chaturvedi, Archana (2009): 'Perspectives on Gandhian Thoughts', Commonwealth Publishers Pvt.

Ltd., New Delhi, p.1.

8. Meena, Hemraj & Fernandez, Preeti (2013): 'Gandhi: A Socio-Political Contribution to Indian Politics', Aadi Publications, Jaipur, pp.236 – 251.

9. Gupta, P. K. (2014): 'Mahatma Gandhi 's Strategy and Indian Politics', Swastik Publications, New Delhi, p.186.

10. Ibid., p.63.

11. Tendulkar, D.G. 'Life of Mohandas Karamchand Gandhi', Vol. V, p. 343.

The Features of Mahatma Gandhi's Thought

Dr. Pulatov Sherdor Nematjonovich
Head of the Department of Social Sciences
Alfraganus University, Tashkent, Uzbekistan,
Email: psherdor88@gmail.com

Abstract

The article analyzes the moral and philosophical worldview of Mahatma Gandhi. The concept of God is at the core of Gandhi's worldview. He sees God and Truth as a single concept. Truth means everything to Gandhi. Ahinsa is the basis of the search for truth. Ahims does not harm any creature.

It is worth noting that when it comes to India for the first time, Mahatma Gandhi will come to mind. His name is so intertwined with the name of India that no one can separate it. Gandhi, with his courage and ideas, left a mark in India and world history.

The study of the socio-political worldview and philosophy of Gandhi is very important. In the modern world its significance is even greater. For example, we can see how the concept of non-violence is necessary both in the world and in political circles. This is because the modern era is very special because of its polarity. In his philosophy, the emergence of man as a primary factor proves its relevance. Therefore, the study of the philosophy of Mahatma Gandhi is relevant.

Keywords and expressions: Mahatma Gandhi, Philosophy, Ethics, Bhavagad-gita, God, Truth, Ahinsa, Satyagraha, Truth, Justice, Love, Mercy, Hatred, Ignorance.

Introduction

India has a rich philosophical history. This is reflected in the development of philosophy, which continues from ancient times to the present day. President of Uzbekistan Shavkat Mirziyoyev called India the largest democracy in the world, noting that the Uzbek people have historical ties. "I am very pleased to be here on hospitable Indian land. India has a special place in the heart of every Uzbek. Our peoples are connected by historical ties, similar traditions, spiritual and cultural proximity of the world. For us, India is a great civilization that radiates the light of kindness and generosity. This is the largest democracy in the world," Mirziyoyev said [1].

The official delegation of Uzbekistan, headed by the President of the Republic of Uzbekistan Shavkat Mirziyoyev, paid tribute to the national hero of India, Mahatma Gandhi, during his official visit to India on October 1, 2018.

The delegation visited the Raj Ghat Memorial in New Delhi and laid a wreath at the eternal flame of Mahatma Gandhi. They made an entry in the book of honored guests [2].

Research and Results

The philosophical views of M. Gandhi (1869–1948), taken together with the teachings of Gandhism, developed under the conditions of the historical era at the turn of the 19th and 20th centuries, which was marked by a special role of the religious factor, which turned out to be a consolidating and mobilizing beginning in an atmosphere of spiritual and socio-political crisis in the country caused by the dominance of the colonial system. Reflecting the most general tendencies in the development of self-awareness of the Indian people, this factor has become an effective means of national and social cohesion in the face of the struggle against the colonialists.

At the same time, this factor, irrespective of the personal motives of Gandhi himself, turned out to be driven in relation to the general desire for national liberation. Despite the deeply religious nature of his worldview, his unlimited commitment to Hinduism and the tendency to consciously perceive him as a convinced Hindu - sanatani xindu, judging by his views and practical activities, his commitment to Hinduism was aimed at certain political goals and objectives. Inspired by religious ideas, it was in them that Gandhi found fertile food and gave his experiments as well as the means to achieve the goals that ultimately took shape in the form of a specific program.

In turn, its program settings turned out to be very effective in terms of ideological influence on the consciousness of the masses and strengthened their determination to rise to the fight against the enslavers. Thus, Gandhi was able to use them to implement this program on the way to India achieving national independence. In this regard, he noted: "A religion that does not take into account practical matters and does not help solve them is not a religion" [3]. Proceeding from this, he considered himself a "practically idealist" and perceived religion as a reference point in the approach to various philosophical problems, as well as the highest criterion and a constant basis for theoretical constructions.

He said that I studied this religion from my hiring teacher, who was very religious and taught me various prayers.

Nanya, the teacher of Gandhi, taught the Ramnan prayer. This blessing has been with him since childhood. "I was very impressed with Ramayana when he was read to my father. A great admirer of Rama was Ladh Maharaj from Bileshwar [4].

Several examples of Ayurveda have become known from the early years of Gandhi. Events in his work affect his life. He is particularly attracted to the image of Rama. In addition to the Ramayana, the life of Gandhi was also influenced by the Bhavagad-gita, another example of Indian philosophy. "A few months later we moved to Rajkot. They did not read Ramayana there. But every night they read the Bhavagad-gita [5]. These circumstances were characteristic of his religious views.

Turning to philosophical views, it should be pointed out that the fundamental principle for him is the perception of God as the primary reality objectively existing and not connected with the will and consciousness of the individual. Therefore, in relation to the main issue, Gandhi's philosophy was in the full sense a supporter of objective idealism.

As for God, in his view - this is an absolutely amorphous reality - this is the root cause and source of all things. In particular, he pointed out: "Running is not a man. God is power. He is the essence of life. He is a pure and fragile consciousness. He is eternal." [6] He further develops his thought: "For me, God is truth and love; God is ethics and morality; God is fearlessness. God is a source of light and life, and yet he is above and beyond all this ..." [7].

 Such vagueness in assessing the essence of God as a primary reality is explained by his substantiation of this concept not from philosophical, but rather from purely religious considerations. Therefore, he formulates his thought without a bluff: "I speak of God exactly as I believe in him ... Reason is powerless to know it ... My logic can create many hypotheses and refuses them. An atheist can defeat me in a polemic. But my faith is so much stronger than my consciousness that I can challenge the whole world and say: "God is, was and always will be" [8].

"In my world there is nothing but Truth and Ahinsa. If you can understand the Truth and Ahimsu, you will understand the true essence of many things in the world. I do not want to speak arrogantly. There are many high rumors in the world, but there is a word of God that can be changed, and the world has its own words. They cannot change the word of God. I think we are losing ourselves, we are forgetting. Therefore, one can understand that the Truth is as great as it can operate in trade. How is it used in everyday life? How does Ahinsa work? When people insult me, some people say that when someone insults you, you also insult them. What is the use of insulting each other? [9]

Moreover, he concluded that "the ultimate goal of man is to comprehend God and all his activities - political, social and religious - should be guided by the ultimate goal of seeing God" [10].

Thus, provided that the divine essence of M.K. Gandhi is considered in the substantial plane as the main point of reference for his philosophical and socio-political views. And this concept essentially runs a red thread through many of the works of M.K. Gandhi.

These statements give reason to believe that he considered the concept of truth in the religious and ethical plane, which provides for the presence and element of knowledge.

Another discovery of Gandhi is the so-called "quiet inner voice", interpreted by him as a unique means of comprehension and knowledge of absolute truth or divine essence. He shared his revelations in the essay "God's Messenger," published in Young India, in which he explains his intuitive sensations, which suggest that this "quiet inner voice" constantly reminds himself of himself as a divine manifestation. However, in his opinion, it is not accessible to everyone, solely because "we close our ears" in front of him [11]. No wonder Gandhi attaches great importance to this mystical phenomenon, which, according to him, helps in comprehending and realizing the "truth in oneself."

Meanwhile, the main tool in the process of perceiving this "voice", in Gandhi's view, is the idea of non-use of violence in the life of mankind. At the same time, he, apparently, puts an equal sign between truth and non-violence, as evidenced by his other maxims. In particular, he points out: "Truth on non-violence is synonymous with God ..." [12]. Whereas "... the root of everything is in Truth, which is also known to me as non-violence" [13].

In ethical terms, the main and leading idea of the concept of M. Gandhi was the concept of "Ahinsa", i.e. "Non-damage to living beings", first elevated to a fundamental principle in line with the Jain religious and philosophical tradition and has undergone a deep development and original interpretation in the teachings of Gandhi.

He recalls an event in his life and says: "I stole a piece of gold from the house and my brother and I sold it, because he owed 25 rupees. So, we somehow paid the debt. But my conscience began to torment me. I promised myself that I would never steal again, and wanted to apologize to my father. In the end, I decided to repent, apologize to my father and write to him about it. My father was sick at the time: he had a hole in his thigh and he had to go to bed. I handed her a letter and sat on the contrary.

My father read the letter and cried. Pearl drops rolled down his face into paper. He closed his eyes for a moment, and then tore the letter. He sat reading a letter, and now lay again. I cried too. I watched my father suffer. If I was an artist, I could paint this picture today - as it is alive in my memory. The pearl of love cleansed my heart and washed away my sins. Only those with such love can feel what it is. In the end, Scripture says that only those who have arrows of love know its power.

It was a practical lesson for me. At that time I saw only a manifestation of fatherly love, but today I know that this is the real Ahinsa. When Ahims becomes widespread, he will change everything he touches. Forgiveness is graciously not my father's custom. I thought he would get angry, frown, and beat me. But he was very calm [14].

The road to Ahinsa is tense, but the results are consistent and good for both sides. But the fist continues to answer. But as a result of this, there is no happy life in the world, and injustice and ignorance live. The main weapon for overcoming it - Ahinsa - this is my opinion [15].

Ahinsa is described as a serious political force in using Gandhi to prove and substantiate political ideas. Gandhi wrote: "Man and his actions are two different things. When one praises a good deed, one condemns a bad deed, whether it is performed good or bad, depending on the circumstances, the person will become respected or sympathetic. "Beware of sin, not sinful." This is a rule that, in fact, is understandable to everyone, but the law is not very effective. That is why hatred is spread all over the world.

Ahinsa is the basis of the search for truth. If you don't rely on Ahinsa, I have the opportunity every day to prove that these searches are useless. Accusation and struggle with the system are possible, but criticism and struggle with its author are similar to condemnation and struggle with each other. In the end, we are all in one place, we are all servants of the same creator, and the divine powers in us are unlimited. Ignoring humanity means ignoring the divine powers and causing evil not only to this creature, but to the whole world".

The concept of "love" is accepted as the most important category within the philosophical and ethical concept of Gandhi, which turns into a very significant property and at the same time an inspiring way to implement the principle of "Ahinsa". In Gandhi's understanding, "love" and "mercy" should be the fundamental beginning for any relationship between people, while the feeling of hatred must be rejected forever. The principle of love, according to the thinker, should be the basis for stable relations between Hindus and Muslims.

"When I look at the name of Mahatma in this sense, I see in him only love. This is nothing but an expression of the firmness of my faith in Ahinsa "[16].

Another indispensable attribute of "non-violence" is "suffering" as a certain pattern. In this sense, according to Gandhi, in the process of following the principle of

"Ahinsa", in addition to the will of a person, as an ardent supporter of non-violence, one has to undergo a certain cycle of suffering. Since a person must proceed from non-damage to his foe and treat him not by force, but by love and mercy, since he must steadfastly and patiently endure the suffering brought upon him by his foe, until he is defeated by the power of love.

In this regard, his statement that "not one of the states of the world has escaped advancement without passing through the cleansing crucible of suffering has been indicative. The hotter the flame in this crucible, the higher the achievement. And it is impossible to gain freedom without such suffering" [17].

It is known that in such a deep understanding of the laws of suffering or "tapasya" on the part of M. K. Gandhi was successful due to his appeal to the centuries-old religious and philosophical foundations on which truly Indian spirituality is based, as a result of which he was able to more specifically develop and implement his socio-political representations in the broad masses. Characteristic in this respect are the statements of J. Neru that "the thought of a certain epithymy, tapasya stops thinking of Indians - both to chosen thinkers and to illiterate lower classes. She is alive now, as she was alive several thousand years ago, and she must be appreciated in order to understand the psychology underlying the mass movements that plague India under the leadership of Gandhi" [18].

According to Gandhi, one of the main goals of promoting society is spiritual and moral perfection. Giving it a divine coloring, he considered it possible for man to strive for that ideal and did not deny his final achievement.

On the way to this, he attached special importance to the principle of refraining from making concessions to one's negative instincts and desires by a person, along with strict regulation of his thoughts, words and deeds, which, according to the teachings of Jainism, was interpreted as a religious and philosophical postulate called "brahmacharya."

In his book, Gandhi sheds light on this issue. At first he understands Brahmacharya as the teaching of Jainism, only as a renunciation of his passion. "Even after I realized this, I failed twice. My failure was due to the fact that the motives of my efforts were destructive. My main goal was not to have more children. In England I read about embryos" [19]. He speaks openly about these things, and then thinks that the Brahmacharya should take care of his essence, not only taking the form and introducing it to society. In this case, Gandhi considered it necessary to make him a lifetime. Controlling your emotions is a prerequisite for taking the oath [20].

They believed that the problem of nutrients should not be a problem, but simple sweeter and as boiled as possible. The role of fasting is also discussed in the Brahmacharya. A person who searches for Brahmacharya always knows about his own shortcomings, searches for passions hidden deep in his heart, and constantly seeks to get rid of them [21]. At the same time, Gandhi also saw other things to which he devoted his life, all his activity, all his physical and spiritual state of independence of India and the people of India. These factors show that this concept is comprehensive and important for Gandhi. In addition to other philosophical and ethical concepts, courage and courage are important. According to the wise advice of the thinker, in order to reach the truth, a person needs fearlessness.

Ahinsa and cowardice are conflicting words. Ahinsa is the quality of family good; fear is the quality of evil. The root of love is love and cowardice is hatred. My aunt is always patient and fear always hurts. The true Ahinsa is a noble hero. My uncle's propagandist is never defeated. Fear always triumphs [22].

"The word "fear" cannot take place in the dictionary of

Ahinsa [23]," he emphasized. He especially pointed out that before courage and courage, all other virtues are insignificant. At the same time, however, this category is not realized in the sense of confronting enemies and evil, but in personal self-sacrifice and voluntary acceptance of torment and suffering. Gandhi repeatedly emphasizes that a truly brave person is by no means obliged to resort to physical violence, but rather is able to defend himself boldly by looking into the eyes of any adversity, using "force of truth" or "willpower".

In the process of spiritual self-improvement, such concepts as "truthfulness" and "justice" are also recognized as important. In accordance with the first, special demands are made on moral behavior and on following the norms of social life.

At the same time, Gandhi drew attention to the importance of personal relations between people in the process of practical implementation and testing of ethical provisions. To this end, he selects the principle of aparigrah as the main criterion, i.e. "Lack of desire for wealth", borrowed from the Jain tradition. He notes that wealth can be a source of propensity for excesses, such as idleness and pomp. Therefore, he believes that this principle is appropriate in conditions when the vast masses cannot afford the minimum means of subsistence and the desire for moral enrichment is fully consistent with the principle of brahmacharya, not to mention the vice of lust for material wealth [24].

Touching upon the totality of moral principles leading, according to M.K. Gandhi, to self-improvement, it should be noted that the most important place here belongs to the ethics of fasting.

Gandhi considered fasting with other similar customs as accessible both ethically and politically, as this is not only a rule of etiquette, but also one of the powerful tools of political struggle. Considering the observance of the post one of the effective methods of the Satyagraha movement, Gandhi at the same time recognized its significance for his daily work as a means of carrying out various political tasks.

The most decisive, leading point in the general system of philosophical and ethical teachings of Gandhi is the principle of "non-violence", which in essence reflects his approach and the development of the concept of "Ahinsa", which in turn serves as an indicator not so much of his ideological creativity as the determining principle of his social political action.

This principle takes in the system of philosophical and socio-political concepts, perhaps the most extensive and universal position, despite the fact that until now it has not received an unambiguous interpretation in scientific use. In particular, by M. Gandhi himself he is identified either with the "Ahinsa" or the "category of love", while the path of truth is determined by the non-violent path.

But at the same time, in the general context of Gandhism, this principle emerges as objective, comprehensive and universal in terms of the position and functioning of the individual in public life. According to M. Gandhi, this principle is by no means sent down from nowhere to earth, but rather, inwardly immanent or peculiar to human nature. In other words, if this concept is as if logical for people, then violence is the lot of predators. Moreover, since non-violence is a law of this kind, it "should fill all being, and not be applied to individual actions" [25]. In addition, the thinker placed special emphasis on the effective nature of this tool, while at the same time drawing a diametrical line between it and its antipodes - inertia and inactivity. He proclaimed at the same time: "Non-violence is the greatest force in the service of mankind. It is stronger than the powerful weapon of destruction invented by the human genius" [26].

On the whole, as a philosophical and ethical principle, this concept, being primarily related to the political sphere, is defined as a distinctive feature of satyagraha. It is important to note that at the same time, this concept was considered by M. Gandhi as an ideological and theoretical platform of satyagraha, as opposed to all other means of struggle for the national liberation of India.

Conclusion

Thus, we can say that the idea of God and truth is at the forefront of his thinking. He knows the truth as God. In all his socio-political and philosophical views, he is based on truth. He believes that truth is above all.

Secondly, at the heart of his moral philosophy lies the achim, the moral principle of Jainism. Based on this principle, Mahatma Gandhi connected it with the truth and created a new path in it: Gandhi is based on several principles of ancient Hindu philosophy.

Thirdly, love is considered the most important category of Gandhi's philosophical and ethical concept, and this category becomes the most important feature of "Ahinsa" and its practical inspiration. "Love" and "mercy," Gandhi believes, should be the cornerstone of all human relationships, and "hatred" must be removed from life. According to Gandhi, in India, based on the principle of "love" relations between Hindus and Muslims must be stable.

Fourth, we see that this principle of satyagraha lies in the branding of Gandhi's socio-political views. The point of this is not to use force, that is, to explain to the enemy that what he or she does without power is a mistake. According to this principle, Mahtama Gandhi left a special mark in the history of mankind.

References:

1. https://www.press-service.uz [Visit of Shavkat Mirziyoyev the president of the Republic of Uzbekistan to India].

2. https://www.press-service.uz [The Uzbek delegation, led by Shavkat Mirziyoyev, honored the memory of Mahatma Gandhi].

3. Gandhi, M. K. (1955): My religion, Ahmedabad, p.4.

4. Gandhi, M. K. (2009): My Life is My Message, T. Uzbekistan, p.24.

5. Ibid, p.24.

6. Pyarelal, Mahatma Gandhi (1956): The Last Phase, Vol.1, Ahmedabad, P. 599.

7. Gandhi, M. K. (1958): All men are Brothers, Peris (UNESCO), p. 58.

8. Gandhi, M. K. (1957): Truth is God, Ahmedabad, p.11.

9. Gandhi, M. K. (17दिसम्बर, 1947): हिरजन सेवक

10. Gandhi, M. K. (1957): All men are Brothers, Ahmedabad, p. 11.

11. Tendulkar, D. G. Mahatma (1951): Life of Mohandas Karamchand Gandhi, Bombay, vol.4, p.190.

12. Ibid, vol. 8, p. 157.

13. Gandhi, M. K. (2009): My Life is My Message,T. Uzbekistan, p.19.

14. Ibid, p.144.

15. Ibid, p,182.

16. Gandhi, M. K. (1958): Satyagtaha (Non-Violent Resistance), Ahmedabad, p.115.

17. Neru J. Otkritie Indiya (1955): (The Discovery of India), Moscow, p.95

18. Gandhi, M. K. (2009): My Life is My Message, T. Uzbekistan, p.108.

19. Ibid, p.111.

20. Ibid, p.114.

21. सम्पूर्ण गांधी वाङ्मय

22. Tendulkar D.G., Mahatma, vol. 5, p.38.

23. Pyarelal, (1956): Mahatma Gandhi: The Last Phase, vol. 1, Ahmedabad, p.599.

24. Gandhi, M. K. (1958): All men are Brothers, Paris (UNESCO), p.58.
25. Ibid, p.85.
26. Po 'Latov, S. N. M. (2022): Mahatma Gandining Inson Tabiati Haqidagi Qarashlari, Academic research in educational sciences, 3(3), pp.10-19.
27. Po 'latov, Sh. N. (2019) Mahatma Gandiijtimoiy-falsafiyqara-shlarigaqadimgi hind falsafasiningta'siri. (TDSHI). – Toshkent., p.120.

The Legacy of Gandhiji's Efforts in India

Dr. Sunita B. John
Assistant Professor
Department of Physical Education
SHUATS, Prayagraj
Email: subijohn2002@yahoo.com

Dr. Priyanka Singh
Assistant Professor
Department of Arts and Social Sciences
SHUATS, Prayagraj
Email: subijohn2002@yahoo.com

Abstract

What did Mahatma Gandhi give to India? This question can have an infinite number of responses. Beyond his involvement in the freedom struggle, he was the first person to bring Indian ideas and aspirations to the world as a pioneer of Indian civilisation. In addition to teaching the Indian populace the value of a unique, nonviolent form of resistance, he also had a significant influence on the political and social climate of the day as well as India's future via the positive social upliftment initiatives he spearheaded.

Gandhiji envisioned an entirely new social structure free from injustice and exploitation. By establishing organisations like Sarvodaya Samaj and Shoshan Vihin Samaj, which sought to shield people from exploitation, he committed himself to this purpose. Gandhiji was adamant that everyone should have equal opportunities for personal growth, regardless of their social or economic standing.

He did not, however, find the concept of maximising happiness for the greatest number of individuals to be satisfactory. Gandhi, on the other hand, favoured the advancement and well-being of all societal segments. Gandhi believed that the welfare of the people as a whole, or Swaraj, hinged on the welfare of each person. Stated differently, people can only thrive in a free and peaceful community.

Gandhi, nonetheless, opposed concentrating solely on worldly advancement because he thought that an excessive amount of material prosperity could result in a number of issues. Gandhi's ideal was based on the conviction that exercising self-control and self-sacrifice, rather than giving in to our wants and cravings, is what leads to the growth of civilisations, cultures, and self-rule (swaraj). This study is focused on the legacy of Gandhiji's efforts in India.

Keywords: Mahatma Gandhi, Sarvodaya Samaj, Swaraj, Society, Social, Human being.

Introduction

The only Indian known worldwide and the one who first placed India on a map of the globe was Mahatma Gandhi. He was the first Indian to achieve political prominence outside of India before returning home. He is credited with bringing millions of men-and particularly women-into the public eye and is the greatest mass mobiliser in Indian history. For 25 years, he dominated Indian politics to such an extent that anyone who offended him risked political suicide. He is the only leader in India, if not the entire globe, to have an impact on a wide range of aspects of life and to have something to say about them, be it high politics, the economy, sexuality, morality, cleanliness or raising children.

Gandhi was so troubled by the widespread violence at the time of India's independence, for which he had fought so hard, that he chose not to raise the national flag or even to deliver a statement. He spent the last two years of his life tending to the wounds caused by intercommunal violence and refused to take on a political role. He traversed the prickly streets of the Noakhali villages alone, fasted until his body could no longer support it and begged the victims to forgive. Despite being threatened with violence on multiple occasions, he turned down all offers of protection and even challenged his critics to try their hardest, which one of them eventually did.

Gandhiji envisioned an entirely new social structure free from injustice and exploitation. By establishing organisations like Sarvodaya Samaj and Shoshan Vihin Samaj, which sought to shield people from exploitation, he committed himself to this purpose. Gandhiji was adamant that everyone should have equal opportunities for personal growth, regardless of their social or economic standing.

He did not, however, find the concept of maximising happiness for the greatest number of individuals to be satisfactory. Gandhi, on the other hand, favoured the advancement and well-being of all societal segments. Gandhi believed that the welfare of the people as a whole or Swaraj, hinged on the welfare of each person. Stated differently, people can only thrive in a free and peaceful community.

Gandhi, nonetheless, opposed concentrating solely on worldly advancement because he thought that an excessive amount of material prosperity could result in a number of issues. Gandhi's ideal was based on the conviction that exercising self-control and self-sacrifice, rather than giving in to our wants and cravings, is what leads to the growth of civilisations, cultures and self-rule (swaraj).

Gandhi ji and freedom struggle

The movement remained empty throughout this time until 1914, when Tilak, fresh out of prison, launched the Home Rule campaign across the nation alongside Annie Besant. This campaign peaked when Mahatma Gandhi visited India. Before he arrived, there had been some opposition to the British, but it had only included a small number of individuals because of the movement's disunity and the exclusion of women and the wider public.

There was no such popularly supported anti-British resistance after the Congress was founded, with the exception of the Swadeshi and anti-Bengal partition movements. Their region was likewise constrained in addition to this. However, although the public's engagement was significant, it was insufficient to address the entire scope of the Home Rule campaign.

Following his arrival in India in 1917, Gandhiji carried out the country's first acts of civil disobedience (Satyagraha in Champaran), the first hunger strike (Ahmedabad Mill Movement, 1918) and the first non-cooperation (Kheda Satyagraha, 1918). These three successful experiments helped the Indian people become involved in the freedom movement and Mahatma Gandhi became a leader who was embraced by the general public as the undisputed leader of the Indian liberation movement. Mahatma Gandhi's inspiring leadership and the realisation that Muslim involvement in the Indian campaign against the British was so widespread for the first time since the uprising in 1857 were the causes behind it. Together, Hindus and Muslims began this unity over the Khilafat issue but their primary goal was to drive the British out of India. On August 1, 1920, Mahatma Gandhi launched the nation's first non-cooperation movement, in which members of every class Hindus and Muslims alike as well as children, the elderly, women, farmers, urban and rural residents, artisans, intellectuals, students, impoverished, wealthy, business owners, employees and so on participated and opposed British rule.

All of India ended up standing with Gandhiji because he prioritised class coordination over class fighting in the national movement. British misconceptions about Indians' lack of consciousness were dispelled by Mahatma Gandhi's leadership. By uniting the Indian freedom movement and introducing them to the force of truth, non-violence and moral strength, Gandhiji not only became the movement's most prominent leader but also proved that the imperialist British power could not defeat them. He fought the British with these values till the very end of his life.

Gandhi ji views on Non-Violence

Morality and nonviolence were preached by religious figures like Ashoka and Mahavira as well as by notable kings like Buddha. It's fascinating to note that movements in India were waging nonviolence as a weapon during the same period that the First and Second World Wars destroyed much of the modern world. The Indian freedom struggle is considered one of the world's biggest struggles because of this feature of Gandhi's movement. The British faced an impossible situation as a result of Gandhi's nonviolent resistance, for which they had no solution. Gandhi had opposed the British military's entire development by fighting them non-violently. In the conflict between the weapons of the two civilisations, Gandhi's nonviolence prevailed. Mahatma Gandhi was a staunch advocate of nonviolence. Mahatma Gandhi adopted the philosophy of his master, Gopal Krishna Gokhale and held that "the means should be as great as the goal." That is, the nation's independence is a sacred ideal and in order to attain it, equally sacred means ought to be employed, making the nation's liberation movement a global model.

Gandhi fought hard to eradicate Indian evils

Gandhi did not, however, advocate the nation's faults or customs in order to prove that Indian civilisation was superior; rather, he waged a protracted war to put an end to these practices and in the process, implemented the necessary reforms to advance Indian civilisation. The great peaceful movement passed down through the generations: A nation's future is determined by the concepts and types of struggles upon which it is founded. Using nonviolent but extremely effective tactics such as fasting, dharna, peaceful protest, strike and moral force, Mahatma Gandhi defeated the British in the liberation campaign. The world's ideas about human values were also growing stronger by that time, so if Britain which prided itself on being the champion of humanity crushed the nonviolent movement with the force of its might, it was fearful of being revealed as a hypocrite to the world at large. The Indians realised the strength of nonviolent action because of their fear of him.

Gandhi ji views on Caste System

Gandhiji asserts that Varnashram and caste are not interchangeable. Class structure, on the other hand, is a response to social systems such as Varnashram, which rely more on Hindu texts than on class structure. The Vedas and other ancient writings, which hold that a person must take up the profession of their ancestors in order to support themselves, are the source of the Varna system's regulations. There is an infinite number of castes, some of which are disappearing and some of which have emerged.

Brahmins, Kshatriyas, Vaishyas, and Shudras are the four main Varnas identified in the tenth Mandal of the Rigveda. Depending on their rank and seniority, the aforementioned Varnas perform a variety of tasks and roles.

Gandhiji asserts that because it violates the Varnas' laws, Brahmins themselves are not entitled to assert their superiority in society. The four Varnas in the Vedas, in his opinion, are comparable to the four body parts. No Varna can be greater than the others; instead, each Varna should be regarded as equal and significant in order to eradicate caste-based prejudice and achieve equality in society. He made an effort to revitalise Varnashram's long-standing customs and employed them to advance social welfare.

Gandhian perspective on Status of Women

Gandhi considered women to be self-aware persons rather than merely objects of reform. Of course, he also included the general public. Indian women's active involvement in local and national social movements was crucial in forming Indian society.

Gandhi urged women to take part in the liberation movement

in India and stressed that their involvement in satyagraha and social reconstruction initiatives was even more crucial than that of males.

Gandhi thought that despite physical distinctions, men and women are equal. Women are viewed as having the same mental capacity as males. He was an advocate for girls' involvement in the social, political and economic sectors and stressed that they shouldn't be viewed as inferior but rather as unique, creative people who contribute to society.

Gandhi promoted women's active engagement in the social, political and economic domains of society in order to improve their status and rights. He pushed women to become independent thinkers and get involved in politics.

Gandhi emphasised the value of education for women and promoted a practical education across a range of areas. He was adamantly against damaging customs that impeded societal advancement, such as child labour, infanticide, homicide and child marriage. Gandhi's persistent efforts to create women's rights in India throughout the post-independence era produced noteworthy outcomes.

Gandhi ji views on Child Marriage

Gandhi condemned child marriage, seeing it as a barbaric and inhumane custom that impairs moral principles and causes bodily degeneration in youngsters. He maintained that religious writings endorsing child marriage are extravagances and do not accurately reflect Hinduism. In addition to having a detrimental impact on mothers' health, child marriage has an adverse effect on the next generation and the country as a whole.

Gandhi felt that only significant reforms to the marital system could lead to the full empowerment of women. The detrimental traditions embedded in the institution of marriage accounted for a great deal of the difficulties women encountered.

The main causes of widowhood among women were child marriage and the restriction of their ability to remarry. Traditional Hindu practices that abused and hampered the growth of Indian women included polygamy, child marriage, the ban on widow remarriage, and dowries.

Gandhi therefore supported marriage in a way that was compliant with Hindu doctrine, such as salvation, reincarnation or transmigration. In an effort to save young females, he was in favour of the creation of unique establishments like Mahila Ashram. He thought that widows who are children shouldn't be regarded as widows in the traditional sense.

Gandhi ji thinking upon Untouchability

Gandhi dismissed the distinctions between castes among other societal groups when discussing the issue of social equality. He opposed the custom of untouchability, sometimes referred to as caste and varna exclusion.

Gandhi thought that the widespread practice of untouchability among Hindus might indicate a rejection of moral values, which could undermine Indian pride. The wicked custom of untouchability stems from a society that flagrantly transgresses the human rights charter. In addition, Gandhi spent his whole political career fighting against untouchability.

Gandhi, nevertheless, persisted in his opposition to untouchability and his desire to eradicate this cruel custom from people's perceptions through his writings, speeches and deeds, even in the face of personal difficulties.

Gandhi pushed for the Harijans' admittance into temples and battled for their uplift, ultimately compelling the Hindu higher castes to grant them access. The Harijans' wounds were healed and their sense of unity was rekindled upon entering the temple, which also gave them confidence that they were not above God.

Conclusion

Gandhi Ji was an inspirational figure to the average man, with a captivating personality. He was revered as the economically downtrodden people's saviour. Gandhi Ji sought to create an ideal social order and used nonviolence to try to alter the discriminatory social structure that exists in India. His support for an equitable social framework advanced the overall development and interdependence of Indian society.

His views and convictions were crucial in driving out social unrest, gender inequity and other forms of customary injustice from Indian culture. Equal opportunity and equality were the cornerstones of GandhiJi's vision of the future society.

With rare exceptions, people in our nation still use nonviolent protests like strikes, dharnas and peaceful marches to pressure the government when they have demands. If we turn our attention to more recent events, precisely ten years ago, Anna Hazare, imitating Mahatma Gandhi, launched a nonviolent movement that sparked a national shift in power. The government was recently forced to rescind its decision over the farmer's bill because to the prolonged and nonviolent movement around the problem of farmers. Gandhi left behind a tradition of nonviolent protest, which has shown that even the power of weapons cannot defeat his moral superiority. Mahatma Gandhi was a symbol of strength, not of weakness.

References:

1. Bonadio, E., Srinivas, K. R., Iyengar, B. P., &Choudhary, A. (2023): Gandhian Philosophy and Indian Intellectual Property, In Relevance of Duties in the Contemporary

World: With Special Emphasis on Gandhian Thought, pp. 343-365, Singapore, Springer Nature Singapore.

2. Casolari, M. (2022): Introduction Gandhi After Gandhi, The Relevance of the Mahatma's Legacy in Today's World, In Gandhi After Gandhi The Relevance of the Mahatma's Legacy in Today's World, pp.1-5, Routledge.

3. Kelley, J., Haynes, A., & Arce-Trigatti, A. (2023): Gandhi: Toward a vision of nonviolence, peace and justice. In The Palgrave handbook of educational thinkers, pp.1-14, Cham: Springer International Publishing.

4. Kurtz, L. R. (2008): Gandhi and his legacies. Encyclopedia of Violence, Peace & Conflict, 837-851.

5. Mukherjie, D., & Majid, I. (2019): Gandhi–India's Greatest Contribution to Mankind, Mukherjie, D. & Majid, I. (2019): Gandhi India's Greatest Contribution To Mankind, Think India Journal, pp.127-140.

6. Rao, R. (2023): Gandhi falling… and rising, Journal of Historical Geography, pp.1-10.

7. Sharma, P. (2023): Public Policy for Sustainable Development: A Gandhian Paradigm, In Applied Spirituality and Sustainable Development Policy, pp. 181-200, Emerald Publishing Limited.

8. Sharma, V. (2023): Indira Files: A Critical Look at The Controversial Side of Indira Gandhi, Indira Files: A Critical Look at The Controversial Side of Indira Gandhi: Analyzing Political Legacy, Prabhat Prakashan.

9. Vickers, E. (2024): Rebranding Gandhi for the 21st century: Science, ideology and politics at UNESCO's Mahatma Gandhi Institute (MGIEP), Compare: A Journal of Comparative and International Education, pp. 785-803.

10. Zeeshan, S., &Kappiarathel, S. M. (2023): Gandhian Thought for Rural Development.

Theoretical Perspective of Mahatma Gandhi: Western Influences and Indian Inspirations

Dr. Shailen Verma
Assistant Professor,
Political Science & I.R.
Sardar Patel Centre for National Integration
DRML Avadh University, Ayodhya, U.P.
Email: shailen123verma@gmail.com

Abstract

This chapter examines the theoretical perspective of Mahatma Gandhi, focusing on the intricate interplay between Western influences and Indian inspirations that shaped his unique philosophical and political worldview. Through a comprehensive analysis of Gandhi's writings, speeches and correspondence, as well as a careful examination of his intellectual influences, this study reveals Gandhi's theoretical framework as a creative synthesis of diverse philosophical traditions.

The research explores key Western influences, including John Ruskin's critique of industrial capitalism, Leo Tolstoy's writings on non-violence and Henry David Thoreau's concept of civil disobedience. It also delves into the Indian philosophical and spiritual traditions that profoundly impacted Gandhi's thought, such as the concepts of Ahinsa (non-violence) from Jainism and Buddhism, and the ethical framework provided by the Bhagavad Gita.

The chapter highlights Gandhi's innovative reinterpretation of both Western and Indian concepts to address the challenges of his time, exemplified in his notions of swaraj (self-rule) and sarvodaya (welfare of all). It also examines Gandhi's approach to modernity, tradition and social reform as reflections of this East-West synthesis. The chapter concludes by emphasizing the significance of Gandhi's cross-cultural philosophical synthesis as a model for developing ethical frameworks that are both locally grounded and universally applicable in our increasingly globalized world.

Keywords: Satyagraha, Ahinsa, Swaraj, Sarvodaya, Civil Disobedience, Synthesis, Non-violence.

Introduction

Mohandas Karamchand Gandhi, widely known as Mahatma Gandhi, stands as one of the most influential figures in modern history, whose philosophical and political ideologies have left an indelible mark on the world. Gandhi's theoretical perspective, a unique blend of Western influences and Indian inspirations, forms the cornerstone of his revolutionary approach to social and political change. This study aims to delve into the intricate tapestry of Gandhi's theoretical framework, exploring the diverse sources that shaped his worldview and the distinctive synthesis he achieved between Eastern and Western thought.

Gandhi's life and work spanned two centuries and three continents, exposing him to a wide array of philosophical, religious and political ideas. His formative years in India, his legal education in England and his transformative experiences in South Africa all contributed to the development of his unique theoretical perspective. This multifaceted background allowed Gandhi to draw upon various traditions and create a philosophy that was both universal in its appeal and deeply rooted in Indian culture.

The complexity of Gandhi's thought lies in its ability to harmonize seemingly disparate elements: ancient Indian spiritual concepts with modern Western political ideals, traditional values with progressive social reforms and individual moral transformation with mass political action. His theoretical perspective not only guided India's struggle for independence but also inspired numerous social and political movements worldwide, from civil rights campaigns to environmental activism.

Gandhi's theoretical perspective was shaped by a diverse array of thinkers and traditions from both the East and the West. Among the Western influences, the works of Leo Tolstoy, John Ruskin and Henry David Thoreau played pivotal roles in shaping Gandhi's ideas on non-violence, civil disobedience and simple living. Tolstoy's concept of non-resistance to evil and his critique of modern civilization resonated deeply with Gandhi, influencing his development of non-violent resistance or Satyagraha. John Ruskin's "Unto This Last" profoundly impacted Gandhi's economic thought, inspiring his ideas on trusteeship and the dignity of labor. Henry David Thoreau's essay on civil disobedience provided Gandhi with a framework for peaceful resistance against unjust laws, which he later adapted and expanded in his own political struggles.

From the Indian tradition, Gandhi drew heavily on the teachings of ancient texts such as the Bhagavad Gita and the Upanishads. The concept of karma yoga (selfless action) from the Gita became a central tenet of Gandhi's philosophy, informing his approach to political activism and social service. The Upanishadic idea of the unity of all life reinforced his commitment to non-violence and universal love. Gandhi was also influenced by contemporary Indian thinkers such as Swami Vivekananda and Rabindranath Tagore. Vivekananda's interpretation of Vedanta philosophy and his call for social reform resonated with Gandhi's vision of a rejuvenated India. Tagore, while often a critic of Gandhi's methods, shared with him a deep concern for India's rural poor and a vision of cultural synthesis between East and West.

Historical Context

To fully appreciate Gandhi's theoretical perspective, it is crucial to understand the historical context in which it evolved. Gandhi's life (1869-1948) coincided with a period of significant global upheaval, marked by the height of European colonialism, two World Wars and the beginnings of decolonization. In India, the late 19th and early 20th centuries saw the rise of nationalist sentiment and the struggle against British colonial rule. This period also witnessed social reform movements addressing issues such as caste discrimination, women's rights and religious conflicts. Gandhi's theoretical framework emerged as a response to these complex challenges, offering a path that combined political liberation with social and moral regeneration.

Gandhi's experiences in South Africa (1893-1914) were particularly formative. It was here that he first developed and applied his methods of non-violent resistance in response to racial discrimination.This period also saw him experimenting with communal living and simple lifestyle, ideas that would later become integral to his vision for India. Upon returning to India in 1915, Gandhi entered a political landscape dominated by the Indian National Congress and a growing independence movement. His theoretical perspective offered a new approach to nationalism, one that emphasized mass mobilization, moral force and constructive programs alongside political negotiation.

This study seeks to examine the theoretical perspective of Mahatma Gandhi, focusing on the interplay between Western influences and Indian inspirations in shaping his unique philosophical and political worldview. By analysing the diverse sources of Gandhi's thought and the way he synthesized them, we aim to provide a comprehensive understanding of his theoretical framework and its relevance in both historical and contemporary contexts.

The objectives of this study are multifaceted. We aim to identify and analyze the key Western thinkers and ideas that influenced Gandhi's theoretical perspective, as well as explore the Indian philosophical and spiritual traditions that shaped his worldview. Furthermore, we will examine how Gandhi synthesized Western and Indian thought to create his unique theoretical framework and assess the evolution of his ideas in response to the historical and political contexts he encountered. The study will also evaluate the practical applications of Gandhi's theoretical perspective in his political and social campaigns and consider the contemporary relevance and global impact of his theoretical contributions. Gandhi's integration of these elements in his theoretical perspective offers valuable insights for addressing complex global challenges in the 21st century.

Literature Review

Mahatma Gandhi, a pivotal figure in India's struggle for independence and a global icon of non-violent resistance, developed a unique theoretical perspective that drew from a diverse array of influences. This chapter examines the intricate tapestry of Gandhi's philosophical and political thought, focusing on the interplay between Western influences and Indian inspirations that shaped his worldview. Through this exploration, we aim to provide a comprehensive understanding of Gandhi's theoretical framework and its relevance in both historical and contemporary contexts.

Gandhi's exposure to Western thought during his time in England and South Africa profoundly impacted his philosophical development. Several key Western thinkers and their ideas played crucial roles in shaping Gandhi's perspective. John Ruskin's work, particularly "Unto This Last," had a transformative effect on Gandhi's economic and social ideas. Gandhi himself acknowledged this influence, stating, "I determined to change my life in accordance with the ideals of the book... Its teaching has never left me and I am always trying to carry them out in Phoenix farm." Ruskin's emphasis on the dignity of labour and the importance of simple living resonated deeply with Gandhi, informing his later concepts of sarvodaya (welfare of all) and swadeshi (self-reliance).

Similarly, Leo Tolstoy's writings on non-violence and civil disobedience significantly influenced Gandhi's approach to resistance. In his correspondence with Tolstoy, Gandhi expressed his admiration: "Your writings have deeply influenced my life. I consider you as one of my guides in my search for truth." Tolstoy's "The Kingdom of God Is Within You" introduced Gandhi to the idea of non-violent resistance based on Christian principles, which Gandhi later adapted to the Indian context.

Henry David Thoreau's essay "Civil Disobedience" provided Gandhi with a theoretical framework for non-violent resistance against unjust laws. Gandhi credited Thoreau for crystallizing his thoughts on civil disobedience: "Thoreau's ideas on civil disobedience influenced my decision to use non-violent resistance to oppose unjust laws in South Africa." Thoreau's concept of individual conscience as a guide for moral action aligned with Gandhi's emphasis on personal ethics in political life. Additionally, Ralph Waldo Emerson's transcendentalist philosophy, emphasizing self-reliance and the inherent goodness of individuals, resonated with Gandhi's own beliefs. Emerson's ideas on the relationship between the individual and society influenced Gandhi's concept of swaraj (self-rule).

While Western thought provided Gandhi with important tools and concepts, his rootedness in Indian philosophy and spirituality was fundamental to his worldview. The Bhagavad Gita was a cornerstone of Gandhi's philosophical outlook. He interpreted its teachings on selfless action (nishkama karma) as a call for ethical engagement in the world: "The Gita is not for those who have no faith. It is for those who want to cultivate faith." Gandhi's concept of anasakti (non-attachment) drew heavily from the Gita's teachings, informing his approach to political action and personal conduct.

Gandhi's upbringing in a Vaishnava Hindu family with strong Jain influences shaped his commitment to Ahinsa (non-violence) and satyagraha (truth-force). Jain principles of non-violence towards all living beings and self-purification through asceticism deeply influenced Gandhi's personal ethics and political strategy. Buddhist teachings on compassion and the middle path also resonated with Gandhi. He often cited the Buddha's teachings in his writings: "The Buddha's teaching of compassion and non-violence is more relevant today than ever before."

The neo-Vedantic interpretations of Ramakrishna Paramahamsa and Swami Vivekananda influenced Gandhi's understanding of religious pluralism and the unity of all faiths. Vivekananda's emphasis on practical Vedanta and social service aligned with Gandhi's vision of spiritually-informed social action. Gandhi once remarked, "I have gone through his works very thoroughly, and after having gone through them, the love that I had for my country became a thousand-fold."

Gandhi's genius lay in his ability to synthesize these diverse influences into a coherent philosophical framework. His concept of satyagraha, for instance, combined Thoreau's civil disobedience with the Jain principle of Ahinsa and the Vedantic notion of the unity of all existence. Raghavan Iyer, in his seminal work "The Moral and Political Thought of Mahatma Gandhi" (1973), argues: "Gandhi's unique contribution was to fuse the Western concept of civil disobedience with the Indian tradition of non-violent resistance, creating a powerful tool for social and political change." Similarly, Bhikhu Parekh, in "Gandhi's Political Philosophy" (1989), notes: "Gandhi creatively reinterpreted both Western and Indian traditions, producing a philosophy that was neither purely Western nor purely Indian, but a unique synthesis that spoke to the universal human condition."

This synthesis is evident in Gandhi's approach to social reform. While he drew inspiration from Ruskin's critique of industrial capitalism, he grounded his economic ideas in the Indian concept of trusteeship, derived from the Isa Upanishad. Gandhi's theoretical perspective was not static but evolved in response to historical circumstances and personal experiences. His experiences in South Africa, for instance, led to a more nuanced understanding of racial and economic oppression, informing his later work in India. Judith Brown, in "Gandhi: Prisoner of Hope" (1989), observes: "Gandhi's thought was constantly evolving, responding to new challenges and experiences. His genius lay in his ability to adapt traditional concepts to modern contexts."

The enduring relevance of Gandhi's theoretical perspective is evident in its continued influence on social and political movements worldwide. From Martin Luther King Jr.'s civil rights movement to contemporary environmental and peace activism, Gandhi's ideas continue to inspire and guide. Gene Sharp, in "Gandhi as a Political Strategist" (1979), argues: "Gandhi's theoretical contributions to non-violent struggle have provided a blueprint for social movements across the globe, demonstrating the universal applicability of his principles."

In conclusion, Mahatma Gandhi's theoretical perspective represents a unique synthesis of Western influences and Indian inspirations. By creatively reinterpreting and combining diverse philosophical traditions, Gandhi developed a framework that was both deeply rooted in Indian thought and responsive to global challenges. His ability to bridge cultural and intellectual divides produced a philosophy that continues to offer valuable insights for addressing contemporary social and political issues. The enduring relevance of Gandhi's thought lies not only in its specific prescriptions but in its demonstration of the possibility of creative cross-cultural synthesis. In our increasingly interconnected world, Gandhi's theoretical perspective offers a model for developing ethical frameworks that are both locally grounded and globally relevant.

This chapter outlines the methodological approach employed in our study of Mahatma Gandhi's theoretical perspective, focusing on the interplay between Western influences and Indian inspirations. The complex nature of Gandhi's thought, which synthesizes diverse philosophical traditions, necessitates a multifaceted research methodology. Our approach combines historical analysis, textual interpretation, and comparative philosophy to provide a comprehensive understanding of Gandhi's theoretical framework.

The study adopts a qualitative research design, primarily relying on interpretive and hermeneutical methods. This approach is particularly suited to the examination of philosophical ideas and their historical context. Our research questions address the primary Western influences on Gandhi's theoretical perspective, the impact of Indian philosophical and spiritual traditions on his worldview, his synthesis of Western and Indian thought, the evolution of his ideas in response to historical contexts, and the contemporary relevance of his theoretical contributions. Thematic analysis is used to identify, analyze and interpret patterns of meaning within Gandhi's texts. We have developed a coding framework based on key themes such as non-violence (Ahinsa), truth (satya), civil disobedience (satyagraha), self-rule (swaraj), economic self-sufficiency (swadeshi), and social equality and justice.

To understand the interplay between Western influences and Indian inspirations in Gandhi's thought, we employ comparative analysis. This involves a systematic comparison of Gandhi's ideas with those of his Western and Indian influences. The process includes identifying key concepts in the works of Gandhi's influences, tracing these concepts in Gandhi's writings, analyzing how Gandhi adapted or reinterpreted these concepts and examining the unique elements Gandhi introduced in his theoretical framework.

Historical contextualization is crucial to understanding the evolution of Gandhi's theoretical perspective. We analyze Gandhi's ideas in relation to the historical events and socio-political contexts of his time, examining how his experiences in South Africa, his involvement in the Indian independence movement and global events shaped his theoretical framework. This analysis draws on a range of primary and secondary sources, including contemporary newspapers, government documents, personal accounts of Gandhi's contemporaries and historical studies.

Given the breadth of Gandhi's thought, our methodology incorporates insights from various disciplines, including philosophy, political science, religious studies and sociology. This interdisciplinary approach allows us to examine Gandhi's theoretical perspective from multiple angles, providing a more comprehensive understanding of its complexity and significance.

We acknowledge several limitations and challenges in our methodological approach, including language barriers, the difficulty of interpreting historical context from a temporal distance, the evolving nature of Gandhi's thought and the challenge of balancing influences and originality in his work. Our data analysis process involves chronological and conceptual mapping, influence tracing, synthesis analysis, contextual analysis and comparative evaluation. The interpretation of our findings is guided by hermeneutical principles, acknowledging the role of both the text and the interpreter in the production of meaning.

Major Debates

Mahatma Gandhi's theoretical perspective, a unique

synthesis of Western and Indian thought, has been the subject of extensive scholarly debate. This chapter explores the major themes and controversies surrounding Gandhi's philosophical framework, focusing on the interplay between his Western influences and Indian inspirations. By examining these debates, we can gain a deeper understanding of the complexity and enduring relevance of Gandhi's ideas.

One of the central debates in Gandhi scholarship revolves around the relative importance of Western and Indian influences on his thought. Some scholars, like Bhikhu Parekh, argue that Gandhi's philosophy is fundamentally rooted in Indian traditions, particularly Hinduism and Jainism, with Western influences playing a secondary role. Parekh contends that Gandhi's concept of satyagraha, often seen as his most original contribution, is deeply grounded in the Indian notion of satya (truth) and the Jain principle of Ahinsa (non-violence). However, others, such as Dennis Dalton, emphasize the significant impact of Western thinkers like Tolstoy, Ruskin and Thoreau on Gandhi's ideas. Dalton points out that Gandhi's first exposure to the Bhagavad Gita was through Sir Edwin Arnold's English translation, suggesting that even Gandhi's engagement with Indian texts was mediated through Western interpretations.

This debate extends to Gandhi's concept of swaraj (self-rule). While Gandhi often presented swaraj as an inherently Indian idea, scholars like Uday Singh Mehta have argued that it also draws heavily on Western liberal notions of individual autonomy and self-governance. Gandhi's interpretation of swaraj as both personal and political self-rule can be seen as a creative synthesis of Indian spiritual concepts and Western political philosophy. This synthesis is evident in Gandhi's writings, where he frequently cites both Indian scriptures and Western political theorists to support his arguments for Indian independence and social reform.

Another significant theme in the study of Gandhi's

theoretical perspective is the tension between tradition and modernity. Gandhi's critique of modern civilization, most famously articulated in "Hind Swaraj," has been interpreted by some as a wholesale rejection of Western modernity in favor of traditional Indian values. However, scholars like Tridip Suhrud argue that Gandhi's position is more nuanced. They suggest that Gandhi selectively appropriated elements of both Western and Indian thought to construct a unique vision of modernity that emphasized moral and spiritual progress over material advancement. This is exemplified in Gandhi's approach to technology, where he advocated for small-scale, locally appropriate technologies (like the spinning wheel) while rejecting large-scale industrialization.

The role of religion in Gandhi's political philosophy is another area of intense debate. Some scholars, like Akeel Bilgrami, argue that Gandhi's use of religious language and symbols was primarily strategic, aimed at mobilizing the masses for political action. Others, such as Margaret Chatterjee, contend that Gandhi's religious beliefs were fundamental to his worldview and inseparable from his political ideas. This debate touches on the broader question of how Gandhi negotiated between the secular ideals of Western political thought and the deeply religious context of Indian society. Gandhi's concept of sarva dharma sambhava (equal respect for all religions) can be seen as an attempt to reconcile these seemingly conflicting perspectives, drawing on both Indian traditions of religious pluralism and Western notions of secularism.

Gandhi's approach to social reform, particularly his stance on caste and gender issues, has also been a subject of scholarly contention. Some critics argue that Gandhi's attempts to reform the caste system without completely abolishing it, and his sometimes-paternalistic attitudes towards women, reflect a conservative adherence to Indian traditions. However, defenders of Gandhi, like Madhu Kishwar, point out that his views on these issues evolved over time and that he consistently pushed for greater equality and justice within the framework of Indian cultural norms. This debate highlights the challenges Gandhi faced in trying to synthesize progressive Western ideas with Indian social structures.

The concept of non-violence (Ahinsa) in Gandhi's thought presents another area of scholarly debate. While Ahinsa is often traced to Indian religious traditions, particularly Jainism and Buddhism, Gandhi's application of non-violence to political struggle was innovative and drew inspiration from Western sources as well. Gene Sharp's work on non-violent action traces the lineage of Gandhi's satyagraha to both Indian and Western precedents, including the writings of Thoreau on civil disobedience. The global impact of Gandhi's non-violent methods, from the Civil Rights Movement in the United States to anti-apartheid struggles in South Africa, demonstrates the universal appeal of this synthesis of Eastern and Western ideas.

Another theme in Gandhi scholarship is the relationship between ethics and politics in his thought. Gandhi's insistence on the unity of means and ends and his emphasis on personal moral transformation as a prerequisite for social change, challenge the conventional separation of ethics and politics in Western political theory. Scholars like Raghavan Iyer have argued that Gandhi's approach represents a unique contribution to political philosophy, one that draws on both the Indian tradition of raja-dharma (ethical governance) and Western critiques of realpolitik. This synthesis is evident in Gandhi's concept of satyagraha, which combines political activism with spiritual self-purification.

The economic dimensions of Gandhi's thought have also been a subject of debate. His critique of industrial capitalism and advocacy for a decentralized, village-based economy have been seen by some as a rejection of Western economic models in favor of traditional Indian economic structures. However, scholars like Ajay Skaria argue that Gandhi's economic ideas also drew inspiration from Western thinkers like Ruskin and Tolstoy, who critiqued industrial capitalism from within the Western tradition. Gandhi's concept of trusteeship, which sought to reconcile private property with social responsibility, can be seen as an attempt to synthesize Western economic concepts with Indian ethical principles.

The relevance of Gandhi's theoretical perspective in the contemporary world remains a point of ongoing debate. Critics argue that Gandhi's ideas are outdated and ill-suited to the complexities of modern global society. However, proponents like Ramachandra Guha contend that Gandhi's emphasis on ethical politics, sustainable living and cross-cultural dialogue is more relevant than ever in an era of global conflicts and environmental crises. The continuing influence of Gandhian ideas on social movements worldwide, from environmental activism to peace initiatives, suggests the enduring power of his theoretical framework. Gandhi's unique synthesis of diverse philosophical traditions continues to challenge scholars and activists alike, offering a rich source of insights for addressing contemporary global challenges. By engaging with these debates, we can gain a deeper appreciation of the nuances and enduring relevance of Gandhi's contributions to political and moral philosophy.

Conclusion

This study has examined the theoretical perspective of Mahatma Gandhi, focusing on the intricate interplay between Western influences and Indian inspirations that shaped his unique philosophical and political worldview. Through a comprehensive analysis of Gandhi's writings, speeches and correspondence, as well as a careful examination of his intellectual influences, we have uncovered a rich tapestry of ideas that defy simple categorization as either "Western" or "Indian."

Gandhi: Ideology, Philosophy and Indian Politics

Our research reveals that Gandhi's theoretical framework represents a creative synthesis of diverse philosophical traditions. From the West, Gandhi drew inspiration from figures such as John Ruskin, whose critique of industrial capitalism in "Unto This Last" profoundly influenced Gandhi's economic thought. Leo Tolstoy's writings on non-violence and Christian anarchism contributed to Gandhi's conception of satyagraha, while Henry David Thoreau's essay on civil disobedience provided a theoretical basis for Gandhi's methods of political resistance. These Western influences were not merely adopted wholesale but were reinterpreted and adapted to the Indian context.

Simultaneously, Gandhi's thought was deeply rooted in Indian philosophical and spiritual traditions. The concept of Ahinsa (non-violence), central to Gandhi's philosophy, has its origins in Jain and Buddhist teachings. The Bhagavad Gita, which Gandhi referred to as his "spiritual dictionary," provided the ethical framework for his idea of selfless action (nishkama karma). The Upanishadic concept of the unity of all existence underpinned Gandhi's holistic approach to social and political reform.

One of the most significant findings of our study is the way Gandhi creatively reinterpreted both Western and Indian concepts to address the challenges of his time. For instance, his concept of swaraj (self-rule) combined Western notions of political sovereignty with the Indian spiritual ideal of self-realization. Similarly, his economic philosophy of sarvodaya (welfare of all) drew on Ruskin's critique of capitalism but was articulated in terms of traditional Indian concepts of trusteeship and non-possession.

Gandhi's approach to modernity and tradition also reflects this synthesis. While he critiqued aspects of Western modernity, particularly its materialism and violence, he did not advocate a simple return to tradition. Instead, he envisioned a new modernity that combined the technological advancements of the West with the spiritual wisdom of the East. This is exemplified in his promotion of khadi (hand-spun cloth) as both a symbol of Indian self-reliance and a critique of industrial mass production.

In the realm of social reform, Gandhi's ideas again reflect a blend of Western and Indian influences. His campaign against untouchability, while rooted in the Indian concept of varnashrama dharma, was also influenced by Western notions of equality and human rights. Similarly, his views on women's empowerment, while often expressed in traditional Indian idioms, were shaped by his exposure to Western feminist thought during his time in London and South Africa.

The global impact of Gandhi's ideas further demonstrates the universal appeal of his theoretical synthesis. The influence of Gandhian non-violence on the American Civil Rights Movement, as evidenced by Martin Luther King Jr.'s adaptation of satyagraha, shows how Gandhi's ideas transcended their Indian origins. Similarly, the application of Gandhian principles in environmental movements worldwide, such as the Chipko movement in India and various Green parties in Europe, illustrates the contemporary relevance of his thought.

In conclusion, this study demonstrates that Mahatma Gandhi's theoretical perspective cannot be understood as simply Western or Indian, but rather as a unique synthesis that transcends these categories. Gandhi's genius lay in his ability to draw from diverse philosophical traditions and create a coherent worldview that addressed the pressing issues of his time and continues to offer insights for our contemporary world.

The enduring relevance of Gandhi's thought lies not only in its specific prescriptions but in its demonstration of the possibility of cross-cultural philosophical synthesis. In our increasingly globalized world, where the challenges we face transcend national and cultural boundaries, Gandhi's approach offers a model for developing ethical frameworks that are both locally grounded and universally applicable.

Future research could further explore the ways in which Gandhi's theoretical perspective continues to influence contemporary social and political movements, as well as how it might be applied to address current global challenges such as climate change, economic inequality and intercultural conflict. Additionally, comparative studies examining Gandhi's synthesis alongside other attempts at cross-cultural philosophical integration could yield valuable insights into processes of intellectual and cultural exchange.

Ultimately, Gandhi's theoretical perspective, with its creative blend of Western influences and Indian inspirations, stands as a testament to the power of cross-cultural dialogue and the potential for diverse philosophical traditions to inform and enrich one another. As we continue to grapple with complex global issues, Gandhi's example of thoughtful synthesis and practical application of diverse ideas remains an invaluable resource and inspiration.

References:
1. Brown, J. M. (1990). Gandhi: Prisoner of Hope. Yale University Press.
2. Brown, J. M. (1990). Gandhi: Prisoner of Hope (1st ed.). Yale University Press.
3. Brown, J. M. (1989). Gandhi: Prisoner Of Hope (cloth). Yale University Press.
4. Brown, J. M. (1989). Gandhi: Prisoner of Hope. Yale University Press.
5. Gandhi, M. K. (1927). The Story of My Experiments with Truth. Navajeevan Trust.
6. Gandhi, M. K. (1927). The Story of My Experiments with

Truth (ed.). Navajeevan Trust.
7. Navajeevan Trust. (1927). The Story of My Experiments with Truth - Deluxe-HC. Navajeevan Trust.
8. Navajeevan Trust. (1927). The Story of My Experiments with Truth. Navajeevan Trust.
9. Navajeevan Trust. (1927). The Story of My Experiments with Truth (Deluxe-HC ed.). Navajeevan Trust.
10. Gandhi, M. K. (1927). An Autobiography, Or, The Story of My Experiments with Truth. Navajeevan Publishing House.
11. Suhrud, T. (Ed.). (2017). An Autobiography or The Story of My Experiments with Truth: A Table of ... Tridip Suhrud.
12. Gandhi, M. K. (1998). An Autobiography, Or, The Story of My Experiments with Truth.
13. Parekh, B. (1989). Gandhi's Political Philosophy: A Critical Examination. Macmillan.
14. Iyer, R. N. (1973). The Moral and Political Thought of Mahatma Gandhi. Oxford University Press.
15. Parel, A. J. (Ed.). (1997). Gandhi: Hind Swaraj and Other Writings. Cambridge University Press.
16. Dalton, D. (1993). Mahatma Gandhi: Nonviolent Power in Action. Columbia University Press.
17. Fischer, L. (1950). The Life of Mahatma Gandhi. Harper & Brothers.
18. Nanda, B. R. (1958). Mahatma Gandhi: A Biography. Oxford University Press.
19. Bondurant, J. V. (1958). Conquest of Violence: The Gandhian Philosophy of Conflict. Princeton University Press.
20. Erikson, E. H. (1969). Gandhi's Truth: On the Origins of Militant Nonviolence. W. W. Norton & Company.
21. Chatterjee, M. (1983). Gandhi's Religious Thought. University of Notre Dame Press.
22. Jack, H. D. (1956). The Gandhi Reader: A Sourcebook of His Life and Writings. Grove Press.

23. Prabhu, R. K., & Rao, U. R. (Eds.). (1967). The Mind of Mahatma Gandhi. Navajeevan Publishing House.
24. Thoreau, H. D. (2008). Civil Disobedience. In Walden and Civil Disobedience (pp. 1-20). New York: Penguin Classics.
25. Weber, T. (1991). Conflict Resolution and Gandhian Ethics. Gandhi Peace Foundation.
26. Sharp, G. (1973). The Politics of Nonviolent Action. Porter Sargent Publishers.

The Relevance of Gandhian Idea of Education in Contemporary Education System

Dr. Md. Afroz Alam
Assistant Professor (Education)
Maulana Azad National Urdu University
School of Education & Training
College of Teacher Education
Chandanpatti, Laheriasarai
Darbhanga, Bihar
Email: afrozmanuu@gmail.com

Abstract

Mahatma Gandhi's educational philosophy, known as "Nai Talim" or "Basic Education" offers a holistic and integrated approach to learning that emphasizes the development of the whole person- physically, mentally and spiritually. Central to Gandhian education are principles such as learning by doing, self-reliance, character building and using the mother tongue as the medium of instruction. Gandhi envisioned an education system where students acquire practical skills through craft-centered curricula, fostering self-sufficiency and community integration. Teachers are seen as role models, embodying the values they teach, which include truth, non-violence and compassion. Additionally, Gandhian education promotes environmental awareness and conservation. The practical implementation of Gandhian education involves creating a curriculum centered around crafts and integrating education with the community's life and work. This approach ensures that schools serve as centers for community development rather than isolated institutions. The relevance of Gandhian education in contemporary society is significant, addressing modern challenges such as sustainable development, the need for skill-based education and moral and ethical crises.

Furthermore, the decentralization of education systems, as advocated by Gandhi, enhances the relevance and effectiveness of schooling by tailoring educational programs to local needs and contexts. Thus Gandhian education offers a timeless and humane model that remains pertinent in addressing current global educational challenges. By revisiting and adapting Gandhian principles, contemporary education can become more holistic, practical and values-driven, contributing to the creation of a more sustainable and ethical world. This paper explores Gandhian educational philosophy, its principles, implementation and its relevance in contemporary education system.

Keywords: Gandhian Education, Nai Talim, Basic Education, Holistic development, learning by doing, Skill-based education, Moral education, Contemporary education system.

Introduction

Mahatma Gandhi, one of the most influential leaders in India's struggle for independence, also had profound ideas about education. His philosophy of education often referred to as "Nai Talim" or "Basic Education" emphasized holistic development and self-reliance. The Gandhian idea of education, rooted in holistic development and ethical living, remains profoundly relevant in the contemporary education system. At its core, Gandhian education emphasizes the integration of intellectual learning with practical skills, fostering a balanced growth of mind, body, and spirit. In an era dominated by technological advancements and a competitive academic culture, Gandhi's vision offers a refreshing alternative that prioritizes character building, self-reliance, and social responsibility.

Today's education system often faces criticism for its narrow focus on rote learning and standardized testing, which can overshadow the importance of moral and ethical development. Gandhian education, with its principles of truth

(Satya) and non-violence (Ahinsa), addresses this gap by nurturing students' ethical and moral values. It encourages experiential learning and community engagement, helping students to connect their academic knowledge with real-world applications and societal needs. Moreover, the emphasis on sustainable living and localism in Gandhian philosophy resonates with current global concerns about environmental sustainability and economic equity. By promoting self-sufficiency and respect for local resources, Gandhian education aligns with contemporary goals of sustainable development and ecological responsibility. Incorporating Gandhian principles into modern education can cultivate well-rounded individuals who are not only academically proficient but also empathetic, socially conscious and equipped to contribute positively to their communities and the world at large.

Principles of Gandhian Education

Gandhian education is built on several key principles:

• **Holistic Development**: Gandhi believed education should cater to the physical, mental and spiritual growth of an individual. He emphasized the development of the whole person rather than focusing solely on intellectual capabilities (Gandhi, 1947).

• **Learning by Doing**: A cornerstone of Gandhi's educational philosophy is the idea of 'learning by doing'. He argued that education should be practical and vocational, enabling students to acquire skills that would make them self-reliant (Prabhu & Rao, 1967).

• **Self-Reliance and Self-Sufficiency**: Education, according to Gandhi, should make individuals self-reliant. This involved imparting skills that would allow them to earn a living and contribute to their community (Gandhi, 1951). Encourages students to be self-reliant and to develop skills that enable them to contribute to their communities.

Promotes local resources and sustainable living, fostering a sense of responsibility towards the environment and society.

• **Character Building**: Gandhi placed significant emphasis on moral and ethical education. He believed that education should cultivate values like truth, non-violence and compassion (Gandhi, 1927). Education should cultivate a sense of honesty, integrity and non-violent conflict resolution in students.

• **Mother Tongue as Medium of Instruction**: Gandhi advocated for primary education to be imparted in the child's mother tongue. He believed that this approach would make learning more effective and meaningful (Gandhi, 1942).

• **Decentralization**: Gandhi's model of education promoted decentralization. He believed that local communities should have control over their educational institutions to reflect their specific needs and context (Gandhi, 1948).

Implementation of Gandhian Education

The implementation of Gandhian education involves several practical steps:

• **Craft-Centered Curriculum**: Gandhi proposed a curriculum centered around crafts, which would serve as the basis for teaching various subjects. For instance, weaving could be used to teach mathematics (through measuring and counting) and history (by exploring the history of textiles) (Gandhi, 1937).

• **Integration with Life**: Education should be integrated with the life and work of the community. Schools should not be isolated from society but should function as centers for community development (Gandhi, 1948).

• **Teacher as a Role Model**: Teachers in Gandhian schools are expected to be role models, embodying the values they teach. This ensures that students learn not just through instruction but through observation and imitation (Prabhu & Rao, 1967). In Gandhian educational philosophy, teachers are seen as crucial role models whose behavior and values significantly influence student development. Gandhi believed that education is not just about academic instruction but also about shaping character. Teachers, therefore, are expected to embody the principles of truth (Satya), non-violence (Ahinsa), simplicity, and self-discipline, providing a living example for students to emulate. The role of teachers as role models is pivotal in instilling ethical and moral values. By demonstrating honesty, integrity and compassion in their daily interactions, teachers instill these values in their students. This direct, personal example is far more impactful than theoretical lessons alone, as students observe and internalize these behaviors. Moreover, teachers who practice simplicity and self-reliance encourage students to adopt sustainable and minimalistic lifestyles, aligning with Gandhian principles. This modeling helps students understand the importance of living in harmony with the environment and society. The impact of such role modeling extends to the development of students' social and emotional skills. By fostering a respectful and supportive classroom environment, teachers help students develop empathy, cooperation and a sense of community. This holistic development prepares students to be responsible, ethical and socially conscious citizens, reflecting the core objectives of Gandhian education.

• **Environmental Awareness**: Gandhian education promotes a deep respect for nature. Students are encouraged to engage in activities that foster environmental awareness and conservation (Gandhi, 1942). Gandhian education fundamentally promotes environmental awareness and conservation through its principles of simplicity, self-sufficiency and respect for nature. Central to this approach is the concept of Swadeshi, which encourages the use of local resources and sustainable practices, reducing dependence on external and often environmentally harmful products. This principle teaches students to value and conserve their immediate environment, promoting a mindset of sustainability. Experiential learning, a cornerstone of Gandhian education, involves hands-on activities such as organic farming, gardening, and recycling. These activities foster a deep connection with nature, teaching students the importance of preserving natural resources. By engaging directly in these practices, students develop practical skills in sustainable living and an understanding of ecological balance. Moreover, Gandhian education emphasizes **simple living and high thinking**. This philosophy encourages minimalism and the reduction of waste, instilling in students a sense of responsibility towards reducing their ecological footprint. It aligns with modern principles of environmental conservation by advocating for lifestyles that do not over-exploit natural resources. Through community service and involvement, Gandhian education also promotes collective action for environmental protection. Students participate in community clean-ups and environmental awareness campaigns, learning the importance of civic responsibility and collective efforts in conserving the environment. These experiences shape environmentally conscious individuals committed to sustainable practices and conservation efforts.

Relevance in Contemporary Education System

Gandhian education, though conceived in the early 20th century, remains relevant today:

• **Sustainable Development**: The emphasis on self-reliance and environmental conservation aligns with modern sustainable development goals. Education that fosters these principles is crucial in addressing contemporary global challenges. The principles of Gandhian education align closely with the goals of sustainable development, emphasizing holistic growth, ethical living and social responsibility. Gandhian education promotes self-sufficiency and sustainable living, encouraging the use of local resources (Swadeshi) and fostering an appreciation for environmental conservation. This directly supports sustainable development goals (SDGs) related to responsible consumption and production, and climate action. Gandhi's emphasis on experiential learning and vocational training integrates practical skills with academic knowledge, preparing students for sustainable livelihoods and economic self-reliance. This aligns with the SDG of quality education by promoting inclusive, equitable and practical learning opportunities. Moreover, the core values of truth (Satya) and non-violence (Ahinsa) in Gandhian education encourage peace, justice, and strong institutions, resonating with the SDG of peace and justice. By cultivating moral and ethical values, students learn to approach societal challenges with compassion and integrity, fostering sustainable communities. Community engagement and service, integral to Gandhian education, align with the SDGs promoting social cohesion and community resilience. This holistic approach ensures that individuals not only pursue personal growth but also contribute to the collective well-being, underpinning the broad objectives of sustainable development.

• **Skill-Based Education**: The focus on vocational training and practical skills is increasingly recognized as essential in today's job market, where there is a growing need for skilled labor. Combines cognitive skills with practical abilities, preparing students for various career paths. Encourages the development of problem-solving, critical thinking and creativity. Integrating vocational training and academic subjects through craft-centered curricula can transform education by making it more relevant, engaging and practical. This approach prepares students not only for academic success but also for meaningful careers and life-long learning. Helps students see the direct application of their academic learning in everyday life and future careers.

• **Decentralized Education Systems**: The push for localized control over education can enhance the relevance and effectiveness of schooling, ensuring that educational programs are tailored to local needs and contexts.

• **Moral and Ethical Education**: In a world facing moral and ethical crises, Gandhian education's focus on character building and values is more pertinent than ever.

• **Experiential Learning**: Gandhi's emphasis on learning by doing ensures that students learn through real-life experiences. This method helps students understand the practical implications of ethical principles and moral values.

• **Community Engagement**: Encouraging students to participate in community service and social work fosters empathy and a sense of social responsibility. Through engagement with their communities, students learn the importance of cooperation, altruism, and civic duty.

• **Value-Based Curriculum**: Integrating stories, biographies, and teachings of great moral leaders, including Gandhi, into the curriculum. Subjects such as literature, history, and social studies can be used to discuss ethical dilemmas and moral choices.

• **Role Modeling**: Teachers and educators serve as role models, demonstrating ethical behavior and moral decision-making. Schools can create a culture of respect, kindness, and integrity that students can emulate.

• **Peace and Conflict Resolution Education**: Teaching students about peaceful conflict resolution and non-violent communication. Programs and activities that promote understanding, tolerance, and respect for diversity.

Conclusion

Gandhian educational practices are intrinsically linked to community development, emphasizing the creation of self-sufficient, ethical, and socially responsible individuals who contribute positively to their communities. Central to Gandhian education is the concept of Nai Talim, or Basic Education, which integrates intellectual learning with manual work. This approach aims to produce well-rounded individuals equipped with both academic knowledge and practical skills, fostering a sense of dignity in labor and self-reliance. One of the key aspects of Gandhian education is its emphasis on community engagement. Students are encouraged to participate in community service and social work, which instills a sense of social responsibility and empathy. By engaging in activities such as village clean-ups, health campaigns and educational outreach, students learn the importance of contributing to the welfare of their communities. These experiences not only enhance their understanding of societal issues but also empower them to take active roles in addressing these challenges.

The principle of Swadeshi further connects Gandhian education to community development. By promoting the use of local resources and skills, students learn to appreciate and sustain their cultural and economic heritage. This focus on localism supports the development of sustainable communities, reduces dependency on external resources and promotes economic self-sufficiency. Students trained in this way are more likely to contribute to the local economy by engaging in agriculture, crafts, and other traditional vocations. Moreover, Gandhian educational practices foster ethical leadership. By prioritizing values such as truth, non-violence and simplicity, these practices cultivate leaders who are committed to justice and the common good. Such leaders are essential for the holistic development of communities, as they are more likely to implement policies and initiatives that promote social equity and environmental sustainability. Finally, Gandhian education emphasizes holistic well-being, considering not just academic success but also physical, emotional, and spiritual health. This comprehensive approach ensures that students grow into balanced individuals who can contribute to the development of harmonious and resilient communities.

Gandhian educational practices contribute significantly to community development by creating self-reliant, ethically grounded and socially responsible individuals. These practices foster a deep connection to local resources and community welfare, leading to sustainable and inclusive growth. Gandhi's ideas on education offer a comprehensive and integrated approach to learning that emphasizes holistic development, practical skills, self-reliance and moral values. While some of these ideas might seem idealistic, their core principles continue to offer valuable insights for creating an education system that is both humane and effective. By revisiting and adapting Gandhian educational principles, contemporary education can address many of the pressing challenges faced by modern societies.

References:

1. Alam, M. A. (2023). Mahatma Gandhi ke Taalimi Afkar aur Gandhiyaee Nizam-e-Taleem (Mahatma Gandhi's Educational Thoughts and Gandhian System of Education). Hindustani Zaban, Vol-9, Issue-4, Oct-Dec 2023, pp.8-20. Hindustani Prachar Sabha, Mahatma Gandhi Memorial Research Centre, Mumbai. https://hindustanipracharsabha.org/Hindustani-Zaban-Urdu.php

2. Avinash, Lingam T. S (1960). Gandhiji's Experiments in Education. New Delhi: Ministry of Education, Govt. of India.

3. Gandhi, M. K. (1927). My Experiments with Truth. Ahmadabad: Navajivan Publishing House.

4. Gandhi, M. K. (1937). Basic Education. Ahmadabad: Navajivan Publishing House.

5. Gandhi, M. K. (1942). Constructive Programme: Its Meaning and Place. Ahmadabad: Navajivan Publishing House.

6. Gandhi, M. K. (1947). Key to Health. Ahmadabad: Navajivan Publishing House.
7. Gandhi, M. K. (1948). India of My Dreams. Ahmadabad: Navajivan Publishing House.
8. Gandhi, M. K. (1951). Self-Restraint vs Self-Indulgence. Ahmadabad: Navajivan Publishing House.
9. Joshi, Sudharma. (2008). Educational Thoughts of Mahatma Gandhi. New Delhi: crescent Publishing Corporation.
10. Patel, M. S. (1953). The Educational Philosophy of Mahatma Gandhi. Ahmadabad: Navajivan Publishing House.
11. Prabhu, R. K., & Rao, U. R. (1967). The Mind of Mahatma Gandhi. Ahmadabad: Navajivan Publishing House.

Gandhian Idea of Education: An Educational Anthropological Perspective

Jaydeep Mondal
Assistant Professor
Department of Anthropology
Acharya Prafulla Chandra College Kolkata
Email: deepjay2014@gmail.com

Abstract

The Gandhian idea of education, rooted in the principles of truth, nonviolence, and self-reliance, presents a transformative approach that emphasizes holistic develop-ment and the integration of moral values in education. This philosophy advocates for "Nai Talim" or basic education, which promotes learning through productive work and the development of character alongside intellectual growth. From an educational anthropological perspective, Gandhian education seeks to harmonize the individual with their community and environment, fostering a sense of social responsibility and collective well-being. It challenges the conventional, exam-centric education system by prioritizing experiential learning, vocational training, and the nurturing of ethical consciousness. The relevance of this approach in contemporary education is profound, particularly in its potential to address social inequalities and empower marginalized communities. By focusing on the intrinsic relationship between education and the socio-cultural context, this perspective underscores the importance of culturally responsive pedagogy and the role of education in societal transformation. This abstract explores the enduring significance of Gandhian educational philosophy in modern educational practices, advocating for its integration to cultivate a more just, equitable, and compassionate society.
Keywords: Gandhian Idea of Education, Educational

anthropology, Social Responsibility, Culturally Responsive Pedagogy

Introduction

Mahatma Gandhi's educational idea, known as "Nai Talim" or "Basic Education," emphasizes the holistic development of individuals by integrating intellectual, physical and spiritual growth. Gandhi advocated for an education system that was accessible, free and compulsory for all, delivered in the mother tongue. His educational model stressed the importance of linking education to the daily lives and environments of students, making it practical and relevant. Gandhi's philosophy was heavily influenced by his experiences in India and abroad, leading him to reject the colonial educational system, which he viewed as alienating and disconnected from Indian culture. Instead, he sought to promote an educational system that fostered self-reliance and cultural pride (Joshi, 2010; Kumar, 2014).

From an educational anthropological perspective, Gandhi's philosophy can be situated within India's broader cultural and social dynamics, illustrating how education can serve as a means of cultural transmission and transformation. The practical aspects of implementing his philosophy in various socio-cultural settings highlight how educational practices are adapted to local contexts. Moreover, Gandhi's educational reforms had significant impacts on both individual and collective identity, as well as on the social structure of Indian society (Patel, 2016). By examining Gandhi's educational philosophy through the lens of educational anthropology, we gain insights into how his ideas were deeply rooted in the socio-cultural context of India and how they sought to transform society. Gandhi's focus on education in the mother tongue and community involvement aligns with the anthropological principle of cultural relevance, ensuring that education is meaningful and accessible to the local population (Batra, 2009). The holistic nature of Gandhi's approach resonates with the anthropological emphasis on considering all aspects of human development- social, physical, intellectual and spiritual (Shukla, 2005). Gandhi's vision of self-sufficiency and community engagement reflects the anthropological interest in education as a tool for social change, aiming to empower individuals and transform society (Chakrabarty, 2011). Educational anthropologists studying Gandhian schools would employ ethnographic methods to gather insights into how these principles are practiced and experienced by students and teachers, contributing to a deeper understanding of their impact and effectiveness (Singh, 2012).

Aims and Objectives

The present study has three main objectives which are written below:

- Understand Education as a Cultural Process
- Explore Educational Practices in Context
- Assess the impact on Identity and Social Structure

Methodology

This paper was meticulously prepared by reading what other researchers have written about the current topic. The current research team has spent a significant amount of time reading primarily project, research or study findings to achieve the stated goals. The authors used desk review to set up the original copy and narrative analysis was used to break down the data. The secondary data used in this paper came from firsthand sources.

Discussions and Interpretations

Gandhian Philosophy: Education as a Cultural Process

Mahatma Gandhi's educational philosophy is a profound example of understanding education as a cultural process. He viewed education not merely as a means of acquiring knowledge but as a transformative tool that shapes and is shaped by the cultural, social, and moral fabric of society.

His approach to education emphasized the integration of local culture, values, and indigenous knowledge, reflecting his belief that education should be closely aligned with the cultural context of the learners.

1. Education as a Reflection of Culture

• **Cultural Identity and Self-Respect**: Gandhi believed that education should reinforce the cultural identity of the learners. In the colonial context, where Western education often alienated Indians from their own culture, Gandhi's educational philosophy sought to reconnect students with their cultural roots. By emphasizing education in the mother tongue and the inclusion of traditional crafts and values, Gandhi's approach helped preserve and promote Indian culture, fostering a sense of pride and self-respect among the learners.

• **Integration of Indigenous Knowledge**: Gandhi's emphasis on incorporating indigenous knowledge into the curriculum demonstrates how education can reflect and sustain local culture. For example, students learned traditional crafts such as spinning and weaving, which were not only economically valuable but also culturally significant. This approach ensured that education was relevant to the learners' lives and communities, grounding them in their cultural heritage.

2. Education as a Tool for Cultural Transmission and Transformation

• **Cultural Transmission**: Through education, Gandhi sought to transmit essential cultural values and practices to future generations. His educational model was designed to instill virtues like truth, non-violence and self-reliance, which were deeply rooted in Indian cultural and spiritual traditions. The focus on moral and ethical education reflects the idea that culture is transmitted not just through language and rituals but also through the values and principles that guide behavior.

• **Cultural Transformation**: Gandhi's educational philosophy was also a means of cultural transformation. He envisioned education as a way to empower individuals and communities to resist colonial domination and rebuild Indian society based on its cultural foundations. By promoting self-sufficiency and community involvement, Gandhi's approach aimed to create a new social order that was rooted in Indian culture but oriented toward justice, equality and sustainability.

3. Education as a Community-Centered Process

• **Community Involvement in Education**: Gandhi's educational philosophy emphasized the role of the community in the educational process. He believed that education should not be confined to the classroom but should involve the entire community. This approach reflects the idea that education is a collective cultural process, where knowledge, skills, and values are shared and reinforced within the community.

• **Education for Social Organization**: By linking education to community life, Gandhi's approach cultivated social organization and cultural continuity. Education was designed to address the specific needs and challenges of the community, whether through teaching agricultural techniques, promoting health and sanitation, or encouraging cooperative living. This community-centered approach ensured that education contributed to the well-being and cultural vitality of the community as a whole.

4. Holistic Development: Mind, Body and Spirit

• **Cultural Holism**: Gandhi's holistic approach to education, which integrated intellectual, physical and spiritual development, reflects the cultural understanding that education should develop the whole person. This view aligns with many traditional cultures that see education as a lifelong process involving the cultivation of wisdom, character and social responsibility, not just academic knowledge.

• **Spiritual and Moral Education**: Gandhi's emphasis on spiritual and moral education is a key aspect of understanding education as a cultural process. He saw education as a means to cultivate inner virtues that are central to the cultural and spiritual life of the community. This focus on character building underscores the cultural dimension of education, where the ultimate goal is to produce individuals who embody the ethical and moral values of their culture.

Educational Practices in Gandhian Philosophy

Exploring educational practices in context, particularly through the lens of Gandhian philosophy, involves understanding how education is shaped by and responsive to the specific cultural, social and economic environments in which it occurs. Gandhian educational practices were deeply rooted in the realities of Indian society during his time, emphasizing self-sufficiency, community engagement and moral development.

• **Contextual Learning- Education Connected to Life:** Gandhi's concept of *Nai Talim* (Basic Education) was based on the principle that education should be closely connected to the learner's environment and daily life. He believed that education should be practical, helping students develop skills and knowledge that are directly applicable to their lives and communities. For example, agricultural practices, spinning, and weaving were integral parts of the curriculum, reflecting the agrarian context of Indian society.

• **Learning through Productive Work:** Gandhi emphasized the dignity of labor and the importance of learning through productive work. Educational practices in his system included engaging students in activities like agriculture, handicrafts and other forms of manual labor. This not only provided practical skills but also instilled values such as self-reliance, cooperation and respect for manual work. By integrating work into education, Gandhi aimed to break down the barriers between intellectual and physical labor, making education relevant to the economic context of rural India.

• **Mother Tongue as the Medium of Instruction:** Recognizing the importance of cultural and linguistic context, Gandhi insisted that education be conducted in the student's mother tongue. He argued that using the mother tongue as the medium of instruction would make education more accessible and meaningful, allowing students to learn without the alienation often caused by colonial languages. This practice also helped preserve and promote local cultures and traditions.

Case Studies: Educational Practices in Context:
Tolstoy Farm (South Africa)

• **Context**: Established during Gandhi's struggle against racial discrimination, Tolstoy Farm served as a communal experiment where education was integrated with daily life. The educational practices at Tolstoy Farm were shaped by the need to create a self-sufficient community that could resist the dehumanizing effects of colonialism.

• **Educational Practices**: Students were involved in agriculture, carpentry and other manual work. Moral education was a key component, with Gandhi emphasizing the importance of living by ethical principles. The curriculum was designed to reflect the social and political context, preparing students to be active participants in the struggle for justice.

Sevagram Ashram (India):

• **Context**: Sevagram Ashram became a center for rural education and self-sufficiency, reflecting Gandhi's vision of a self-reliant India. The educational practices at Sevagram were directly influenced by the rural context and the need to address the challenges faced by the local community.

• **Educational Practices**: The curriculum included spinning, weaving, agriculture and community service. Instruction was conducted in the local language and education was closely linked to the economic and social realities of rural life. The focus on self-sufficiency and community involvement made education relevant to the context of rural India, where economic independence and social cohesion were critical.

Impact on Identity:

Assessing the impact of Gandhian educational practices on identity and social structure reveals how his philosophy of education sought to transform both the individual and society. Gandhi's approach was designed to reshape the social fabric by fostering a sense of identity rooted in cultural pride, self-reliance and moral integrity, while simultaneously challenging and restructuring existing social hierarchies.

• **Reinforcement of Cultural Identity**: Gandhi's insistence on education in the mother tongue and the inclusion of indigenous knowledge and local crafts in the curriculum helped students reconnect with their cultural roots. This approach reinforced cultural identity, promoting pride in one's heritage and traditions. By grounding education in the cultural and linguistic realities of the learners, Gandhi's philosophy fostered a strong sense of belonging and identity, especially in a colonial context where Western education often alienated Indians from their own culture.

• **Development of Ethical Identity**: Gandhian education emphasized character building, with a focus on values such as truth (Satya), non-violence (Ahinsa) and simplicity. This moral and ethical education was central to the development of a strong personal identity rooted in integrity and social responsibility. Students were encouraged to internalize these values, which shaped their sense of self and their role in society. The emphasis on ethical living and personal discipline cultivated individuals who saw themselves as part of a larger moral community, dedicated to the principles of justice and non-violence.

• **Empowerment and Self-Reliance**: By integrating productive work and vocational training into the curriculum, Gandhian education promoted self-reliance and dignity in labor. This focus on practical skills and economic self-sufficiency empowered individuals, in ruparticularly ral areas, to take control of their lives and contribute to their communities. The cultivation of self-reliance as a core aspect of identity challenged the dependency fostered by colonial rule and created a sense of agency and autonomy among learners.

Impact on Social Structure:

• **Challenging Social Hierarchies**: Gandhi's educational practices were deeply egalitarian and aimed at breaking down the social hierarchies of caste, class and gender. By emphasizing the dignity of labor and integrating students from diverse backgrounds into a common educational experience, Gandhi's approach challenged the rigid social stratification that characterized Indian society. His educational model sought to democratize access to knowledge and skills, promoting social equality and reducing the power imbalances that sustained traditional hierarchies.

• **Transformation of Economic Structures**: The integration of vocational training and productive work into education had a significant impact on local economic structures. By teaching skills such as spinning, weaving and agriculture, Gandhian education promoted economic self-sufficiency and reduced dependence on industrialized and colonial economies. This focus on local crafts and sustainable livelihoods helped to revitalize traditional economies and provided a foundation for the economic empowerment of rural communities.

• **Resistance to Colonial Power Structures**: Gandhian education was also a form of resistance to colonial power structures. By promoting an indigenous model of education that valued local knowledge and cultural practices, Gandhi's approach directly opposed the colonial education system, which aimed to produce subservient subjects. This resistance was not only educational but also political, as it sought to empower individuals and communities to resist colonial domination and build a self-reliant and independent nation.

Conclusion:

Through Gandhian philosophy, education is understood as an inherently cultural process that both reflects and shapes the values, practices and social structures of a society. Gandhi's approach to education highlights the importance of grounding learning in the cultural context of the learners, integrating indigenous knowledge and fostering a deep connection between education and the community. Gandhian educational practices are a prime example of how education can be effectively contextualized to meet the needs of a specific society. By integrating practical skills, moral education and community involvement, Gandhi's approach ensured that education was not just about academic learning but also about empowering individuals to improve their lives and contribute to the well-being of their communities. Gandhi's educational philosophy had a profound impact on both identity and social structure. By fostering a strong sense of cultural identity, moral integrity and self-reliance, Gandhian education empowered individuals to redefine their roles in society. At the same time, it challenged and transformed existing social hierarchies, promoting social equality, community solidarity and economic self-sufficiency. Gandhi's approach to education was not just about learning but about reshaping society in ways that aligned with his vision of justice, equality and sustainable living.

References:

1. Batra, P. (2009). Reclaiming the idea of education: Back to the basics with Mahatma Gandhi. *Journal of Educational Planning and Administration, 23*(1), 5-22.
2. Chakrabarty, A. (2011). Education for social change: Gandhi's vision in contemporary times. *International Journal of Gandhi Studies, 8*(2), 55-70.
3. Joshi, D. (2010). Nai Talim: Education for life. *Journal of Indian Education, 36*(1), 42-50.
4. Kumar, K. (2014). Educational philosophy of Mahatma Gandhi and its impact on modern education in India. *Journal of Educational Thought, 48*(1), 78-93.
5. Patel, S. (2016). Gandhian philosophy of education and its relevance in the present context. *Journal of Humanities and Social Sciences, 21*(3), 105-112.
6. Prasad, G. (2019). Nai Talim: Its past, present and future. *Contemporary Education Dialogue, 16*(2), 171-186.
7. Shukla, S. (2005). Holistic education and Gandhi: An ethnographic exploration. *Journal of Indian Anthropology, 9*(2), 49-63.
8. Singh, R. (2012). Ethnography of a Gandhian school: Understanding Nai Talim from the ground. *Anthropology and Education Quarterly, 43*(4), 413-429.
9. Sykes, M. (1988). Experimental schools in Gandhi's India: The Sevagram and Jamia Millia Islamia. *History of Education Quarterly, 28*(1), 55-74.
10. Gandhi, M. K. (1956). *Satyagraha in South Africa.* Navajivan Publishing House.
11. Brown, J. M. (1989). *Gandhi: Prisoner of hope.* Yale University Press.
12. Narayana, S. (1988). *Gandhi and Tolstoy Farm: Experiments in self-sufficiency.* Navajivan Publishing House.
13. Parekh, B. (1997). *Gandhi: A very short introduction.* Oxford University Press.

14. Prasad, D. (1972). *Gandhi: The educator*. Navajivan Publishing House.
15. Mishra, R. P. (1984). *Sevagram: The heart of Mahatma Gandhi's philosophy*. Concept Publishing Company.

Relevance of Trusteeship as per The Gandhian Philosophy

Dr. Antara Dey
Assistant Professor, Department of Education
Tezpur University, Assam, India.
Email: antaradey666@gmail.com

Kirtee Kanya Sharma
M.A. Education Student, Department of Education
Tezpur University, Assam, India.
Email: kirteesharmakuki@gmail.com

Prof. Nil Ratan Roy
Professor, Department of Education
Tezpur University, Assam, India.
Email: niledn@tezu.ernet.in

Abstract

Trusteeship is a concept developed by Mahatma Gandhi as part of his broader socio-economic and ethical framework. At its core, trusteeship revolves around the idea that wealth and resources should be managed not as personal possessions but as trusts for the welfare of others. Trusteeship emphasizes for a transformative approach to wealth management that aligns with equity, responsibility, and sustainability values. Mahatma Gandhi's concept of trusteeship is a socio-economic philosophy advocating for the ethical stewardship of wealth. Trusteeship, as articulated by Gandhi, suggests that wealth should not be considered personal property but held in trust for the benefit of society. In contemporary times, Gandhian education remains relevant as it addresses the growing need for educational systems that go beyond mere knowledge transmission to cultivate ethical and socially conscious citizens. By incorporating principles such as sustainability, community engagement and peace education, Gandhian education can contribute to addressing modern global challenges. Trusteeship posits that wealth should be held not as personal property but as a resource for societal benefit, challenging both capitalism and socialism. Key principles of trusteeship are examined, including moral ownership, voluntary commitment, equitable distribution, non-violence and sustainable development. Practical applications are discussed, focusing on wealth sharing, corporate responsibility and community development and organizations embodying these ideals.

Keywords: Trusteeship, Ethical Stewardship, Moral Ownership, Voluntary commitment, Community engagement, Sustainability.

Introduction

Mahatma Gandhi, a great figure in India's liberation fight, made an everlasting effect on education. Trusteeship is a socio-economic concept that Mahatma Gandhi advocated as an alternative to both capitalism and socialism. The idea centres on the belief that wealth and resources should be managed by individuals not for their own benefit but for the welfare of society as a whole. Gandhi envisioned trusteeship as a means to create a just and equitable society where wealth does not lead to exploitation or social disparity. It is a blend of ethical capitalism and social responsibility, encouraging individuals to live simply and dedicate their excess resources to the greater good (Gandhi, 1942). Mahatma Gandhi, a towering figure in the movement for Indian freedom, also made substantial contributions to socio-economic theory. His notion of trusteeship stands out as a distinctive alternative to both capitalism and socialism, calling for a moral and ethical approach to wealth and resource management. The complexities, practical applications, philosophical underpinnings and applicability in modern society of trusteeship are all examined in this chapter. Gandhi's trusteeship is a plea for moral stewardship of resources and wealth, prioritizing moral obligation and voluntary action over forceful redistribution (Gandhi, 1942). Gandhi was deeply concerned about the vast economic disparities he witnessed, particularly in colonial India, where the accumulation of wealth by a few often led to the exploitation and marginalization of the many. He believed that the unchecked accumulation of wealth was a form of violence against the poor and that a just society could not be built on such foundations (Gandhi, 1942). To address these concerns, Gandhi proposed the idea of trusteeship, where the wealthy would act as trustees of their wealth, using it to benefit the less fortunate and promote the common good. Mahatma Gandhi's philosophy of trusteeship represents a profound and innovative approach to addressing social and economic inequalities, rooted in his broader principles of non-violence (Ahinsa) and truth (Satya). Developed as an ethical alternative to both capitalism and socialism, trusteeship challenges the conventional notion of wealth as private property and proposes instead that wealth is a trust held for the benefit of society. Gandhi's trusteeship is not merely an economic doctrine but a moral and spiritual framework that seeks to harmonize individual rights with social responsibilities (Gandhi, 1942).

Philosophy of mahatma Gandhi's trusteeship

Mahatma Gandhi's philosophy of trusteeship is a distinctive and influential socio-economic doctrine that challenges conventional views on wealth and property. Developed as part of his broader ethical framework, trusteeship embodies Gandhi's deep commitment to non-violence (Ahinsa), truth (Satya) and social justice. It presents a middle path between the extremes of capitalism and socialism, advocating for a system where wealth is not seen as the personal property of an individual but as a trust to be used for the welfare of society. Gandhi's concept of trusteeship is rooted in his belief that economic disparities are not merely a political issue but a profound ethical concern. He argued that vast inequalities in wealth and resources lead to social unrest and injustice, which in turn disrupt the moral fabric of society (Gandhi, 1927). To address these issues, Gandhi proposed trusteeship as a way to harmonize economic activity with moral and social responsibility. He believed that those who possess wealth should act as trustees, holding their assets in trust for the benefit of others, particularly the less fortunate (Iyer, 1973). Gandhi asserted that wealth is not an absolute right of the individual but a trust given by society. This perspective contrasts sharply with capitalist notions of private property and unrestricted accumulation of wealth. Gandhi emphasized that while individuals have the right to earn and possess wealth, this right comes with the responsibility to use that wealth for the common good (Bornstein, 2007). He stated, "The rich man should take the initiative in dispossessing himself of his wealth. He must be a trustee, doing the best by his wealth not for himself but for others" (Gandhi, 1942). Gandhi's philosophy of trusteeship offers a moral and practical framework for addressing economic disparities and promoting social justice. By advocating for voluntary wealth sharing, moral ownership and non-violence, trusteeship provides a unique and enduring approach to creating a more equitable and just society (Nanda, 1998).

Historical Context and Development

Early Influences

Gandhi's ideas on trusteeship were shaped by various sources, including his upbringing, religious beliefs and experiences. Raised in a devout Hindu family, he was deeply influenced by the teachings of Jainism, particularly the principles of non-violence (Ahinsa) and self-discipline. His exposure to Christian ethics, especially the teachings of Jesus Christ, also shaped his views on compassion and self-sacrifice (Gandhi, 1957).

South African Experience

During his time in South Africa, Gandhi witnessed the exploitation and discrimination faced by the Indian community. This period was crucial in shaping his socio-economic thoughts. He began to formulate the idea that those with wealth and power had a moral duty to use their resources for the benefit of the oppressed and disadvantaged (Gandhi, 1953).

Indian Independence Movement

Upon returning to India, Gandhi's involvement in the independence movement provided a broader platform to develop and advocate for trusteeship. He saw economic exploitation as a significant cause of social injustice and believed that political freedom must be accompanied by economic equity. His experiences with Indian industrialists and landlords further refined his ideas on trusteeship, leading to its formal articulation (Gandhi, 1942).

Core Principles of Trusteeship

Mahatma Gandhi's philosophy of trusteeship is built on a foundation of ethical and moral principles aimed at creating a more just and equitable society. Below are the core principles that define Gandhi's trusteeship:

Moral Ownership

The cornerstone of trusteeship is the idea of moral ownership. Gandhi believed that wealth and resources should not be regarded as personal possessions to be used at the owner's discretion. Instead, they should be considered as assets held in trust for society's welfare. This principle challenges the capitalist notion of absolute property rights, advocating instead for a stewardship model where wealth is managed for the common good (Parekh, 1989). Gandhi challenged the traditional notion of absolute ownership of wealth and property, arguing that individuals are merely custodians or trustees of the wealth they possess (Bhatt,

2006). He believed that wealth should be used for the benefit of society rather than for personal gain. Gandhi stated, "Wealthy people should consider themselves trustees of the wealth they possess. They should use it for the benefit of society" (Gandhi, 1942). This principle redefines wealth as a social resource, emphasizing the responsibility of the wealthy to use their resources for the common good.

Voluntary Commitment

A key aspect of trusteeship is its reliance on voluntary action. Gandhi believed in the power of moral persuasion and the innate goodness of individuals. He argued that the wealthy should voluntarily renounce their excess wealth and use it for social welfare. This approach differs fundamentally from socialist doctrines that advocate for state intervention and compulsory redistribution. He believed that individuals should willingly share their wealth with others, driven by a sense of moral duty and compassion. This voluntary aspect reflects Gandhi's deep faith in the inherent goodness of people and his commitment to non-violence. He argued that social change should be achieved through persuasion and moral appeal, rather than coercion or force. This principle underscores the importance of personal integrity and ethical conduct in the management of wealth (Iyer, 1973).

Equitable Distribution

Trusteeship aims to bridge the gap between the rich and the poor by promoting equitable distribution of resources. Gandhi envisioned a society where no one would be excessively rich or miserably poor. He believed that the concentration of wealth in the hands of a few leads to social imbalance and injustice. Gandhi was deeply concerned with the vast economic inequalities that existed in society. He believed that trusteeship could help bridge the gap between the rich and the poor by ensuring that wealth is distributed more fairly. According to Gandhi, those who have surplus wealth should voluntarily use it to meet the needs of the less fortunate, thus promoting social and economic justice. He envisioned a society where the basic needs of all individuals are met and extreme disparities in wealth are minimized (Nanda, 1998).

Non-violence

Non-violence (Ahinsa) is the bedrock of Gandhi's philosophy. Trusteeship, too is grounded in non-violent principles. Gandhi rejected violent means of wealth redistribution, advocating instead for peaceful and ethical approaches. He believed that true social change could only be achieved through non-violent means. He believed that economic justice could not be achieved through violent or coercive means. Instead, trusteeship promotes peaceful and non-violent methods of addressing social and economic inequalities. Gandhi maintained that true social change must be rooted in love, compassion and respect for all individuals, including those who possess wealth. This principle is consistent with Gandhi's broader philosophy of non-violence, which seeks to create a just and harmonious society through peaceful means (Weber, 1999).

Sustainable Development

Gandhi's concept of trusteeship highlights the responsible and sustainable utilization of resources. He supported environmental conservation early on and promoted a lifestyle that avoids harming the environment or using up resources for future generations. This principle is fundamental today, especially with the current global environmental issues (Weber, 1999). Gandhi was worried about the social and environmental effects of unbridled consumption and industrialization. To preserve resources for future genera-tions, he promoted sustainable living and economic activities. Trusteeship requires the prudent management of resources, guaranteeing that economic operations are carried out in a way that protects the environment and advances the long-term well-being of society (Gandhi, 1942). Gandhi's holistic approach to development, which takes into account the welfare of both people and the environment, is reflected in this idea.

Practical Implementation of Trusteeship

Wealth Sharing

Wealth sharing is a fundamental component of trusteeship. Gandhi proposed that individuals and businesses with surplus wealth should voluntarily share a significant portion of their profits with the community. This could be achieved through donations to social welfare projects, investments in education and healthcare and support for infrastructure development (Gandhi, 1942).

Case Studies

Jamnalal Bajaj: An Indian industrialist and close associate of Gandhi, Bajaj exemplified trusteeship by using his wealth for social causes. He established educational institutions, supported rural development projects and contributed significantly to the independence movement (Nanda, 1998).

Tata Group: The Tata Group has engaged in a wide range of charitable endeavours, including as healthcare, education, and community development, all of which are motivated by Gandhi's teachings. The group's founders founded the Tata Trusts, which are still vital to social welfare programs. (Weber, 1999).

Corporate Responsibility

In the context of businesses, trusteeship implies a strong sense of corporate responsibility. Companies should operate not solely for profit but also with a commitment to the well-being of their employees, customers and the environment. This includes fair wages, good working conditions and environmentally sustainable practices (Parekh, 1989).

Modern Examples

• **Corporate Social Responsibility (CSR)**: Many modern corporations adopt CSR policies that align with the principles of trusteeship. They invest in community development, environmental sustainability and social welfare programs (Porter & Kramer, 2006).

• **B Corps**: Benefit corporations (B Corps) are businesses that meet high standards of social and environmental performance, accountability and transparency. They integrate social responsibility into their business models, reflecting the ethos of trusteeship (Honeyman, 2014).

Community Development

Trusteeship encourages active participation in community development. This involves initiatives that promote self-reliance and empowerment of local communities. Wealthy individuals and businesses can support vocational training programs, microfinance schemes and other initiatives that help people build their own livelihoods (Iyer, 1973).

Examples from India

Amul: The dairy cooperative movement in India, particularly the success of Amul, reflects the principles of trusteeship. The cooperative model empowers local farmers and ensures fair distribution of profits (Kurien, 2005).

SEWA (Self-Employed Women's Association): SEWA is a trade union for poor, self-employed women workers. It works towards improving their economic conditions through training, microfinance and collective bargaining (Bhatt, 2006).

Relevance of Trusteeship in Contemporary Society

Addressing Economic Inequality

Economic inequality remains a significant challenge globally. The principles of trusteeship offer a framework for addressing this issue by promoting voluntary wealth sharing and equitable distribution. While state interventions and policies are essential, the moral and ethical dimensions of trusteeship can complement these efforts (Piketty, 2014).

Corporate Ethics and Responsibility

Corporate ethics and responsibility are becoming more and

more important in today's business world. Businesses can use the trusteeship principles as a guide for implementing more environmentally and socially conscious procedures. This benefits society well-being and long-term profitability in addition to improving their reputation (Porter & Kramer, 2006).

Conclusion

Mahatma Gandhi's concept of trusteeship offers a moral and ethical framework for resource and wealth management. It asks for a fair and voluntary allocation of resources and questions accepted ideas of ownership. Trusteeship provides a way forward for a fair and inclusive society since it is based on nonviolence and sustainable development. The concepts of trusteeship are still applicable to today's concerns about corporate social responsibility, environmenttal sustainability and economic injustice, notwithstanding criticisms and obstacles to their use. Gandhi's vision continues to motivate attempts to create a society that is more sustainable and egalitarian.

References:
1. Bhatt, E. (2006). We Are Poor but So Many: The Story of Self-Employed Women in India. Oxford University Press.
2. Bornstein, D. (2007). How to Change the World: Social Entrepreneurs and the Power of New Ideas. Oxford University Press.
3. Gandhi, M. K. (1927). The Story of My Experiments with Truth. Navajivan Publishing House.
4. Gandhi, M. K. (1942). Constructive Programme: Its Meaning and Place. Navajivan Publishing House.
5. Gandhi, M. K. (1953). Basic Education. Navajivan Publishing House.
6. Gandhi, M. K. (1957). Hind Swaraj or Indian Home Rule. Navajivan Publishing House.

7. Honeyman, R. (2014). The B Corp Handbook: How to Use Business as a Force for Good. Berrett-Koehler Publishers.
8. Iyer, R. N. (1973). The Moral and Political Thought of Mahatma Gandhi. Oxford University Press.
9. Kumarappa, J. C. (1949). Economy of permanence: A quest for a social order based on non-violence. Navajivan Publishing House.
10. Kurien, V. (2005). I Too Had a Dream. Roli Books.
11. Nanda, B. R. (1998). Mahatma Gandhi: A Biography. Oxford University Press.
12. Parekh, B. (1989). Gandhi's Political Philosophy: A Critical Examination. University of Notre Dame Press.
13. Piketty, T. (2014). Capital in the Twenty-First Century. Harvard University Press.
14. Porter, M. E., & Kramer, M. R. (2006). Strategy and Society: The Link Between Competitive Advantage and Corporate Social Responsibility. Harvard Business Review, 84(12), 78-92.
15. Weber, T. (1999). Gandhi's Peace Army: The Shanti Sena and Unarmed Peacekeeping. Syracuse University Press.

Trusteeship in the Philosophy of Mahatma Gandhi

Dr. Rishika Verma
Assistant Professor
Department of Philosophy
HNB Garhwal University
Srinagar (Garhwal), Uttarakhand
Email: rishika.verma75@gmail.com

Abstract

Trusteeship is a socio-economic philosophy that was propounded by Mahatma Gandhi. It provides a means by which the wealthy people would be the trustees of trusts that looked after the welfare of the people in general. This concept was condemned by socialists as being in favor of the landlords, feudal princes and capitalists, opposed to socialist theories. Gandhi believed that the wealthy people could be persuaded to part with their wealth to help the poor. Putting it in Gandhiji's words, "Supposing I have come by a fair amount of wealth-either by way of legacy or by means of trade and industry- I must know that all that wealth does not belong to me; what belongs to me is the right to an honorable livelihood by millions of others. The rest of my wealth belongs to community and must be used for the welfare of the community". Gandhi along with his followers, after their release from prison formulated a "simple" and a "practical" formula where Trusteeship was explained. A draft practical trusteeship formula was prepared by Gandhi's co-workers. The founder of the Tata Group, J.R.D. Tata was influenced by Gandhi's idea of Trusteeship. He developed his personal and professional life based on this idea.

Keywords: Trusteeship, Mahatma Gandhi, Capitalist, Trustee, Ownership, Industry

Introduction

Gandhiji was a multi-dimensional man. There was hardly any aspect of our life to which he did not give deep thought and come out with original observations. We accept that technology answers all our problems. In the event, we had almost stopped asking the right questions. Gandhiji's greatness lay in raising pertinent questions on the technological and industrial society we are creating. His other concern was to consider the moral position of the "rich" man. And Gandhiji knew that technology and industrialisation would make any skilled and talented man rich, and a time would come when a poor villager may question the basis of higher wages of not only capitalists but also the manager or the organised industrial or bank worker as is happening in our country. Thus, when Gandhiji was asked. "How would you, in a word, describe the rich man's legitimate position?" he replied, "That of a Trustee". He advised the rich, the talented, the skilled, "Take what you require for your legitimate needs and use the remainder for Society."

Gandhi's theory of trusteeship stipulates that the rich should consider their property as what God trusted them to manage for the benefit of the poor. This theory legitimated the positions of the former, as long as they behaved as "trustees". Therefore, Marxists severely condemned it as conservative, while some scholars re-evaluated it as consonant with capitalist or mixed economies during the post-Cold War period. However, the theory is observed to have some aspects concessive to socialist or aspects not really observed in the past evaluations. Here I would trace in what way Gandhi presented this theory from the 1920s to the 1940s, in order to evaluate it as a form of "non-violent" social reform, which was far different from any of existing theories based on capitalism or socialism.

For Gandhi political freedom from the British rule was not

the only important issue for India in the early 20th century. His travels throughout the country exposed him to the poverty and misery of the downtrodden masses. Economic development for India was of vital importance to him. The inequalities present in the Indian Society did not escape Gandhi's notice. He believed that unless the landowners, the rich did not take into account the ferment brewing in the peasant and labor class, there would be an entire overthrow of the politico-economic system. The ownership of property and resources has always been a thorny issue between those who favored capitalism and the communist economists. The former believes that right to property is absolute and needs no intervention by the state. They believe that each man is the best judge of his own interest and would make efforts to better his own lot and also promote general good. The communists reject the |Capitalist model on the ground that it inevitably led the growth of monopolies and imperialism on one hand and the constant exploitation of the working class on the other.

The core of Gandhian economic thought is the protection of dignity of human person and not mere material the prosperity. He aimed at the development, upliftment and enrichment of human life rather than a higher standard of living with scant respect for human and social value. Feconomic idea undamental ethical values dominated his. He wanted to liberate the modern economic philosophy from the quagmire of materialism and bring it to a higher spiritual plane. Human actions were motivated by social objectives of teh protection of human rights. Gandhi's efforts ritualizing economics" are truly reflected in his towards"sp ceoncept of Trusteeship. He based his doctrine of trusteeship on the first sloka of Isopanisad, according to which one is asked to dedicate everything to God and then use it only to ncipal condition laid down in it is required extent. The pri that one must not covet what belongs to others. In other words, in the first instance, everything must be surrendered to God and then cut of it one may use only that which is according to ,necessary for the service of God's creatoion one's strict needs. This makes it clear beyond doubt that it is not in industrail adn bussiness sectors only that the doctrine of trusteeship is to be made applicable. the spirit of this rtues doctrine is detachment and service. unless these two vi are inculcated, it is impossible to obey the command "covet not anybody's riches". therefore Gandhi's idea of trusteeship possession. it was -arose from his faith in the law of non founded on his religious belief that eeverything belonged to as from God. therefore the bounties of the world God and w were for His people, as whole, not for any particular individual. when an individual had nore than his respective portion, he beccame a truestee of that portion for God's no need to store. He powerful has-people. God who is all creates things afresh everyfay. therefore man should also live his life from day to day without tryilng to store things for the future. if this principle was inbibed by peopl in general, it ould have would have become legalised and trusteeship w become a legalised instituion. Gandhi wished it became a .gift from India to the world

Basically, Gandhi suggested this doctrine as an answer to the economic inequalities of ownership and income- a kind of nonviolent way of resolving all social and economic conflicts which grew out of inequalities and privileges of the present social order. Gandhi never ceased to believe in trusteeship in theory from the beginning or, at any rate, towards the later part of life, thought the method was proving ineffective. He believed in the indispensability of nonviolence, non-co-opration and Satyagraha in converting the privileged classes into trustees. He even advocated violence as a last resort to dispossess property-owners of their wealth. Therefore, man's dignity and not his material prosperity, is the center of Gandhian economics. Gandhian economics aims at a distribution of material prosperity keeping only human dignity in view. Thus it is dominated more by moral values than by economic ideas. According to Gandhi, Trusteeship is the only ground on which he can work out an ideal combination of economics and morals.

Mahatma Gandhi's Views on Principle of Trusteeship

1. According to Mahatma Gandhi those who sought to attain God through social service, even if they controlled vast possessions, should not regard any of it as their own. They should rather hold their possessions in trust for the benefit of those less privileges than themselves.

2. The theory of trusteeship applies equally to both tangible and intangible property such as the muscular energy of the laborers and the talents.

3. By trusteeship he meant that the wealthy should not just claim their possessions to be theirs entirely as that they cannot accumulate their wealth without the labor and cooperation of workers and the poorer sections of society.

4. According to him, wealthy people are morally bound to share their wealth in a fair manner with their workers and poor.

5. Just as it is proposed to give a decent minimum living wage, a limit should be fixed for the maximum income that would be allowed to any person in society. The difference between such minimum and maximum incomes should be reasonable and equitable and variable from time to time, so much so that the tenancy would be towards the obliteration of the difference.

6. It does not exclude legislation of the ownership and use of wealth. Wealthy people should voluntarily surrender part of their wealth and hold it in trust for those working for them. But by the 1940s, he had come to believe that state legislation would be necessary to ensure compliance with the principle of trusteeship.

7. It does not recognize any right of private ownership of property except so far as it may be permitted by society for its own welfare.
8. He believed that adoption of this doctrine at an individual and national level is the only way to form an egalitarian and non-violent society.
9. He said that rich man should spend his wealth only when reasonably required for his personal needs and should act as a trustee for the remainder to be used for society.
10. The whole idea of possessing wealth only to guard it from being misused and to distribute it equitably aims at protecting human dignity.
11. Gandhi did not believe in inherited wealth as a trustee has no heir other than the people.
12. By trusteeship he does 'not mean compulsion to surrender the wealth as the forcible dispossession of the wealthy would deny to society the talents of people who could create national wealth. His method was to persuade the wealthy to act as trustees, failing which satyagraha could be adopted.

Trusteeship provides a means of transforming the present capitalist order of society into an egalitarian one. It gives no quarter to capitalism, but gives the present owning class a chance to reform itself. It is based on the faith that human nature is never beyond redemption.

Trusteeship Formula

The Trusteeship formula that has been handed down to us was derived from a draft prepared by prof. ML Dantwala, the noted economist, in which Gandhiji made a few changes. It reads as follows:

1. Trusteeship provides a means of transforming the present capitalist order of society into an egalitarian one. It gives no quarter to capitalism, but gives the present owning class a chance of reforming itself. It is based on the faith that human nature is never beyond redemption.

2. It does not recognise any right of private ownership of Property, except so far as it may be permitted by society for its own welfare.
3. It does not exclude legislative regulation of the ownership and use of wealth.
4. Thus under state-regulated Trusteeship, an individual will not be free to hold or use wealth for selfish satisfaction or in disregard of the interest of society.
5. Just as it is proposed to fix decent minimum living wage, even so a limit should be fixed for the maximum income that would be allowed to any person in society. The difference between such minimum and maximum incomes should be reasonable and equitable and variable, from time to time, so much so that the tendency would be towards obliteration of the difference.

Under the Gandhian economic order the character of production will be determined by social necessity and not by personal whim or greed. Although this formula was approved by Gandhiji in 1942, nothing was done to promote the concept of Trusteeship till 1965 when Mr. Jayaprakash Narayan organised an international seminar on Social Responsibilities of Business followed by another on Responsibilities of Trade Unions in 1966. Between 1965 and 1972 J.P. made many efforts to persuade the large business houses to subscribe to social obligations by requesting them to include a clause in their articles of association and submit to social audit but without much success. The late Dr. Ram Manohar Lohia tried in 1967 to get a bill on Trusteeship passed by the Parliament but the then Congress Government discouraged all such efforts.

Conclusion

Gandhi in his concept of 'Trusteeship believes in the goodness of heart and humanitarian nature of other fellowmen too. His concept of Trusteeship has been thus criticized for being naïve and not propagating equality in society. Many critics and even his protégé Jawaharlal Nehru believed that the concept of Trusteeship carried forward a feudal society and promoted capitalism.

According to Professor M.L. Dantwala, "The division of the society into the property owning and the property less classes, which is the characteristic of capitalism, is sought to be retained in Gandhism also. The only difference in Gandhism is that the erstwhile capitalist, property owning classes will consider itself trustee on behalf of the proletariat. The change is purely on the subjective sphere. The objective conditions of production will continue by remaining as they were in capitalism. Production will continue by unplanned private competition among the individual trustee. These conditions of production have a compelling logic of their own which will lead to the same contradictions as are witnessed under capitalism today.

At last, I can say that The Gandhian model of Trusteeship is an interesting and innovative model of ownership and management of industrial and business organizations basically deriving inspiration from the philosophy of Bhagavat Gita. As such, it is a theory based on the Indian thought and ethos. In the trusteeship theory the owners and managers of industry/business are to consider their wealth and assets ad belonging to God and society and not as their personal property. They are to manage and handle all these assets only as trustees and would be entitled to the reasonable amount needed for their sustenance out of the earnings of these assets as their remunerations.

References:
1. Anjaria, J. J. An Essay on Gandhian Economics. Vora & Co. Bombay. 1945.
2. Biswas, S. C. 'Gandhian View on Trusteeship', Gandhi Sewagram Ashram.

3. The Collected Work of Mahatma Gandhi. Publications division. Ministry of Information and Broadcasting. Government of India. New Delhi. 1961.

4. Dr. Sundar Sarukkai, Friday, 27 May 2005, "The Idea of Trusteeship in Gandhi and JRD Tata hi rancho".

5. Harijan: A Journey of Applied Gandhism. Garland Publishing Inc. New York. 1973.

6. Gandhi, M. K. 'Gandhi's Concept of Trusteeship'. Institute of Gandhian Studies, PDF, 12 chap.

7. Gandhian trusteeship in theory and practice, Raghavan Iyer, crest associates, Vallabh Vidyanagar, Gujarat (India) 388 120.

8. M. K. Gandhi, complied by Ravindra Keledar, Trusteeship, April 1960, Printed and Published by: Jitendra T Desai Navajivan Mudranalaya, Ahemadabad-380014 India, ISBN 8172290918.

9. Trusteeship concept, precepts and practice, M/s Link Publications, 250, Shanwar Peth, Pune 411 030.

10. Trusteeship: A Possible Solution to Problems of Power, Exploitation, Conflict and Alienation Edited by: George Goyder, Proceedings of an International Seminar held in Bangalore, (India), October 1979

Revisiting Gandhian Economics: S. D. Javadekar's Vision of Non-Violent Social Transformation

Dr. Vijay Srivastava
Associate Professor
Department of Humanities
Maharishi School of Science & Humanities
MUIT, Lucknow
Email: vijaygunjan1986@gmail.com

Dr. Anuj Kumar
Assistant Professor
Department of Economics
Amity University Lucknow
Email: anujsharma21@rediffmail.com

Abstract

In the domain of Gandhian political economy, one can witness the remarkable contributions from the many writers, scholars and political activists. In the world of Gandhian thought and its ideological foundation inter connection of all existing literature make Gandhian thought more effective. To explore deeper analysis of Gandhian social philosophy this chapter rediscover the socio-political thought of S.D Javdekar one the prominent freedom fighter, writer and Marathi scholar of 20th century. S. D Javdekar is widely considered as 'Acharya Javdekar'. Javdekar was a social diplomat in his political thinking, and was influenced by the political and social views of 'Mahatma Gandhi' and 'Vinona Bhave'. His political and economic thinking was based on his mastery over Gandhism and Marxism. In year 1952, he discovered the concept of 'Sarvodaya Samajawad'. His contribution towards Gandhian literature is unparallel in comparison to contemporary scholars of dependent India.

Reflection of revolutionary socialistic ideas can be seen in his scholarly work and editorials. He was journalist by profession and editor of news dailies 'Nava Shakti' and 'Lok Shakti'. In the next section of this paper, we will try to understand the theological perspective of ideas of S. D Javdekar. Main reference point of our analysis will be prime work of S.D Javdekar and his writings including his editorials[1]. His economic and social understandings are mainly available in the published volume including '(Adhunik Bharat, 1938) and (Sarwodaya and Samajwad, 1954). In this study, we will also try to find out similarities and differences between his thought and Gandhi's thought. Even he contributed in Gandhian literature and Gandhism but there are some differences also.

Keywords: Gandhian Social Thinker, Acharya Javadekar, Satyagrahi, Sarvodaya

Introduction

In the realm of Gandhian political economy, numerous writers, scholars and political activists have made significant contributions to its development and discourse. The interconnectedness of this literature enhances the impact and relevance of Gandhian thought. This chapter aims to delve deeper into the socio-political thought of S. D. Javadekar, a prominent freedom fighter, writer, and Marathi scholar of the 20th century, widely known as 'Acharya Javadekar.' Javadekar's political philosophy reflects his deep understanding of both Gandhism and Marxism, which he synthesized into his unique concept of 'Satyagrahi Sarvodaya's.' His contributions to Gandhian literature, as well as his revolutionary socialist ideas, distinguish him from

---

[1] His main writings are available in Marathi Language, so all references are use here from the translated version of his work. Rajshewri Deshpande and Chitra Redkar have provided translated materials.

his contemporaries. As a journalist and editor of the dailies 'Nava Shakti' and 'Lok Shakti,' Javadekar's writings captured his advocacy for democratic decentralization, economic self-sufficiency, rural development, and the principles of non-violent social transformation. This chapter will explore Javadekar's ideological foundation, particularly through his major works, such as *Adhunik Bharat* (1938) and *Sarvodaya and Samajwadi* (1954), while also comparing and contrasting his ideas with those of Gandhi and other key figures in Gandhian thought.

Satyagrahi Sarvodayism

He was the founder of concept of Satyagrahi Sarvodayism. To him main motive of Satyagrahi Sarvodayism is self motivation. Like Gandhi he believed in the philosophy of self purification. Satayagrahi Sarvodayism is a higher order of non-violent society. Satayagrahi Sarvodayism demands for social, economic and as well as cultural revolution. The non-violent revolution which changes the attitude of human beings. Acharya Javedkar was familiar the role of individual as Satyargarhi to achieve the goal of social equality. Social equality cannot achieve without the individual Satyagrahi. To him, Satyagraha must be universal principle applicable to all. He quoted *"**The final goal of this self motivation it to merge with the universe. The attitude of human intelligence gang towards truth form untruth is itself a self motivation. The revolution of Satyagraha should happen in social, economic and political field of society as well as inner fields of Satyagrahi**[2] "*(Javedkar,1953). Vinoba Bhave's conception of Satyagraha. Vinoba stated that, *"**There may be individual Satyagraha in a society where corporate problems are decided with the consent of all. Our ways of life and attitudes of mind must**

---

[2] Javadekar, S.D, "Rashtrawad Samajwadi, Chitramaya Jagat, Dec 1953, pp 954.

be so shaped that the principles of unanimous decision not hold up all progress. People will have to learn how to work together so that their work does not suffer, in this new notion that Satygraha has no place in a democracy. We must make up our minds about it".[3] (**Bhave, 1962**).

Javedkar developed his political philosophy under the core parameters of Gandhian political economy. He believed in democratic decentralization, self sufficiency, small scale industries, rural economy and 'Antodaya'. His Sarvodayism is innovative version of Kumarappa's 'Economy of Permanence'. To achieve goal of non-violent socio-economic order individual, play an important role as stake holder. To Him, true revolution is 'Satyagrahi Revolution'. Non violent social transformation through Gandhian way is ultimate goal of his 'Satygrahi Sarvodayism' society. He was having opinion that

"Satygraha revolutionaries have to take complete care to protect the individual freedom and independence in the society after establishing social ownership of wealth. The arrangements should be made to see that every unit and every family in the society is made self sufficient about the basic needs like food, clothing and shelter. The principle of decentralization is implemented. It was decided by resolution at the 'Sarvodayism' that the rural industries would encourage at its ways also decided that things which were produced in big factories would be boycotted. There should be self dependent society in regard to food and clothing. Rural industries must be independent and economically self dependent village are the economic bases of future society[4]" (**Javadekar, 1953**).

---

[3] Bhave, Vinoba, "Democratic Values", Sarv Seva Sangh Prakashan, Varanasi, Pp 100-101.

[4] Javedkar, S. D, "Samajwad Krantika Satyagrahi Deeksha", Article no 4, Sadhana, 1954, p 12.

Acharya Javadekar believed that India had embraced secular nationalism alongside democracy, and this combination instilled self-confidence and strength in its people. He argued that secular nationalism, democracy, and socialism were crucial for shaping Modern India. Additionally, he emphasized the necessity of implementing Mahatma Gandhi's concept of Satyagraha. Javadekar stressed that the foundation of Modern India should be grounded in the principles emerging from the Indian Freedom Struggle.

On Marxism, Socialism and Democracy

Javedkar believed in the philosophical base of democratic values propagated by the Vinoba Bhave. He wanted self rule state not the representative democracy. He was an advocator of land reforms movements especially *'Bhoodan Yagya'*. Classless society can be formulated when there is freedom from government and not absence of government.[5] He criticized the Marxian way of social reconstruction and violent social change. In the words of Javedkar

"We have to go from representative democracy to self-ruled state. Establishment of stateless and classless society was our aim. It was unambiougsly explained by 'Bhoodan' movement. The way to self-government wants through social ownership of wealth and classless society. Class systems and individual ownership of property were two obstacles in the way of self government. Those who wanted to establish stateless society should take economic revolution as immediate goal. But in Marxism the means of revolution were different. Marxism tries to have revolution by forming one party dictatorship. On the other hand, Gandhian tries to do this with the help of people's power"[6]
(Javedkar, 1953).

---

[5] Bhave, Vinoba, "Democratic Values", Sarv Seva Sangh Prakashan, Varanasi, Pp 30.

[6] Javedkar, S. D, "Samajwad Krantika Satyagrahi Deeksha", Article no 4, Sadhana, 1954, p 12.

For Javedkar, eradication of private ownership of capital is a necessary condition for achieving the goal of principle of trusteeship. Trusteeship is a way to achieve democratic values and classless society.

Ultimate Goal of Self-Government

Acharya Javadekar highlighted that both Acharya Vinoba Bhave and Jayprakash Narayan had embraced the objectives of socialism and Gandhi's concept of 'Atmarajya' (self-rule). While Marxism shared the same ultimate aim, it sought to achieve it through violent means. However, Indians were opposed to violence because it led to communist dictatorships in Europe. The American hydrogen bomb had failed to eliminate the threat of such dictatorships, but a 'Satyagrahi' revolution, based on non-violence, could succeed. Javadekar believed that the spiritual power derived from a Satyagraha-based revolution would lead to the social ownership of wealth and the creation of a free society. He had opinion that

"Satyagrahi revolutionaries have to take complete care to protect individual freedom and independence in the society after establishing social ownership of the wealth. The arrangements should be made to see that every unit and every family in the society is made self-sufficient about the basic needs like food, clothing and shelter. The principle of decentralization be implemented. It was decided by the resolution at the Sarvodaya Puri that the rural industries would be encouraged and it was also decided that the things which were produced in big factories would be boycotted"[7] *(* **Javadekar, 1954**)

Satyagraha and the Role of Religion in Social Transformation

Satyagraha is described as a method for social revolution

---

[7] Javadekar, S.D. "Samajwadi Krantila Satyagrahi Deeksha", p. 12, Article No. 4, Sadhana, May 1954.

where spiritual and religious elements are crucial. The Bhoodan Movement, led by Vinoba Bhave, exemplifies how religious and spiritual values can drive progressive change rather than perpetuate reactionary views. Despite the fact that many religious institutions are seen as oppressive and sectarian, the underlying spiritual and religious instincts are viewed as progressive forces capable of fostering social transformation.

Acharya Javadekar emphasized that it is India's historical responsibility to demonstrate that religion and spirituality are not inherently reactionary. Instead, they can be harnessed for progressive purposes, such as the establishment of a classless society. This involves adopting principles like trusteeship, where resources are managed for the benefit of all rather than for personal gain, and the eradication of class struggle through non-violent means. By creating a new civilization grounded in these values, the aim is to promote human progress and liberation.

"I have to teach the society that there should not be any one's right on the land. As the rich think themselves (to be) owners of the land, the poor, too, think themselves (to be) the owners of the land. I see to free both of them from. the feeling of ownership" (Javadekar ,1954)

The text critiques the Indian Constitution from a socialist perspective, emphasizing its perceived failure to align with Gandhian principles, particularly regarding land reforms. It highlights a fundamental tension between constitutional provisions that protect individual ownership of land and the Gandhian ideals of trusteeship and community ownership. Gandhi's concept of trusteeship envisions individuals managing resources not for personal gain but as custodians for the benefit of the broader community. This principle inherently challenges the notion of private land ownership that perpetuates social and economic inequalities. Furthermore, the text underscores the importance of community ownership, a cornerstone of Gandhian thought, which argues that land and resources should serve the needs of the entire community rather than being concentrated in the hands of a few. The critique also touches on the ideal of non-violent socialism, where equitable distribution of resources is achieved without conflict or coercion. The content suggests that the existing constitutional framework does not facilitate these Gandhian principles, arguing that any genuine attempt to integrate them would require a fundamental constitutional amendment, thus calling into question the authenticity of claims that Gandhian values are embedded within the current constitutional structure

On Representative Democracy

Javadekar opined that the transition from a representative democracy to a self-ruled state was essential for achieving a stateless and classless society, a goal clearly articulated by the Bhoodan movement. According to Javadekar, the path to self-government involved the social ownership of wealth and dismantling the class system, with economic revolution as an immediate objective. However, he pointed out a fundamental difference between Marxism and Gandhism in achieving this vision. While Marxism advocates revolution through a one-party dictatorship, Gandhism emphasizes the use of people's power and non-violent means for social transformation. For Javadekar, Gandhism's reliance on moral authority and self-discipline contrasts with Marxism's focus on state control and coercive measures, underscoring the Gandhian belief in decentralized governance and voluntary cooperation over authoritarian rule

"We have to go from representative democracy to self-ruled state. Establishment of stateless and classless society was our aim. It was unambiguously explained by Bhoodaan movement. The way to self-government went through social ownership of wealth and classless society. Class system and individual ownership of property were two obstacles in the

way of self-government. Those who wanted to establish stateless society, should take economic revolution as immediate goal. But in Marxism the means of revolution were different. Marxism tries to have revolution by forming one-party dictatorship. On the other hand, Gandhism tries to do this with the help of peoples' power." (Javadekar, 1954)

On Economic Policies of Socialist Planners

Javadekar was in Favor of the nationalization of fundamental industries, especially those involved in international trade, and advocated for national ownership of these sectors. He supported allowing private capitalists to manage secondary businesses and trade, albeit with certain regulatory controls to ensure alignment with national interests. While the Congress highlighted various obstacles and difficulties in implementing such policies, Javadekar believed these challenges could be effectively managed. He argued that with proper national planning, the obstacles were not insurmountable; resources could be mobilized, and the efficiency of industries and trade could be enhanced. According to Javadekar, the Congress's hesitation was unwarranted, and he viewed the Socialist Party's program as not only practical but also likely to succeed, as reflected in the manifesto of the Congress Socialist Party.

"Nationalization of fundamental industries of international trade, national ownership, secondary business and trade be kept for private capitalists but certain controls be imposed on them. Thus, the Socialist Party pleaded national planning. The Congress tried to show that there were obstacles and difficulties in the implementation of this policy, but Acharya Javadekar held that these obstacles and difficulties could be overcome and the resources mobilized and the efficiency of the industry and trade increased. All these things had been put in detail in the manifesto of the CSP. The difficulties that the Congress tried to show as an

excuse were baseless and from this point of view Socialist Party's programme was practical and was bound to succeed"[8](Javadekar, 1954)

Conclusion

Acharya Javadekar's vision was centred on achieving a non-violent socio-economic order through democratic decentralization and the concept of 'Satyagrahi Sarvodaya's,' where every individual acts as a stakeholder in social transformation. He critiqued Marxism for its emphasis on a one-party dictatorship and violent means of change, instead advocating for a non-violent, people-powered revolution to establish a stateless and classless society. Javadekar believed that India's path to modernization must be grounded in principles derived from the Indian Freedom Struggle, combining secular nationalism, democracy, and socialism. He also saw the importance of land reform, rural self-sufficiency, and decentralized governance in achieving these goals. While Javadekar aligned closely with Gandhian principles, he offered his own unique interpretations, particularly in his call for the nationalization of key industries and his vision of a self-ruled state. His contributions to the Gandhian literature provide a nuanced perspective on the interplay between social, economic, and spiritual dimensions in achieving an equitable and just society.

References:

1. Acharya Javadekar. (1953). Adhunik Bharat.
2. Acharya Javadekar. (1954). Sarvodaya and Samajwad.
3. Bhave, V. (1962). Satyagraha and Social Change.

---

[8] Javadekar, S.D. "Samajwadi Pakshyachi Kutalki", p. 2, Sadhana, 26 May 1950.

4. Javadekar, S. D. (1953). Satyagrahi Sarvodayism: A Higher Order of Non-Violent Society. Nava Shakti.
5. Javadekar, S. D. (1954). Satyagrahi Revolutionaries and the Principles of Decentralization. Lok Shakti.
6. Javadekar, S. D. (1954). The Role of Religion in Social Transformation. Sarvodayapuri.
7. Javadekar, S. D. (1954). Transition from Representative Democracy to Self-Ruled State. CSP Manifesto.
8. Javadekar, S. D. (1954). The Principles of Trusteeship and Social Ownership of Wealth.

The Role of The Gandhian Economic Approach towards Large Farmers

Dr. K. S. Sivakumar
Assistant Professor
Department of Sanskrit and Indian Culture
Sri Chandrasekharendra Saraswathi Viswa Mahavidyalaya
(SCSVMV) Enathur, Kanchipuram, Tamil Nadu
Email: sivakumarks07@yahoo.co.in

Abstract

With the objective of improving the conditions of the small and marginal farmers, the Government is channelizing its effort from production-centric approach to income-centric approach and are implementing a number of effective schemes.

The paper brings out the need and the implications of persuading large farmers to imbibe and implement the Gandhian economic philosophy for the growth and development of the agricultural sector. Towards this end, the paper expounds the Gandhian economic principles of Simplicity, Non-possessiveness, Non-violence, Trusteeship and Sarvodhya. The relevance of these economic principles to large farmers is also presented. With proper implementation, every Indian village would turn out to be a self-sufficient and democratic unit.

The paper concludes by stating that a **synthesized paradigm** may be evolved wherein the Governmental agricultural policies may be employed for small and marginal farmers, the Gandhian economic perspectives may be persuaded to be implemented by the large farmers, in the agricultural sector of India. Such a synthesis would make Indian villages a qualitatively better place to live in for the entire farming community and would propel India as a self-sufficient and self-reliant nation.

Keywords: Governmental Agricultural Policies, Small and Marginal Farmers, Large Farmers, Gandhian Economic Philosophy, Synthesized Paradigm.

Introduction

Covid-19 has adversely affected all sections of the Indian economy. The pandemic has disrupted the pattern of production, distribution and consumption in the Indian agricultural system. The production and distribution is affected by financial, labour and logistical constraints, while negative income, restricted access to markets and increased prices of food commodities have affected the consumption pattern. Hence, there arises a need to revisit the domain of agricultural sector.

The Three Sectors of the Indian Economy

Indian economy consists of three main sectors, namely, the agricultural sector, the industrial sector and the services sector. The agricultural sector includes agriculture, forestry, fishery, etc. The industrial sector includes mining, quarrying, manufacturing, electricity, gas, water supply, construction, etc. The services sector includes trade, transport, communication, finance, banking, insurance, real estate, community services, social services, personal services, etc.

Importance of Agricultural Sector in India

It is often said that India lives in its villages and agriculture is still the backbone of our nation. The truth behind the statement may be made clear with the following facts:

1. Agriculture sector provides employment to the vast army of uneducated and unskilled labour in Indian villages
2. Agriculture sector contributes to the gross domestic product (GDP) and per-capita income of our country
3. Agriculture sector reduces poverty in Indian villages
4. Agriculture sector mitigates inequalities of income and wealth in villages

5. Agriculture sector creates demand for goods and services produced in the non-agricultural sectors (ie. industrial and services sectors) of our economy
6. Agricultural sector earns valuable foreign-exchange through export of surplus agricultural products
7. Agricultural sector endeavour to create a self-sufficient and dynamic India

Classification of Indian Farmers

Based on operational land holdings, Indian farmers are classified under Five categories, namely:

1. Marginal farmers: less than 1.00 hectare
2. Small farmers: 1.00 - 2.00 hectares
3. Semi-medium farmers: 2.00 - 4.00 hectares
4. Medium farmers: 4.00 - 10.00 hectares, and
5. Large farmers: 10.00 hectares and above

It must be pointed out that the majority of Indian farmers fall under the categories of marginal, small and semi-medium farmers. Some of the vital present issues faced by them are:

1. Inadequate finance/capital
2. Inadequate storage facilities
3. Small and fragmented land-holdings
4. Exposed to the vagaries of nature-drought, floods, etc.
5. Decease in the varieties of crops and livestock produced
6. Loss of agricultural land due to soil erosion, soil degradation, conversion for urban use, etc.
7. Lack of irrigational facilities
8. Inadequate marketing facilities
9. Perennial poverty
10. Inequalities of income and wealth

Governmental initiatives for Small and Marginal farmers

With the objective of improving the condition of the small and marginal farmers as well as double the income of farmers by 2022, the Government is channelizing its effort from production-centric approach to income-centric initiative. Towards this end, some of the schemes that are implemented by the Government, includes:

1. Pradhan Mantri Fasal Bima Yojana (PMFBY)
2. Soil Health Card Scheme (SHCS)
3. Paramparagat Krishi Vikas Yojana (PKVY)
4. National Agriculture Market Scheme (E-NAM)
5. Pradhan Manthri Krishi Sinchai Yojana (PMKSY)
6. Farmer Producer Organization (FPO)
7. Financing of Joint Liability Groups (JLGS)
8. National and State Disaster Relief Fund (NSDRF)
9. Coordinated programmme on Horticulture Assessment and Management (CHAMAN)
10. National Food Security Mission (NFSM)
11. Rashtriya Gokul Mission (RGM)
12. Attracting and Retaining Youth in Agriculture (ARYA)
13. Pradhan Mantri Gram Sadak Yojana (PMGSY)
14. Fisheries and Aquaculture Infrastructure Development Fund (FAIDF)
15. Animal Husbandry Infrastructure Development Fund (AHIDF)
16. Pradhan Mantri Kisan Samman Nidhi (PM-KISAN)
17. Neem Coated Urea (NCU)
18. Rainfed Area Development under National Mission for Sustainable Agriculture (NMSA)
19. National Mission on Oilseeds & Oilpalm (NMOOP)
20. Mission for Integrated Development of Horticulture (MIDH)
21. Rashtriya Krishi Vikas Yojana (RKVY)
22. National Mission on Agriculture Extension & Technology (NMAET)

Other Schemes

(a) Kisan Call Centres (KCC) (b) Agri-Clinics and Agri-Business Centres (ACABC) (c) Agri-Fairs and Exhibitions, and (d) Kisan SMS Portal.

Need for Persuasive Approach towards Large Farmers:
It is indeed laudable that the Government (Central and State), with the National Bank for Agriculture and Rural Development (NABARD), are taking great effort to uplift the standard of living of small and marginal farmers through implementation of various income-generating schemes. These schemes involve, among others, increasing productivity of various agricultural crops through promoting the practice of multiple cropping, inter cropping and integrated farming systems.

Bare Necessities Index (BNI): According to the *Economic Survey2020-2021*, the agricultural sector is expected to grow by 3.4%. Even though it is an healthy growth rate in the given economic conditions, the disturbing feature lies with regard to the Bare Necessities Index. This index takes into account five dimensions, namely, (1) Access to water (2) Housing (3) Sanitation (4) Micro-environment, and (5) Other facilities (electricity, cooking gas, etc.). The value of index range from 0-1 and higher the value, better the access to the bare necessities. According to the *Economic Survey 2020-2021*, only Four States, namely, Punjab, Kerala, Haryana and Gujarat have the highest (above 0.70) BNI. The rest of the 24 States and 8 Union territories have only Medium (0.50-0.70) and Lowest (below 0.50) BNI. This clearly shows high inequality in the access to the bare necessities for both urban and rural India. This would be a great hurdle in the growth and development of the agricultural sector.

The Objective of the paper
In the context of the above scenario, it may be stated that while the government machinery is focusing its entire effort on addressing the issues of small and marginal farmers, there is an imperative need to persuade the large farmers to actively and effectively participate in the growth and development of the agricultural sector, especially during the present pandemic crisis engineered by Covid-19. This

persuasion of large farmers is to be effected through non-violence and an appeal to the higher ethical values of large farmers. Hence, we resort to the perspectives of the Gandhian Economic Philosophy.

The Gandhian Economic Philosophy

By 'Gandhian Economic Philosophy', we refer to the economic thoughts based on the spiritual and socio-economic principles expounded by Mahatma Gandhi. His economic ideas are part of his general philosophy of life in which the combination of economic, moral and spiritual well-being of 'man' is of supreme consideration. Therefore, Mahatma Gandhi's economic philosophy revolves around an individual, his attitude and behavior at the village level.

Some of the economic ideas of Mahatma Gandhi that would enable to persuade the larger farmers are:

The Economic Philosophy of Simplicity

According to Mahatma Gandhi 'simple living and high thinking' should be the guiding principle of a man's life. Happiness is a mental condition. The mind is a restless bird and the more it gets, the more it wants and still remains unsatisfied. The famous statement of Mahatma Gandhi is that: The earth provides enough to satisfy every man's needs but not for every man's greed.

Relevance to Large Farmers

By making a clear-cut distinction between want and need, Indian villages would be free from unnecessary/unwanted and harmful goods and services. It would also bring about a pollution-free environment in the villages. As far as large farmers are concerned, they would avoid unscrupulous consumption. They may be persuaded to utilize their savings for providing common irrigation, storage and other agricultural facilities for the welfare of the entire village. This would address the problem of inadequate finance as well as poverty experienced by small and marginal farmers.

This would enhance their health and also make them debt-free. It is often said that and Indian farmer is born in debt and die in debt. Simple and contended life would also pave the way for their happiness and peace.

The Economic Philosophy of Non-possessiveness

Along with simplicity, Mahatma Gandhi emphasized the quality of non-possessiveness as the bedrock for the emancipation of the Indian masses/poor. By 'non-possession', Mahatma Gandhi does not refer to complete renunciation of every possession of man. Non-possessiveness is contentment and non-acceptance. Mahatma Gandhi states that the tendency to possess things is the root cause of all evils. Therefore, one must cultivate the discipline of living with what one has and with what one needs.

Relevance to Large Farmers

Non-possessiveness on the part of large farmers, as a policy, would lead to automatic and natural redistribution of income and wealth in the village communities. This would put an end to class-struggles and ensures smooth and harmonious functioning of the village-activities. Non-possessiveness would mitigate unchecked desires, greediness, crimes, etc. of large farmers. This would also enhance their physical, moral and spiritual well-being.

The Economic Philosophy of Non-Violence

According to Mahatma Gandhi, non-violence must be practiced in thought, word and deeds. Even though no activity is possible without a certain amount of violence, Gandhi advocated activities with least possible violence. Gandhiji's economics may be called as non-violent economics. Mahatma Gandhi states that a non-violent occupation is one which is fundamentally free from violence and which does not involve exploitation or envy of others. The basis of capitalism is the exploitation of human labour to create surplus value. Society must be based not on exploitation but on justice.

Relevance to Large Farmers

Violence is any form is always attended by completion, exploitation, alienation, hatefulness, etc. Violence breeds greater violence. This leads to a number of problems that affects the production and distribution of goods and services, in society. When Large farmers are persuaded to perform their activities with non-violence, it leads to a harmonious development of social, economic, cultural and political well being of the entire village community. Labour-intensive tools and machinery mitigates exploitation of labour and concentration of wealth in the hands of few. Non-violence ensures a smooth give and take policy among all farmers, thereby bringing peace and prosperity to the individual and community. True democracy and real growth of human personality are only possible in a non-violent community.

The Economic Philosophy of Trusteeship

Mahatma Gandhi's belief in trusteeship comes from his belief in non- violence and non-possession. According to him, trusteeship, a socio-economic philosophy, involves wealthy people to consider themselves as trustees of their wealth and utilize it for the welfare of the entire community. Mahatma Gandhi states that if an individual has acquired large amount of money through inheritance or from trade, the entire amount of money does not belong to that individual alone, but also to the entire community. One who had accumulated that money is entitled to only that part of it which is necessary for an honourable living. The rest of the accumulated wealth belongs to the entire nation and must be spent for the welfare of all. It must also be noted here that Mahatma Gandhi was against the idea of confiscation of wealth from the wealthy and the capitalists, by using force or violence. The rich could be persuaded through moral pressure, non-cooperation and through legislation.

Relevance to Large Farmers

Mahatma Gandhi addresses the problem of economic

inequality and the concentration of wealth, through the principle of trusteeship. Possession of wealth necessarily implies storage of wealth and violence is inevitable in defending the stored wealth. Thus, the concept of trusteeship ensures economic equality. At the same time, trusteeship also leads to the elimination of classes in society. When the Large farmers are persuaded to adopt the doctrine of trusteeship, it mitigates the problem of poverty in society. They would feel morally satisfied that they are doing the right action and the needy small and marginal farmers would feel that they are also recognized and not alienated in community. This ensures smooth functioning of the entire village community.

The Economic Philosophy of Sarvodaya

Mahatma Gandhi perceived Sarvodaya, meaning 'upliftment/ welfare of all', as a tool to revive the system of village self-governance in India. He felt that Sarvodaya would enable every Indian village to be prosperous in agriculture as well as decentralized small scale and cottage industries with participation of people at all levels. His earnest desire is that every Indian village should be converted into a little self-sufficient republic. Mahatma Gandhi's Sarvodaya principle is based on the values of freedom, equality, justice and fraternity.

Relevance to Large Farmers

The Sarvodaya society would function as an organic whole rather than being disjointed into economic classes or social classes. The practice of non-violence, respect for other religion, serving others and eradicating untouchability are the core principles of Sarvodaya. When large farmers are persuaded to understand, adopt and implement the policy of Sarvodaya, it would change the entire structure of the village society. The idea of village self-governance would address many issues faced by small and marginal farmers. Sarvodaya society ensures that production is for immediate use and not for distant market. This would address the issue of inadequate storage and marketing facilities. The revival of village Panchayats with prosperous agriculture and decentralized small-scale/cottage cooperative organizations would ensure better use of small and fragmented agricultural lands, better soil conservation and irrigation facilities, generating adequate/needed finance, reduces inequalities of income and wealth, thereby, poverty, both at the individual and village levels.

Conclusion

From the foregone discussion, we are able to clearly understand the vital potency of persuading large farmers to imbibe and implement Mahatma Gandhi's economic philosophy in order to mitigate the problems faced by the agricultural sector, in general, and the small and marginal farmers, in particular. We are also aware of the steps/efforts taken by the Government to enhance the agricultural sector in India.

In this situation, we propose to moot a <u>Synthesized paradigm</u> that would involve both the policies of the government as well as Gandhian economic perspectives in order to revive the agricultural sector of India. While the Governmental agricultural policies may be employed for small and marginal farmers, the Gandhian economic perspectives may be implemented as a persuasive tool towards large farmers, in the agricultural sector of India.

Such a synthesis would enhance the growth and development of Indian villages as well as the entire agricultural sector of our country, during the present pandemic times. This would ensure a high standard of living and standard of life for all farmers, thereby, evolving Indian villages as a qualitatively better place to live in for the village masses. It would also propel the growth and development of industries and service sectors of India. This would go a long way in ensuring India as a self-sufficient and self-reliant nation.

References:
1. Fischer Louis (2006). Mahatma Gandhi-His Life and Times, Mumbai: Bhartiya Vidya Bhavan.
2. Gandhi M.K. (1947). India of my Dreams, compiled by R. K. Prabhu, Ahmadabad: Navajeevan Publishing House.
3. Kripalani Krishna (1968). Gandhi: A Life, New Delhi: National Book Trust.
4. Kumarappa J. C. (1962). Gandhian Economic Thought, Rajghat, Varanasi: Sarva Seva Sangh Prakashan
5. Maharajan M. (2008). Economic Thought of Mahatma Gandhi, New Delhi: Discovery Publishing Pvt. Ltd.
6. Narayan Shriman (1970). Relevance of Gandhian Economics, Ahmadabad: Navajeevan Publishing House.
7. Nirmal Kumar Bose (1972). Studies in Gandhism, Ahmadabad: Navajeevan Publishing House.
8. Shanti Swarup Gupta (1994). Economic Philosophy of Mahatma Gandhi, New Delhi: Concept Publishing Company.

Gandhiji's Approach of Non–Violent Protest and its Influence on Future Social and Political Movement

Dr. Priyanka Singh
Assistant Professor
Dept. of Arts and Social Sciences
Sam Higginbottom University of Agriculture, Technology
and Sciences, Prayagraj, Uttar Pradesh
Email: dr.priyankasingh999@gmail.com

Ms. Manjishtha Callen
Pursuing B.A, LL.B. Hons.
University Institute of Legal Studies, Chandigarh University
Mohali, Punjab
Email: manjishthacallen.9@gmail.com

Abstract

This review paper examines the Gandhiji's approach of Non–Violent protest and its influence on future social and political movement. Social and political movements all throughout the world have been impacted by Mahatma Gandhi's peaceful protest methods and dedication to nonviolence. According to Gandhi, "just means lead to just ends" and nonviolence is morally necessary to establish democracy. He battled against social ills like racial discrimination and untouchability as well as colonialism, caste prejudice, gender inequity, and injustice by nonviolent means. Civil disobedience movements like the 1930 Salt March were promoted by Gandhi as a means of nonviolent resistance. He held that practicing nonviolence affects families, communities, cities, countries, and the entire world from the heart. In addition, he held that fighting for justice and human rights should be done so without using violence since it is an inside struggle that nonviolence resolves.

With Gandhi's democratic worldview, the plurality of cultures and faiths in the Indian subcontinent gained anti-monistic and pluralistic characteristics. Based on an inclusive and dialogical concept of coexistence, he made an appeal to nonviolent democratic theory. Fanaticism in any form, whether it be religious or patriotic, was strongly disapproved of. It was therefore suggested that nonviolence may be used for more than merely social and political liberation. Moreover, it was stated as a fundamentally moral requirement for establishing democracy.

Keywords: Non-Violence, Democracy, Gandhi's philosophy, Social evils, Untouchability.

Introduction

The "father of India" and a "great soul in beggar's garb," as some have dubbed him. After over a century of British colonial control, India gained independence because to his nonviolent approach to political reform. A weak man with an iron resolve, he set the standard for later global social revolutions. He was and is still regarded as one of the most important people in contemporary history—Mahatma Gandhi.

On October 2, 1869, Mohandas Karamchand Gandhi was born in the Gujarati town of Porbandar. He attended school close to Rajkot, where his father was a local ruler's advisor. Even though India was ruled by the British at the time, more than 500 kingdoms and principalities were known around the world for their peaceful passive resistance attitude. In his book, he said that as a young boy, he and his buddies would sneakily consume meat in order for them to grow up to be as powerful as the English. It was determined that he should move to England to study law after some local schooling. By vowing to abstain from liquor, women, and meat, he won his mother's approval, but he disobeyed his caste's rules prohibiting travel to England. He enrolled in London's Inner Temple Law College. He became persuaded of vegetarianism's concept after reading Henry Salt's A Plea for Vegetarianism while looking for a vegetarian restaurant. He met individuals who shared his theosophical and humanitarian goals and founded a vegetarian group. He read Edwin Arnold's poetic version of the Bhagavad-Gita, The Song Celestial, and shared what little Sanskrit he knew with others. Afterwards, the Sermon on the Mount and this Hindu text served as his spiritual manuals and bibles. He would repeat the Gita in its original Sanskrit at his prayer gatherings, having committed it to memory while brushing his teeth every day.

Non-Violent Revolution

Non-violence literally means acting without using violence. Humans and wild animals should not be killed. They shouldn't be harmed in any way. The term "non-violence" comes from the Sanskrit word "Ahinsa," which means "lack of desire to harm or kill." Non-violence is the individual practice of being non-violent toward oneself and others in all circumstances. It refers to a general philosophy of refraining from violence based on moral, religious, or spiritual beliefs and originates from the idea that harming people, animals, or the environment is not necessary to attain a result.

The best leaders' weapon of choice is nonviolence. It is the most basic technique of persuasion. The divine attributes of non-violence draw us closer to God. Consequently, nonviolence and the reasons behind it should be understood by all. Freedom of conscience is ensured by nonviolence, allowing individuals to act according to their most deeply held beliefs. The use of violence in the modern world has conveyed a message of extreme injustice, encouraged greed among a select few and ignored the needs of the overwhelming majority of people. It has also heavily favored a small number of wealthy nations over innovative nonviolent resistance strategies that could preserve humanity.

Gandhian concept and philosophy of Non-Violence

Gandhi gave the concept of nonviolence a unique significance. A strong proponent of nonviolence, Mahatma Gandhi preached and practiced it from an early age throughout the world. It is the weapon of the courageous and the strong, he remarked. He meant strong people to be those who possess strong moral and spiritual qualities. He asserted that nonviolence is far more powerful and effective than violence. In Gandhi's Non-Violence, truth is sought after.

The most essential component of Gandhi's nonviolent ideology is truth. Gandhi found the principle of non-violence in the book "Experiments with Truth," which is a collection of his quest for truth. He expounded on this principle in his autobiography, saying that "Ahinsa is the basis of the search for truth." I'm coming to see that without Ahinsa as its foundation, this search is pointless. The hills are as old as truth and non-violence. In addition to his theories, he embraced non-violence as a philosophy and the ideal way of living. He helped us realize that the non-violent ideology is a weapon that everybody can use, not only the weak. Gandhi did not invent nonviolence.

Gandhi distinguished between two types of violence: physical and passive. Consciously and unknowingly, passive violence is a daily practice. Once more, it is the gasoline that starts the fire of physical aggression. Gandhi is aware that the Sanskrit word for violence is "hinsa," which signifies harm. Gandhi believes that the person who possesses non-violence is blessed, even in the midst of extreme violence. Blessed is the one who, amidst the boiling fire of himsa all around him, is able to discern the law of Ahinsa, or non-violence. By his example, we bow down in adoration to such a man. His need for release from the bondage of flesh, which serves as his vehicle, grows more acute the worse the circumstances around him get. Gandhi rejects violence as a means of fostering animosity.

Gandhi recognized that a nonviolent global order required the institutionalization of democratic world government and federated democratic government at all levels of governance, as well as the spiritual commitment of people worldwide. Four foundations of Ahinsa, or the Nonviolent Revolution, that Gandhi proposes be maintained 1. The Sarvodaya 2. The Swaraj 3. Swadeshi 4. The Satyagraha.

Non-Violence and Democracy

Mahatma Gandhi was a strong believer in nonviolence and believed that all institutions created by men, especially "State-like" ones, carry some level of risk. He held that nonviolence is the only way for a state, especially a democracy, to endure. It cannot mature into its form unless and until it is fully encompassed by non-violence. Gandhi, though, was unsure of it himself. "I am making efforts in this direction," he said.

For this reason, democracy is crucial in a nation like India. A true Ram Rajya can be established or earnest attempts can be made to attain that status if we eradicate cases of democracy being abused. Gandhiji proposed nonviolence and satyagraha as a way to start in this path from India and lead by example for the other countries of the world. When discussing the establishment of a democratic society, Gandhiji gave priority to and favored discussing economic matters. "A non-violent form of government is obviously unachievable as long as the enormous disparity between the millions of hungry and the rich continues to exist," he declared.

Gandhi changed the idea of democracy by coming up with ways to incorporate the ruling class. Gandhi fiercely opposed the consolidation of power in the hands of a select few. Regarding the devolution of power, he had strict guidelines. Concentration of power refers to the retention of authority in the hands of a small number of people, who may abuse it whenever it suits them. "Twenty men seated in the center cannot function as a true democracy. Every village's residents must work at it from the bottom up. All citizens must have access to power for it to operate within the bounds of morality in a democracy. Although the people's representatives will wield power on behalf of the people, the people themselves will hold the exclusive authority to assign power. Since the people are the Guardians of democracy, the responsibility for any abuse of power rests with their representatives.

Gandhi's democratic ideology gave the Indian subcontinent's diversity of cultures and faiths anti-monistic and pluralistic features. His defense of a nonviolent democratic ideology rested on the notion of inclusive and dialogical coexistence. This ideology rejected all types of extremism and self-centeredness, whether it be religious or national. Consequently, nonviolence was promoted as a tool for more than merely social liberation and political conflict. It was also stated that establishing democracies is fundamentally morally required.

Relevance of Non-Violent Revolution in the present scenario

A brief while back, every violent incident was viewed with much alarm. But today's world has grown so rife with violence that the majority of these instances happen on a regular basis and receive little notice from the public. The best way to curb violence is a topic of discussion whenever anything horrifying or horrific occurs. But in today's world, it's just another method of treating badly with more evil. Promoting violence as a means of authority and defending the use of weapons as a must to uphold law and order are the fundamental tenets of the arms proliferation debate. Is there ever a justifiable reason to use violence? Today, a clear response is necessary to this important subject, to which the majority of people would respond by citing crimes associated with terrorism, the need to protect disadvantaged segments of society, and other similar arguments.

Before a developed world can be established, there must be peace and nonviolence. Such a community or country can focus on improving standards in order to reach the pinnacles of spirituality, science, business, the arts, education, and other areas of human endeavor. In terms of connection and work quality, they are able to achieve the pinnacle of human experience. Such a world is achievable in the present and is not just a utopian fantasy. People used to live in a fully non-violent manner and adhere to the principle of shared brotherhood at a time in human history known as Satyuga, or heaven. Truth be told, vices like lust, rage, greed, attachment, and ego have taken over the entire human race and made it their hostage.

Gandhi's nonviolent teachings have always been relevant since nonviolence is the core idea. We cannot envision this society without non-violence since, should everyone turn aggressive and nasty, they will battle among themselves, leading to high-minded national goals that will ultimately be in jeopardy and endanger global existence. Hence, in order to have a peaceful world, his ideal must become the most crucial one to follow. The independence movement benefited greatly from Gandhi's nonviolent revolution. Gandhi's insightful speech from the era of the freedom movement still has application in modern society.

Conclusion

Mahatma Gandhi's ideology is still relevant today, which is evidence of the continuing value of his teachings. We have looked at several aspects of Gandhi's ideology and its significant influence on modern society in this review study. Gandhiji has always envisioned a peaceful society where everyone is blessed. The peaceful phenomena of non-violence is extremely important. It is the most creative and motivating solution to every issue and conflict that exists in the community, the country, and the entire planet. The promotion of an Ahinsa and non-violent culture is the cure to violence. All religious, political, and social leaders will create a utopia if they support non-violence as the ideal ethic and way of life. The current global context of violence and its connected branches has once again highlighted the significance of this issue.

Reverting to Gandhi's belief in non-violence and truth as a last resort would be extremely beneficial for nations suffering from corruption, communalism, dictatorship, and power struggles. These countries may effectively eradicate their social, political, economic, and religious problems by implementing the Non-Violence policy. Without a question, the social theory of non-violence, which Mahatma Gandhi promoted, is today essential to maintaining the new social and political order. It is not outdated, but rather has a bright future if properly implemented globally.

References:
1. Chandra, S. & Pal, R. P. (2017). The Impact of Gandhi on the US Peace Movement. Samajbodh, 7(1), 101-109.
2. Du Toit, L. (2022). Gandhi and the Gender of Nonviolent Resistance. Religions, 13(5), 467.
3. Gandhi, M. K. (2012). Non-violent resistance. Courier Corporation.
4. Ghosh, B. (Ed.). (2024). Exploring Social Movements: Theories, Experiences, and Trends. Taylor & Francis.
5. Gregg, R. B. (2018). The power of nonviolence. Cambridge University Press.
6. Jahn, E. (2021). The National and Universal Importance of the Non-violent Policy of Mohandas K. Gandhi. Decolonising Conflicts, Security, Peace, Gender, Environment and Development in the Anthropocene, 245-277.
7. Jahn, E. & Jahn, E. (2020). The Fatal Glorification of Mohandas K. Gandhi as a Saint: His Role in the National

Independence Movement in India. War and Compromise Between Nations and States: Political Issues Under Debate–Vol. 4, 79-95.

8. Khundrakpam, P. & Sarmah, J. K. (2024). Comparative political theory and Gandhi: A systematic review. Social Sciences & Humanities Open, 9, 100887.

9. Mantena, K. (2018). Showdown for nonviolence: The theory and practice of nonviolent politics. To shape a new world: Essays on the political philosophy of Martin Luther King, Jr, 78-102.

10. May, T. (2015). Nonviolent resistance: A philosophical introduction. John Wiley & Sons.

11. Nepstad, S. E. (2013). Nonviolent civil resistance and social movements. Sociology Compass, 7(7), 590-598.

12. Rai, D. & Tiwary, R. M. (2021). Gandhi and Satyagraha—A quest for global transformation: A review essay on the international seminar. Social Change, 51(1), 121-133.

13. Roberts, A. & Ash, T. G. (Eds.). (2009). Civil resistance and power politics: the experience of non-violent action from Gandhi to the present. Oxford university press.

14. Scalmer, S. (2011). Gandhi in the West: The Mahatma and the rise of radical protest. Cambridge University Press.

15. Sharma, N. (2021). Gandhi, Value Creation, and Global Education: Intercultural Perspectives on Education for Citizenship. In Teaching and Learning in Higher Education: The Context of Being, Interculturality and New Knowledge Systems (pp. 237-247). Emerald Publishing Limited.

16. Tripathi, A. K. (2022). Dissent and Protest Movements in India: Revisiting Gandhi's Ideas of Peaceful Protest. In Gandhi in the Twenty First Century: Ideas and Relevance (pp. 199-210). Singapore: Springer Nature Singapore.

Mahatma Gandhi's Approaches to Social Reform

Mr. Vijay Kumar Mishra
Assistant Professor
Department of Studies in Social Management (DSSM)
School of Social Sciences (SSS)
Central University of Gujarat (CUG)
Gandhinagar, Gujarat
Email: vijaymishra2k8@gmail.com

Abstract

M. K. Gandhi a well-known figure of the Indian freedom Movement and social reform in India. Moreover, he is popularly known as Mahatma Gandhi for his practice of truth and non-violence and involvement of masses in his movements. He led so many movements in India as well as in outside of India through nonviolence and involvement of masses. His focus on nonviolence and involvement of masses seeks social reform social based on equality, cooperation, harmony, nonviolence, simple living and respect for all living beings which is known as *Swaraj and Sarvodaya.* Gandhiji involved masses in his movements to achieve independence as well as for social reform. He led movements against racial discrimination, peasant exploitation, class repression, untouchability, gender discrimination, British rule and to establish a self-reliant society through his various establishments and practices. He wanted changes or reform in society through individual transformation. He started such kind of ideal practices like simple and community living and advised the people to follow those ideas. It was Gandhiji who gave unique theory of movement i.e. *Satyagraha* which he started when he was in South Africa. He gave a chance to the common people to participate in social transformation as well as in national movement. In this regard he introduced *Ekadshvrata* (Eleven Vows) for individual transformation, constructive programme for social transformation and Satyagraha for problems which cannot solve through rest of concept of given by him to make a society based on justice and equality.

Keywords: Social Reform, Self-Reliant, Swaraj, Satyagraha, Sarvodaya

Introduction

Mahatma Gandhi is a renowned figure of the Indi's struggle against British rule. He is also known for social reform movement in India. He led several social movements in both South Africa and India. He led movements against racial discrimination in South Africa. He led movement against peasant exploitation in Champaran a district of Bihar and Kheda a district of Gujarat. Beside he also struggled against class repression, untouchability, gender discrimination and British rule etc. through mass actions. He has established a number of organizations and settlements like Natal India Congress, Phoenix Settlement, Tolstoy Farm, in South Africa and Kocharab Ashram and Sabarmati Ashram and Sewagram Ashram in India. In addition, he also established many other organisations and published newspapers to reach to the common people to raise their consciousness, make them aware and develop collective action among them and to achieve *Swaraj*. He introduced constructive programme in this regard which is eighteen in number; Communal unity, Removal of untouchability, Prohibition, Khadi, Other village industries, Village sanitation, Basic education (Nai Talim), Adult education, Emancipation of women, Education in health and hygiene, Provincial languages, National languages, Economic Equality, Peasants, Labour, Tribals, Leprosy patients and Students.

Gandhiji also tried to bring about a radical change of the mindset of the individuals to that end, he introduced *Ekadashvrata* (eleven vows) which are (Satya-Truth,

Ahinsa-Nonviolence, Brahmacharya-Celibacy, Asteya-Non-stealing, Asangraha or Aparigraha-Non-possession, Sharira-Shrama; Physicallabour or Bread Labour, Asvada-Control of Palate, Abhaya-Fearlessness, Sarva-Dharma-Samanatva or Sarva-Dharma-Sambhava- Equal respect for all Religions, Swadeshi-Duty towards Neighbour and Asprishyatanivarana - Removal of Untouchability). In addition, Gandhiji introduced *Satyagraha* to solve the problems which cannot be solve through Ekadshvrata and constructive programme and to make a society based on justice and equality. Gandhiji struggled against British rule in South Africa as well as in India through the Satyagraha. He took these practices from Indian tradition which imbibed perfectly could really change the individual consciousness or new consciousness among the people. Now it would be relevant to note here that there were many views about the social movements for radical change or social reform.

For instance, there was a view that radical change or reform should start at the individual level. If such a change turns into a mass movement that would lead to the emergence of good society or society based on equality and nonviolence. On the contrary there was another school of thought which think that change at individual level would take hundreds of years. Hence, they would have to be carried out at systematic level. In particular, Marxist believed in such approach to social change. They also believe that state power is the key factor and major instrument in any scheme or programme of the social change (Mishra, 1975). In sharp contrast to above Marxian perspective Gandhi believed that in the absence of state power civil society organisation could bring about radical change in a given a society. He did not have much faith in the institution of state as he looked at it as a symbol of organised violence. Therefore, he transcended the debate about individual verses systematic change. He suggested that in any scheme of social movement one must work both at individual and systematic level (Thomson, 1993). To that end, he suggested three major instruments viz. eleven vows (for the individual and constructive programme and Satyagraha at collective level. This is the distinct nature of Gandhi's approach to social movement. If we closely examine the social political movements led by Gandhi at different time and different places, we could find that he attempted to apply all the three above instruments of social change in his scheme of themes. The present paper seeks to examine some of the Gandhian social movements to see to what extent he succeeded in apply these instruments of change and to what results. In this view, it is essential to focus on major contribution Gandhi towards social reform.

Major Contribution of Mahatma Gandhi for Social Reform

With his experience of vegetarian club from England, Gandhiji formed Natal India Congress, Phoenix settlement and Tolstoy Farm in South Africa and Sabarmati Ashram, Sewagram Ashram, *Harijan Sewak Sangh*, *Sarvodaya Mandal*, All India Charkha Sangh, *Satyagraha Sabha*, Gandhi Seva Sangh, Adim Jati Seva Sangh, Gujarat Vidyapith (Educational), Dakshin Bharat Hindi Prachar Samiti, Rahstra Bhasha Prachar Samiti, Puna Naturopathy Centre and many other educational, and social reform organisations in India. Though these organization and establishment he attempted to put his ideas on social movement in practice (Thomsaon, 1993: Gandhi, 1955).

Gandhiji rejected class or caste approach to social movement and really put his faith in mass action and got cross sectional support that comprised different section of society. It was such a perspective that built up 'Indian National Congress' (INC) a new Congress organization across caste, class, creed, and religion thus congress became a fighting organization committed to the nation cause. Earlier INC was known as organization of elite people. Apart from that, Gandhiji raised a number of social organizations as stated above for regeneration of Indian social economic cultural and educational field (Thomsaon, 1993: Gandhi, 1955). The main objective of his numerous establishment and practices were to inter to the masses and mobilise the masses to carry out his ideas and approaches to social movements in the context of social reform and to attain the freedom. In this view, it is essential to Gandhiji's contribution towards fight against discriminations based different social stratification.

Mahatma Gandhi's Movement against Racial Discrimination

Gandhiji went to South Africa in 1893 to practice law under one-year contract. He faced racism in South Africa due to a law based on discrimination. Gandhiji found that this law restricted the rights of Indians in South Africa. During a journey Gandhi was forced to leave the first-class compartment of the train. However, Gandhiji refused to leave the first-class compartment, therefore; he was thrown off from the train. After this incident, Gandhiji decided to fight against injustice and defend the rights of Indians who were living in South Africa.

When his contract with Abdula Seth expired, Gandhiji spontaneously decided to remain in South Africa. He launched a campaign against a legislative law because this law had provision to denies right to vote for Indians in South Africa. He formed the Natal Indian Congress and drew international attention to the plight of Indians in South Africa. In 1906, the Transvaal government brought another law, which restricted the rights of Indians. This law had provision to legitimate only Christian marriages. Gandhiji organized a campaign against this law. It was his first campaign of *Satyagraha,* or mass civil disobedience in South Africa. After seven years of protest, he negotiated a compromise agreement Thent with African government where it was provision that non-Christian marriages would also be recognized (Nauriya, 2006: Gandhi, 1968).

Mahatma Gandhi's Movement against Peasant's Exploitation

Mahatma Gandhi's early activities in India was very much connected with peasant groups, the reasons for that connection were his focus on reform in rural area. Gandhiji's thought and action seeks wellness of common man and rural people because majority of Indians resided in rural area, and they were depended on agriculture. Therefore, it can be said that his emphasis on rural areas is directly connected with the wellness of peasants. However, through the Champaran peasant struggle Gandhiji directly came into contact with the peasants. Champaran and Kheda movements are recognized as major agitations against peasant exploitation led by Gandhiji.

Gandhiji went to Champaran at the request of Rajkumar Shukla. There he saw the problems of peasants. The problem of peasants at Champaran was related with *Tinkathiya* rule. According to *Tinkathiya* rule, peasants had to cultivate indigo plants in three *Kattha* out of every *Bigha*. Gandhiji saw that farmers were afraid of their landlords and government servants. Gandhi thought to make them fearless, therefore; he requested some lawyers for their advocacy. Gandhi along with landlords, met with collector and their officers but collector asked him to live Tirhut. However, Gandhi refused it. Gandhi was summand to the court. This news spread everywhere like wildfire. A large number of farmers came to the court to see Gandhiji. So, magistrate gets back summon. Now peasants became fearless, and Gandhiji felt face to face with Ahinsa. This was Gandhi's first movement in India for peasants.

Gandhiji visited different villages of Bihar. He saw the actual condition of Bihar. He found dirt at in villages, dirt on roads and dirt at every place, and untouchability. Gandhiji realized that villagers were not practicing organized work. Therefore, he thought their mode of living required a change. As per his experience, he thought that work of permanent nature was not possible without proper village education. Therefore, Gandhiji decided to open primary schools in six villages. He gave one condition to villagers that they would provide boarding and lodging for the teachers and his colleagues would see after to the other expenses (Gandhi, 1927: Tendulkar, 2016: Prasad, 1957).

The Kheda movement was second major move of Gandhiji for peasants. It was the consequence of the financial atrocities afflicted by the landlords of Britishers on the farmers of the Kheda a village in Gujarat near Anand. In 1918, the villages of Kheda were massively affected by the floods and famine that resulted in the destruction of the crop. The farmers requested the British government to exempt them from the payment of taxes. However, the authorities refused to give exemption. Therefore, villagers started movement under the leadership of Sardar Vallabhbhai Patel and Mahatma Gandhi. They launched a campaign against the government and in addition to it they took pledged for the non-payment of taxes. As a result, the government threatened the peasant that government would seizure their land. However, the peasants remain undeterred. After five months of persistent struggle, the British government agreed to off the payment of taxes and also returned the seized properties of the peasants, in May 1918 (Gandhi, 1927).

Bardoli movement was third major move of Gandhiji for peasants. It was launched in mid-February 1928. The reason of Bardoli movement was quite like Kheda. Gandhi selected Bardoli as a suitable place for launching civil disobedience campaign and stated some constructive work in the entire Bardoli taluka. Peasants of Bardoli participated in constructive work with great enthusiasm. Therefore, Gandhi said that peasants of Bardoli were the child of the non-cooperation movement. Sardar Vallabhbhai Patel became the principal figure of this movement. Later, Sardar Patel advocated farmer's cooperatives for the benefit of farmers (Vasava, 2017: Mandal, n.d).

Mahatma Gandhi's Movement against Untouchability

Gandhiji wanted a just society. Therefore, he advocated for total eradication of untouchability. According to him, untouchability was one of the questions of life and death for Hinduism, he repeatedly said it. Gandhiji believed that if untouchability remained in Hinduism, it would perish Hinduism and if untouchability would eradicate from the Hinduism, Hinduism would give a definite message to the world (Gandhi, 1980; Rao, 2017). Therefore, Gandhiji started the temple-entry campaign and the travelling campaign against untouchability in 1932 and got greater success. He established an extensive organisation, the *Harijan Sevak Sangh* to eradicate untouchability and got massive support.

The *Harijan Sevak Sangh* (hereafter HSS) was founded by Gandhi in 1932. The main cause for its establishments was Gandhiji's worried about Harijan service and the promotion of village industries. Gandhiji selected Sewagram due to a number of reasons. Harijan Seva was one of them. He wanted to make HSS a laboratory to fight against untouchability and other social evils. It was a non-profit organization to work the issues of untouchability as well as the upliftment of the Harijans i.e. scheduled castes and Dalits in India. In addition, the objective of the HSS was to enable the depressed classes to access public spaces like temples, schools, water resources and roads because in those days these things were severely restricted to the untouchables in parts of the locality. The acts of inter caste marriages and inter dining were also restrained. The HSS worked on these issues under the leadership and guidance of Gandhiji. These were the attempts by Gandhi and his colleague to create a society based on equality for all and bringing change among the people and community (Gandhi, 1980; Gandhi 1936; Rao, 2017).

Mahatma Gandhi's Movement against Gender Discrimination

There were two schools of thoughts, which explained the condition of women in India. The first school of thought believed that the status of women has never been good in Indian society, while second school of thought believed that the position of women in Indian society was quite respectable. Shrimati Sarojini Naidu, who played an important role in the Indian independence movement, believed that the position of women in the ancient Indian society was very respectful. In this connection, the example of Maitreya and Gargi is given. Therefore, she emphasized that women should get rights as they enjoyed in ancient India. The historians of first category say that the condition of women worsened during the Mughal period. Due to renaissance of nineteenth century in India, women got some respectful position in the society because of the efforts of some thinkers and reformers like Iswarchandra Vidyasagar, Verislingam, Swami Vivekananda and Jyotiba Phule etc (Pradhan, 2008). Gandhi believed that women have a key role to play in the family and women are superior to men because of their moral and spiritual strength. They had greater powers of self-sacrifice and suffering. Gandhi believed women are capable of infinite strength, which they needed to realize. During Indian national movement, Gandhi played important role in women emancipation. He advocated for gender justice and brought women into Indian national movement.

Gandhiji opposed those practices that were injurious to women, girls and gender equality. He was against the practice of female infanticide. He observed that the birth of a girl was generally unwelcome because of customs like girl was to be married off and had to live and work in her marital home and dowry. He considered these practices evil or sin and found that lack of education and information was the root cause of all kinds of women's exploitation. Therefore, Gandhiji emphasized that education is necessary for women as it is for men because education is an essential aspect for enabling women to assert their rights. He was also in favour of economic independence of women while some people were afraid that economic independence of women would lead to disrupt domestic life. Gandhiji recommended the work like spinning that would help the women to get economic empowerment without disturbing the domestic life. Moreover, Gandhi recommended equal payment for men and women and equal property rights to women (Kaushik, n.d). When Gandhi started active participation in the Congress, he contributed to associate women in the freedom movement. He organized several conferences that were held at national and provincial levels in various cities of the country. As a result of it, women participated in the freedom movement. They burned Holi of foreign clothes, raised their voice for prohibition and Sarojini Naidu led salt movement (Pradhan, 2008).

Mahatma Gandhi's Movement for Self-Reliant Society

Gandhiji was a prominent leader of the freedom movement. He wanted to make India free from British rule as well from inequality, injustice and poverty etc. He called it *Swaraj* and wanted to work out a path towards it. He fought against inequality, extreme poverty, backwardness, and socio-economic challenges throughout of his life. In other word, it can be said that he wanted a society based on decentralized economy, self-sufficiency and involvement of common people. In his all moves he emphasised on *Swadeshi*, constructive work (1. Communal Unity 2. Removal of Untouchability 3. Prohibition 4. Khadi 5. Other Village Industries 6. Village Sanitation 7. New or Basic Education 8.

Adult Education 9. Women 10. Education in Health and Hygiene 11. Provincial Language 12. National Language 13. Economic Equality 14. Kisans 15. Labour 16. Adivasis 17. Lepers and 18. Students'. *Panchayti Raj*, nonviolence and non-cooperation. He also presented a scheme of basic education or *Nai Talim* and built institution on the idea of it. His institution built on the idea of basic education cantered on the principles of economic self-sufficiency and Self-Reliant Society (Gandhi, 1921: Bhuimali, n.d).

Mahatma Gandhi's Movement against British Rule:

As it has been discussed above Mahatma Gandhi a most recognized figure of the Indian Nationalist Movement led so many movements against British Rule in South Africa as well as in India through nonviolence, started with South Africa. He led three major movements against British rule in India. Gandhiji wanted a society based social justice and social harmony. He struggled throughout his life against social discrimination. His struggle against British rule was also a part of it as he considered that British rule impoverished the Indian people by destroying their village-based great tradition, education system and industries basically the cloth-making industry. In this view, it is essential to analyse the Gandhiji's movements against British rule.

The Non-Cooperation Movement

The non-cooperation movement was the first freedom movement led by Gandhiji. It was started in September 1920 after Jallianwala Bagh massacre and continued till February 1922. Gandhiji called it non-cooperation because he believed that the main reason for British success in India was the support of Indians to British administration and the east India Company. Gandhiji was of the view that if Indians would stop co-operating with the Britishers, they would be forced to give rights to Indians because Britishers were in minority. This movement gained popularity; millions of people came to boycott establishments of British Government. Many people left their jobs, removed their children from government schools, and avoided government offices. In addition, boycott of schools and colleges became an integral part of the movement. They organized hartals, led processions and courted arrest in big numbers in Punjab, Bengal, UP and Bombay. National education institutes like Kashi Vidyapeeth, Bihar Vidyapeeth, Jamia Millia Islamia, Bengal National University, and Gujarat Vidyapeeth were established during this movement. Out of these five Vidyapiths Gujarat Vidyapith was one, estalished by Gandhi himself on October 18, 1920. Gandhiji wanted to prepare the youths for the task of national reconstruction and usher in 'Hind Swaraj' (the India of his dream) through Gujarat Vidyapith However, the Non-Cooperation Movement ended when a violent mob erupted at Chauri Chaura in Uttar Pradesh. The mob burned a police station and killed twenty-three police officials (Pradhan, 2008: Chandra, Mukherjee, Mukherjee, Panikkar & Mahajan, 2016).

The Civil Disobedience

Gandhiji launched the civil disobedience movement on March 12, 1930. It is also known as Salt Satyagraha as it was a satyagraha against the British-imposed tax on salt, which affected the poorest section of the community. The Dandi March was a part of this movement. Gandhi also practised *Satyagraha* in this movement. For Gandhi, this movement was second move towards freedom. Dandi march was a campaign designed to oppose the British monopoly on salt. Gandhi started it with 79 followers and ended with thousands. They marched for 240-mile in 24 days. The protesters reached to the coastal town of Dandi and produced salt from saltwater without paying tax to the British government. Gandhi gave moving speeches about the inhumanity of a salt tax and told the salt Satyagraha as a struggle of the poor people. British authority arrested

Gandhi. However, the movement earned national and international attention and increased the number of Gandhi's followers (Pradhan, 2008: Chandra, Mukherjee, Mukherjee, Panikkar & Mahajan, 2016).

The Quit India Movement

During the Second World War the British Government promised Indians that they would be given some independence after the war. However, they offered only some concessions to the Indian demands such as the right to make independent provincial constitutions. This proposal was not acceptable for the leaders of Indian national movement. This disagreement resulted into the quit Indi movement. The Quit India Movement began on August 8, 1942. The India National Congress Committee, under the leadership of Gandhi, called for a mass movement against the British government. Gandhiji made a "Do or Die" speech. British authority acted immediately and arrested active members of the Indian National Congress party. However, the nation once again entered mass civil disobedience and introduced the idea that now the British government would not be able to control Indian emotions. This movement somehow, made it clear that British would not remain in India for long time. And, at last, India gained independence from British rule in 1947 (Pradhan, 2008: Chandra, Mukherjee, Mukherjee, Panikkar & Mahajan, 2016).

Mahatma Gandhi's Movement for Communal Harmony

Gandhiji felt the need of religious unity during his stay in South Africa. He worked hard to establish harmony between Hindus and Muslims. He worked for it in India also. Gandhi supported the Khilafat Movement. The Khilafat issue greatly agitated the minds of Muslims Gandhiji delivered speech at the Khilafat Conference held on 24- 11-1919 to bring the two communities together. Gandhiji felt that there are no huge differences between Hindu-Muslim. Therefore, Hindu-

Muslim unity could easily be strengthened. He never found serious differences between the Hindus and Muslims and among other minorities as well. He insisted that the Hindus who are in a majority in the country should help the minority community and should never entertain any idea of enforcing their rights but try to win the hearts of the minority community (Mazmudar, 2003).

Gandhiji tried to unite all sections of Indian people against British rule and get independence. We got independence on August 15, 1947. However, independence came at a huge cost. Hindus and Muslims who fought solder to solder against the British Rule. On the eve of independence, they fought against each other that led ultimately to the partition of the country. They became enemy of each other. The Noakhali riot that began on 10 October 1946 is generally considered as a reaction to the 'great Kolkata killings' of 16 August 1946. However, it had certain characteristics that make it imperative to study it differently. Gandhiji worked hard to stop communal violence. When India was becoming independent, Gandhiji fasted in Kolkata to stop communal riots that began on 10 October 1946 (Batabyal, 1997).

Conclusion

Gandhi successfully led different movements through his idea of non-violence and *Satyagraha* and engaged common masses in social reform and freedom struggle. He worked for the betterment of the society. He fought for right of Indian residing in South Africa through various establishments. Gandhi established Ashrams in India to bring social change and attain the Independence or his idea of Swaraj. He launched non-cooperation movement, civil disobedience/ salt Satyagraha and quit India movement to make India free from British rule. At the same time, he worked for Swaraj that seeks a society based on equality, cooperation, harmony, nonviolence, simple living and respect for all living beings etc. Gandhi made different establishments, practised eleven vows, constructive programmes etc. to achieve freedom and social transformation. He introduced eleven vows as an instrument of individual and constructive programme as an instrument of social reform. Gandhi Therefore, it is essential to understand Gandhi's role to meet the problems that we are facing today. He made establishment as per need and time that is still relevant in present Indian context. India still needs the same kinds of establishments that Gandhi did, to tackle contemporary problems.

References:
1. Batabyal, R. (1997). Communalisin, the Noakhali riot and Gandhi. Studies in Humanities and Social Sciences, IV(l), 135-174.
2. Bhuimali, A. (n.d). Relevance of M. K. Gandhi's ideals of self-sufficient village economy in the 21st century. Retrived from:
3. https://www.mkgandhi.org/articles/bhuimali.htm. Accessed on 20.03.2019.
4. Chandra, B., Mukherjee, M., Mukherjee, A., Panikkar, K. N., & Mahajan, S. (2016). India's struggle for independence. Penguin UK.
5. Gandhi, M. (1955). Ashram observances in action. Ahmedabad, India: Navajivan Publishing House.
6. Gandhi, M. (1980). All men are brothers: Autobiographical reflections. A&C Black.
7. Gandhi, M. K. (1921). Hind Swaraj or Indian home rule. GA Natesan and Company, Madras.
8. Gandhi, M. K. (1968). Satyagraha in South Africa. Ahmedabad, India: Navajivan Publishing House.
9. Gandhi, M.K. (1927). An Autobiography or The Story of my experiments with truth, Ahmedabad: Navajivan Publication.

10. Kaushik, A. (n.d). Gandhi on Gender Violence and Gender Equality: An Overview. Retrieved from: https://www.mkgandhi.org/articles/gender_equality.htm. Accessed on: 13.03.2019.

11. Mandal, P. (n.d). Bardoli Satyagraha: Useful Notes on Bardoli Satyagraha of 1928. Retrieved from: http://www.yourarticlelibrary.com/sociology/bardoli-satyagraha-useful-notes-on-bardoli-satyagraha-of-1928/31983. Accessed on: 12.09.2019.

12. Mazmudar, B. (2003). Gandhiji on communal harmony. Mani Bhavan Gandhi Sangrahalaya Mumbai.

13. Mishra, R. (1975). Marx and welfare. The Sociological Review, 23(2), 287-313.

14. Nauriya, A. (2006). The African Element in Gandhi. National Gandhi Museum.

15. Pradhan, R. (2008). Raj to Swaraj: A textbook on colonialism and nationalism in India. Macmillan India Ltd., New Delhi.

16. Prasad, R. (1957). Satyagraha in Champaran (Second revised edition), Ahmedabad: Navajivan Publication.

17. Rao, U. S. M. (2017). The Message of Mahatma Gandhi. Publications Division Ministry of Information & Broadcasting.

18. Tendulkar, D. G. (2016). Gandhi in Champaran: Publication Division Ministry of Information and Broadcasting.

19. Thomson, M. (1993). Gandhi and his Ashrams. Popolar Prakashan Pvt. Ltd.

20. Vasava, B. B. (2017). Bardoli Satyagraha and leadership of Vallabhbhai Patel. Research guru, 11(3). Retrieved from:http://www.researchguru.net/volume/Volume%201 1/Issue%203/RG11-BV-6.pdf. accessed on: 15.09.2019.

Reinterpreting Swaraj: From Gandhi's Era to the Digital Age

Dr Anju Sachan
Assistant Professor
Department of English
Jagran College of Arts, Science and Commerce, Kanpur
Email: anjusachan10@gmail.com

Abstract

The Gandhian idea of Swaraj, as articulated in his seminal work *Hind Swaraj,* presents a vision of self-rule rooted in ethical and spiritual autonomy, emphasizing moral and communal responsibility over mere political independence. "Hind Swaraj," written in 1909, serves as a manifesto of Gandhi's vision for India's independence and self-governance, known as Swaraj. Central to Gandhi's philosophy are the principles of nonviolence (Ahinsa), truth (Satya), and civil disobedience (Satyagraha). These tenets were not only foundational to his approach in resisting colonial rule but also in shaping the moral and ethical framework for post-independence India. In the chapter discussing 'true civilization,' it is described as 'mode of conduct which points out to man the path of duty'. Additionally, it is emphasized that moral behavior involves achieving 'mastery over one's mind'. The paper explores Gandhi's trenchant critique of modern civilization and industrialization, advocating for a return to traditional village-based economies and self-sufficient communities. This concept, which advocates for a decentralized and self-sufficient society, remains profoundly relevant in contemporary times. In an era marked by globalization, environmental degradation, and social inequities, Gandhi's principles of non-violence, sustainability and local governance offer critical insights for creating resilient and equitable communities. By examining the core principles of self-rule, self-discipline, and true civilization, the paper seeks to bridge Gandhi's philosophical ideals with contemporary societal challenges posed by the rise of social media and digital interconnectedness. Revisiting *Hind Swaraj* enables a deeper understanding of sustainable development, civic engagement, ethical leadership, and tutelage a framework to address modern challenges through the lens of Gandhian philosophy.

Keywords: Gandhian Swaraj, Self-rule, Sustainability, Non-violence, Local governance, Contemporary relevance

Introduction

The Gandhian idea of Swaraj, articulated in *Hind Swaraj*, transcends the conventional notion of political independence to embrace a comprehensive vision of self-rule. Gandhi's interpretation of Swaraj, which emphasizes moral, ethical, and spiritual autonomy, is deeply intertwined with his principles of non-violence (Ahinsa) and truth (satya). In the context of *Hind Swaraj*, Gandhi critiques modern civilization and advocates for a return to simpler, more self-reliant communities. This vision remains strikingly relevant in today's globalized world, which faces numerous challenges such as environmental degradation, social inequities, and the erosion of local cultures. The Gandhian idea of Swaraj as presented in *Hind Swaraj* and examines its relevance to contemporary issues, particularly in the realms of sustainability, local governance, and ethical leadership. As the world transitions into the digital age, characterized by pervasive social media and digital communication, it becomes imperative to reinterpret Gandhi's ideas to address current societal dynamics.

Hind Swaraj, written in 1909, is a foundational text in Gandhian thought. It was composed as a dialogue between the 'Editor' and the 'Reader,' a format that allowed Gandhi to address and refute the prevailing ideas of the time. In it,

Gandhi articulates his vision of Swaraj (self-rule) as not merely the attainment of political independence from British rule but as a profound moral and spiritual awakening of the individual and the community. Gandhi's concept of Swaraj is deeply philosophical, drawing from Indian tradition of dharma (duty) and the pursuit of truth (satya). He envisions Swaraj as a state where individuals govern themselves according to the principles of morality and righteousness, mastering over their own desires and actions, extending to the collective self-governance of communities. Gandhi asserts that true freedom is achieved not through external liberation but through inner discipline and ethical living.

In "Hind Swaraj," the outline of a new societal framework is introduced, offering a basic blueprint for an alternative civilization. The book is a critique of modern Western civilization, which Gandhi viewed as inherently violent, materialistic, and dehumanizing. Instead, he advocated for a return to a simpler, more self-reliant way of life, a society rooted in ethical and spiritual values. He had a vision of Swaraj and his concept of Swaraj was just like Rama Rajya or kingdom of God on the earth. (Nehru 1962). As society transitions into the digital age, characterized by pervasive social media and digital connectivity, it becomes essential to reinterpret Gandhi's principles to address contemporary challenges. This chapter also explores the relevance of Gandhi's ideas in the context of today's digital landscape.

Principles of Swaraj

Non-violence (Ahinsa): Non-violence, or Ahinsa, is a cornerstone of Gandhian thought. Gandhi's understanding of non-violence goes beyond the absence of physical violence to include non-harm in thought, word, and deed. He believed that a society practicing non-violence fosters harmony, reduces conflicts, and promotes genuine cooperation among its members. This principle is integral to the Gandhian idea of Swaraj, ensuring that self-rule is grounded in compassion and respect for all life. "Darkness cannot drive out darkness; only light can do that. Hate cannot drive out hate; only love can do that."(Harper & Row 1963)

In a practical sense, Gandhi's commitment to non-violence influenced his approach to political activism. The non-violent resistance movements he led, such as the Salt March and the Quit India Movement, demonstrated the power of collective, peaceful action in challenging oppression and injustice. These movements not only aimed at achieving political independence but also at fostering a culture of non-violence and ethical living.

In the globalized world, where conflicts both inter-state and intra-state are prevalent, Ahinsa offers a powerful framework for conflict resolution. Mahatma Gandhi's principle of *Swaraj* (self-rule) and non-violence remains profoundly relevant in today's era, particularly in the context of international conflicts like the Ukraine-Russia war and the rising tensions between global powers like the U.S. and China. Gandhi's vision of *Swaraj* emphasized not just political independence but also moral and ethical self-governance, which would discourage the aggressive expansionism and power struggles we see today. His advocacy for non-violence as a means to resolve conflicts or reconciliation as alternatives to violence and warfare offers a stark contrast to the devastation of modern warfare, suggesting that sustainable peace can only be achieved through dialogue, mutual respect, and a commitment to the well-being of all humanity. This principle is critical in peace-building efforts, as it encourages the resolution of disputes through peaceful means rather than through force.

Non-violence extends beyond human interactions to encompass our relationship with nature. In a time of ecological crisis, Ahinsa can inspire a commitment to environmental stewardship, advocating for sustainable practices that do not harm the earth. This principle aligns with the growing global emphasis on climate change mitigation and the protection of biodiversity. The tension between globalization and the principles of Swaraj highlights the need to balance global interconnectedness with local autonomy and self-reliance promoting a culture of peace and non-violence in both personal and political spheres. Contemporary societies can strive to integrate these principles by promoting global cooperation while preserving local cultures, economies, and governance systems. In this age, Gandhi's ideals serve as a crucial reminder that the true strength of a nation lies in its ability to pursue justice and harmony without resorting to violence.

Self-sufficiency: Gandhi advocated for self-sufficiency at both the individual and community levels. He believed that dependence on external resources and centralized power structures leads to exploitation and loss of autonomy. Instead, he promoted local production and consumption, decentralized governance, and the empowerment of local communities. His book 'Hind Swaraj' encapsulates this vision, emphasizing khadi (hand-spun cloth) and village industries, symbolizing economic independence and social equity. 'It is true, Bengal encourages the mill industry of Bombay. If Bengal had proclaimed a boycott of all machine-made goods, it would have been much better.' (Gandhi 1909)

Self-sufficiency, in Gandhi's view, is not merely economic but also cultural and social. He envisioned vibrant, self-reliant communities where individuals are connected to their local environment and traditions. This approach counters the alienation and homogenization brought about by industry-alization and globalization, fostering a sense of belonging and responsibility within communities. Gandhi wanted to deploy "the ascesis of patience and self-knowledge". (Mehta 2011).

The principle of self-sufficiency within the framework of Swaraj offers a powerful vision for contemporary society. It encourages communities and nations to build resilience, reduce dependency on external forces, and create sustainable, self-reliant systems. By applying this principle in areas such as the economy, agriculture, energy, and governance, societies can address some of the most pressing challenges of our time, including economic inequality, environmental degradation, and social injustice. In doing so, the principle of self-sufficiency remains as relevant today as it was during the struggle for independence, providing a blueprint for a more equitable and sustainable future.

Gandhi's emphasis on self-sufficiency and simplicity resonates with contemporary principles of sustainability. Modern civilization, characterized by consumerism and industrialization, has led to severe environmental degradation. Gandhi's vision of a self-reliant and decentralized society offers a viable alternative to the exploitative practices of modern economies. By promoting local production, sustainable agriculture, and minimal consumption, Gandhi's ideas provide a framework for achieving environmental sustainability.

The concept of "localization" in sustainable development echoes Gandhi's advocacy for local governance and self-sufficiency. Localization involves empowering local communities to produce their own food, energy, and goods, reducing dependence on global supply chains, and minimizing ecological footprints. This approach supports environmental sustainability and enhances community resilience and social equity.

One contemporary example is the organic farming movement in India, which promotes sustainable agricultural practices, aligns with Gandhi's advocacy for self-sufficiency and environmental stewardship. By encouraging farmers to adopt organic methods, reduce chemical inputs, and diversify crops, the movement seeks to create a more sustainable and resilient agricultural system.

Similarly, the global transition towards renewable energy sources, such as solar and wind power, echoes Gandhi's vision of decentralized and sustainable development. Community-led renewable energy projects, which provide clean energy while empowering local communities, exemplify the practical application of Gandhian principles in addressing modern environmental challenges.

Ethical Leadership: For Gandhi, true leadership is rooted in ethical behavior and selfless service. He believed that leaders should lead by example, embodying the values of truth, non-violence, and self-discipline. Ethical leadership, according to Gandhi, is essential for achieving Swaraj, as it inspires trust and fosters a culture of integrity and accountability.

The contemporary world faces a crisis of ethical leadership, with widespread corruption, dishonesty, and abuse of power undermining public trust in institutions. Gandhi's insistence on ethical behavior and selfless service as the hallmarks of true leadership offers a compelling antidote to this crisis. His example of leading by example and prioritizing the common good over personal gain is a powerful model for contemporary leaders.

Ethical leadership, grounded in principles of integrity, transparency, and accountability, is essential for addressing the complex challenges of today's world. By fostering a culture of ethical leadership, organizations and governments can rebuild trust, inspire collective action, and promote social cohesion.

The leadership of figures like Nelson Mandela and Martin Luther King Jr. exemplifies the enduring influence of Gandhian principles on ethical leadership. Both leaders, inspired by Gandhi's philosophy, championed non-violence, justice, and equality. Their commitment to ethical leadership and moral integrity had a profound impact on their respective movements for civil rights and social justice.

In the corporate world, initiatives such as the B Corp certification reflect a growing recognition of the importance of ethical leadership. B Corps are businesses that meet rigorous standards of social and environmental performance, accountability, and transparency. By prioritizing ethical practices and social responsibility, these companies embody the Gandhian ideal of leadership rooted in moral values.

Social Equity: Gandhi's critique of modern civilization includes a condemnation of the social inequalities perpetuated by industrialization and capitalism. He advocated for a society where resources are equitably distributed, and every individual has the opportunity to live with dignity. In today's world, where economic disparities and social injustices are rampant, Gandhi's principles of equity and justice are more relevant than ever.

The growing movement for social equity, encompassing issues such as income inequality, access to education, and healthcare, aligns with Gandhi's vision of a just society. Initiatives aimed at reducing poverty, empowering marginalized communities, and promoting fair trade can draw inspiration from Gandhian thought. By prioritizing the well-being of the most vulnerable, societies can move closer to achieving true Swaraj.

Organizations like SEWA (Self-Employed Women's Association) in India embody Gandhi's commitment to social equity and empowerment. SEWA supports the economic and social empowerment of marginalized women, reflecting Gandhi's vision of a society where everyone has the opportunity to thrive. Globally, the FairTrade movement aligns with Gandhian principles by promoting ethical production and equitable trade practices. Fair Trade initiatives ensure that producers receive fair wages and work in safe conditions, addressing the exploitative practices of conventional trade systems. This movement's focus on social justice and economic equity resonates with Gandhi's vision of a just and humane society.

Civic Engagement: Mahatma Gandhi's concept of 'Hind Swaraj' (Indian Home Rule) emphasizes self-governance, moral development, and active civic engagement. Civic engagement, in Gandhi's view, is essential for the realization of true Swaraj, which goes beyond mere political independence to include the moral and social empowerment of the individual and the community. Civic engagement ensures that individuals take responsibility for their actions and contribute to the welfare of society. 'The common people lived independently, and followed their agricultural occupation. They enjoyed true Home Rule.' (Gandhi 1909)

Gandhi's idea of Swaraj places significant emphasis on active civic engagement and participatory democracy. He believed that individuals should take responsibility for their communities and work collectively towards common goals. This vision of grassroots democracy is reflected in contemporary movements advocating for greater citizen participation in governance. The rise of community-based organizations, participatory budgeting, and grassroots activism demonstrates a growing recognition of the importance of civic engagement. These initiatives empower individuals to have a direct say in the decisions that affect their lives, fostering a sense of ownership and accountability. In cities like Porto Alegre, Brazil, and New York City, participatory budgeting allows residents to directly decide how public funds are allocated. He envisioned a decentralized form of government where local communities (villages) would be self-reliant and govern themselves. Civic engagement is crucial in this context, as it allows for the active participation of citizens in local governance, ensuring that decisions reflect the needs and values of the community. In present time, civic engagement remains essential for strengthening democratic institutions.

Gandhi's Enduring Ideals in a Changing World

In another chapter of the *Hind Swaraj* he examines the English educational system introduced in India and describes it as 'false education'. For him the basic aim of education should be to bring our senses under our control and to help imbibe ethical behaviour in our life. He attacks the newly emerged elite, a by-product of the Macaulay system of education, as they have enslaved India. He concludes his critique of modern civilization by comparing it to an *Upas* tree, a poisonous plant which destroys all life around it.

Elsewhere in *Hind Swaraj* he rejects the British thesis that India was never a nation. Rather it has always been a conglomerate of different creeds and communities. He asserts that our seers and sages laid the foundation of our national unity and Indian nationhood by establishing centres of pilgrimage on the four corners of India. In the process, they fired the imagination of our people with the idea of nationhood. Thus in *Hind Swaraj* Gandhi lays a real foundation of secular nationalism for which he lived and died for.

In the chapter discussing 'true civilization' from Mahatma Gandhi's "Hind Swaraj," it is described as a 'mode of conduct which points out to man the path of duty.' (Gandhi 1909) Additionally, it is emphasized that moral behavior involves achieving 'mastery over one's mind.' Relating this to today's generation, which is deeply engaged with social media and Instagram reels, we can see significant relevance. 'Control over the mind is alone necessary, and, when that is attained, man is free like the king of the forest'. (Gandhi 1909)

Social media platforms, including Instagram, often captivate users with a constant stream of content designed to entertain and engage. While this can be a source of connection and inspiration, it can also distract individuals from their duties and responsibilities. Gandhi's idea of 'true civilization' suggests that people should focus on behaviors "good conduct" that guide them towards fulfilling their obligations and living purposeful lives (Parel 2009).

Moreover, the concept of 'mastery over one's mind' is particularly pertinent in the context of social media. The incessant scrolling and the pursuit of likes and followers can lead to a lack of self-control and an overemphasis on external validation. Gandhi's teaching encourages the cultivation of self-discipline and mental resilience. For today's generation, this means consciously choosing how to engage with social media, setting boundaries, and prioritizing content that contributes to personal growth and well-being. Embracing Gandhi's vision in contemporary contexts allows us to navigate the complexities of modern life while staying true to the values of self-rule and moral integrity.

The Gandhian idea of Swaraj, as articulated in *Hind Swaraj*, offers a timeless and profound vision of self-rule that extends beyond political independence to encompass ethical, spiritual, and communal dimensions. The principles of Swaraj and Ahinsa are not just historical concepts but living ideals that can guide contemporary society toward more equitable, peaceful, and sustainable futures. In an era marked by environmental crises, social inequities, and a deficit of ethical leadership, Gandhi's principles of non-violence, self-sufficiency, and moral integrity provide invaluable insights for contemporary society. By revisiting *Hind Swaraj* and embracing its principles, we can address modern challenges and work towards creating a more just, sustainable, and compassionate world that upholds the dignity and rights of all people while fostering harmony with the environment. By applying Gandhi's principles, individuals can navigate the digital world more mindfully, ensuring that their online activities support their personal duties and foster inner strength rather than detracting from them. Gandhi's vision of

Swaraj remains a beacon of hope, guiding us towards a future where true freedom and self-rule are realized through ethical living and collective responsibility.

References:
1. Parel A. J. (2009). Ed. Hind Swaraj and Other Writings, Delhi, Cambridge University Press, New Delhi. p- 67.
2. Parekh, Bikhu. (1995). Gandhi's Political Philosophy, A Critical Examination, Delhi, Ajanta.
3. Gandhi, M. K., (1909). Ḥind Swaraj or Indian Home Rule. Navajivan Publishing House, Ahmedabad. https://www.jmu.edu/gandhicenter/_files/gandhiana-hindswaraj.pdf. p-37-65.
4. Gandhi, M. K. (1988). An Autobiography or The Story of My Experiments with Truth, Ahmedabad, Nava Jivan Publishing House.
5. Gavaskar, M. (2009). Gandhi's Hind Swaraj: Retrieving the sacred in the time of modernity. Economic and PoliticalWeekly,44(36),5-11.
www.jstor.org/stable/25663507
6. Harper & Row (1963). Strength of love: A collection of Kings writing. Oxford University Press p.37.
7. Iyer, R. N. (1983). The Moral and Political Thought of Mahatma Gandhi. Oxford University Press.
8. Mehta, U. S. (2011). 'Patience, Inwardness, and Self-Knowledge in Gandhi's Hind Swaraj', Public Culture, vol. 23, issue 2. p. 429
9. Nehru, J. L. (1962). The Discovery of India′, Bombay. p. 422
10. Kumarappa, J. C. (1945). Gandhian Economic Thought. Vora & Co. Publishers.
11. Prasad, Nageshwar. (1985). (ed) Hind Swaraj: A Fresh Look, New Delhi, Gandhian Peace Foundation.

12. Prabhu, R. K., & Rao, U. R. (!967). The Mind of Mahatma Gandhi. Navajivan Publishing House.
13. Narayan, Shriman (1968). The Selected Works of Mahatma Gandhi, Volume three: The Basic Works, Ahmedabad, Navajivan Publishing House.

Role of Gandhiji's view on Swaraj in Social Change

Dr. Dhananjoy Mahato
Assistant Professor
Department of Philosophy
Murshidabad Adarsha Mahavidyalaya
Islampur, Murshidabad.West Bengal.
Email: pintumahatopurulia@gmail.com

Abstract

Over the ages, all the ancient Aryas - Sages, Munis, Monks, saints, of the Indian subcontinent have appeared and understood the nature of the world and life and have protected and carried the precious Indian civilization and culture by showing different ways or paths for the welfare of the country and nation as well as humanity. It emphasizes how M.K.Gandhi, a prominent modern Indian thinker and politician,Philosophers upheld these traditions even under British colonial rule, focusing on non-violence, truth, and moral integrity.The abstract stresses the relevance of Gandhi's ideals, particularly his concepts of "Swaraj" (self-rule) and "Satyagraha" (non-violent resistance), in addersssing the devaluation of humanity and cultural erosion in today's technologically advanced yet morally challenged society.The need to reintroduce these values to counter the negative effects of blind competition, social inequality, and the degradation of natural resources is underscored. Gandhi's vision of an equitable society free from divisions and untouchability is portrayed as a vital guide for modern human values, emphasizing the Vedic principle of "Vasudhaiva Kutumbakam" that means, the whole world is our family. Keeping this Vedic educational thought and social reform intact, Gandhi also incarnated the concept of self-control and self-realization called "Swaraj" (Self Rule) as a form of social change.He realized that the society would be one where truth and non-violence should be established in life to form an equal society. Where there will be no high-low rich-poor communal and religious divide, everyone in the society will enjoy the right to everything and the right to wealth equally. His Swaraj thought was a social image based on non-violent love and Satyagraha. In my prepared essay this great ideal of Gandhiji seems to be very necessary in view of present human values.

Keywords: Swaraj, Satyagraha, Ahinsha, Vasudhaiv Kutumbakam, Humanity, Degradation

Introduction

Etymologically the word 'Swaraj' (Self Rule) means self i.e. own and raj means rule or better to say good governance. The word swaraj was first used by Swami Dayananda Saraswati. Then Bal Gangadhar Tilak declared that "Swaraj is my birthright" in 1916 while founding the Home Rule League. Mahatma Gandhi first said in 1920 that "Swaraj will be formed for my India for the Indians.", which would be formed on the basis of adult suffrage. Gandhiji here articulated the concept of Swaraj. He said that Swaraj means a strong government based on the needs and aspirations of the people. Swaraj is the rule of the people, especially the 'Swaraj of the poor', which inspires the emancipation or freedom of the poor and emphasizes decentralization of power.

So Swaraj's major is self-governance or self-control or self-governance. The term swaraj means the rule of the people to overcome this self-determining social condition. Gandhiji's idea of swaraj was not limited to achieving independence in the political sphere. He said "Swaraj of my dream is poor man's swaraj" This swaraj does not mean any religious distinction.... This swaraj is for the good of all. By swaraj he did not mean freedom from foreign rule or independence, he meant swaraj to establish a homeland. Swaraj is complete freedom in all aspects, social, political, cultural etc. Real Swaraj will be established when all the human clans of the country will be fully inspired by indigenous thoughts and ideas. There will be indigenous management in everything from education, civilization, culture and clothing. We can see some of its influence in the modern India plan. Swaraj is not only an external management but also an inner aspect of Swaraj. This inner aspect of Swaraj is its spirituality. To bring about self-realization through the full development of spiritual consciousness in man. And for this self-realization, it is necessary to follow the path of truth and non-violence, because Gandhiji thought that only through the path of truth and non-violence can there be self-realization, and self-realization can make people realize their full freedom, it is through this self-realization that the meaning of Gandhiji's word Swaraj lies. Helped me stand on my own feet and realize my true nature. **In reference to the Swaraj in the journal named " Young India"- "It has been stated that The Swaraj of my…. our…dream recognise no race or religious distinction. Nor is it to be the monopoly of the lettered person nor yet of moneyed men. Swaraj is to for all, including the farmer, but emphatically including the maimed, the blind, the starving toiling millions"** He meant by this line that the whole of India should be initiated into the mantra "atmavat sarvabhuteshu, sarbe bhavantu sukhin: sarbesantu sukura" and forget the differences between people and embrace everyone. When the people of all communities rule the country together, the social system established by this justice will be Hind Swaraj. Gandhiji wanted a form of governance where the majority of people would devote themselves to the national interest, striving for the betterment of the country and the nation. Full swaraj will be established when working and the necessaries of life are enjoyed equally by both the rich and the poor, with a patriotic attitude towards all matters of national welfare, even personal gain above loss.

Gandhiji said, "I will try to build an India where even the poorest man will feel that it is his country and I am fully involved in its creation." He believed that swaraj would be formed on the basis of public opinion and democracy. He wanted to establish swaraj in a vision where even the least man would have a role, freedom and right to all resources. Gandhiji laid great importance on the character of the individual for the formation of Swaraj and he said that the character of the individual should be pure whether in his own life or public life. There will be characters where "Udarcharitam Vasudhaiv Kutumbakam" will be published. Being steadfast in the religion of truth - non-violence, Sarvodaya will adopt the way or the means. Every person in the country will be blessed with spiritual strength, a conviction will arise in the heart of the individual that is "Sarvajan Hitaya Sarjana Sukhaya" Swaraj will be the welfare of all and the rise of all.

Gandhi's swaraj focused on the welfare of the poor and encouraged decentralization of power through village swaraj. He believed that 'the best state is that which governs least'. He said that if the society is run by a majority community, it will increase the communal agitation and disorder in the society. Therefore, he wanted a swaraj where the people of all communities would rule the country together, forgetting the communal differences, then the rule of justice and the social system of justice would be established. When we are freed from religious dogma and learn to accept humanity as the best religion, then this spirit of true swaraj will be established in us. By the call to go back to the village, he meant that a bond of kinship would develop between every citizen of the country when they were bound to each other. He also considered decentralization of power as an essential political step in self-governance, just as everyone's participation was essential in the democracy he sought to govern the state and society. He named the decentralized state power "Gram Raj". To him, this village raj or swaraj should not exclude the city, but should exclude the domination of the city, a civilized society in which they would devote themselves to the service of the people as a complement to each other. He realized that through centralization, governance is never in the hands of a handful of people, which is reflected in autocratic rule. Therefore, he decentralized power and governed from the lower levels of society to maintain unity among all classes of people. It will help to move the society towards a better and better society only through the mutual sense of unity among people. Gandhiji realized that the various provinces or territories could not be self-sufficient unless decentralization of authority took place. Decentralization policy can make every region of India self-sufficient in every village. Each person in the village will equally enjoy the production of food items essential for the livelihood of the villagers. There will be no high-level differences in the village society, they will be able to establish their own opinions about their own happiness, prosperity, justice, injustice, good and bad, etc. This swaraj system of Gandhi's thought could re-establish the Indian tradition.

Even though nearly 100 years of independence have passed, we still have not fully established the country's swaraj. The day we can establish swaraj, self-reliant India will be established.The recent formulation of the National Education Policy 2020 will help India re-establish itself as a socially, financially and culturally prosperous nation by providing timely and better education.The moral, spiritual, cultural and social heritage of the ancient Indian civilization which was famous all over the world, the irreparable damage done to the cultural heritage of India during the British period and before, may be if we return to India and the glory of India in the thinking of Gandhi and other thinkers. If we try to bring it, surely we will be able to sit on the best seat of civilization again.

Before British rule, India was one of the largest economies in the world. To strengthen the economy, it is important to promote self reliant businesses and villages as well as total national contribution. It is also necessary to reform the judicial system, ensure equality for all classes and regulate the policy of appeasement. Efforts should be made to eradicate poverty and unemployment with strong determination and strong will.

Gandhi viewed Swaraj for the country as not merely political freedom from the clutches of British rule but more substantive including freedom of each individual to regulate their own lives without harming others. Swaraj is government by many and not acquisition of power by a handful few. Realization of Swaraj is a difficult path to tread as it requires fearlessness, patience and perseverance of the people wherein patriotism and sacrifice reigns supreme. It empowers the masses through education to regulate and resist authority when required and encourages freedom of speech. Swaraj is never granted but has to be earned through morality and sacrifice.

References:
1. Bandyopadhyay Nikhilesh: Samakalin Bharatiya Darshan Sadesh,101C, Vivekananda Road, Kolkata-700006, 15/8/2005.
2. Ghosh Govinda Charan, Samakalin Bharatiya Darshan .pub-Progressive Publishers, 37A, College Street, Kolkata -700073, Oct 2020.
3. Bhattacharya Sujit Kumar: Mahatma Gandhi - page no.49 to 60. Progressive Publisher, July 2011
4. Choudhary Ranjit: Fragments of Gandhian Mind. (Some Essay on Gandhian Thought) Published by progressive

publishers, 37A College Street Kolkata 73,2nd October 2002.Page no-101

5. Lahiri Ashutosh: Gandhi in Indian politics; A critical review. Published by Firma KLM Private limited, 257B Bipin Behari Ganguly Street, Kolkata 700012,1976(First Edition) Page no:54-56

6. Gandhi M. K, An autobiography or the story of my experiments with truth, Published by Rupa publication India PVT. LTD -2011.7/6 ansary road, dardang new Delhi 110002. ninth edition -2016.

7. Dr.Bhattacharya Samarendra & Mukhopadhyay Goutam, Samakalin Bharatiya Darshan. Pub-Progressive Publishers,37A, College Street, Kolkata -700073, 2021.

8. Munsi Ramesh Chandra & Syanal Padma, Samaj Darshan o Rashtra Darshan, Baikuntha Book House

9. Bhattacharya Samarendra, Samaj Darshan o Rashtra Darshan, Pub-Book Syndicate Private limited ,35, College Street, Kolkata -700073, July 2009.

Gandhi's Green Vision: Timeless Wisdom for a Sustainable Future

Dr. Renu Pandey
Assistant Professor
Department of History
Babasaheb Bhimrao Ambedkar (A Central) University
Lucknow
Email: renupandeybbau21@gmail.com

Abstract

The world is facing an unprecedented environmental crisis, threatening the very foundation of human existence. The relentless pursuit of economic growth, technological advancements, and consumerism has led to devastating consequences, including climate change, biodiversity loss, and ecosystem degradation. This essay argues that a fundamental transformation in our economic paradigm is necessary, prioritizing qualitative development over quantitative growth and recognizing the intrinsic value of natural resources. Drawing inspiration from Mahatma Gandhi's philosophy of simple living, self-sufficiency, and reverence for nature, we can adopt sustainable practices, reduce waste, and preserve natural habitats. The Indian tradition of revering nature, as embodied in Gandhi's ideas, offers a powerful alternative to the Western approach of dominating and exploiting nature. The essay emphasizes the urgent need for collective action, sustainable practices, and a paradigm shift in our relationship with the natural world to ensure a resilient and thriving planet for future generations. Gandhi critiqued the Western notion of conquering nature, advocating for harmonious coexistence instead. He championed Swadeshi, promoting the judicious use of local resources without exploiting nature. Gandhi believed in minimizing wants, living simply, and maintaining ecological balance. His philosophy offers a solution to the contemporary environmental crisis, which is largely man-made, including ozone depletion, global warming, and natural disasters. By embracing Gandhi's principles, we can restore the delicate balance between humanity and nature, ensuring a sustainable future. His wisdom is a timely reminder to adopt a more mindful and sustainable approach to nature.

Keywords: Sustainability, Ecological Balance, Minimalism, Environmentalism, Simple Living, Mindful Consumption.

Introduction

As the world grapples with the far-reaching consequences of environmental degradation, embracing sustainable practices, renewable energy, eco-friendly technologies, and conscious consumption becomes crucial. By adopting a circular economy, reducing waste, and preserving natural habitats, we can mitigate the effects of climate change, protect biodiversity, and ensure a resilient, thriving planet for future generations. The time for action is now – individual and collective efforts can drive meaningful change and create a sustainable future.

If our ancestors had exploited nature with the same reckless abandon that we do today, the delicate balance of the ecosystem would have been disrupted, and the very foundation of our existence would have been threatened, leaving us to face the dire consequences of a depleted and degraded natural world.

This ego-centric approach has led to a commodification of nature, where the intrinsic value of the earth and its resources is overshadowed by their utility and profit potential, further estranging us from the harmonious coexistence that is essential for the well-being of both humans and the planet.

In the words of J. Krishnamurti, "That sensitivity does not come in the mere hanging of a few pictures, or in painting a tree, or putting a few flowers in your hair; sensitivity comes only when this utilitarian outlook is put aside". However, in this capitalist/consumerist world where everything is looked at from its utilitarian perspective, nature is bound to bear the brunt. Ozone depletion, rising sea level, and natural catastrophes have increased in recent years and still no concrete and concerted effort is being taken globally to address this issue despite many international and national level summits.

In his classic book, "Small is Beautiful", E. F. Schumacher, a German-British statistician, and economist, wrote: "Modern man does not experience himself as a part of nature but as an outside force destined to dominate and conquer it. He even talks of a battle with nature, forgetting that if he won the battle, he would find himself on the losing side". The true cost of development has been revealed, and the planet is bearing the brunt of our environmental neglect, suffering from rampant pollution and degradation. It's a stark reminder that our pursuit of comfort and convenience must be balanced with a deeper respect for the delicate harmony of nature. The cumulative impact of these global and localized environmental issues is staggering, and if left unchecked, poses an existential threat to the health, security, and survival of our planet, underscoring the urgent need for collective action, sustainable practices, and a paradigm shift in our relationship with the natural world.

Additionally, the population explosion has put a huge strain on Earth's natural resources. While technological growth has immensely aided our civilization's advancement, it has also adversely affected the environment globally. The uncontrolled greed and reckless use of technology is the core of environmental degradation and it's causing pressure on earth's finite resources.

Highlighting these issues, Joseph Stiglitz in his book, "Making Globalization Work" stated how the relentless pursuit of economic growth and profit in Western nations has led to the exploitation and degradation of the environment, perpetuating a false dichotomy between economic development and environmental protection, and undersco-ring the need for a more balanced and sustainable approach to globalization that prioritizes both human well-being and the health of the planet. This conundrum highlights the need for a fundamental transformation in our economic paradigm, one that prioritizes qualitative development over quantitative growth, recognizes the intrinsic value of natural resources and ecosystem services, rather than treating them as mere commodities to be exploited for short-term gains, and seeks to balance human well-being with the planet's ecological limits.

If we make a comparative analysis of the Western and Indian approaches, we notice that in the Western world, the emphasis has been on how to control and win over nature whereas Indian tradition believes in having proximity with nature. Indian philosophical tradition believes that nature is the source of life. According to Atharvaveda, "Mata Bhumih Putohum Prithivya' means the earth is the mother and I am the son of this earth. In other words, we have had a tradition to revere and respect nature but with the onset of globalization, the exploitation of nature has increased manifold.

Gandhi: The Original Environmentalist

While talking about Gandhi and the Environment, we have to keep in mind that the word "environment" is not found in Gandhi's writings. It first appeared in English. Although the word environment may be new, the consciousness associated with it is not new and it has been part of Indian tradition and culture. We find its manifestation in Gandhi. In Indian tradition, we pray to Mother Nature. Against this backdrop, let us discuss Gandhi and his ideas vis-a-vis the environment. Gandhi's philosophy of simple living, self-sufficiency, and reverence for the natural world, as reflected in his concepts of 'Satyagraha' and 'Swadeshi', implicitly embodied environmental principles, foreshadowing modern environmentalism's emphasis on sustainability, localism, and the intrinsic value of nature, even if he did not explicitly frame his ideas in contemporary environmental terms. He once said, "that earth, air, land, and water are not our property inherited from our ancestors. They are the heritage of our children. They have to be handed over to future generations in the same conditions as we have received them".

This statement reflects his approach towards nature. Even 76 years after his death, Mahatma Gandhi and his ideas remain relevant. In other words, the whole world is getting inspired by his thoughts and ideas in one way or the other. His contribution in the form of Swadeshi, swaraj, Truth, and Non-Violence is globally known through his exemplary life and philosophical musings, he embodied a profound understanding of the interconnectedness of human existence and the natural world, inspiring a quiet revolution in thought and action, and leaving behind a legacy that continues to influence contemporary environmental thought and sustainable living practices. Gandhi's pragmatic wisdom and grassroots approach to sustainable living, though not rooted in modern scientific ecology, intuitively grasped the interconnectedness of human and natural systems, earning him the moniker 'apostle of applied human ecology' as his ideas and practices continue to inspire and inform contemporary environmental thought, particularly in the realms of eco-philosophy, sustainable development, and environmental justice. Gandhi's prescient wisdom, echoed in his iconic statement, continues to resonate with eerie relevance, as we grapple with the devastating consequences of unchecked consumption, climate change, and ecological degradation, underscoring the urgent need to reexamine our values and embrace a more equitable, sustainable, and compassionate relationship with the natural world.

He was deeply influenced by Adolph Just's book "Return to Nature", which reinforced his opinion that to lead a decent life, a man must learn to share it with all the creatures-plants, birds, animals, and the entire ecosystem.

Gandhi's view towards nature was shaped by both Indian and Western traditions/scholars. He was deeply inspired by Jainism as well as Hinduism. Both treat nature as a living entity and give equal reverence to all life forms. "He also drew on several Western thinkers, who were not wholly against the modernist project but romantically cherished the pre-industrial order. For example, John Ruskin was highly critical of industrialization as it had destroyed the harmonious relationship humans had with nature. Henry David Thoreau, the American poet and naturalist, whose essay on civil disobedience had influenced Gandhi, believed that nature could exist without humans. He was also influenced by Edward Carpenter who wanted to lead a life that was simple and close to nature. What is special about all these thinkers is a kind of romanticism about nature and a general distaste for industrial civilization and urbanization. We also have statements of Gandhi expressing similar romanticism".

Additionally, "Gandhi had been a major influence on several writers like E F Schumacher and deep ecologist, Arne Naess, who called his brand of environmentalism 'biospheric egalitarianism' and pointed out that he was influenced by the Mahatma's metaphysics". Petra Kelly, founder of the Green Party in Germany was greatly influenced by Gandhi. Gandhi has been, and continues to be, the major influence on the environmental movements in India. There is Gandhian tradition in the Indian environmental movement as it has drawn inspiration from Gandhi. He left an indelible impression on the Indian environmental movement. Leaders of the environmental movement were inspired by Gandhi and his vision of social change. It emerged as a response of the people to safeguard their existence. Chipko Movement, Narmada Bachao Movement, Silent Valley Movement, etc. are the largest environmental movements in Asia and its leaders like Chandi Prasad Bhatt, Sundalal Bahuguna, Medha Patekar, and Baba Amte were inspired by Gandhi. Similarly, environmental historians such as Vandana Shiva, Anil Agarwal, Madhav Gadgil, and Ramachandra Guha have acknowledged their debt to Gandhi's ideas. Guha has described him as the "single most important influence on the environmental movement". Prof. Guha describes him as an early environmentalist.

The concern of Gandhi about the environment, urbanization, and mechanization was evident in his speeches, writings, and messages. With remarkable foresight, Gandhi warned against the pitfalls of unchecked industrialization, highlighting the dangers of exploiting nature's resources without regard for the consequences and advocating for a more harmonious relationship between human progress and the natural world, his words now echoing prophetically in the face of climate change, pollution, and ecological degradation. He was an early critic of the dehumanizing character of modern industrial civilization. Gandhi's prophetic vision recognized that the relentless march of mechanization and industrialization would not only displace traditional crafts and livelihoods, but also ravage the natural world, leaving in its wake a trail of pollution, resource depletion, and ecological devastation, a warning that remains eerily relevant as we grapple with the consequences of unchecked technological progress and environmental degradation. He stated in Young India, "God forbid that India should ever take to industrialism after the manner of the West". Gandhi's critique of unbridled industrialization laid bare its dark underbelly, exposing how the insatiable quest for wealth and material pleasure has led to the exploitation of the earth's resources, the erosion of traditional ways of life, and the imperilment of the very web of life, his words serving as a clarion call to reexamine our values and seek a more sustainable, equitable, and harmonious relationship between humanity and the natural world. He was equally against urbanization. For Gandhi, "India lives in villages and he believed that urbanization may prove suicidal for Indian villages and its residents".

Gandhi's vision of 'production by the masses' offered a radical alternative to the dominant paradigm of mass production, prioritizing decentralized, local, and small-scale economic activity that not only promotes self-sufficiency and community resilience but also harmonizes human endeavor with the natural environment, paving the way for a more regenerative and sustainable economic system that balances human needs with the earth's ecological limits.

With uncanny prescience, Gandhi's Hind Swaraj, penned in 1909, sounded the alarm on the catastrophic consequences of unchecked industrialization and modernization, warning of the devastating impact on the natural world, and urging a radical shift towards a more sustainable, self-sufficient, and eco-friendly path, his prophetic words now resonating with eerie relevance as humanity confronts the existential threats of climate change, ecological collapse, and planetary degradation. He criticized modern civilization as satanic and said that it is the machinery that has impoverished India.

Minimalism

Gandhi practiced and preached minimalism, believing that one should only possess what is truly necessary. For Gandhi, the human race has survived for centuries without any scientific advancement and it happened just because mankind during the ancient times used to live near nature and they used to respect nature whereas in the modern world, excessive emphasis is on overexploiting nature. Gandhi's philosophy of simple living and self-sufficiency starkly contrasts with the relentless pursuit of material progress and consumerism that defines modern civilization, as he advocated for the reduction of wants to align with the natural limits of the earth, whereas modern society perpetuates the myth of infinite growth and the endless multiplication of desires, fueling ecological degradation and social discontent. Modern civilization believes that everything is meant for consumption forgetting in the process that natural resources like land, water, flora, and fauna are limited. Gandhi's emphasis on self-sufficiency, minimalism, and mindful consumption offers a powerful antidote to the rampant consumerism and unsustainable practices that have pushed our planet to the brink, inviting us to reevaluate our priorities, redefine our notion of progress, and cultivate a more mindful and regenerative relationship with the natural world.

Gandhi's holistic vision and critique of industrial civilization's disconnection from nature and human well-being offers a prophetic warning, urging us to reconsider our values and embrace a more integrated, equitable, and sustainable approach to living, one that harmonizes economic, social and environmental spheres, and recognizes the intrinsic limits and interconnectedness of our world.

Gandhi's wisdom cautions us that the relentless pursuit of material prosperity and comfort can lead to a life of emptiness, disconnection, and ecological degradation, and that true freedom and fulfillment can only be achieved by embracing a simpler, more mindful way of living, one that balances physical comfort with spiritual growth and harmony with nature.

Gandhi's pragmatic approach to ecological living acknowledges the inevitability of some impact on the natural world but urges us to adopt a mindful and restrained approach, taking only what is necessary, and striving to minimize harm, thereby cultivating a sense of reciprocity, respect, and responsibility towards the earth and its resources, and ensuring a more sustainable and harmonious coexistence. Gandhi's vision of a harmonious relationship between humans and nature is rooted in a profound understanding of the natural order, where hard work, self-sufficiency, and moderation are the guiding principles, and the relentless pursuit of wealth and accumulation is seen as a violation of the fundamental laws of nature, leading to suffering, inequality, and ecological degradation.

This also makes Gandhi relevant in contemporary times when we see on the one hand the number of billionaires is rising and wealth is getting concentrated in their hands and on the other hand inequality is widening and millions of people around the world are struggling for two squares meal per day. This ever-growing inequality is highlighted by Thomas Piketty in his magnum opus "The Economics of Inequality" in detail. Gandhi had long suggested in his trusteeship model that one should treat oneself as a trustee of one's wealth rather than the owner.

From a Gandhian perspective, the current environmental crisis is a stark reminder of the consequences of prioritizing economic growth and material prosperity over ecological harmony and social equity, and calls for a radical transformation of our values and systems, one that seeks to uplift the entire web of life, rather than merely treating the symptoms of a deeper malaise, and recognizes the intrinsic interconnectedness of human well-being, social justice, and environmental sustainability.

Gandhi's reverence for nature was not about romanticizing the wild or seeking to escape into it, but about recognizing the intricate web of life that binds us all, and living by that understanding, as evident in his simple, self-sufficient ashram life, where humans, animals, and plants coexisted in harmony, and even the most feared creatures, like snakes, were treated with respect and compassion, reflecting his profound belief in the sacredness and interconnectedness of all living beings.

He conveyed the value of conserving resources for future generations and asked for judicious use of natural resources. Through his championing of decentralized, village-based economies and technologies, Gandhi embodied a pioneering spirit of ecological wisdom, recognizing the intrinsic value of local self-sufficiency, human-scale production, and intimate connection with the natural world, and foreshadowing the modern concepts of sustainable development, environmental stewardship, and bioregionalism, which prioritize the health of the planet and the well-being of all living beings. Gandhi's skepticism towards technological progress as a measure of true progress resonated with E. F. Schumacher's philosophy of 'intermediate technology', which prioritizes human-scale, decentralized, and labor-intensive technologies like the Charkha, over large-scale, capital-intensive, and labor-replacing ones, emphasizing the importance of preserving human dignity, community, and environmental sustainability in the face of technological advancement.

With remarkable foresight, Gandhi anticipated the ecological consequences of unchecked industrialization and modernization, recognizing the inherent tension between nature's limits and humanity's aspirations, and thus, his ideas on simple living, self-sufficiency, and local economies, though formulated decades ago, remain strikingly relevant to contemporary environmental debates, offering a prophetic warning and a wisdom-filled guide for navigating the sustainability challenges of our times. Indeed, he was "an early critic of the dehumanizing character of modern industrial civilization".

The Modern Relevance of Gandhi's Timeless Wisdom

Gandhi's notion of respect for nature, simple living, self-sufficiency has become pertinent in contemporary times. Embracing Gandhi's timeless wisdom and principles offers a beacon of hope in our quest for a sustainable future, providing a framework for transformative change that prioritizes simplicity, self-sufficiency, and harmony with nature, and empowering us to mitigate the environmental crisis through collective action, conscious choice, and a renewed commitment to living in balance with the natural world, ensuring a healthier, more peaceful and regenerative existence for generations to come.

When the world is now under serious environmental threat, concern is being shown globally. Right from Stockholm to Rio to Kyoto, the threadbare discussion is going on as to how to control the situation, and nothing concrete has happened so far. Had we followed the path shown by Gandhi, things would have been different.

Gandhi was a strong critique of the Western notion of man's conquest of nature as it would lead to man's estrangement from nature's order. Rather, "he believed in harmonious coexistence with nature and all living beings. He was a champion of Swadeshi which suggests that locally available resources be used without being aggressive against nature. He believed in the judicious use of natural resources and not in the destruction of the beauty of nature, forests, and rivers".

Gandhi ji was in favor of making judicious use of natural resources so that ecological balance is maintained. He believed in the minimization of wants. His prescription for a simple life prevents unlimited consumption and endless exploitation of natural resources. Mankind is now paying the price for not paying heed to what Gandhi said. The majority of our contemporary environmental crisis is man-made be it ozone depletion, global warming, rising sea levels, air and water-borne diseases, landslides, flood and famine, etc. They all are the byproduct of excessive and haphazard use of nature.

We find a solution to our entire contemporary environmental crisis in Gandhi. He believed that humankind has survived for centuries while being near nature but of late, due to excessive and over-exploitative use of nature, the relation between man and environment has deteriorated beyond repair.

Conclusion

The world's environmental crisis requires a comprehensive damage control approach if we are to maintain a peaceful and healthy existence and Gandhi's environmental philosophy offers a profound and holistic vision for a sustainable future, one that seamlessly integrates ecological wisdom, social justice, and personal transformation. By embracing his principles of simple living, self-sufficiency, and moral restraint, we can foster a more harmonious relationship with nature, prioritize human well-being, and cultivate a more regenerative and equitable world. As we navigate the complexities of the environmental crisis, Gandhi's timeless wisdom reminds us that a better future is possible, one that is rooted in the timeless values of compassion, reciprocity, and reverence for the natural world.

Gandhi's enduring legacy as a champion of ecological sustainability and social justice continues to inspire contemporary environmental movements, from eco-villages and permaculture initiatives to climate justice activism and sustainable development programs, offering a powerful reminder that a more equitable, peaceful, and regenerative world is within reach. Time magazine in its 9th April, 2007 issue published 51 methods to save the world from global warming and the 51st method is limited consumption and simple living. Through the growing recognition of Gandhi's ecological wisdom, the Western world is tacitly acknowledging the limitations of its own industrial and consumerist paradigm, and seeking a more sustainable and equitable path forward, one that echoes Gandhi's call for a simpler, more self-sufficient, and nature-centered way of living, a testament to the enduring relevance and universal appeal of his philosophy. "Earth provides enough to satisfy every man's need, but not every man's greed". This quote highlights the distinction between need and greed, emphasizing that the earth's resources are sufficient to meet our basic needs, but not our excessive desires. However, it underscores the importance of living simply, consuming mindfully, and recognizing the limits of the natural world.

References:

1. Gandhi, M. K. (1928, Dec 20). Young India.
2. Guha, R. C. (1998). Mahatma Gandhi and Environmental Movement in India, in Arne Kalland and Gerard Persoon (ed.), Environmental Movement in India. Nordic Institute of Asian Studies & Routledge, London.
3. Khoshoo T. N. (1995). Mahatma Gandhi: An Apostle of Applied Human Ecology. TERI. New Delhi.
4. Moolakkattu, J. N. (2019, Oct 1). Mahatma Gandhi and the Environment. TERI.
https://www.teriin.org/article/mahatma-gandhi-and-environment
5. Moolakkattu, J. S. (2020, Oct.3). Gandhi and Environment, Daily Chhattisgarh.
https://dailychhattisgarh.com/article-details.php?article=57427&path_article=11
6. The Statesman (2022, Oct 23). A Gandhian Future, The Statesman.
https://www.google.com/amp/s/www.thestatesman.com/opinion/a-gandhian-future-1503124553.html/amp
7. Vyas, K. G. (2020, Jan.7), Gandhi's Contemplation on Nature. Indiawaterportal.
https://hindi.indiawaterportal.org/articles/gaandhai-kaa-parakartai-cainatana)

Eco-Development Debates with Special Reference to Gandhi

Dr. Manisha Misra
Assistant Professor,
Department of Political Science,
Vasanta College for Women Rajghat, Varanasi
Email: polsciencemanishamisra@vasantakfi.ac.in

Abstract

"Prithiwi Shanti, Aakash Shanti, Vanaspati Shanti" is the prayer we offer in our tradition to protect nature. In the 21st century, we find that the "anthropocentric" model is replacing the "eco-centric" model, which is detrimental to mankind and paves the way for environmental disasters such as ozone depletion, global warming, green house gases (GHG) emissions, climate change and others. At the global level, several initiatives have been taken against this non-traditional security threat. The principle of common but differentiated responsibilities and respective capabilities denotes that developing countries, such as India, have no obligation to reduce GHG emissions. Most industrial *countries* are expected under the convention to have binding commitments to reduce their emissions for the sake of humanity. On the other, they are putting pressure on developing nations to take the initiative. In this scenario, the Gandhian view of the environment becomes very relevant. The philosophy of simple living and high thinking could save mankind from the invasion of the consumerist approach in the present time. The world has enough resources to fulfil our necessities but cannot satisfy the greedy nature of the people, everyone has to realize this fact. Against this background, the present chapter deals with the various facets of eco-development debates along with the Gandhian viewpoint of tackling the environmental crisis and adopting an "eco-centric" approach in its true sense.

Keywords: Eco-Centric, Environment, Sustainable, Development, Growth, Economy

Introduction

The study of the environment is a story of a relationship which mankind has with nature. The three fundamental resources of nature land, water and air are potentially powerful living constituents of the environment because they are habitats to an innumerable variety of life forms both big and the microscopic. Environmental protection is the base of our survival. But what we find is that due to excess stress on blind development and economic advancement, we are neglecting the essential safeguards for our mother-earth. As a result, human beings and other species are facing the adverse effects of climate change, global warming, environmental disasters and other calamities.

One analyzes environmental degradation because mankind has pursued its advancement at the cost of these other life forms and as a result fallen into a trap from where its survival has become threatened. Environmental awareness and concerns emerged in the late 1960s and since the 1970s. Thereafter, a wide range of agreements, institutions and regimes for international ecological governance have developed gradually. The global environmental debate is often seen as a debate between developed and developing countries on issues of economic growth versus environmental sustainability. The primary challenge of the twenty-first century is to shape a pattern of development to promote sustainability that includes preserving biodiversity and preventing damaging climate change. The huge size of the world's population is now seriously being realized on the ecosystem. Damaged sea, stratospheric ozone depletion and climate change are major global challenges arising from atmospheric pollution worldwide. The impacts are global and the challenges can only be sorted out through cooperation on a world level. Everyone has to understand that environmental protection and economic development are the two sides of the same coin. We cannot separate them. Global eco-development debate-related dialogue is tilted towards developed countries at the cost of developing nations. The eco-development debates are intimately linked to the dynamics of political decision-making and economic process. A better alternative could be adopting the Gandhian vision of the environment for protecting the earth from a consumerist approach and saving the world from further environmental crisis. The present chapter delves into Gandhi's theoretical and realistic position concerning the environment and sustainable practices. It emphasizes their pertinence in dealing with the present-day ecological and developmental challenges by reexamining Gandhi's insights.

Objectives

➢ To examine how globally environment is facing severe challenges in many forms and the wide range of agreements, institutions and regimes that have been initiated at the international level as coping mechanisms for protecting the ecosystem.
➢ To comprehend the politics behind the global environmental protection-oriented negotiations and the challenges in implementing the concept of sustainable development.
➢ To contextualize the Gandhian vision of the environment for coping with the challenges of environmental disasters.

Environmental Challenges

Some of the major environmental challenges of the contemporary world could be categorized as follows:

- Chronic shortage of food.
- Global warming: Greenhouse effect, deforestation, Problems of biodiversity.
- Reduction in the ozone layer: use of chemicals like Chlorofluorocarbons (CFCs).

- Depletion of natural resources and fossil fuels: Coal, petroleum and gas extraction.
- Soil degradation and erosion.
- Atmospheric Pollution: sewage, oil spills, dumping of waste products into the sea, acid rain and climate change.
- Omission of sulphur dioxide by one state will be carried by winds and waters as acid rain on other states.
- Unsustainable agricultural practices.
- Exploitation of global commons: oceans, deep sea bed, atmosphere and outer space.

Global Environmental Negotiations and Eco-Development Debates

The United Nations Conference on the Environment (June 1972) in Stockholm was a major step in the direction of raising global environmental consciousness. It was the first event where the political, social and economic challenges of the ecosystem were understood at an intergovernmental level with a perspective of taking concrete steps in terms of policy at ground level. The most important result of this conference was the creation of the United Nations Environment Programme (UNEP) for global negotiations.

The second wave of the global environment movement since the 1980s produced an interest in comprehending the economic and political dimensions of environmental challenges. Several initiatives were taken globally for environmental protection such as Session of the UN General Assembly (June 1997) New York, Millennium Summit (September 2000), New York, World Summit on Sustainable Development (August - September 2002), Johannesburg, World Summit (September 2005) , Special Event towards Achieving the Millennium Development Goals (September 2013), New York, United Nations Summit on Sustainable Development (September 2015), New York and Stockholm +50 (June 2022) Stockholm in this direction.

The World Commission on Environment and Development

is generally known as the Brundtland Commission. It strongly attached the economy and environment through its concept of 'sustainable development'. It also promoted a landmark international conference held at Rio de Janeiro in 1992 popularly called as Earth Summit. In this summit, three new conventions were agreed with Agenda 21:

1. The Framework Convention on Climate Change (FCCC): Emphasized the role of developed countries in the production of GHGs; came into force in 1994, and 153 states signed it.
2. The Convention on Biodiversity: Under UNEP; the monopoly of developed countries on R&D was examined; and strict patent regimes were studied. It came into force in 1993; 155 states signed it.
3. The Forest Principle: The sovereign right of individual states to exploit forest resources within the general principles of forest management and protection was adopted.

Agenda 21 was adopted to ensure that the concept of sustainable development became an important principle of the UN by integrating the goals of environmental protection and economic development, based on local community and free market principles. Similarly, the Kyoto Protocol (1997) mandated that thirty-seven industrial nations plus the European Community cut their Green House Gas emissions; 192 parties have ratified (191 states and 1 regional economic integration organization). However, the US dropped out in 2001. Further, during the Johannesburg Summit (2002): UN Conference on Environment and Development, all the states repeated their commitments to eco-centric development initiatives.

Major Findings: Global Regime for Addressing Environmental Challenges

In response to the concerns about the need to address climate change, an international regime of action was agreed to by the UNFCCC in 1992. As per the principle of 'common but differentiated responsibilities and respective capabilities', developing countries, including India, have no obligation to reduce Green House Gas emissions. All industrial countries are required under the convention to have binding commitments to reduce their emissions. But as we all know these seminars and conferences alone are not able to tackle the problem of environmental degradation. There is no provision for compulsory implementation and binding commitments on states to reduce their emission. In most of the conferences blame game was played between developed and developing nations instead of taking the stern measures for implementation of the provisions of any convention. As a result, due to the environmental crisis, the suffering of people worldwide is increasing day by day.

Gandhian Vision of Environment

Mahatma Gandhi, a well-known leader and philosopher of the twentieth century, championed an exclusive and insightful standpoint on ecological awareness and sustainable progress. Gandhi's respect for the environment, simplicity, and self-reliance are initial characteristics of his visualization of a harmonious relationship between humans and the environment. Renewable sources of energy, evils of large-scale industrialisation and the dangers of environmental pollution were recognised by Gandhi several decades ago.

The eminent Gandhian thinker, J.C. Kumarappa drew attention towards these critical matters of environmental pollution and preservation of natural resources and urged that mankind should strive to establish an 'Economy of permanence,' rather than reckless destruction of natural resources. This could be achieved by judicious minimum use of non-renewable resources, thereby saving them for future generations and adopting a productive system in which whatever is drained out of nature is restored through the natural process.

Gandhi was very much aware of the utility of machines in few cases. In a place he says, "...the heavy machinery for the work of a public utility which cannot be undertaken by human labour has its inevitable place." But primarily he urged for labour oriented production process for work in more hands. Investment in the human capital of the poor is not only consistent with faster long-term growth, but they also contributed to it.

Similarly, Gandhi suggested for more investment in spinning wheel because he considered it very significant for the upliftment of the domestic economy along with job opportunities. In Gandhi words, "The entire foundation of the spinning wheel rests on the fact that there are crores of semi-unemployment people in India... the spinning wheel is destructive of no enterprise whatsoever."

All decentralized technological systems which make use of built-in processes demand a settlement pattern different from the heavy one that forms our preference now. But if we take a broader view, they can become the indicators of advancement, leading to development with the help of eco-friendly technology. When the basic problems of the Indian economy are analyzed we find that the pattern of income distribution, inequality, poverty, and unemployment still exists as they were during Gandhi's time.

In this context, the eleven Vratas of Gandhi which are Non-violence, Truth, Non-stealing, Brahmacharya, Non-avarice, Physical labour, Control of Palate, Religious harmony, Fearlessness, Swadeshi and Abolition of untouchability are very important. The significance of each of the vratas could be elaborated in the context of preserving the environment.

Concluding Remarks

According to Gandhi, Earth has provided sufficient to satisfy any man's need but not that much to satisfy any man's greed. Gandhi's beliefs of simplicity, self-reliance, and agreement with nature shaped the foundation of his ecological stance. He supported for an evenhanded coexistence connecting people and the environment. Gandhi's assessment of unrestrained industrialization, consumerism, and misuse of natural resources underlines the call for an accountable and just advancement. Gandhi's thoughts can encourage current movements and practices that endorse ecological righteousness, social fairness, and natural equilibrium. It put forward a holistic pattern combining moral contemplations with sensible policies for a further sustainable future.

References:
1. Ahuja, Ram (2014). Social Problems in India. Jaipur: Rawat Publications.
2. Anand, Sudhir and Sen, Amartya. (1992). 'Sustainable Human Development: Concepts and Priorities'. Human Development Report Office, Occasional Paper, UNDP.
3. Basu, Rumki (Ed.). (2012). International Politics: Concepts, Theories and Issues. New Delhi: Sage.
4. Baylis, John & Smith, Steve (Ed.). (2005). The Globalization of World Politics: An Introduction. New York: Oxford University Press.
5. Bhatia, Ravi, P. (2014). Protection and Sustenance of the Environment- Role of Education and Gandhian Principles. Gandhi Marg, 36 (1). April-June 2014.
6. Dutt, Gautam & Eaisli, Fablan. (2007). Coping with Climate Change. Economic and Political Weekly, (Oct. 20, 2007).
7. Chatterjee, Aneek (2010). International Relations Today: Concepts and Applications. New Delhi: Pearson Education.
8. Gandhi's Views on Nature and Environment. Retrieved April 13, 2024, from

https://egyankosh.ac.in/bitstream/123456789/33724/1/Unit-16.pdf.

9. Ghosh, Peu (2014). International Relations. Delhi: PHI Learning Private Limited.

10. Goldstein, Joshua, S. (2006). International Relations. New Delhi: Pearson Education.

11. Lal, Vinay. Mahatma Gandhi: An environmentalist by nature. Retrieved May 05, 2024, from https://www.thehindu.com/news/national/mahatma-gandhi-an-environmentalist-by-nature/article29566196.ece.

12. Malhotra, Vinay Kumar (1993). International Relations. New Delhi: Anmol Publications Pvt.Ltd.

13. Mehta, V. R. (1996). Foundations of Indian Political Thought. New Delhi: Manohar Publishers & Distributors.

14. Pantham, Thomas & Deutsch, Kenneth. L. (Ed.). (1986). Political Thought in Modern India. New Delhi: Sage Publications India Pvt Ltd.

15. Sasikala, A.S. Environmental Thoughts of Gandhi for a Green Future. Retrieved March 28, 2024, from https://www.mkgandhi.org/articles/green_future.php.

16. Suchak, Kavita Y. Development and Environment Issues with Special Reference to Gandhian Perspective. Retrieved January 08, 2024, from https://www.gandhiashramsevagram.org/gandhi-articles/development-and-environment-issues-with-special-reference-to-gandhian-perspective.php.

17. The Paris Agreement. Retrieved January 11, 2024, from https://unfccc.int/process-and-meetings/the-paris-agreement.

18. United Nations Conferences: Environment and Sustainable Development. Retrieved June 02, 2024, from https://www.un.org/en/conferences/environment.

19. Verma, Sarika. Et.al. Mahatma Gandhi's View on Environment and Sustainable Development. Retrieved June 18, 2024, from https://www.researchgate.net/publication/375892421_Mahatma_Gandhi's_View_on_Environment_and_Sustainable_Development#:~:text=He%20emphasized%20the%20interconnectedness%20of,for%20responsible%20and%20ethical%20development.

20. Verma, V.P. (2014) Modern Indian Political Thought. Agra: Lakshmi Narain Agrarwal Educational Publishers.

21. World Commission Environment and Development. (1987) One Common Future. Retrieved July 16, 2024, from https://sustainabledevelopment.un.org/content/documents/5987our-common-future.pdf

Gandhi's View on Women Empowerment

Alice Mathew
HOD, Associate Professor
Department of Political Science
Mount Carmel College, Autonomous, Bangalore
Email: alice.mathew@mccblr.edu.in

Abstract

Mahatma Gandhi's revolutionary approach to women's empowerment significantly influenced the freedom movement and reshaped women's roles in Indian society. His efforts went beyond advocating for legal equality, emphasizing the importance of women's moral and spiritual strength in driving societal change. Gandhi challenged deep-rooted social issues like the dowry system, widowhood, and gender-based discrimination, urging women to actively participate in the struggle for independence. He believed that women's involvement would bring ethical clarity to national politics and that they were inherently suited to lead in the pursuit of truth and nonviolence. Gandhi's initiatives empowered women to redefine their roles within the social framework, freeing themselves from traditional constraints. His vision of social reform and gender equality laid the groundwork for a more just society, where both men and women could equally contribute to the nation's progress. Gandhi's enduring commitment to women's rights and his advocacy for their emancipation in India are encapsulated in this summary.

Introduction

The leadership of Mahatma Gandhi significantly transformed the societal role and status of women in India. When he took charge of the Indian independence movement, the average life span of an Indian woman was just twenty-seven years. High mortality rates plagued babies and pregnant women, child marriage was rampant, and there was a large population of widows. A mere two percent of women had any form of education, and many women lacked personal identity, especially in North India, where the purdah system was practiced. Women were not allowed to leave the house unless accompanied by men and had to cover their faces with cloth. Those fortunate enough to attend school had to commute in covered tangas (carts).

In this challenging context, Gandhi's work was revolutionary. He firmly believed in and practiced the principle of gender equality. Under his influence, thousands of women, regardless of their educational background or social status, participated in the freedom movement. For Gandhi, the struggle for independence was not solely a political fight; it encompassed economic and social reforms on a national scale. As a result of his efforts, gender equality became more accepted and natural in Indian society.

After India's independence and the adoption of the constitution, which emphasized gender equality, the Hindu Code was formulated. Remarkably, the populace accepted these changes, reflecting Gandhi's profound impact on societal attitudes toward women. His leadership not only galvanized the participation of women in the freedom struggle but also paved the way for lasting reforms that improved their status in society.

Background to the status of women during Gandhian time

Mahatma Gandhi, originally Mohandas Karamchand Gandhi, was deeply influenced by his mother, Putlibai, who instilled in him a strong sense of ethics, compassion, and spirituality. Her dedication to daily prayer and strict adherence to vows left a lasting impression on him. Gandhi's favorite prayer, "Vaishnav Jan To," by the 15th-century reformer Narsinha Mehta, reflects the values she imparted, emphasizing empathy and selflessness. Putlibai's influence was so profound that when Gandhi sought her permission to study in England, he took a solemn vow to abstain from wine, women and meat—promises that protected his moral integrity during his stay abroad.

Gandhi married Kasturba at thirteen and initially sought to assert his authority over her. However, Kasturba's passive resistance, especially through fasting during disputes, deeply impacted Gandhi and inspired his concept of Satyagraha, a nonviolent resistance central to India's independence movement. Throughout their life together, Kasturba remained a steadfast partner, embodying strength and independence, while Gandhi affectionately called her "Ba," meaning mother.

Gandhi's deep respect for women, especially mothers, stemmed from his admiration for Putlibai and Kasturba. He believed that the selfless care inherent in motherhood was a model for both India's liberation and his personal growth. Convinced that India's freedom was impossible without the empowerment of women, Gandhi saw the need to cultivate a "mother's heart" to purify and reform society.

In addition to the influence of his immediate family, Gandhi was also shaped by the broader women's movement in India. The concept of the "bhadra mahila," or the responsible new woman, emerged in the 19th century through the efforts of Indian social reformers. These women, primarily from the upper-middle class, established organizations such as the All India Women's Council and Bhagini Samaj, advocating for education and women's empowerment. While Gandhi is often recognized for mobilizing women in the nationalist movement, the foundation for this activism had already been established by these earlier women's organizations.

Women leaders who influenced Gandhi

Mahatma Gandhi was significantly influenced by prominent women such as Annie Besant, Sarojini Naidu, Kamaladevi Chattopadhyaya, Rajkumari Amrit Kaur, and Pushpaben

Mehta. Sarojini Naidu, in particular, envisioned India as a "house" with its people as a "joint family" and women as the "Mother," a vision Gandhi shared. Gandhi and these women leaders believed that the nation's progress and women's empowerment were closely linked, with this familial model vital for social and national transformation. Rajkumari Amrit Kaur highlighted Gandhi's nurturing influence, describing him as both a father and mother figure. While advocating for equal rights for women, Gandhi emphasized that true societal progress required unity and dignity, believing that women's recognition of their own dignity could greatly uplift humanity.

Equality of Sexes

In his autobiography, Gandhi acknowledged the male-dominated nature of Indian society and shared how he initially tried to dominate his wife. He recognized that paternalism causes inequality and expressed regret for past behavior, resolving never to hurt her again. Despite their intellectual gap, their marriage remained strong, with Kasturba exceeding expectations in following him. After her passing, Gandhi mourned deeply, acknowledging that without Ba, his life would have been meaningless. Their bond defined their 62-year marriage.

Gandhiji championed "Sarvodaya," meaning comprehensive progress, and believed that the only difference between men and women was physical. He felt that women excelled in tolerance, patience, and sacrifice. He stated that women are intellectually, mentally, and spiritually equivalent to men. Throughout his political career, his belief in women's empowerment grew stronger, as reflected in his writings in "Harijan" and "Young India." Although he didn't create specific programs for women, they played integral roles in all his initiatives.

Gandhi believed that womanhood should not be confined to the kitchen, asserting that women's true potential could only be realized once they were freed from this traditional role. He did not suggest that women stop cooking but advocated for shared household responsibilities among men, women, and children. Gandhi urged women to move beyond traditional roles and engage in national affairs. He also criticized India's preference for male children, stating that the nation would remain in darkness until girls were valued as equally as boys.

Gandhi believed in the fundamental equality of men and women, asserting that both should not suffer any legal disadvantages that the other does not. He viewed men and women as complements, with nature assigning them different roles, but emphasized that these roles should be a matter of personal choice rather than societal expectation. Gandhi argued that men and women are equal because the same atma (soul), which is sexless, resides in both. Therefore, in the eyes of God, they are perfectly equal. He opposed the rigid sexual division of labor, recognizing that while traditionally defined roles existed, men and women should be free to choose their vocations without any imposed limitations.

Gandhi believed that while women might naturally avoid certain roles traditionally associated with men, this did not justify inequality. He strongly advocated for equal pay, recognized women's mental capacities as equal to men's, and emphasized their right to fully participate in all aspects of life, including those traditionally dominated by men. Gandhi's vision was to elevate women's status while preserving family harmony, ensuring that women had equal standing with men in all spheres.

Reflecting on Indian history, the progress women have made since Gandhi's time is significant. His vision inspired a eneration of women, leading to a society where many women in India can now work in offices, educational institutions, and factories without fear. Gandhi and his followers laid the groundwork for this transformation. Although inequality persists, there is now a widespread recognition of the importance of gender equality.

Unlike in Western countries like the U.S.A. and U.K., where women had to struggle for basic rights such as voting, property ownership, and child custody, Indian women were granted economic, political, and voting rights through the Constitution from the outset. In the West, women had to fight against entrenched stereotypes and take to the streets to secure their rights. Gandhi, however, believed that women are equal companions to men, endowed with the same mental capacities and deserving of full participation in all aspects of life. He argued that women should share the same freedom and liberty as men, holding a supreme place in their own spheres of activity, just as men do in theirs.

Gandhi also criticized the deeply ingrained customs that allowed even the most ignorant and unworthy men to enjoy undeserved superiority over women. He pointed out that many social movements falter because of the oppressed condition of women and that much legislation, often crafted by men, has failed to be fair or impartial. Gandhi believed that the regeneration of women required eliminating the flaws portrayed in shastras as inherent characteristics of women. He asserted that when women are freed from male-dominated legislation and institutions designed to constrain them, their nonviolent rebellion would be immensely powerful, marking the beginning of a new era of equality and mutual respect.

Men must learn to give women their rightful place, as a society that honors women is truly civilized. Currently, few women participate in politics, and many rely on their parents or husbands for decisions, which fuels their demand for rights. Rather than just advocating for rights, women leaders should focus on empowering women by encouraging voter registration, offering practical education, fostering independent thinking, and breaking the chains of caste. This empowerment will transform society, compelling men to recognize and honor women's strength and capacity for sacrifice.

Gandhi on widow remarriage

Gandhi was considerate of the young widows. As a nation if we have progressed on the matter of child widows, it is due to the reformers like Gandhiji and his contemporaries. He declared the marriage in which the girls were not consulted were unholy. He gave a call to the young to marry the widows and to boycott child marriage. Gandhi was very disturbed by the plight of low caste and untouchable section of the society namely, Devadasis. He was hurt by the miserable way children of brothels were treated. He made elaborate plans to rehabilitate and protect their honour. Even though on paper we have abolished the system of Devadasis, rampant exploitation of women as sex servants has continued. Today, it has emerged in a newer garb called prostitution. Gandhiji certainly identified it's a social evil and tried to fight it.

He criticized the hypocrisy of those who, in the name of religion, advocated for cow protection but neglected the welfare of widows, whom he referred to as "human cows." Gandhi argued that forcing widowhood on young girls who could not even grasp the significance of marriage was a cruel crime. He condemned the practice of imposing widowhood on these young girls, calling it a brutal act for which society, especially Hindus, was paying a heavy price daily.

Gandhi was firmly against any social or religious barriers that prevented widow remarriage, emphasizing that it was unjust to impose such a harsh fate on young widows who were incapable of understanding the consequences of marriage.

Gandhi believed that voluntary widowhood, consciously adopted by a woman who has experienced the affection of a partner, adds grace and dignity to life, enriches the home, and elevates religion. In contrast, widowhood imposed by religion or custom is an oppressive burden that defiles the home with hidden vices and degrades religion. To save Hinduism, we must eliminate this harmful practice. Reform should start with those who have girl widows under their care, encouraging them to ensure that these young widows are well and duly married, not remarried, as they were never truly married initially.

Marriage, according to Gandhi, establishes the right of union between two partners, excluding all others, when both partners mutually agree that such a union is desirable. However, marriage does not give one partner the right to demand compliance from the other regarding their desire for union. The issue of what should be done when one partner, on moral or other grounds, cannot conform to the other's wishes is a separate matter. Personally, if divorce were the only option, Gandhi believed it should be accepted rather than hindering one's moral progress, especially if one wishes to exercise restraint based on purely moral grounds.

Gandhi's view on Dowry

Gandhi wanted the dowry system to be abolished, denouncing it as a cruel and degrading custom that undermined the dignity of women. He believed that marriage should not be a financial arrangement made by parents. The dowry system is closely tied to the caste system. As long as the choice of marriage partners is limited to a few hundred young men and women within a particular caste, the dowry system will persist despite any opposition. For middle-class and poor families, dowry was nothing short of a nightmare, turning the birth of a girl into a burden and fueling gender discrimination across society. This led to the celebration of the birth of male children while the birth of female children was met with silent sorrow. Gandhi argued that any man who demanded dowry should be ostracized from society. He advocated for the formation of strong public opinion against dowry and encouraged women to wait for a suitor who would marry them without any exchange of dowry.

To eradicate this issue, girls, boys, and their parents must break free from the bonds of caste. Education is crucial in revolutionizing the mindset of the nation's youth. Parents should educate their daughters to refuse marriage to any man who demands a price for marrying. It is better to remain single than to accept such degrading conditions. The only honorable foundation for marriage is mutual love and mutual consent.

Crime against Women

Gandhi always held a woman's honour is inviolable if she possesses the strength of purity and courage. True violation occurs only when she succumbs to fear or forgets her inner strength. Like Sita, whose purity protected her from Ravana, a woman's moral strength can be more powerful than any physical force. A fearless woman, who holds her purity as her shield, can never be dishonored; even the most beastly of men will be shamed by her courage. Women should be taught to cultivate this fearlessness, rooted in faith in God, their unfailing protector. In the face of assault, a woman's primary duty is self-protection, using any means necessary, including her nails and teeth. If needed, she should be prepared to die defending her honour, for one who fears not death can protect themselves and others.

Dying bravely and with honour requires no special training but a deep, living faith in God. Non-violent individuals should die without retaliation in defending their own or others' honour, embodying the highest form of bravery. India's salvation, Gandhi believed depends on the sacrifice and enlightenment of women.

Women and Politics

Gandhi was a rare advocate for women's liberation, encouraging their active participation in the freedom struggle. He believed that women, through their innate capacity for non-violence, could lead society by embracing truth and Ahinsa. Gandhi's call for women to join the national movement brought about significant change, both in women's self-awareness and in the humanization of politics. Women responded by organizing meetings, selling Khadi, picketing, and even facing police brutality, all while challenging traditional norms. Although Gandhi did not directly challenge the traditional societal structure, he inspired women to reshape it from within, empowering them to protest against injustice and develop their own perspectives.

Gandhi saw women as inherently connected with service rather than power. He advised women to focus on educating others, breaking free from caste restrictions, and influencing the political atmosphere by demonstrating their strength and capacity for sacrifice. While advocating for women's right to vote and equal status, Gandhi emphasized that their true impact would begin once they influenced the nation's political deliberations.

Conclusion

Mahatma Gandhi's approach to women's empowerment was both progressive and deeply rooted in his belief in truth, non-violence, and equality. He recognized the immense potential of women in shaping society and the nation, advocating for their active participation in the freedom struggle and beyond. Gandhi's efforts to uplift women extended to challenging social evils like the dowry system, widowhood, and gender-based discrimination. He encouraged women to break free from the shackles of traditional norms, urging them to carve out their own destinies within the societal framework while maintaining their inherent dignity and strength.

Gandhi's vision for women was not merely about achieving legal equality; it was about transforming society by recognizing and harnessing the unique capacities of women to bring about moral and social change. His belief in the equal spiritual potential of men and women, coupled with his advocacy for their equal rights, laid the foundation for a more just and humane society. Gandhi's legacy in promoting women's liberation continues to inspire generations, demonstrating that true social reform requires the active participation and empowerment of all, regardless of gender.

Refrences:
1. Rao, Anupama. "Women and Gandhi in Colonial India: The Struggle for Swaraj", University of Illinois Press, 2010.
2. Bakshi, S. R., 'Gandhi and His Social Thought', Criterion Publication, 1986, p. 174- 175.
3. Gandhi, M. K., Woman's Role in Society, Navjjivan Publishing House, Ahemdabad, 1959, p.32.
4. Gandhi, Mahatma., edited by Raghavan Iyer "The Essential Writings of Mahatma Gandhi", Oxford University Press, 1999.
5. Gandhi, M. K., Gandhi on Women, Navjivan Publishing House, Ahemdabad, 1958, p. 22.
6. Gandhi, M. K., Women and Social Injustice, Navjivan Publishing House, Ahemdabad, 1942, p. 96.
7. Kishwar, Madhu., 'Gandhi on Women', Economic and Political Weekly Vol. 20, No. 40 (Oct. 5, 1985), pp. 1691-1702
8. Guha, Ramachandra, 'Makers of Modern India', Penguin, New Delhi, 2012.
9. Guha, Ramachandra, "Gandhi: The Years That Changed the World, 1914-1948, publisher Alfred A. Knopf, 2018
10. Gandhi on women Empowerment, https://www.mkgandhi.org 9. Gandhi on women, https://www.jstor.org>stable

11. Ranjan, Ravi., 'Reading Gandhi', Anmol Publications Private Limited, 2010.
12. Relevance of Mahatma Gandhi's ideas on Women Empowerment, https://www.ijeponline.org
13. Kumari Jayawardena, "Feminism and Nationalism in the Third World" Verso Books, 1986
14. Gandhi and his view on women Empowerment, https://www.xajzkjdx.cn
15. Gandhi's contribution in Women Empowerment, https://legalservicesindia.com
16. Mahatma Gandhi's thought on women empowerment and present scenario, https://www.researchgate.net
17. Gandhi and women empowerment, https://gandhiashramsevagram.org
18. Susanne Hoeber Rudolph and Lloyd I. Rudolph "The Power of Women: A Top-Down Exploration of Gandhi's Ideas on Gender Equality" Harvard University Press, 2008

The Role of Women in Gandhiji's Satyagraha Movements

Abhinav Choudhary
UGC-NET (History)
SET (History), Rajasthan
Email: abhinavchoudhary1996@gmail.com

Abstract

The article explores the pivotal role of women in Mahatma Gandhi's Satyagraha movements, highlighting their contributions to India's struggle for independence and the broader fight for gender equality. Gandhi's philosophy of nonviolence and civil disobedience, which emphasized moral and spiritual strength, resonated deeply with women, whom he saw as natural leaders in the fight against colonial rule. Women's participation in key movements such as the Non-Cooperation Movement, Civil Disobedience Movement, and Quit India Movement was transformative, challenging societal norms and expanding the scope of the nationalist struggle.

Leaders like Sarojini Naidu, Kasturba Gandhi, Kamaladevi Chattopadhyay, Aruna Asaf Ali, and Usha Mehta played crucial roles, mobilizing women across India to engage in acts of defiance against British authority. Their involvement not only contributed to the success of these movements but also redefined their roles within Indian society, shifting from passive observers to active participants and leaders in public life.

Gandhi's vision of women's empowerment was a double-edged sword. While it provided women with a platform to challenge traditional gender roles, it also reinforced some existing stereotypes. Nevertheless, the Satyagraha movements marked a turning point in the history of women's rights in India, laying the foundation for future struggles for gender equality.

The legacy of women's involvement in Gandhi's movements continues to inspire contemporary movements for social justice and gender equality in India. Their courage, resilience, and leadership remain a testament to their critical role in shaping the nation's path to independence and beyond. This article underscores the enduring impact of Gandhi's vision, reminding us of the importance of gender equality in the pursuit of a just and free society.

Keywords: Satyagraha, movements, nonviolence, civil disobedience

Introduction

Mahatma Gandhi's Satyagraha movements, rooted in nonviolence and civil disobedience, were instrumental in India's struggle for independence. Central to these movements was the participation of women, whose involvement challenged the traditional gender norms of the time. Gandhi believed in the innate strength of women, particularly their capacity for self-sacrifice and nonviolence. As historian Judith Brown notes, **"Gandhi's inclusion of women in the political arena was revolutionary, opening up new possibilities for their role in public life"** (Brown, 1989). This paper examines the role of women in Gandhi's Satyagraha movements, analyzing their contributions, the challenges they faced, and the impact of their involvement on both the nationalist struggle and the broader movement for women's rights in India.

Gandhi's Philosophy and the Inclusion of Women

Gandhi's philosophy of Satyagraha emphasized the power of nonviolence, truth, and self-discipline. He believed that women possessed these qualities in abundance, making them ideal participants in the struggle for freedom. As he famously stated, **"To call women the weaker sex is a libel; it is man's injustice to woman"** (Gandhi, 1927). Gandhi's belief in the moral superiority of women was central to his strategy, as he saw them as natural bearers of nonviolence and moral fortitude.

Renowned scholar R. P. Dutt highlighted the significance of this belief, noting that **"Gandhi's respect for the spiritual and moral strength of women was pivotal in mobilizing them for the nationalist cause" (Dutt, 1955).** This mobilization not only expanded the reach of the Satyagraha movements but also began to erode the rigid societal norms that had long confined women to domestic roles.

Women in the Non-Cooperation Movement (1920-1922)

The Non-Cooperation Movement marked a watershed moment in the involvement of women in the Indian independence struggle. Gandhi's call for the boycott of British goods, especially textiles, resonated with women, who took up the spinning of khadi as a symbol of resistance. **"The charkha [spinning wheel] became a symbol of women's agency in the nationalist movement,"** writes historian Sumit Sarkar (Sarkar, 1983).

Sarojini Naidu, a leading figure in the movement, used her eloquence to inspire women across the country. She declared, **"We want deeper sincerity of motive, a greater courage in speech and earnestness in action" (Naidu, 1925).** Naidu's leadership galvanized women to step out of their traditional roles and participate actively in the boycott of foreign goods, picketing of liquor shops, and other acts of civil disobedience.

Kasturba Gandhi, another key figure, demonstrated the principles of Satyagraha through her actions, becoming a role model for many women. As historian B.R. Nanda observes, **"Kasturba's involvement in the Non-Cooperation Movement underscored the critical role of women in Gandhi's campaigns, serving as a beacon for others to follow" (Nanda, 1998).** Her participation, along with that of countless other women, marked a significant departure from the norms of the time and set the stage for their continued involvement in the freedom struggle.

Women in the Civil Disobedience Movement (1930-1934):

The Civil Disobedience Movement saw an even greater involvement of women, with Gandhi's Salt March serving as a catalyst for mass participation. Women from all walks of life joined the movement, defying the British salt laws by making and selling salt. Kamaladevi Chattopadhyay, a prominent leader, boldly confronted British authorities and encouraged others to do the same. She stated, **"Freedom is not given; it is taken. Women must take their place in the front lines of the fight for independence"** **(Chattopadhyay, 1986).**

The movement also witnessed the formation of women's organizations that played a crucial role in organizing protests and boycotts. The All India Women's Conference (AIWC), for instance, became a platform for women to voice their demands for both political and social reforms. **"The AIWC was instrumental in broadening the scope of the nationalist movement to include issues of gender equality and social justice,"** notes historian Geraldine Forbes (Forbes, 1996).

Despite the nonviolent nature of the movement, women faced severe repression. Many were arrested and imprisoned, yet their resolve remained unshaken. Gandhi acknowledged their contributions, stating, **"In courage and self-sacrifice, the women of India have proved themselves the equals of men" (Gandhi, 1931).** This acknowledgment not only validated their efforts but also encouraged more women to join the movement.

Women in the Quit India Movement (1942)

The Quit India Movement, launched in 1942, was a turning point in India's independence struggle, with women playing a leading role. The movement called for an immediate end to British rule and women, inspired by Gandhi's call, participated in protests, strikes and acts of civil disobedience on an unprecedented scale.

Aruna Asaf Ali, a prominent leader during this period, became a symbol of resistance when she hoisted the Indian National Congress flag at the Gowalia Tank Maidan in Mumbai. Her actions inspired many and as political scientist Ramachandra Guha notes, **"Aruna Asaf Ali's leadership during the Quit India Movement exemplified the courage and determination of Indian women in the face of colonial repression" (Guha, 2007).**

Another key figure was Usha Mehta, who set up an underground radio station to broadcast messages and keep the spirit of resistance alive. Reflecting on her role, she stated, **"The Quit India Movement was a watershed moment for women in India, marking their transition from passive participants to active leaders in the struggle for independence" (Mehta, 1995).**

The involvement of women in the Quit India Movement was not limited to urban areas; rural women also played a significant role, challenging the British authorities and participating in acts of defiance. This widespread participation highlighted the movement's broad appeal and its capacity to unite people across different sections of society.

Impact on the Nationalist Struggle and Society

The participation of women in Gandhi's Satyagraha movements had a profound impact on the Indian nationalist struggle. Women's involvement brought a new dimension to the movement, demonstrating the power of nonviolent resistance and challenging the colonial authorities' perception of Indian women as passive and submissive. As historian Amrita Basu notes, **"The mass participation of women in the Satyagraha movements was a transformative moment in Indian history, reshaping both the nationalist struggle and the social fabric of the nation" (Basu, 2012).**

The mass mobilization of women in the Satyagraha movements also challenged traditional gender norms. As women stepped into the public arena, they began to question and resist the social and cultural practices that oppressed them. This shift was evident in the growing demands for gender equality, women's education, and social reforms during and after the independence struggle. **"The involvement of women in the nationalist movement laid the foundation for the post-independence feminist movement in India," writes historian Radha Kumar (Kumar, 1993).**

Gandhi's encouragement of women's participation also had a lasting impact on their self-perception and societal roles. By involving women in the struggle for independence, Gandhi empowered them to see themselves as active agents of change rather than passive recipients of societal norms. **"Gandhi's movement was as much about the liberation of women as it was about the liberation of India,"** asserts historian Aparna Basu (Basu, 1990).

Gandhi's Vision for Women's Empowerment

Gandhi's vision for women's empowerment was integral to his broader philosophy of social reform. He believed that the liberation of India from colonial rule was inseparable from the liberation of its women from social and cultural oppression. Gandhi advocated for the education of women, the abolition of practices such as child marriage and dowry, and the promotion of women's rights within the framework of a nonviolent and just society.

In his writings, Gandhi often emphasized the importance of women's education and self-reliance. **"If you educate a man you educate an individual, but if you educate a woman you educate an entire family,"** he wrote in *Young India* (Gandhi, 1929). This belief underpinned his efforts to promote literacy and education among women, which he saw as essential for the development of a free and just society.

Gandhi's vision extended beyond political independence to encompass social and economic reforms that would empower women. He believed that true independence could only be achieved through the upliftment of all sections of society, including women. His emphasis on spinning khadi, for example, was not just an economic strategy but also a means of promoting self-reliance and dignity among women.

Challenges and Criticisms

Despite Gandhi's efforts to involve women in the independence struggle, his views on women's roles were not without criticism. Some feminists argue that while Gandhi provided a platform for women's participation, his vision was still rooted in traditional gender roles. He often emphasized women's roles as caregivers, moral guardians, and embodiments of nonviolence, which, critics argue, reinforced existing stereotypes rather than challenging them.

Moreover, Gandhi's insistence on nonviolence and self-sacrifice sometimes placed women in vulnerable positions, especially in the face of physical violence and repression by colonial authorities. While Gandhi believed that nonviolence was the most powerful weapon for the oppressed, some feminists contend that this approach limited women's ability to assert their rights and challenge patriarchal structures more aggressively.

Despite these criticisms, it is undeniable that Gandhi's Satyagraha movements provided a significant platform for women's involvement in the nationalist struggle. The participation of women in these movements not only contributed to India's independence but also laid the groundwork for future struggles for gender equality and women's rights.

Conclusion

The role of women in Gandhiji's Satyagraha movements was transformative, both for the Indian independence struggle and for the societal position of women in India. By encouraging women's active participation in these movements, Gandhi not only broadened the base of the nationalist struggle but also challenged the deep-seated patriarchal norms that had confined women to the domestic sphere. Women's involvement in the Non-Cooperation Movement, the Civil Disobedience Movement, and the Quit India Movement showcased their courage, resilience, and leadership, qualities that significantly contributed to the success of these movements.

Gandhi's vision of women as moral and spiritual leaders in the struggle for independence was a double-edged sword. While it empowered many women and provided them with a platform to challenge societal norms, it also reinforced traditional gender roles in some respects. Nevertheless, the Satyagraha movements marked a crucial turning point in the history of women's rights in India, paving the way for future generations to continue the fight for gender equality and social justice.

The legacy of women in Gandhi's Satyagraha movements is evident in the ongoing struggles for women's empowerment in India. Their contributions laid the foundation for a more inclusive and equitable society, and their courage and commitment continue to inspire movements for social change today. Gandhi's belief in the potential of women to lead and transform society remains a powerful reminder of the importance of gender equality in the quest for a just and free nation.

References:
1. Basu, A. (1990). Women's Struggles: Personal and Political. Manohar Publishers.

2. Basu, A. (2012). Indian Women in Politics: From Independence to the Present. St. Martin's Press.
3. Brown, J. M. (1989). Gandhi: Prisoner of Hope. Yale University Press.
4. Chattopadhyay, K. (1986). Inner Recesses Outer Spaces: Memoirs. Navrang.
5. Dutt, R. P. (1955). India Today. Gollancz.
6. Forbes, G. (1996). Women in Modern India. Cambridge University Press.
7. Gandhi, M. K. (1927). The Story of My Experiments with Truth. Navajivan Publishing House.
8. Gandhi, M. K. (1929). Young India. Navajivan Publishing House.
9. Gandhi, M. K. (1931). Young India. Navajivan Publishing House.
10. Guha, R. (2007). India After Gandhi: The History of the World's Largest Democracy. HarperCollins.
11. Kumar, R. (1993). The History of Doing: An Illustrated Account of Movements for Women's Rights and Feminism in India 1800-1990. Zubaan.
12. Mehta, U. (1995). Gandhi's Political Philosophy: A Critical Examination. Clarendon Press.
13. Nanda, B. R. (1998). Gandhi: A Pictorial Biography. Oxford University Press.
14. Naidu, S. (1925). Speeches and Writings of Sarojini Naidu. G.A. Natesan & Co.

The Tenets of Freedom in Gandhi's Thought

Dr. Saraswati Kumari
Associate Professor
Department of History
MMV, BHU, Varanasi
Email: saraswatikumari64@yahoo.co.in

Abstract

Many books have been written on Gandhi since, the first decades of the 20th century. Most of these books have been biographical or episodic. Some have dealt with some of his campaigns, some with his programmes for building a new society, some with his methods of struggle, some with his perception of God and religion, some with his experiments in education, some with his experiments in the field of health. There is hardly a field of human life that Gandhi did not concern himself with and therefore there is hardly an area in relation to which Gandhi's views have not been studied and expounded But Gandhi himself claimed that all that he had done, said and written about all through his life had only one objective and that is self-assertion, self-realisation, self-attainment or the persuade of truth towards one's freedom from everything. The philosophy of Karam which leads to the attainment of his realisation towards the goods and evils of the society due to the environment in which he lives are the core to the Gandhi's thought. Gandhi's philosophy of freedom is inherent in his concept of religion with the basis of Karm which decides his future faith. This chapter throws light on how the thought of Gandhi leads towards the thought of freedom by which the ultimate freedom from the shackles of exploitation whether be social, economic or political are ameliorated.

Keywords: Philosophy, Karma, Struggle, life, Religion, Truth, self, Freedom

Introduction

Philosophy is a branch of human inquiry and as such it aims at knowledge and understanding. We might expect that the value of philosophy lies in the value of the ends that it seeks, the knowledge and understanding it reveals. But philosophy is rather notorious for failing to establish definitive knowledge on the matters it investigates. I'm not so sure this reputation is well deserved. We do learn much from doing philosophy. Philosophy often clearly reveals why some initially attractive answers to big philosophical questions are deeply problematic, for instance. But granted, philosophy often frustrates our craving for straightforward convictions. In our first reading, Bertrand Russell argues that there is great value in doing philosophy precisely because it frustrates our desire for quick easy answers. In denying us easy answers to big questions and undermining complacent convictions, philosophy liberates us from narrow minded conventional thinking and opens our minds to new possibilities[1].

In Indian philosophy the main emphasis is in the integral approach to truth which pervades life and which when found or even in the process of finding must guide life itself. A philosophy which does not lead to a way of life and does not inspire the activities of life has generally no attraction for the Indian mind[2]. In India the impact of philosophy was not limited to the elite circle of intellectuals and academics but its influence was pervasive. In the Indian tradition. A philosopher established his philosophy by living it and not by mere logical argumentation the entire stress in Indian philosophy lies in the mode of living and the primary concern of the Indian philosopher has always been not merely information about nature and man but also transformation of life a radical changing of Man's nature. That is why the term darshan is deeply rooted in the Indian tradition and as there is complete harmony between theory and practise, in Gandhi this similarity has an added significance in this study which will well unfold the philosophy of Gandhi towards freedom[3].

If philosophy is wisdom Mahatma Gandhi was among our fore most philosophers. He had the wisdom of Socrates, the humility of St Francis, of Assisi, the mass appeal of Lenin, the St Cleanness of the ancient Indian Rishis and the profound love of humanity of the Buddha. He was a revolutionary who was committed to the overthrow of all forms of tyranny and social injustice. But who never had any ill will towards anyone who led a mighty movement against British imperialism, but never allowed the movement to be accompanied by hatred, rancour resentment against Englishmen[4]. He was not an intellectual in the conventional sense of the term and was also not an academic philosopher propounding his philosophy in a precise dry and formal manner .it would not be difficult to find inconsistencies and contradictions in some of his statements. He was supremely consistent in his devotion to truth. He was like the ancient sagas and earnest seeker after truth or spiritual, explorer or a scientist, experimenting all his life to discover truth and apply it to the practical problems facing man. His source of inspiration was not confined to his country or to his religion, his deceptive mind was open to various influences and find the solutions of the problems[5].

From his very childhood he was brought into contact with religious and moral ideas. He studied the Ramayan, The Bhagavad. The Vaishnav poets of Gujarat and the popular writings of the Jains. During his Stay in England, he studied Buddhism and the Gita, met quakers and missionaries read the Upanishad in translation. *Ruskin's unto this last,* theosophist literature and books on Islam also. He was also profoundly impressed by *Thoreau* and *Tolstoy.* Thoreau taught him that it was more honourable to be right than to be law abiding a revolutionary concept which inspired his philosophy of passive resistance *Tolstoy's The Kingdom of God is within you* taught him how man could liberate himself and control evil through suffering[6].

While talking about India's freedom Gandhi points much more forcefully to the moral failure, he says, 'the English have not taken India, we have given it to them, they are not in India because of their strength but because we keep them recall the company Bahadur, who made it bahadur? they had not the slightest intention at the time of establishing the kingdom who insisted the company's officers? who was tempted at the site of their silver? who bought their goods? History testified that we did all this, when our princes fought among themselves, they sought the resistance of company Bahadur that corporation was versed alike in commerce, in war. it was un hampered by questions of morality is it not then useless to blame the English for what we did at the time it is truer to say that we gave India to the English than, that India was lost[7].'

Gandhi wanted to free India from the shackles of modern civilization, he was of the view that the moral failure of the part of India led to the conquest of India and in exploring reasons behind this moral failure .Gandhi answers the causes behind it, he says that it is not because Indian society lack the necessary cultural attributes that it was unable to face up to the power of the English ,it is not the backwardness or lack of modern values or modernity of India's culture that keeps it in continued subject but the task of achieving freedom would not be accomplished by creating a new modern culture for the nation[8]. For Gandhi it is precisely because Indians were seduced, affected by the modern civilization, that they became a subject people and he was also the view that until and unless the Indians are free from the illusions of the progressive world of modern civilization, they will remain a subject nation. Even if physically, they drive the Englishman, out of India English rule without the

Englishman will definitely persist because it is not the physical presence of the English which makes India's subject nation, it is civilization which subjects[9].

To Gandhi modern civilization leads to disease, war and suffering, he discloses the reason behind all these three things as fundamentally, Gandhi attacks the very notion of modernity and progress and the central claim made on behalf of those notions, he says that the modern world has the implications of a new organisation of society in which the productive capacities of human being as a labour are ,multiplied several times creating increased wealth, prosperity, leisure, comfort and happiness and in return of these things what modern civilization does is make man a prisoner of his craving for luxury and self-indulgence and release the forces of unbridled competition which leads society the evils of poverty so he wanted to free the world from the shackles of modernity. He says,' when I read Mr Dutts economic history of India I wept, and as I think of it again my heart sickens, it is machinery that has impoverished India it is difficult to measure the harm that Manchester has done to us, it is due to Manchester that Indian Handicraft has all but disappeared[10].'

Again describing towards the disadvantage of the modern civilization or the machine made civilization Gandhi goes on to say that, we noticed that the mind is a restless bird, the more it gets the more it wants, and still remains unsatisfied the more we indulge our passions the more unbridled they become, our ancestors therefore set a limit to our indulgences, they saw that happiness was largely a mental condition… observing all this our ancestors dissuaded us from luxuries and pleasures[11].' we have managed with the same kind of plough as existed thousands of years ago, we have retained the same kind of cottages that we had in former time, and our indigenous education remains the same as before, we have had no system of life corroding competition, it was not that we did not know how to invent machinery but our forefathers knew that if we set our hearts after such things we would become slaves and lose our moral fibres they therefore after due deliberation decided that we should only do what we could with our hands and feet. So, he says that the solution to the social evils of industrialism is not just to remove its defects because he thinks these so-called defects are the Root Cause, way to the very fundamentals of the modern system of production so his solution is to give up industrialism altogether.

Gandhiji was throughout his life a god conscious man. He never passed through the valley of doubt and darkness, nothing could, shake his confidence and faith in God and his scheme of life. God with him was not an abstraction or a mere metaphysical concept but an intensely felt reality. Mahatma described God in various ways god to him was kind, just and loving who always responded to prayer and love. His was truth and love a logical corollary to this belief is that the universe is organised on moral principles and that it presents a harmonious design. There being no contradiction or inconsistence in the laws of nature and moral and spiritual principles. Gandhiji's faith in God was not shaken when he held nature, read in truth and claw. when he saw earthquakes, floods and other natural calamities overwhelming man and causing in finite suffering[13]. Evil and destruction also had a meaning, a significance of purpose despite appearances to the contract. So as early as in Hind swaraj Gandhi dismisses all historical objections to his projection of freeing India not by the strength of arms but by the force of the soul by saying,' To believe that what has not occurred in history will not occur at all is to argue disbelief in the dignity of man.' He says that history therefore does not record the truth, truth lies outside history, it is universal, unchanging, truth has no history of its own.

Mahatma Gandhi's bold affirmation of faith in God, in the

moral nature of the universe, in human society as an association of kind souls and in free will may be criticised by the modern Cynics on the ground that no valid intellectual grounds have been offered but none can dispute the fact that his faith leads to a way of life which is incomplete, harmony with the needs of the time[14]. He was of the view that to discover the truth one would of course have to interpret the text to the best of once knowledge and belief. He goes on saying,' Who is the best interpreter? not learned man surely. learning there must be. But religion does not live by it. It lives in the experiences of its Saints and sheers in their life and sayings. When all the most learned commentators of the scriptures are utterly forgotten, the accumulated experience of the sages and Saints will abide and be an inspiration for ages to come.'

Religion does not divide people unless it is understood in the sense that it is a matter of dogma. A church it emphasises, the fundamental unity of the human race. Gandhi has the way of universal love and tolerance of profound reverence for all great religious, which are so many ways of apprehending, the reality and identifying ourselves with its purposes. Distinctions of race, nationality and sect have no room in Gandhi ethics. Patriotism is not enough. A true religious man does not restrict his allegiance to any country or nation his loyalty is to the whole of humanity he acknowledges all great regions as embroiding the truth and therefore worthy of deep reverence Mahatma Gandhi was an admirer of all religions, Hinduism, Buddhism Jainism, Sikhism, Islam, Christianity and others this does not mean that he accepted everything they preached[15]. If God is truth and if truth is God, then there is nothing which stands in the way of persons of various religions affiliations coming together on the same platform as seekers after truth. Even an earnest atheist trying to explore the reality is a truly religious man. what is repugnant to the Gandhian, way of life is dogmatism, fanatism, intolerance, selfishness. Gandhi was a secularist in the sense that he was against any discrimination between citizen and citizen on grounds of religion, Sect, caste but he firmly believed that a state of society would be stable only to the extent to which it was based on ethical and spiritual ideals.

Gandhi always preached Satyagraha as a way for all kinds of freedom. Truth, Force nonviolence, universal love of man he argued, was a spiritual being. love and nonviolence were part of his nature, force, hatred, vindictiveness was contrary to it. Non variance was not the weapon of the weak and the timid but of a strong man of a bold man who would not tolerate any manifestation of evil or injustice or tyranny but would resolutely fight it and willingly suffer the consequences of rebellion. What Gandhiji condemned most was covered his weakness of will acquiescence in evil. He wanted man, to create an ideal society by his soul force not to remain satisfied with things as they were[16]. He was a great revolutionary, a great rebel a great social reformer but his weapon always was man's defiant spirit, permanently committed to nonviolence and love. Gandhiji was an apostle of nonviolence and love because while violence and hatred brutalised men, love enhances them and brought out the best in them.

Christ and Buddha liberated mankind from misery and tyranny. They achieved this liberation through their gospel of love, charity, gentleness and sympathy. Nonviolence as a method of agitation, the Mahatma believed was bound to succeed because there was no man however tyrannical domineering and acquisitive who could indefinitely hold out against Satyagraha, against, the appeal of the fighter for justice voluntarily submitting himself to suffering and sacrifice.

Those who were not moved by appeals to reason or by display of physical force would not fail to respond to the appeal to their heart and to their soul. Underlying Gandhiji's faith in Satyagraha is his belief that man is fundamentally a spiritual being and cannot long deny the spirituality within himself. Satyagraha enables both the fighter for justice as well as the wrongdoer. Fasting, civil disobedience and non-cooperation with the tyrant are the means through which the conscience of the evil Doer is aroused. They are not a kind of blackmail or pressure, tactics; they are not intended to coarse a man or to intimidate him they are not a form of exploitation.

In fact, Gandhi viewed life as a whole an integrated and indivisible whole and every aspect and part of it he understood as vitally significant in the Constitution of the whole. It is this holistic approach that makes Gandhi's worldview unique and relevant in the search for alternative paradigms. Gandhi himself has claimed that all that he had done said and written about all through his life had only one objective that is self-realisation or the pursuit of Truth. The Great philosopher and Saviant Romain Ronald was one of the early biographers of Gandhi who referred to this basic element in Gandhi's philosophy as the crypt he wrote:'' To understand Gandhi's activity it should be realised that his doctrine is like a huge edifice composed of two different floors or grades[17]. Below is the solid groundwork, The basic foundation of religion. On this vast and unshakable foundation is based the political and social campaigns... These developments are interesting, but the essential part of the edifice is the crypt which is deep and well-built and meant to uphold a very different cathode, from the structure rapidly rising above it. The crypt alone is durable, the rest is temporary and only designed to serve during the transition years... An understanding of the principle on which the vast subterranean crypt is based is essential, therefore for here Gandhi's thought finds its real expression....''

Gandhi believed as God was manifest in man, he was

endowed with free will, reason and conscience. And therefore' we are the makers of our destiny we can mend or mar the present on that will depend the future.' Man is free did not mean to Gandhi that he had unlimited or unfettered freedom nor did it indicate the arbitrariness of will. For him freedom was essentially moral and hence the sine qua non of any system of ethics which aimed at explaining the phenomena or moral obligation, if a man would determine by natural forces the question of any moral response should not raise. In this context in order to decide how Free man was and what law determined the freedom of will, Gandhi accepted the position of the Hindu theory of Karma.

Karma literally means action deed. All facts produce their effects which are recorded both in the organism and the environment. Their physical effects may be short lived but their moral efforts (Sanskar) are worked into the character of the self. Every single thought, word and deed enters into the living chain of causes which makes us what we are, our life is not at the mercy of blind chances or capricious fate[18]. While talking about the philosophy of logic and the theory of Karam Radha Krishnan emphasise the importance of right action as follows,' All things in the world are at once causes and effects. They embody the energy of the past and exert energy on the future. Karma or connection with the past is not inconsistent with creative freedom. On the other hand, it is implied by it. The laws that link us with the past also asserts that it can be subjugated by our free action… The law of Karma says that each individual will get the return according to the energy he puts forth.'

Freedom acquires A new meaning and significance when it is being placed against the backdrop of the theory of Karma and that was also why Sri Aurobindo emphasised its importance and wrote,' The doctrine of renunciation and Karma tells us that the soul has a past which shaped its present birth and existence ; it has a future which our present action is shaping; our past has taken and our future will take the form of recurring terrestrial births and karma, our own action is the power which by its own continuity and development as a subjective and objective force determine the whole nature and eventually of these repeated existences. There is nothing here to depreciate the importance of the present life. On the contrary the doctrine gives its immense vistas and enormously enhances the value of effort and action. The nature of the present act is of an incalculable importance because it determines not only our immediate but our subsequent future[19].'

Gandhi also understood the law of Karma as the law of moral continuity and accepted the logic of its argument. That was why He said, 'The law of Karma is inexorable and impossible of evasion.' According to Gandhi though inexorable it was not completely deterministic and was not to be confused with either a hedonistic or a judicial theory of rewards and punishments. Gandhi thought that Karam or connection with the past was consistent with creative freedom. Karma was not mere mechanical action performed under the influence of blind impulse or custom. According to him, 'No action which is not voluntary can be called moral so long as we act like machines, there can be no question of morality if we want to call an action moral it should have been done consciously as a matter of duty.' Thus, Gandhi did not see any basic contradiction between the law of Karam and free will or moral freedom19. On the other hand, the possible arbitrariness of will could be put to continual check by the creative urges that spring from within. That's why Gandhi said that the free will which we enjoyed was less than that of a passenger on a crowded deck.

To sum up it is clear that implicit in Gandhi worldview is his concept of man as the manifestation of self-freedom. Gandhi formed his notion of the human self in the light of his religious beliefs and metaphysical presuppositions. He accepted the Hindu view that man is a manifestation of God and a complex multi-dimensional being including within him different elements of matter, life, consciousness, intelligence and the divine spark which is the Godhead within him. Gandhi believes that as a man is a manifestation of God human nature is basically good. This implicit faith of his in the innate goodness of the human individual did not make him blind to the element of error and evil in a man with his deep inside into human nature. He knew that side by side with the divine, there was also the brute in man. That's why Gandhi made a distinction between the higher self and the lower self in a man. But as man is essentially and basically good, Gandhi argued that he was also perfectible[20]. it was possible for a man to extricate himself from the downward pulls of the lower self and realise the higher self in him. In fact the chief emphasis in the Gandhian Praxis is on how to bring out the Divinity inherent in human nature, towards freedom and as a consequence of his belief in the essential divinity of human nature and the Oneness of life, Gandhi contented that if a man gained spiritually, the whole world gained with him and so it was his duty to regulate his behaviour and actions in a way that would benefit the whole community which later on led to Gandhi's lead in India's freedom struggle. Gandhi also believed in the Hindu theory of Karma and rebirth so he understood the law of Karma as the law of moral continuity and rebirth its natural corollary as a chance obtained by the self for attaining its withheld completeness thus Gandhi's concept of Man of self is comprehensive and fits well into the metaphysical framework of his worldview of freedom.

References:
1. Sing Ramjee, Gandhi and The New Millennium, Wealth publishers, New Delhi 2000.
2. Speeches and writings of Mahatma Gandhi Madras Natesan, 4th Edition, p-685.
3. Edward Carpenter, Civilization its cause and cure and other essays, London George Allen and Unwin 1889.
4. Collingwood R. G., Ruskin's philosophy, Chichester Sussex Quentin Nelson,1971.
5. Ronald Romain, Mahatma Gandhi: A Study in Indian Nationalism, in LV Ramaswamy I hear Madras S Ganesan 1923.
6. Ibid
7. Hind Swaraj in the collected works of Mahatma Gandhi, New Delhi publication division 1958.
8. Chatterjee Partha, Omnibus Comprising Nationalist Thought and the colonial India the Nation and its Fragments a possible India, OUP, New Delhi ,1999
9. Ibid.
10. Ibid.
11. Mathai. M. P., Mahatma Gandhi's world-View, D.C. Press, Kottayam,2000.
12. Ibid.
13. Young India October 11th 1928.
14. Sharma. D. S., Essence of Hinduism, Bombay, 1971.
15. Ibid.
16. Dr. S. Radhakrishnan, The Bhagavad Gita, Introductory essay
17. Mathai. M. P., Mahatma Gandhi's world-View, D.C. Press, Kottayam, 2000.
18. Datye. Dr. S. N., Rethinking Mahatma Gandhi: Relevance of Gandhian Thought and Leadership in 21st century, Kalinga publication, New Delhi, 2001.
19. Rolland Romain, Mahatma Gandhi, New Delhi, 1990.
20. Ibid.

Mahatma Gandhi`s Vision on Sustainable Tribal development in India with special reference to Tana Bhagats

Mr. Sandesh Bandhu
Research scholar,
Department of Geography, Institute of Science
Banaras Hindu University, Varanasi
Email: sandeshbandhu69@gmail.com

Kunvar Chandra Verma
Research scholar,
C.M.P. Degree College Prayagraj
(A Constituent college of the University of Allahabad)
Email: alanpatel1999@gmail.com

Prof. Vishwambhar Nath Sharma
Professor
Department of Geography, Institute of Science
Banaras Hindu University, Varanasi
Email: drvnsharmabhu@gmail.com

Abstract

Mahatma Gandhi had a clear vision of rural development and tribal welfare. He believed that the tribal community is the original resident of India and their welfare must be ensured. He included the tribal community in many of his freedom movements and the tribal community also supported him wholeheartedly. Mahatma Gandhi aspired to provide tribal communities with an indigenous livelihood plan, self-sufficiency, habitat development, education and literacy, infrastructure and connectivity, and Gram Swaraj (village self-governance) and these things are useful for sustainable tribal development. Approximately 476 million Indigenous people, or 6.2 percent of the world's population, reside in 90 various countries. Out of them, the United Nations lists over 5,000 distinct groups. In particular, in India, the Scheduled Tribes are commonly referred to as Adivasis, which is an acronym for Indigenous Peoples. With an estimated 104 million people, they make up 8.6percent of the nation's total population. (Census of India, 2011) So Gandhian approach is very relevant for the development of these tribal communities, not only in India but it is applicable all over the world. Some tribal communities literally follow Gandhian ideology. Tana Bhagats is one of them. They are part of the Oraon tribal community of Jharkhand. They worship Mahatma Gandhi like a God and follow the principles of Gandhian philosophy.

Keywords: Gandhian philosophy, Gram Swaraj, Tribal welfare, Tribal community, Tana Bhagats.

Introduction

Mahatma Gandhi's vision for tribal development was based on principles of non-violence, self-reliance, and cultural preservation. He believed in inclusive, sustainable development that preserves indigenous people's cultural and spiritual integrity. Gandhi ji believed that India is a country of villages so the character of the nation is found in rural areas. He emphasized tribal care and the developed world's responsibility to support the comprehensive development of India's indigenous populations. Gandhi Ji was aware of their social and economic circumstances. His vision for India's development includes social and economic goals. The central tenet of this ideology is the economic conception of human welfare. Gandhian approach towards the development of tribal communities lies in the economic construction including empowerment of these communities, self-sufficiency, social justice, and also many other aspects and this ideology is totally towards Sustainable development goals, which is definitely needed today.

Key Elements of Gandhian Vision for Tribal Economic Empowerment:

Gandhian Principle	Application in Tribal Development	Outcome
Swadeshi	Promotion of local crafts, agriculture, and small-scale industries	Economic self-sufficiency and reduced dependency
Non-Exploitation	Opposition to the exploitation of tribal lands and resources	Protection of tribal land rights and natural resources
Village Industries	Support for the establishment of village-level industries	Local employment generation and economic stability

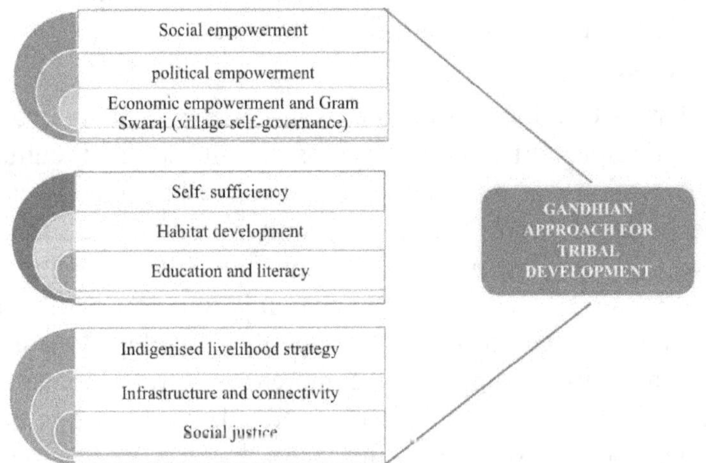

Impact of Gandhian model of development on Government plans for the welfare of tribal communities:

The ideology of Mahatma Gandhi is very important for the sustainable development pf the tribal society because it includes all those aspects through which the welfare of the tribes can be achieved. At present, the major schemes running in India for the development of tribal society are also inspired by the Gandhian approach in which self-sufficiency, habitat development, education, social justice, and empowerment are considered important. Examples of these types of schemes are the following-

Schemes for tribal development in India are following Gandhian approach of development and these are the following major schemes-

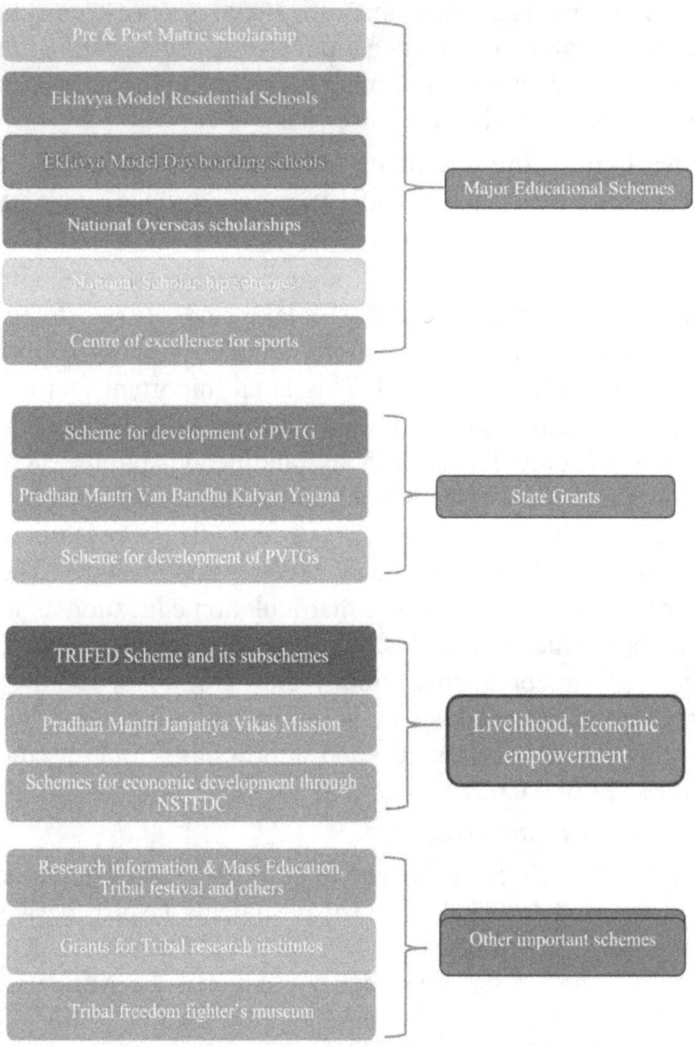

Empowering the Tribal Communities:

Government of India understands the importance of preserving the tribal people's socio-cultural aspect and their role in nation-building so specific provisions for the advancement of Scheduled Tribes and the preservation of tribal culture are include in the Indian Constitution. These provisions are providing them financial security, ensuring that their rights to an education are upheld, safeguarding their language, culture and other elements, and also working towards socio-political empowerment.

Educational Empowerment:

The purpose of Eklavya Model Residential Schools (EMRS) is to offer ST students (Class VI-XII) in rural locations a high-quality education through residential schooling facilities. There are now about 1.2 lakh students registered in 401 EMRS. EMRSs have more female students (60,815) than male students (59,255). This is an important fact to be aware of. Furthermore, for the Ekalavya Model Residential Schools, which will serve 3.5 lakh indigenous pupils, 38,000 teachers and support personnel are being hired. To help ST students with their studies, a variety of Fellowship and Scholarship Programs have been established. These programs cover pre- and post-matriculation education as well as higher education and study abroad. Notably, over the course of the preceding nine years—from April 2014 to September 2023—a total of 3.15 crore tribal students have been awarded scholarships and fellowships totaling more than Rs. 17,087 Crore.

Economic Empowerment:

Over Rs. 17,087 crore in scholarships and fellowships have been awarded to 3.15 crore tribal students (April 2014 till September 2023).In acknowledgment of the importance it places on the welfare of tribal populations, the Ministry of Tribal Affairs has increased its budget allocation significantly, "from Rs. 4295.94 crore in 2013–14 to Rs.

12461.88 crore in 2023–24, or an increase of roughly 190.01%. The Indian tribal groups' efforts to develop their means of subsistence through retail marketing are supported by TRIFED or the Tribal Cooperative Marketing Development Federation of India". The annual budget projection for the fiscal year 2023–2024 also includes a provision of Rs. 288 crores to be executed through TRIFED, namely through the establishment of producer firms and Self-Help Groups. On April 18, 2023, in Manipur, a Central Sector Scheme named "Marketing and Logistics Development for Promotion of Tribal Products from North-Eastern Region (PTP-NER)" was introduced under TRIFED for the benefit of the Northeastern Region's Scheduled Tribes. So in these ways, GOI is trying to uplift the economic condition of tribal communities of the country. The government is continuously increasing its budget and ensuring the welfare of tribal communities.

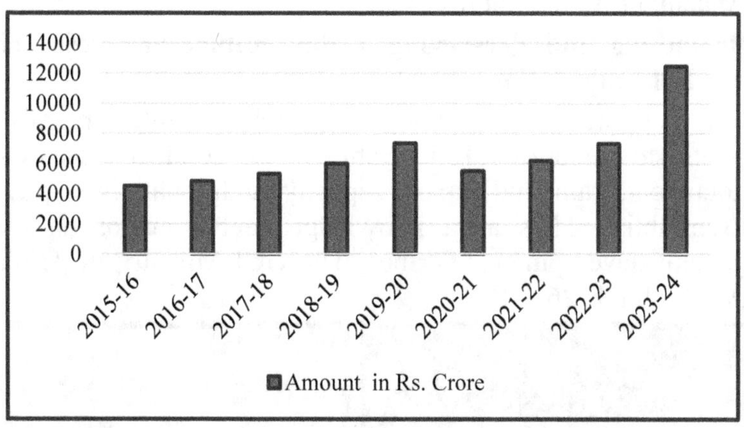

Ministry of Tribal Affairs increases in budget in last 9 years, Source- Ministry of Tribal Affairs

Improved Infrastructure and Livelihood Opportunities:

In villages with a significant tribal population, the PMAAGY ("Pradhan Mantri Adi Adarsh Gram Yojana") aims to construct the basic infrastructure. 500 Scheduled Tribes

(STs) and 36428 villages with 50% tribal population have been identified as part of the project. These villages are to provide basic infrastructure facilities; they also involve villages in the Aspirational Districts that NITI Aayog has designated. 10509 villages are covered by PMAAGY in 86 common districts out of the total number of Aspirational Districts.

Initiatives for Better Health Outcomes:

The National Health Mission, which is part of the Ministry of Health and Family Welfare, has created and distributed detailed guidelines for the management and prevention of hemoglobinopathies, such as sickle cell disease, to the states. The government has made efforts to guarantee that Sickle Cell disease, a genetic blood ailment that affects the tribal population in Central, Southern, and Western India, has been virtually eradicated. In this aim, on July 1, 2023, the Prime Minister of Madhya Pradesh announced the Sickle Cell Anaemia Elimination Mission.

Promoting and Preserving Tribal culture and research work through TRIs:

The Support to TRI (Tribal Research Institute) initiative seeks to enhance TRI`s ability to conduct research, document, train, and expand capacity; additionally, it aspires to establish TRIs as a knowledge center supporting the general development of tribes. The GOI Ministry of Tribal Affairs funds 26 TRIs.

Note: Tribal research institutes and museums are promoting tribal research work as well as tribal culture. (Pictures clicked by the researcher during TRI Bhopal visit)

Honoring and Celebrating India's Tribal Communities:

Ten authorized Tribal Freedom Fighter's museums are located in states where native people once resided, fought the British, and refused to submit. Prime Minister Narendra Modi requested the creation of a plan on November 1, 2022, for the development of Mangarh Dham in the Banswara district of Rajasthan. Near the boundary between Rajasthan and Gujarat, Mangarh Dham is the location of the mass shooting by the British in 1913 that claimed the lives of over 1500 Bhil independence fighters. The governments of Gujarat, Rajasthan, Maharashtra, and Madhya Pradesh will collaborate to build the Mangarh Dham, a national memorial showcasing the tribal people's rich cultural heritage and legacy.

Tana Bhagats, their movement, and their attachment to Gandhian philosophy:

A tribal community in the Indian state of Jharkhand is known as Tana Bhagat. Basically they belongs to Oraon tribal community and started the Tana Bhagat Movement (1914). The Tana Bhagat Movement (1914–1920) opposed the corrupt commercial practices of the zamindars and the local British government policies in Chhota Nagpur, British India. Jatra Bhagat was the main leader of this movement.

Years before Mahatma Gandhi's parallel campaign against British authority, the Tana Bhagats staged a Satyagraha (civil disobedience movement) in opposition to the taxes levied on them by the British colonial administration. They were against the British and the Zamindars. Tana Bhagats adhere to Ahinsa (non-violence) and are disciples of Mahatma Gandhi. At present time, their total population, as reported by Ganga Tana Bhagat former MLA, is approximately 45,000. Ranchi, Khunti, Gumla, Lohardaga, Latehar, Chatra, Palamu, and Hazaribagh are basically the main areas of Tana Bhagats.

Influence of Mahatma Gandhi on Tana Bhagats:

1. Non-Violent Resistance:
The Tana Bhagats were influenced by Gandhi's principles of non-violent resistance (Satyagraha). Gandhi's emphasis on peaceful protest and civil disobedience resonated with the Tana Bhagats, who were engaged in a struggle against oppressive systems and colonial rule.

2.Religious Reform and Self-Reliance:
Gandhi's ideas on self-reliance and economic independence found echoes in the Tana Bhagat movement. The movement promoted social and religious reforms among the tribal communities, seeking to uplift them by encouraging local self-reliance and rejecting external oppression.

2. Spiritual and Social Upliftment:
The Tana Bhagats incorporated Gandhi's ideas on moral and social reform. They aimed to purify their social practices and emphasized ethical living, which aligned with Gandhi's vision of moral and spiritual regeneration.

Relationship with Gandhi's Vision:
While the Tana Bhagats were not directly organized by Gandhi, their movement reflected his broader ideas of non-violence, self-reliance, and social reform. The overlap in their objectives demonstrated how Gandhi's principles were interpreted and adapted by various groups across India,

including tribal communities striving for justice and empowerment. In summary, the Tana Bhagats were influenced by Gandhi's ideas, particularly his principles of non-violence and social reform. Their movement represents an example of how Gandhi's philosophy was embraced and adapted by diverse communities in India, including tribal groups seeking to address their own unique challenges. Tana Bhagats adhere to Ahinsa (non-violence) and are disciples of Mahatma Gandhi. They worship Mahatma Gandhi like God.

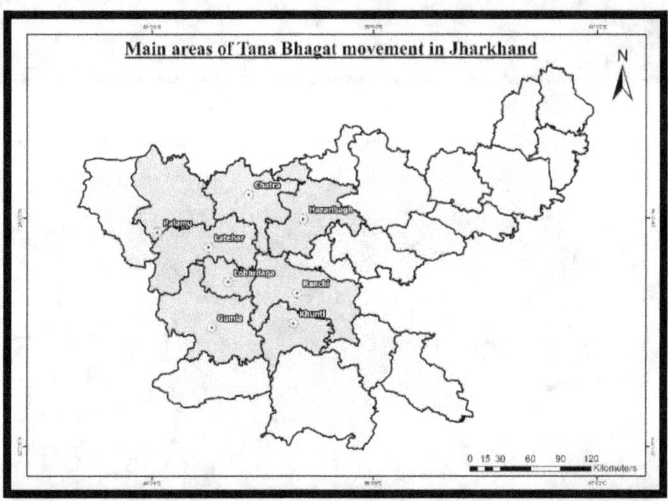

Tana Bhagats in their traditional white dress.

Tana Bhagat with Gandhian Charkha

Tana Bhagat Community in a village of Jharkhand

One of the remarkable features of the Tana Bhagat movement was that the entire foundation of the movement was based on non-violence. They believe in non-violence, nature conservation, hygiene, and affection towards animals and one special thing that they practice is the worship of the National flag (Tiranga). For Tana Bhagats, Mahatma Gandhi and the National flag are the most important.

Legacy and Contemporary Relevance

The Tana Bhagat movement continues to have an impact on

society today. Its history of nonviolent protest and social change has served as an inspiration for numerous Indian movements. Furthermore, in the current global setting, the movement's message of social equality and environmental

Influence on Future Generations

The people who follow Jatra Bhagat's teachings are known as Tana Bhagats, and they still do. They are an inspiration for social justice and sustainability because of their commitment to a life of social justice, communal harmony, and simplicity.

Lessons for Modern Society

- Sustainable living: The movement's emphasis on living an austere lifestyle encourages discussion about modern sustainable living.
- Social activism: Modern social activists might draw inspiration from the nonviolent strategy of confronting injustices.

Offering significant lessons on the strength of faith and the significance of resisting injustice, the Tana Bhagat movement weaves a complex web of spiritual renewal and social engagement. It is evidence of the close relationship that can exist between spirituality and the pursuit of social justice and equality. Tana Bhagats are really a promising example of how they are following Gandhian principles till today. They are promoting a sustainable way of living which is really needed in the present time but the promotion of these ideologies and ways of living is also required for the modern generation.

Conclusion

Mahatma Gandhi's vision of tribal development emphasized rural upliftment and self-reliance, emphasizing harmony, respect for traditions, and local control. His principles continue to influence discussions on tribal development in India and other regions. Today, tribal development projects empower indigenous communities to take charge of their own development, safeguard their cultural legacy, and manage their natural resources responsibly. The Government of India has adopted Gandhian approaches to address socio-economic disparities and promote inclusive growth in tribal areas. This approach aims to preserve tribal identity and autonomy, promoting sustainable development in tribal areas.

References:
1. Bagachi, T., & Pandey, S. (2023). Gandhi, Tribes and Rural Development. Rawat Publication
2. Basu, R. (2022). Gandhian Approach to Education and its Relevance for Tribal Development. Journal of Educational Development, 45(3), 289-305.
3. Chakrabarti, A. (2023). Environmental Sustainability in Gandhian Thought. Journal of Environmental Philosophy, 52(4), 415-432.
4. Chatterjee, S. (2022). Mahatma Gandhi's Vision for Tribal Upliftment. Indian Journal of Social Work, 63(2), 123-137.
5. Chattoraj C, A. K. (1999, January). The Tana Bhagat movement: An appraisal. In Proceedings of the Indian History Congress (Vol. 60, pp. 639-644). Indian History Congress.
6. Dasgupta, S. (1999). Reordering a World: The Tana Bhagat Movement, 1914-1919. Studies in History, 15(1), 1-41.
7. Duary, N. A. B. A. K. U. M. A. R. (2008). The Tana Bhagat movement. The unrest axle: Ethno-social movements in Eastern India, 147-152.
8. Gupta, K. A. (2012). "Tana Bhagats want early solution to their problems. Ranchi News - Times of India". The Times of India.

9. Gupta, S. D. (2003). Constructing a Tribe A Case Study of the Oraons and the Tana Bhagats in Late Nineteenth and Early Twentieth Centuries. Changing Tribal Life: A Socio-philosophical Perspective, 15.

10. Kumar, N., & Patel, R. (2022). Sustainable Development in Tribal Areas: Lessons from Gandhian Philosophy. Development Studies Journal, 38(2), 224-241.

11. Kumar, S. (2008, January). The Tana Bhagat Movement in Chotanagpur (1914-1920). In Proceedings of the Indian History Congress (Vol. 69, pp. 723-731). Indian History Congress.

12. Mehta, P., & Jain, S. (2021). Gandhian Principles in Contemporary Tribal Development. Journal of Tribal Affairs, 34(1), 45-60.

13. Mishra, S. S. (2008). The Bhagat movement among the Oraon. The unrest axle: Ethno-social movements in Eastern India, 135-146.

14. Mishra, S. S. (2008). The Bhagat movement among the Oraon. The unrest axle: Ethno-social movements in Eastern India, 135-146.

15. Roy, T. (2021). Non-Violence and Tribal Welfare: A Gandhian Perspective. Journal of Peace Studies, 19(3), 89-102.

16. Shah, A. (2023). Gram Swaraj and Tribal Autonomy in Gandhi's Thought. Rural Development Review, 48(2), 150-167.

17. Sinha, S. P. (1993). Conflict and Tension in Tribal Society. Concept Publishing Company. ISBN 978-81-7022-493-8.

18. Sundar, N. (2023). Gandhian Philosophy and Its Impact on Tribal Development. Journal of Social Sciences, 41(5), 345-363.

19. Tripathy, H. The Tana Bhagat Movement: From Socio-Religious Reform to Political Rebellion. Contemporary Social Sciences, 109.

20. Tripathy, H. The Tana Bhagat Movement: From Socio-

Religious Reform to Political Rebellion. Contemporary Social Sciences, 109.

Web Sources

Gurpreet Singh Ranchi, CC BY-SA 4.0
https://creativecommons.org/licenses/by-sa/4.0
https://avenuemail.in/tana-bhagats-of-jharkhand-have-kept-mahatma-gandhis-legacy-alive/
https://indianexpress.com/article/political-pulse/jharkhand-adivasis-tana-bhagat-self-rule-5th-schedule-8227462/
https://lagatar24.com/jharkhand-tribal-research-institute-conducting-research-on-tana-bhagats/87977/
https://philosophy.institute/tribal-philosophy/tana-bhagat-movement-tribal-purification-resistance/
https://sfe.org.in/pdf/Tana%20Bhagats.pdf
https://theindiantribal.com/2022/05/07/tana-bhagats-struggle-to-preserve-old-glory/
https://timesofindia.indiatimes.com/city/jamshedpur/mahatma-still-alive-among-jharkhand-tana-bhagats/articleshow/71397661.cms
https://timesofindia.indiatimes.com/city/ranchi/Tana-Bhagats-want-early-solution-to-their-problems/articleshow/17596646.cms
https://www.indiatoday.in/coronavirus-outbreak/story/jharkhand-tana-bhagats-show-how-to-beat-covid-19-waves-no-positive-case-yet-1815290-2021-06-15
https://www.newindianexpress.com/good-news/2019/Sep/30/practising-satya-and-Ahinsa-the-community-which-holds-gandhi-as-god-2041063.html
https://www.prabhatkhabar.com/state/jharkhand/ranchi/independence-day-2023-tana-bhagats-said-in-1916-itself-british-run-away-used-to-chant-that-maa-bharti-be-free-grj
https://www.inextlive.com/jharkhand/ranchi/nine-freedom-fighters-from-ranchi-took-part-in-the-freedom-struggle-1711732234

Gandhiji and Rural Reconstruction in India: Reviving India's Villages for a Self-Reliant Nation

Raj Kumar Pal
Research Scholar
Department of Education
Tezpur University
Email: rajkpal112@gmail.com

Antara Dey
Assistant Professor,
Department of Education,
Tezpur University
Email: antara9@tezu.ernet.in

Abstract

Mahatma Gandhi, revered as the Father of the Nation, significantly influenced the course of rural reconstruction in India. His approach to rural development was not merely a response to colonial exploitation but a comprehensive vision aimed at creating self-reliant, self-sufficient, and sustainable village economies. Central to this vision was his concept of Gram Swaraj (village self-rule), where decentralized governance and local self-sufficiency were emphasized as pillars of true independence. Gandhi's focus on agriculture and Khadi as foundational elements of the rural economy highlighted his belief in sustainable practices and the revival of traditional industries. Gandhi's *Nai Talim*, further complemented his rural reconstruction efforts by integrating productive work with learning, thus aligning education with the socio-economic needs of rural communities. This model sought to promote self-worth, dignity of labour, and social equality, essential for uplifting marginalized communities in the deeply hierarchical rural landscape.

Gandhi's efforts extended beyond philosophy to practical initiatives, including the establishment of ashrams that served as centers of rural development and social reform. His promotion of cottage industries, particularly through the Khadi movement, aimed at providing employment, preserving traditional skills, and fostering economic independence. The legacy of Gandhi's rural reconstruction efforts is evident in India's post-independence policies, non-governmental organizations, and global sustainable development movements. While his ideas have faced criticisms related to economic viability, technological advancement, and scalability, they continue to offer valuable insights into creating a just, equitable, and sustainable society. Gandhi's vision remains a guiding light for contemporary rural development efforts, emphasizing the importance of self-reliance, community-based learning and social justice in building a resilient and inclusive rural India.

Introduction

Mahatma Gandhi, fondly known as the Father of the Nation, remains a beacon of inspiration for millions around the world. His philosophy and actions have profoundly influenced various aspects of Indian society, including rural reconstruction. Gandhi's vision of rural India was not just a reaction to colonial exploitation but a holistic approach towards creating a self-reliant, self-sufficient, and sustainable rural economy. This article delves into Gandhiji's perspectives, contributions and works on rural reconstruction in India, providing a comprehensive understanding of his enduring legacy.

Gandhiji's Perspectives on Rural Reconstruction

Vision of Self-Reliant Villages

Gandhiji envisioned a self-reliant village economy as the cornerstone of India's development. He believed that India's soul resided in its villages, and true independence could only be achieved through the upliftment of rural areas. In his words, "The true India is to be found not in its few cities but in its 700,000 villages" (Gandhi, 1942).

His concept of Gram Swaraj (village self-rule) emphasized local self-sufficiency and governance. He advocated for decentralized administration, where each village would function as a self-contained republic, managing its affairs and meeting its needs independently. This vision aimed to eliminate the dependence on urban centres and industrialization, fostering a more equitable distribution of resources.

Importance of Agriculture and Khadi

Gandhi saw agriculture as the backbone of the rural economy. He stressed the need for sustainable farming practices, crop diversity, and organic farming. He believed that modern industrial farming methods would erode traditional agricultural knowledge and harm the environment.

Khadi, the hand-spun and hand-woven cloth, was another pillar of Gandhi's rural reconstruction philosophy. He promoted Khadi as a means to revive the rural economy, create employment, and reduce dependency on foreign goods. Gandhi's emphasis on Khadi was not merely economic but also symbolic of self-reliance and national pride.

Social Equality and Upliftment of Marginalized Communities

Gandhiji's approach to rural reconstruction was inclusive, addressing the social inequalities prevalent in rural India. He worked tirelessly to eradicate untouchability and uplift marginalized communities, ensuring that the benefits of rural development reached all sections of society. His establishment of ashrams in rural areas served as centres for social reform, education, and community development.

Gandhiji's Nai Talim in the Context of Rural Reconstruction in India

Mahatma Gandhi's *Nai Talim*, or Basic Education, was a revolutionary concept that sought to transform not just the education system in India but also the broader socio-economic fabric of rural society. Conceived as a holistic and practical approach to learning, *Nai Talim* emphasized education through productive work, aligning intellectual development with the needs of rural communities. This educational philosophy was integral to Gandhi's vision of rural reconstruction, aiming to foster self-reliant, sustainable, and socially equitable village economies.

The Essence of Nai Talim

Nai Talim, literally meaning "New Education", proposed a radical departure from the existing education system, which Gandhi believed was overly focused on rote learning and alienated from the realities of rural life. He envisioned an education system where knowledge would be acquired through engaging in productive activities, particularly those rooted in traditional village industries like spinning, weaving, and agriculture. This method was intended to make education more relevant and accessible to the rural masses, who constituted the majority of India's population.

Central to *Nai Talim* was the idea that education should integrate intellectual, physical, and moral development. By learning through work, students would not only gain practical skills but also develop a sense of self-worth and dignity of labour. Gandhi believed that this would prepare them to contribute meaningfully to their communities and live in harmony with their environment.

Nai Talim and Rural Reconstruction

Gandhi's vision of rural reconstruction was based on the concept of Gram Swaraj, or village self-governance. He believed that India's strength lay in its villages, and that true independence could only be achieved by making villages self-sufficient and sustainable. *Nai Talim* was conceived as a key instrument in this process of rural reconstruction.

Through *Nai Talim*, Gandhi sought to empower rural communities by reviving traditional crafts and industries that had been undermined by colonial policies. By integrating these activities into the education system, Gandhi aimed to provide students with the skills necessary to support themselves and their communities, thereby reducing unemployment and poverty. This focus on vocational education was not just about economic survival but also about preserving the cultural heritage of rural India.

Moreover, *Nai Talim* was a deliberate attempt to promote social equality. Gandhi recognized that the existing education system perpetuated social hierarchies by devaluing manual labour and privileging intellectual work. By making productive work a central part of education, he sought to break down these barriers and create a more just and equitable society.

Relevance of Nai Talim Today

In contemporary India, Gandhiji's *Nai Talim* remains a relevant and powerful model for rural development. The challenges of unemployment, poverty, and the erosion of traditional livelihoods continue to plague rural areas. The principles of *Nai Talim*, with its emphasis on vocational training, community-based learning, and sustainable practices, offer valuable insights for addressing these issues.

Furthermore, as the world grapples with environmental crises and the need for sustainable development, Gandhi's vision of an education system that is in harmony with nature and the local environment is more relevant than ever. By fostering self-reliance, dignity of labor, and social equality, *Nai Talim* provides a blueprint for a more just and sustainable rural economy.

In conclusion, Gandhiji's *Nai Talim* was not just an

educational reform but a comprehensive approach to rural reconstruction. It aimed to empower individuals and communities, preserve cultural heritage, and promote social justice. Its principles continue to offer important lessons for contemporary efforts to revitalize rural India and build a more equitable society.

Contributions to Rural Reconstruction

Establishment of Ashrams

Gandhi established several ashrams across India, which became hubs for rural development and social reform. The Sabarmati Ashram in Gujarat and the Sevagram Ashram in Maharashtra are notable examples. These ashrams were not just places of residence but centres of learning and experimentation in sustainable living, agriculture, and cottage industries.

In these ashrams, Gandhi and his followers practiced and promoted various activities such as spinning Khadi, organic farming, and basic education. The ashrams embodied Gandhi's principles of simple living, self-sufficiency, and community service, serving as models for rural reconstruction.

Promotion of Cottage Industries

Gandhi championed the cause of cottage industries as a means to provide employment and sustain rural livelihoods. He believed that industrialization would lead to the exploitation of labor and resources, creating economic disparities. Instead, he advocated for small-scale, decentralized industries that could be managed and run by local communities.

The promotion of Khadi and other village industries like soap-making, oil extraction, and handicrafts were integral to his rural reconstruction efforts. These industries provided employment, preserved traditional skills, and reduced dependence on urban and foreign goods.

Education and Health

Gandhi's approach to education was holistic, focusing on the overall development of an individual. He advocated for Nai Talim, or basic education, which emphasized learning through productive work. This model integrated vocational training with basic literacy and numeracy, preparing individuals to contribute effectively to rural economies.

Health was another critical area of focus. Gandhi promoted simple, natural remedies and preventive healthcare practices. He established clinics and trained volunteers to provide basic medical care in rural areas, addressing issues like sanitation, hygiene, and nutrition.

Works and Initiatives in Rural Reconstruction

Champaran and Kheda Satyagraha

Gandhi's early experiments with rural reconstruction began with the Champaran Satyagraha (1917) and Kheda Satyagraha (1918). In Champaran, Bihar, indigo farmers were subjected to exploitative practices by British planters. Gandhi's intervention led to the abolition of the oppressive system and initiated socio-economic reforms in the region. He focused on education, sanitation, and self-reliance, setting up schools and encouraging villagers to adopt hygienic practices.

The Kheda Satyagraha in Gujarat was a response to a devastating famine. Gandhi organized peasants to demand relief from taxes, which the British authorities eventually conceded. These movements highlighted the power of non-violent resistance and laid the foundation for Gandhi's future rural reconstruction efforts.

The Khadi Movement

The Khadi Movement was central to Gandhi's rural reconstruction strategy. He saw Khadi as a symbol of self-reliance and economic independence. The All India Spinners Association (AISA), established in 1925, coordinated the production and distribution of Khadi. Gandhi encouraged every Indian to spin their own cloth, reducing reliance on British textiles and empowering rural artisans.

The movement also had a significant social impact, bridging the gap between urban and rural populations. Urban elites who adopted Khadi showed solidarity with rural workers, fostering a sense of national unity and shared purpose.

The Village Industries Association

In 1934, Gandhi established the Village Industries Association (VIA) to promote and support various cottage industries. The VIA aimed to revive traditional crafts and provide rural employment opportunities. It focused on industries like pottery, carpentry, tanning, and food processing, ensuring that villagers could sustain themselves economically.

Gandhi's efforts through the VIA helped preserve traditional skills, reduce migration to cities, and create a self-sufficient rural economy. The association also played a crucial role in providing training and resources to rural artisans, enhancing their productivity and market reach.

Constructive Programmes

Gandhi's Constructive Programme, outlined in 1941, was a comprehensive blueprint for national regeneration. It included 18 points, focusing on areas like communal harmony, education, sanitation, women's empowerment, and rural industries. The programme aimed to build a self-reliant and morally robust society, with a strong emphasis on rural development.

Key components of the Constructive Programme included the promotion of Khadi, village sanitation, basic education, and the upliftment of marginalized communities. Gandhi believed that real freedom could only be achieved through the holistic development of rural areas, making them self-sufficient and resilient.

Legacy and Impact on Contemporary Rural Development

Influence on Government Policies

Gandhi's vision of rural reconstruction has significantly influenced India's post-independence policies. The principles of self-reliance, decentralized governance, and sustainable development have been integral to various rural development programs. The Community Development Programme (1952) and the establishment of Panchayati Raj institutions are direct reflections of Gandhi's ideas.

The Five-Year Plans, initiated by the Indian government, incorporated many of Gandhi's principles. The emphasis on rural industries, agriculture, and decentralized planning can be traced back to his vision. Programs like the Mahatma Gandhi National Rural Employment Guarantee Act (MGNREGA) continue to uphold his legacy by providing employment and sustaining rural livelihoods.

Non-Governmental Organizations and Movements

Gandhi's influence extends beyond government policies to various non-governmental organizations (NGOs) and social movements. Organizations like the Self-Employed Women's Association (SEWA) and the Khadi and Village Industries Commission (KVIC) draw inspiration from his ideas.

SEWA, founded in 1972, empowers women in the informal sector, promoting self-reliance and economic independence. KVIC continues to promote Khadi and other village industries, ensuring that rural artisans have access to markets and resources.

Sustainable Development and Global Influence

Gandhi's principles of sustainability and self-sufficiency have found resonance in global movements for sustainable development. His emphasis on local economies, organic farming, and community-led development align with contemporary environmental and social justice movements.

The concept of Gandhian economics, which advocates for a non-exploitative, human-centric economic model, has influenced thinkers and activists worldwide. Gandhi's vision of rural reconstruction serves as a guiding light for those seeking to create sustainable and equitable societies.

Challenges and Criticisms:

Economic Viability

One of the primary criticisms of Gandhi's rural reconstruction model is its economic viability. Critics argue that small-scale, traditional industries may not be able to compete with large-scale industrial production in terms of efficiency and cost-effectiveness. The globalized economy poses challenges to the sustainability of localized, self-sufficient models.

Technological Advancements

Gandhi's emphasis on traditional methods and self-reliance is sometimes seen as being at odds with technological advancements. Critics argue that modern technology and innovation are essential for development and that Gandhi's model may hinder progress by rejecting industrialization and modern methods.

Implementation and Scalability

Implementing Gandhiji's vision on a large scale has proven to be challenging. While his principles are sound, translating them into actionable policies that can be scaled up across a vast and diverse country like India requires significant effort, resources, and political will.

Conclusions

Mahatma Gandhi's perspectives, contributions, and works on rural reconstruction in India continue to resonate in contemporary discussions on sustainable development and social justice. His vision of self-reliant villages, emphasis on agriculture and cottage industries, and commitment to social equality laid the foundation for a holistic approach to rural development. Despite the challenges and criticisms, Gandhi's ideas remain relevant, offering valuable insights into creating a just and equitable society. His legacy endures in the policies, programs, and movements that strive to uplift rural communities and build a sustainable future.

References:

1. Dey, S. K. (1964). Community Development: A Movement and Its Evolution.
2. Gandhi, M. K. (1942). Harijan. Retrieved from Gandhi Heritage Portal
3. Khadi and Village Industries Commission (KVIC). (2020). Annual Report.
4. Kumarappa, J. C. (1945). The Gandhian Plan of Economic Development for India.
5. Ministry of Rural Development, Government of India. (2020). Annual Report.
6. Self-Employed Women's Association (SEWA). (2020). Annual Report.
7. University of Delhi. (2021). Course Materials on Gandhian Thought and Rural Development.
8. World Bank. (2020). Rural Development in India: Policies and Practices.

Mahatma Gandhi and Religion

Surabhi Shrivastava
Research Scholar
Department of History
Shri J.J.T University, Jhunjhunu

Dr. Najiya Hussain
Research Director
Department of History
Shri J.J.T University, Jhunjhunu

Abstract

Mahatma Gandhi's life and worldview were profoundly shaped by his deep religious beliefs and spiritual practices. This paper examines the various religious influences and philosophical perspectives that informed Gandhi's teachings and led to his distinctive approach to nonviolence, social justice, and interfaith harmony. Gandhi's engagement with Hinduism, as well as his exposure to and appreciation of other faiths such as Islam and Christianity, are explored in detail. The study also analyses Gandhi's interpretations of key religious concepts and scriptures, his critique of dogmatic religiosity, and his advocacy for religious pluralism and tolerance. The paper ultimately highlights the central role that spirituality and the ethical foundations of various religious traditions played in shaping Gandhi's transformative leadership and enduring legacy.

Introduction

Mahatma Gandhi's life and teachings were profoundly shaped by his religious beliefs and practices. Mahatma Gandhi was a towering figure of the 20th century, known for his unwavering commitment to nonviolent resistance and his tireless efforts to achieve Indian independence. However, Gandhi's life and work were also deeply rooted in his religious beliefs and spiritual practices. This paper will explore the intersection of Mahatma Gandhi's life and teachings with his religious worldview, examining how his understanding of Hinduism, as well as his engagement with other faiths, profoundly shaped his approach to social and political change. Mahatma Gandhi, the iconic Indian independence leader, was a deeply spiritual individual whose life and teachings were profoundly shaped by his religious beliefs and practices. From a young age, Gandhi displayed a profound fascination with the world's religious traditions, driven by a desire to understand the underlying unity that connects them all. This lifelong spiritual journey would go on to have a transformative impact on Gandhi's worldview and approach to social and political reform Mahatma Gandhi's life and teachings were deeply influenced by the multifaceted nature of religion in Indian society. His worldview was shaped by his nuanced understanding of Hinduism as well as his exposure to other faiths such as Islam.

Gandhi Early Life and Spiritual Influences

Gandhi's early life was marked by a deep fascination with religious teachings and a desire to understand the underlying all faiths. Mohandas Karamchand Gandhi, fondly known as Mahatma Gandhi, is an iconic figure who left an indelible mark on the world. Gandhi's early life was shaped by his family's strong spiritual values and traditions. He was born in 1869 in Porbandar, a coastal town in the western Indian state of Gujarat, to a family with deep Hindu roots. Gandhi's father, Karamchand Gandhi, was the chief minister of Porbandar, while his mother, Putlibai, was a deeply religious woman who instilled in him the importance of truth, nonviolence, and vegetarianism (Gardner, 1993). Growing up, Gandhi was influenced by the teachings of the Bhagavad Gita, a Hindu sacred text that emphasizes the importance of duty, selfless action, and the pursuit of spiritual enlightenment. (Dhillon, 2023) His early experiences and the spiritual environment of his upbringing would later have a profound impact on his worldview and the development of his unique approach to social and political change. As he grew older, Gandhi's spiritual beliefs and practices became increasingly intertwined with his political activism. He was greatly inspired by the writings of American philosopher Henry David Thoreau, particularly his essay on civil disobedience, which advocated for non-violent resistance to unjust laws. Gandhi's commitment to nonviolence, or "satyagraha," became the cornerstone of his political strategy, as he sought to liberate India from British rule through peaceful means. (Dhillon, 2023)

Gandhi's religious and spiritual beliefs were deeply rooted in his understanding of the Bhagavad Gita, which he saw as a source of wisdom and guidance for both personal and political transformation. He believed that the Gita's message of nonviolence and the realization of the divine within each individual was essential to achieving true freedom and justice. (Lal, 2013)

Gandhi's religious and spiritual beliefs were not confined to Hinduism; he had a deep respect for other faiths and believed in the unity of all religions. As a result, his influence extended beyond the borders of India, inspiring civil rights movements and nonviolent resistance around the world. (Gardner, 1993) Gandhi viewed religion as inseparable from life and believed in the fundamental unity of all religions. He advocated for "Sarva Dharma Sama Bhava," meaning all religions are different paths leading to the same truth (Sarva Dharma Sama Bhava - Wikipedia, 2007). He emphasized the shared values of love, compassion and non-violence found in all faiths.

Gandhi's understanding of religion was deeply personal and influenced by his own Hindu beliefs, particularly the Bhagavad Gita, which he interpreted through the lens of non-violence and self-realization. However, he didn't believe any single religion held a monopoly on truth (Mahatma Gandhi's Discovery of Religion, 1998). He respected all faiths equally and encouraged interfaith dialogue and understanding.

Gandhi's concept of "Truth is God" (Truth is God, n.d) further illustrates his perspective. He believed that seeking truth was the highest form of religious practice and this pursuit transcended dogma and rituals. He saw religion as a guiding force for ethical living and believed that true religion manifested in actions that upheld truth, justice and non-violence.

Gandhi's Thought on Hinduism

Gandhi was born into Hinduism and remained deeply connected to it throughout his life. However, his understanding of Hinduism was nuanced and emphasized its philosophical and ethical core over rituals and dogma. He believed in the inherent truth of all religions (Mohandas Gandhi on Conversion Being Unnecessary, 2023) and saw Hinduism as a path to realizing that truth, not as the only path.

Gandhi was critical of certain aspects of Hinduism, such as caste-based discrimination and untouchability, which he considered distortions of its true essence. He actively campaigned against these social evils, advocating for equality and the rights of all people.

Gandhi's interpretation of the Bhagavad Gita (Dhillon, 2023) significantly shaped his view of Hinduism. He saw the Gita's message of selfless action (karma yoga) and non-violence (Ahinsa) as central to Hindu philosophy and drew upon these principles in his personal life and political activism.

He believed that Hinduism's emphasis on non-violence had the highest expression and application compared to other religions (62. Religious Tolerance in India, n.d) (22. Why I Am a Hindu, n.d). However, he also acknowledged the presence of valuable teachings in other faiths and encouraged Hindus to be open to learning from them.

Gandhi's Hinduism was inclusive and outward-looking. He believed in the universality of its core principles and sought to live by them in a way that resonated with people of all faiths. He saw no contradiction in being a devout Hindu while respecting and learning from other religions.

To further explore Gandhi's perspective on Hinduism, you might find it helpful to examine his writings on specific topics like:

- His views on the caste system and untouchability.
- His interpretation of the Bhagavad Gita and its relevance to modern life.
- His interactions with people of other faiths and his efforts to promote interfaith harmony.

You could also consider adding some of his writings to your library for a more in-depth analysis. For example, his book "One's Own Religion" (10. One's Own Religion, n.d) might offer valuable insights into his personal understanding of Hinduism.

Gandhi's Thought on Islam

Gandhi studied the Quran and engaged with Islamic principles, seeking common ground between Islam and his own philosophy (Gandhi on theory and practice of Islam, 2015). He acknowledged that violence and fundamentalism, often associated with Islam in global conflicts, raised questions about the religion's peaceful nature (Gandhi on theory and practice of Islam, 2015). However, he believed that judging an entire faith based on the actions of some was inaccurate and unjust.

Gandhi emphasized that India's history demonstrated periods of both peaceful coexistence and conflict between Muslims and people of other faiths (Gandhi on theory and practice of Islam, 2015), suggesting that the issue was complex and not inherently tied to Islam itself.

He championed interfaith dialogue and understanding, believing that respecting diverse religious experiences was crucial. While he advocated for individuals to follow their chosen faith sincerely (17. Conversion, n.d), he opposed proselytization that required discarding one's existing religion, seeing it as a threat to global peace (17. Conversion, n.d).

Gandhi's focus remained on shared values like non-violence, truth, and compassion, which he believed transcended religious boundaries. He saw these principles as essential for peaceful coexistence and sought to highlight them in his interactions with people of all faiths, including Islam.

Gandhi's Thought on Christianity

Gandhi engaged with Christianity throughout his life, particularly during his time in South Africa and England. He studied the life and teachings of Jesus Christ, expressing admiration for his emphasis on love and forgiveness (Gandhi, Christ and Christianity, 1998). He was particularly drawn to the concept of "turning the other cheek" (Gandhi, Christ and Christianity, 1998), seeing it as a powerful example of non-violent resistance.

However, Gandhi was critical of what he perceived as hypocrisy within Christianity, particularly the actions of some Christians that contradicted the teachings of love and compassion (Gandhi, Christ and Christianity, 1998). He questioned the concept of conversion, believing that true faith came from within and shouldn't involve discarding one's existing beliefs (17. Conversion, n.d). He advocated for interfaith understanding and encouraged Christians to live by the values of Christ, emphasizing love and service (Gorski, 2003).

Gandhi's views on Christianity were complex and sometimes seemingly contradictory. He admired Christ and his teachings but remained critical of institutionalized religion and its role in colonialism and violence. He saw value in the ethical teachings of Christianity but believed that true spirituality transcended religious labels and manifested in actions that upheld truth, love, and non-violence.

To gain a deeper understanding of Gandhi's perspective on Christianity, you might find it helpful to explore his writings and speeches where he directly addresses Christian principles and figures. For example, his book "Gandhi, Christ and Christianity" (Gandhi, Christ and Christianity, 1998) could offer valuable insights into his complex relationship with this faith. You can add this book to your library for further study.

Gandhi's Thought on Buddhism

While Gandhi didn't leave behind extensive writings specifically focused on Buddhism, his emphasis on Ahinsa (non-violence) and his practice of satyagraha (truth force) resonated with core Buddhist principles.

Although he primarily studied and drew inspiration from the Bhagavad Gita (Dhillon, 2023), Gandhi acknowledged the profound impact of Buddha's teachings on India and the world. He recognized Buddhism's significant contribution to the philosophy and practice of non-violence, a principle central to his own life and work.

Gandhi's emphasis on self-suffering as a means to awaken compassion and effect social change aligns with the Buddhist concept of dukkha (suffering) and the path to liberation through understanding and transcending it.

Given his deep respect for all religions and his belief in their shared truth (Mohandas Gandhi on Conversion Being Unnecessary, 2023), it's likely that Gandhi saw Buddhism as a path to truth, just like Hinduism, Islam, and other faiths. He might have seen its emphasis on non-violence, self-reflection, and compassion as valuable practices for spiritual growth and societal harmony.

Unfortunately, without specific writings or documented

statements from Gandhi directly addressing Buddhism in detail, it's difficult to provide a more comprehensive analysis of his thoughts on this particular faith

Gandhi's Thought on Jainism

While there isn't extensive information readily available on Gandhi's specific commentary about Jainism, it's known that he deeply admired the Jain principle of Ahinsa, non-violence in thought, word, and deed.

Gandhi's emphasis on Ahinsa as a cornerstone of his philosophy and activism aligns closely with Jainism's core tenet. He recognized the profound impact of Jainism on Indian culture and its contribution to the philosophy of non-violence.

Given his deep respect for all religions and his belief in their shared truth (Mohandas Gandhi on Conversion Being Unnecessary, 2023), it's likely that Gandhi viewed Jainism as a path to truth, just like Hinduism, Islam, Christianity, and other faiths. He might have seen its emphasis on non-violence and self-discipline as valuable practices for spiritual growth and societal harmony.

However, without specific writings or documented statements from Gandhi directly addressing Jainism, it's difficult to provide a more detailed or nuanced analysis of his thoughts on this particular faith.

Thought on Conversion

Mahatma Gandhi believed that conversion should be a matter of self-purification and self-realization rather than a business transaction (Mahatma Gandhi on Conversion, 2001). He felt that India, particularly Hindus, did not need conversion in the sense of changing faiths (Mahatma Gandhi on Conversion, 2001).

Gandhi emphasized the importance of understanding all faiths and believed that all religions hold truth, despite their errors (Mohandas Gandhi on Conversion Being

Unnecessary, 2023). He held deep respect for all religions, equating his veneration for them to his own faith, Hinduism (Mohandas Gandhi on Conversion Being Unnecessary, 2023). This perspective made the idea of conversion inconceivable to him (Mohandas Gandhi on Conversion Being Unnecessary, 2023).

Instead of seeking conversion to a different faith, Gandhi suggested that individuals should focus on becoming better followers of their own religion. He believed that true goodness stemmed from within, not from changing one's religious affiliation.

Furthermore, Gandhi stressed that methods of conversion should be ethical and transparent, emphasizing that faith is conveyed through genuine emotion, not forceful tactics

Critical Analysis of The Thought of Religion

Mahatma Gandhi's religious views were complex and deeply intertwined with his personal experiences and socio-political activism. While often lauded for his inclusive approach to faith, his perspective also attracted criticism. This analysis delves into the nuances of Gandhi's religious outlook, highlighting both its strengths and limitations. Gandhi advocated for a syncretic approach to religion, believing in the inherent truth of all faiths (Lal, 2013). He famously stated, "Truth is God," suggesting that different religions were merely diverse paths leading to the same ultimate reality (Lal, 2013). This inclusive stance challenged the traditional boundaries between religions, promoting interfaith dialogue huand understanding. His interpretation of the Bhagavad Gita, for instance, emphasized non-violence and self-realization rather than literal interpretations of war (Dhillon, 2023). This resonated with many, particularly in the context of India's diverse religious landscape.

However, critics argue that Gandhi's idealistic view of religion sometimes overlooked the realities of religious conflict and dogma. His emphasis on the ethical core of religion, while noble, could be seen as simplifying the complexities of religious doctrines and their potential to incite violence (Nakhre, 1976). For instance, his concept of "trusteeship," where the wealthy safeguard societal resources, drew criticism for potentially perpetuating existing power structures (Rolnick, 1962)

Gandhi's religious views, though rooted in his personal interpretation of Hinduism, transcended religious boundaries, advocating for interfaith harmony and self-transformation. While his idealistic approach had limitations, his emphasis on truth, non-violence, and the inherent goodness within all religions continues to inspire individuals and movements striving for a more just and compassionate

Conclusion

Mahatma Gandhi's approach to religion transcended the confines of dogma and ritual, positioning faith as a catalyst for personal and societal transformation. His unwavering belief in the inherent truth of all religions, encapsulated in his famous declaration "Truth is God," fostered interfaith dialogue and challenged religious exclusivism. Gandhi's emphasis on self-purification and ethical conduct, rather than blind adherence to scripture, resonated with individuals seeking a more experiential and socially engaged form of spirituality.

While his idealistic vision, particularly his concept of "trusteeship," attracted criticism for potentially overlooking the complexities of power dynamics and religious

References:
1. Rolnick charity, trusteeshipand social changes in india: A study of a political ideology, Cambridge University press:1962
2. Nakhre,1976

3. Lal 2013
4. Dhillon 2023
5. Gandhi basic education, navjeevan publishing house
6. Gandhi, M. K., Basic Education, Navajivan Publishing House, Ahmedabad: 1960.
7. Gandhi, M. K., Hind Swaraj and other writings, Cambridge University Press, Cambridge: 1997.
8. Gandhi, M. K., The Collected Works of Mahatma Gandhi, Vol. 39, Letter to C. P. Mathew, 3 November 1929.
9. Amar Chitra Katha., Mahatma Gandhi: The Early Days, Amar Chitra Katha Pvt. Ltd, Mumbai: 2009.
10. Andrews, C. F., "VII – The Teaching of Ahinsa". Mahatma Gandhi's Ideas Including Selections from His Writings.
11. Pierides Press, 2008
12. Easwaran, Eknath., Gandhi the man: how one man changed himself to change the world. Nilgiri Press, 2011

Gandhiji: Idea of Education

Prasanta Kumar Ghata
Asst. Professor of Education
Midnapore City College, West Bengal
Email: prasantasp77@gmail.com

Abstract

Education is a process of human development. It moulded and purified the learning experiences among children as well as human being. Gandhiji was a utopian who had reconstructed the new educational idea in India. His major principle of philosophy of education focus on activity and craft centered education; self-supporting and self-sufficient education; the medium of instruction is mother tongue; non-violence environment in education; the ideal of citizenship is an important feature of education, the spirit of citizenship is filled in the child. Gandhi believed in the total development of the human personality through education. He advocated that education should start with hand. It should promote dignity of labour; it should depend more on practice than theory; it should develop social awareness and the spirit of service. According to him the education should be practical which is craft based. Also he was focused on self- supporting aspect of education. Gandhi shown a keen sense for change in the education pattern and discussed at length as to the genesis and implementation schemes. He indicate to it as the synthesis between vocation and education as he had viewed it. Gandhi's concept of education is highly relevant to this day. He had clearly voiced the affairs of the deteriorating education system, about the necessity of craft-centred training, building up of character, issues of unemployment, student unrest and relevant message to the students. To this day, many of these issues have remained unaddressed, inspite of several educational reforms. Akin to the issue of politics, Gandhi did not annul the relation between religion and education. Rather, it was a effective means to inculcate cultural and moral values as prescribed in various texts and the best way to practice the virtues.

Education is one of the most defining features in the life of an individual. It enables one to acquire literacy, to analyse the situations with logic and wisdom and also use it greatly for individual as well as social development. Education, in this context, is more a way of life, a crucial instrument in character-building which enables us to determine the course of our thoughts and actions and also achieve goals and ideals of life. It is this logic to which Gandhi attached greater importance. He was undeniably one of the greatest proponents of modern education in India and his scheme of education sought to further the moral, individual, social, political and economic progress of man. His scheme of education aimed at the truthful and non-violent way of life and the ultimate goal of self-realisation. His methods were simple and practical and this was evident in his scheme of education.

Gandhi's disclosure to realities of life in South Africa taught him about life much more than what he had learnt in formal institutions of learning. It is this considerate of life which gave shape to his views on the nature of education that a free India needed.

According to Gandhiji education means "By education I mean an all-round drawing out of the best in child and man - body, mind and spirit. Literacy is not the end of education nor even the beginning. It is only one of the means whereby man and woman can be educated. Literacy in itself is no education. I would, therefore, begin the child's education by teaching it a useful handicraft and enabling it to produce from the moment it begins its training. I hold that the highest development of mind and the soul is possible under such system of education. Only every handicraft has to be taught not merely mechanically as is done today, but scientifically, i.e. the child should know the why and the wherefore of every process."

Gandhi's stayed at Africa 21 years and first experiments in education began at the Tolstoy Farm ashram in South Africa. It was much later, while living at Sevagram and in the heat of the Independence struggle, that Gandhi wrote his influential article in *Harijan* about education.

Educational Philosophy of Gandhi

With the object of realising God in an ideal moral society Gandhiji evolved a dynamic philosophy of Education. He adhered that education should bring about the development of the whole man. He explored as one of the masters of the mankind, one of the great teachers of the human society. The main principles of Gandhiji's educational philosophy are free and compulsory education from 7 and 14 years of age; activity and craft centered education; self-supporting and self-sufficient education; the medium of instruction is mother tongue; non-violence environment in education; the ideal of citizenship is an important feature of education, the spirit of citizenship is filled in the child. Gandhi believed in the total development of the human personality through education. He advocated that education should start with hand. It should promote dignity of labour; it should depend more on practice than theory; it should develop social awareness and the spirit of service.

Aims of Education

According to Gandhiji, "Physical, handicrafts drawing and music should go hand in hand in order to draw the best out of the boys and girls and create in them a real interest in their tuition." He firmly believes that the true education of mind and heart can come through a proper exercise of the bodily organs.

According to Gandhi along with the development of body, mental and soul development is also being must. He said that as the mother milk is necessary for the development of body, similarly education is necessary for the development of mental development.

Gandhi felt more urgency of the training of the heart than the training of the mind. In his opinion, "Culture of the mind must be subservient to the culture of the heart." Without education of the heart,

In the Harijan of May 27, 1939 Gandhi wrote "I value individual freedom, but you must not forget that man is essentially a social being. He has risen to his present status by learning to adjust his individualism to the requirements of social progress. Unrestricted individualism is the law of last of the jun."

Gandhi considers that cultural aspect of education as more essential than its academic aspect. Culture is the main foundation and an essential spirit of education. According to him the cultural aspect of education is more important than then a literary aspect. Culture refines personality. Pulsar is not the product of intellectual work. A man's culture cannot be jazz by the amount of his knowledge and information. It is the quality of mind and of soul which is reflected in the daily conduct of a man and in all states of human behaviour, it is the reflection of life.

The Gandhian vision of education, as mentioned earlier, has character-building as one of its aims. It is the education that guides and enables an individual to develop into a better human being and provides direction in the diverse aspects of human development. Gandhi made considerable references to religion as the sole guide from which he drew various examples to mould his attitude and views. Education also enables an individual to develop tolerance, love and humaneness which are necessary preconditions to imbibing the virtues of non-violence. Love, according to Gandhi, is akin to non-violence and truth. In the Gandhian scheme of character-building, righteousness, passion for self-help and attitude of peace are some of the astounding qualities that can be developed through right education.

Education makes it possible to develop a balanced personality and Gandhi rightly insisted on morality and spirituality as necessary ingredients for such development. No other leader has so passionately advocated the importance of moral and spiritual development as Gandhi did. Gandhi drew heavily from his life experiences and adhered to the notion of moral superiority throughout his life. He advocated faith in God as the first step towards the right education and often lamented the waning belief of the youth in God. Gandhi firmly believed that apart from imparting physical and mental training to a child, training in the moral and spiritual aspects are also crucial to personality development. While teaching the students at the Farms in South Africa, he made constant endeavours towards this training. He relied primarily on religious books and acquainted the students with a general knowledge of the scriptures; he strongly believed in the futility of imparting any training without the training of spirit and without any knowledge towards God and self-realisation. He trained the young minds through the recitation of hymns and verses from various scriptures and imparted moral training based on such readings. He realised the significance of a good teacher in imparting such education. He abhorred misconduct on the part of students and corporal punishment by teachers. His sole aim was to build moral and spiritual character through love, tolerance and non-violence. To set himself as an example, he often resorted to fasting to bring about a positive change in the attitude of the pupils.

Education for self-reliance should be job oriented to act as a safeguard against economic exploitation. They want all men to make self-supporting. So they forces in the fevour of craft-centered, self-supporting and industrial education.

Gandhiji's scheme of education emphasises dignity of manual labour through active participation in productive work. Manual labour is not at all disgraceful, it rather enlarges the heart and enriches the personality.

Gandhiji watch of the growing complexities of life in the present world and accordingly he formulated his scheme of education which would feed the child in later life. According to him education must prepare the child to face the dream realities of life and enable him to adjust with his immediate environment for complete living.

Basic education is based on the principle of activity centering round a productive and useful craft. It is activity-centred education. Here the child is not a passive recipient of knowledge but active participant in the learning process. It fosters learning by doing. Gandhiji had realistic and pragmatic view of education. He laid stress on imparting knowledge and acquisition of productive efficiency and practical skills through a craft. He followed the principle of practice preceding theory. Most of the time in the time table would be given to acquisition of practical skills and productive efficiency.

Another important aspect of the educational philosophy of Gandhiji is service and development of social awareness Service includes love for the motherland. "The end of all education should surely be service", said Gandhiji Social awareness and responsibility can be developed through the involvement of students in programmes of community service.

Gandhiji had synthetic view of life, education and culture. He synthesised all the three basic philosophies of education into his philosophy of education-idealism, naturalism and pragmatism. Like a naturalist Gandhiji emphasised self-discipline among children.

Curriculum

Gandi formulated a suitable curriculum which was intented for primary and junior Basic schools i.e., upto class V. The curriculum was same for both boys and girls. This curriculum was mainly implemented in Basic education. This curriculum is an activity-centered. He was emphasised more on 3H's (head, heart and hand) than on 3R's (reading, writing and arithmetic). The content of education were basic craft in accordance with the local needs and conditions, mother-tongue, arithmetic, social studies, general science including nature study, botany, zoology, philosophy, hygiene, chemistry and physics, art work, music and domestic science for girls in place of general science after class-V.

Gandhi on Medium of Instruction

Gandhi was totally averse to English education. Gandhi attaches greatest importance to learning in the language into which a child is born. He notes that 'English is today admittedly the world language. I would therefore accord it a place as a second, optional language, not in the school, but in the university course. We and our children must build on our own heritage'. Gandhi noted that by borrowing from another, we impoverish our own. His stress was on building knowledge in the languages spoken by people. 'I want the nation to have the treasures contained in that language and, for that matter, in other languages of the world, through its own vernaculars into Indian languages. Bringing knowledge from across the world and from within the country was to be addressed by good translations'.

Gandhi's Colonial Education

As we have seen, Gandhi had not only rejected colonial education but also put forward a radical alternative. To understand the alternative system he proposed, we need to understand his disposition towards industrialisation, which was centric to western education. Gandhi through his writings and lectures has expressed his absolute opposition to modern machinery. In his collected works, he refers to 'machinery as having impoverished India and that it was difficult to measure the harm that Manchester had done to them by producing machine-made cloth, which, in turn, ruined the internal market for locally produced hand woven goods'.

Gandhi on Higher Education

Gandhi's views on higher education are need based. To him, the aim of university education should be to turn out true servants of the people who will live and die for the country's freedom. He was of the opinion that university education should be brought in line with basic education.

Gandhi planned to revolutionise college education and relate it to national necessities. Universities would offer only those degrees which are going to absorb the knowledge for the betterment of society. According to him graduates are to be attached to different industries which should actually pay for the training of the graduates they need.

Methods of Teaching

Gandhi advocated the activity method– 'learning by doing'. Education is through the medium of and in correlation with a productive work. The industry should be such that the child is able to achieve gainful work experience through practical work. He says "Children take in much more and with less labour through ears than through their eyes." Follow- up (anukaran), lecture, explanation, question-answer, discussion, experiment, experiment, project project and shrawan, manan nidhhdhyasan (listenning, thinking and practice) methods were given great importance by Gandhi in the craft-centered method.

School

The school should be an activity school. It should be situated in a natural atmosphere. As M.S. Patel has observed "The school of Gandhi's imagination will not be a place of passive absorption of information imparted second-hand, but will be a place of work, experimentation and discovery, because it will follow an activity curriculam. The child acquires his knowledge activity and utilises it for the understanding and better control of his social environment".

Textbooks

He believed that the true text-book for the pupils is their teacher. He did not want to load the student with innumerable textbooks. Gandhi's views on textbooks are similar to that of Rousseau.

Women Education

Gandhi especially focuses on women education. He says that women are not only our sister, mother, and wife but also human creature, social creature and God's super article (kriti). So they wants to give safety to the women same as men. A wife is not a slave of the husband. Gandhi strongly favored the emancipation of women, and urged "the women to fight for their own self-development" development". He says that men-women are same as two wheel of any vehicle. He wants provide ideal form in women as Sita, Dropadi etc., with the help of education.

Co-Education

Education He accepted co-education. According to Gandhi co-education can be arranged only on primary and higher education but not on adolescence.

Adult Education

According to Gandhi the adult education is a type of mass education. Gandhiji were very unhappy because the most adults are illiterate. Gandhi wants to educate him with the help of Basic education. He wants to character development in the adult education.

Religious education

Gandhiji attach great importance to religious education. He said "life without religion is life without principle add life without principle is like a say without a radar". Religion Gandhiji does not mean dogmas or rituals. Gandhiji emphasised the moral aspect of education. He said "True religion and true morality are inseparable bound up with each other". Believes in the universal religion propounded by swami Vivekananda.

We can draw a conclusion that his concept of education is not only the eradication of illiteracy but learning by doing. He ambush the doctrine of simple living and high thinking. His education system are greatly emphasizing the culture of peace, sincere work, adherence of the cause of the nation, social minded, friendliness, right feelings, economic advancement, physical improvement and socio-cultural development. It is based on work-centre education which can give the necessary economic self-sufficiency and self-reliance.

References:

1. Gandhi, M. K., Towards New Education, Navajivan Publishing House, 1953, (ed by Bharatan Kumarappa).
2. Mukalel, Joseph C., Gandhian Education, Discovery Publishing House, New Delhi, 1997.
3. Patel, M. S., The Educational Philosophy of Mahatma Gandhi, Navajivan Publishing House, Ahmedabad, 1953.
4. Shriman Narayan, Mahatma Gandhi, The Atomic Man, Somaiya Publications Pvt.Ltd, Bombay, 1971.

Gandhi and National Spirit: Understanding Through Symbols

Vinay Kumar Hind
Research Scholar,
CMP Degree College
University of Allahabad
Email: Vinayrajhindau@gmail.com

Abstract

In this paper author is signifying the relation between the symbol and the rise of nationalism in India & the way symbolism helped in developing a sense of nationalistic spirit, by giving a brief understanding of what is symbol and how it works psychologically in a particular society. Scholars like Benedict Anderson are of the view that Indian Nationalism emerged in India because of British rule. Referring this argument the author is concentrating that how the British interference in the cultural and religious affairs pushed the third world nations in general and Indian population in particular to re-think about their glorious past having some sort of nationalist feeling and at the same time conveying the exploitative nature of imperial colonialism. What symbols did in the scenario is that it eased the medium of communication and gave a clear line of action to achieve the independence. Gradually society accepted & adopted those symbols, which now had a different meaning than before, as a method of protest. Albeit rhetoric of symbolism, was mostly circulated by the western educated middle class in India to aware masses that how the British policies are intervening the cultural and religious affairs of Indian's as a whole. Prior to that there was no such widely accepted symbols having concept of nationalism in India which can unify them against one common enemy. Considering that it becomes important to signify that how Gandhian entry into Indian politics impacted the larger section of the society and how he reinvented symbolism as a tool to fight back the imperial power and motives. Gandhi's nationalism was based on Ahinsa karma yoga, ram-Rajya, tapasya & moksha, which Gandhi has propogate well to the masses through symbolic gesture.

What is Symbolism

Symbolism was a late 19th-century art movement of French and Belgian, origin in poetry and other arts seeking to represent absolute truths symbolically through language and metaphorical images, mainly as a reaction against naturalism and realism. It is the use of signs and objects in art, films, etc to represent ideas. Symbolism isn't a new arena in the field of research & study. Based on our ability for symbolic behavior, that sets humans apart from all other species. Only the human brain has the capacity for analogic behavior or ability to think beyond immediate and obvious correlations. Humans alone have the ability to classify a diversity of objects and actions into abstracted, analogic categories and to communicate using a complex and interrelated system of symbols which we call as language. Long time's ago, pictograms were utilized by ancient Egyptians, Sumerians, and Chinese to develop their written languages. Even today, people in certain regions use pictograms to communicate concepts and messages. Pictogram is a graphical symbol that conveys meaning through its visual resemblance to a physical object.

A different way to think about symbolism is to understand that objects only have symbolic meanings in specific situations – and sometimes they don't symbolize anything at all, but we as a human has developed various meanings according to our convenience. In the words of Gertrude Stein, there are times when a rose is simply a rose. It doesn't always represent love, courtship, passion, desire, or devotion

– it is just a flower. Some flowers are red, while others are white or blue, and they don't hold any symbolic significance, in reality or in stories.

Symbols are used by people to show emotion's, ideas, or concepts in a concrete way. In fiction, authors may use basic words or events as symbols to represent deeper or more important meanings in a story. Similarly different religions use symbols to represent their beliefs. These symbols can be objects like the Christian cross or gestures like standing during prayers in Judaism. Muslims have a symbol for Muhammad that is not shown in human form. Symbols were also introduced to public consciousness in the early period through religions; in Buddhism & Jainism various symbols represent the identity of different Tirthankara's. Symbols were also used to convey the essence of religions to people. Such as Buddhist symbolism is the use of symbols (In Sanskrit pratīka) to represent certain aspects of the Buddha's Dharma (teaching). Early Buddhist symbols which remain important today include the Dharma wheel, the Indian lotus, the three jewels and the Bodhi tree. According to Karlsson, Buddhists adopted these signs because "they were meaningful, important and well-known to the majority of the people in India."

While moving to the next aspect it is important to notice that symbols have a powerful capacity to convey its internal spirit and meaning to the masses at large scale. As a point of reference Indian national movement and French revolution are the best example of ethno-symbolism & how the symbols can be utilized to create a psychological and spiritual awareness appealing the masses for one single cause. As the radicals and Jacobins gained traction in the revolutionary period, there was a dissatisfaction with 'high-fashion' because of its extravagance and association with royalty and aristocracy. It was replaced by a new form of "anti-fashion" for men and women that emphasized simplicity and modesty.

The men wore plain, dark clothing with short hair. The sans-culottes' work day outfits symbolized Jacobin egalitarianism during the terror of 1794, similarly Liberty cap and Liberty tree has also a special symbolic relationship, though it assumes new meaning with time. Semiotics sometimes changes its meaning as in, adaptation of *Swastika* doesn't always symbolizes for well being or pious, it can be mean as destruction if adopted by a extreme jingoistic leader as Hitler in Nazi Germany. Talking in Indian context the Mughal throne in India viewed as a symbolic political authority during British expansion, though it was weekend after the death of Aurangzeb. Moreover the flags of Azad Hind Fauj & the establishment of Rani Laxmibai regiment symbolizes the crucial role of women in the Independence. There are countless examples of such symbols which was established by the individuals, government and authorities to convey their ideas to the masses or with which people felt connected.

While analyzing the nature and structure of symbolic representation in general context it appears that mostly it follows the bottom to top structure based on the advancement of any society and polity. Earlier people don't have loyalty toward their king instead they obey their just next feudal lords and zamindar in west & east respectively, and it was these lords or zamidars who owe their loyalty to the supreme king, giving it a down to top structure of loyalty. In the early 20th century though India was captive of British colonialism, but it witnessed the development of modern factory system in India based on the European lines which is completely new but exploitative & it played a crucial role in creating a middle class in India. With the growth of English education in British India, people were becoming aware at that time and when the fight for India's independence started, these middle class educated people exposed the economic loot of the Raj and in the meantime it also unveiled the unnecessary interference of British in the religious and social customs of India through symbols to connect with their minds. It is not essential that the symbols always carry some meaning in direct sense but it gives essence to the appeal of collective individuals for one common goal.

Concept of Nationalism & Ethno-Symbolic Aspect

Nationalism is a belief and movement that suggests the nation should synchronize with the state. It assumes the presence and works to advance the interests of a specific nation, primarily to achieve and uphold its independence. It asserts that each nation should self-determine itself, free from outside interference (self-determination), that a nation is a natural and ideal foundation for a governing body, and that the nation is the only legitimate source of political authority. Further, its goal is to create and uphold a unified national identity by emphasizing common social traits like culture, ethnicity, geography, language, government, religion, traditions, and belief in a shared history. Additionally, it seeks to encourage national unity and solidarity.

Indian and Western scholars have expressed varying opinions on the origins of Indian nationalism. Anderson believed that the British invented, print media and railways played a role in fostering nationalism. Valentine Chirol, on the other hand, rejected the idea of Indian Nationalism, despite giving Bal Gangadhar Tilak, the title of the father of Indian unrest. Tilak initiated the Ganesh festival to promote national sentiments, which later became a symbol of unity in India. Christopher Belle, another British scholar, attempted to trace the roots of Indian nationalism back to ancient India, suggesting that concepts of good governance and patriotism have always been present in the country. In third world countries, the concept of Nationalism was used to get freedom from the Colonial powers. In this way, idea of nationalism has been used in a different sense in European and third world countries according to their socio-political and economic basis. Marxist scholars have seen Nationalism and national movement as a struggle against colonial and feudal powers.

As S. C. Dash has argued that nationalism is an abstract concept and a concrete reality. It is a positive consciousness of unity, homogeneity and national aspiration. The positive and negative aspects of nationalism are provided by the history of its development. It is linked with Sovereignty. The nationalism can be different for the different social groups in multi-cultural countries like India because of different culture, identity and political Status. Religion, culture, language, ethnicity etc. are the main sources of nationalism in Asian and African countries. Swami Vivekananda advocated spiritual nationalism, he was not opposed to borrowing ideas from other cultures, but he did emphasizes that Hindus should not abandon his faith. It was a revival of religion for Vivekananda, which would give vitality to nationalism. He was of the believe that Indian nationalism could be effective as a mass movement only if it had a religious component. Vivekananda attempted to link Hinduism and spirituality to Indian nationalism in this way. The emblem of the Ramakrishna Order designed by Swami Vivekananda is a unique and unparalleled symbol of harmony and synthesis for reverent meditation in this present age of conflict and disharmony. This symbol symbolizes his message of harmony and synthesis, leading to the perfection of life. It is indeed the clearest expression of what he really preached, what he wanted every man and woman to realize, whether in the East or the West. The goal is in this very life, to realize your true self or the self-effulgent soul, like the swan in the symbol, and through this realization to be free from all limitations, all bondages, all trivialities.

From the late 1700s onwards, starting with events like the French Revolution, promotion of popular sovereignty, development of scientific temperament & the concept of people governing themselves began to be explored by political thinkers. Slowly and gradually three main theories took shape to understand the rise of nationalism. First one is 'Primordial' which suggests that nations or ethnic identities are inherent, unchanging, and ancient, with proponents arguing that each person possesses a predetermined ethnic identity that is not influenced by historical events. Second is "Modernization theory" as advocated by leading scholars like Benedict Anderson, Ernest Gellner, and Eric Hobsbawn, attributes the rise of nationalism to the period of modernization in the late 18th century as key factors contributing to the development of nationalism include industrialization and democratic uprisings. Supporters of this idea, view nations as "imagined communities" and nationalism as a "created tradition" where a common feeling fosters a sense of collective identity and unites individuals in political unity. And third theory is of "Ethno-symbolism" which describes nationalism as the result of symbols, myths, and traditions. This theory is connected to the research of Anthony D. Smith. Ethno symbolism was created to challenge modernist ideas about nationalism. It focuses on how nations have historical ties to ethnic symbols, myths, values, and traditions that were passed down from past generations. Ethno-symbolist scholars, like the modernists, believe that nationalism is a product of modern times, which sets them apart from primordialists.

Symbolic Representation in history

Symbols move along in history, as time passes, the social role becomes important in legitimizing it. There are presence of many such symbols in history which were used in one or another sense in the past but with the time due to social, political, economic and religious changes, the same symbols were used as a new weapon with new meaning of it. And this language of symbols have long history from wagging wars and sending peace forces to establish the world order and to impose authority in the political and social ladder in India or else were. In the context of India the usage and significance of symbolic representation has been gradually changed over a period of time from ancient to modern times and to many extent it's still going on in contemporary period.

There are symbols which helped the ruling elite to establish their authority as pointed out by Upinder Singh in her book that ancient literature's speak of 'Ashvamedha yagya working as a tool to legitimize rule. The Ashvamedha was a horse sacrifice ritual followed by the Śrauta tradition of Vedic religion. Ancient Indian kings used a special way to show they were in charge: If anyone, in the area the horse traveled through tried to challenge the king's power by fighting the soldiers, they could. But if no one was able to harm the horse during the year, it would be brought back to the king's city. Then, the horse would be sacrificed, and the king would be officially declared as the rightful ruler.

In medieval India, symbolic legitimacy played a crucial role in reinforcing monarchic authority. The Tamil tradition's "Sengol" exemplified this, reminding kings of their duty to rule justly. Similarly, Delhi Sultanate's Sultans obtained symbolic charters from Caliphs, legitimizing their authority in Sindh. Under the Mughal regime, a symbolic relationship existed between supreme kings and regional rulers. Despite Aurangzeb's demise, the Nawab of Bengal and Nizam of Hyderabad continued paying token taxes and printing coins bearing Mughal emperors' names. This persisted even as Mughal authority waned, underscoring the throne's enduring symbolic supremacy.

Throughout medieval India, iconographic representations conveyed complex meanings to the masses through available means. Symbolism facilitated the expression of power dynamics, cultural values, and legitimacy, shaping the region's cultural and political landscape.

The significance of symbolism in modern Indian nationalism warrants analysis through a rural social context lens. Researchers note that symbols like the lotus and bread represented rebellion during the 1857 war against British rule. The Chapatti movement, emerging in Mathura, utilized chapattis as a symbol of resistance, with protesters distributing them widely. Magistrate Mark Thornhill discovered chapattis were transported up to 300 kilometers nightly. J. W. Sherer, Collector of Fatehpur, observed that this movement effectively created unease among the population.

Indian handicrafts, preferred in British households, were adopted as symbols to boycott foreign markets and undermine imperial economic power. Historians argue that cultural and religious symbols profoundly impacted the Indian masses, particularly given widespread economic unawareness. Symbols facilitated unity, as seen in Bengal's anti-partition agitation, where Rabindranath Tagore and Ramendra Sunder Trivedi promoted Hindu-Muslim unity through symbolic gestures like "raksha-bandhan" and "arandhan". Effective symbolism helped unite India's uneducated masses against western imperialism, leveraging religious and cultural lines to foster nationalism.

While investigating the Gandhian phase of movements it shows sign that Gandhi's national sprit is all inclusive and based on Ahinsa, Karma yoga, Ram-Rajya, Tapasya & Moksha, which Gandhi has propogate well to the masses through symbolic gesture. The Ram Rajya being discussed here is not to be confused with today's popular concept of Ram Rajya. Gandhi dreamed of a Ram Rajya where there is complete good governance and transparency. He wrote in Young India "By Ram Rajya I do not mean Hindu Raj. My Ram Rajya means the Kingdom of God. For me, Rama and Rahim are one and the same; I accept no other God than the God of truth and righteousness. Whether the Rama of my imagination ever lived on this earth or not, the ancient ideal of the Ramayana is undoubtedly one of true democracy in which even a very bad citizen is assured of speedy justice without a complicated and costly process". Though earlier, religious and cultural means were used to unite a large uneducated Indian class against the imperialism and colonialism of the British rule, whereas during Gandhi's era, efforts were made to unite people with the understanding of morality, mutual & universal brotherhood, economic exploitation etc. And when a large uneducated class has to be made to understand the exploitation being done on them, the role of symbols becomes important. Focusing on the Gandhian symbolism by emphasizing the women aspect, Madhu Kishwar writes, "The Sita or Draupaadi of Gandhi was not the commonly accepted lifeless stereotypes of subservience. They were symbols, versatile enough to incorporate the qualities that he chose to endow with them. In fact, sometimes, he tended to overburden the symbols with meanings they were ill-equipped to carry. For instance, Sita was used as a symbol of swadeshi, to convey an anti-imperialist message, she only wore 'cloth made in India' or home-spun and thus kept her heart and body pure. Further more, 'Sita was no slave of Rama'. She portrayed as being able to say no even to her husband if he approached her carnally against her will. Gandhi's Sita was not a helpless creature". This notion of pureness gave a huge impetus to the women's participation in congress session and their constructive programs during Swadeshi movement. At a meeting at Allahabad in November 1920, Gandhi convey to women that in the days of Ravana's rule, even goddess Sita had to wear for 14 years a rough garment made from the barks of trees (Gandhi, Vol 19: 44-45). Wearing swadeshi was thus a pious duty of women for the liberation of the country from the imperial loops.

Beside the genesis of Gandhian ideology to establish symbolic representation he believed that the Charkha was important for giving respect to manual labor & khadi was seen as a symbol of self-reliance and regeneration, it seemed to provide solutions to various socio-economic problems. He saw it as a way to bring together the people of India. By listening to the spinning wheel, Gandhi found a connection to the unity of life and the harmony of the world. The Charkha also gave people something new to focus on during their daily spinning time. Gandhi's persistent promotion of spinning yarn with a charkha and wearing khadi aimed to instill a sense of nationalism and freedom in every household, reaching even the most isolated villages.

For Gandhi, the spinning wheel was a way to identify with the poor. It was intimately connected to basic needs of millions, i.e., food and clothing which are essential. He wanted them to be self-sufficient. He believed that poverty resulted in moral deterioration. Charkha wanted to help the homeless and marginalized. Several of his tours were intended to organize and finance the spinning wheel project. The spinning wheel was once the symbol of India's poverty and backwardness, which later became a symbol of self-reliance and non-violence, as Gandhi used it. Khadi helped him to carry his message of swadeshi and swaraj to the people and establish contact with them. And this effort of symbolic representation helped to make the fight against colonial rule more tangible and relatable to the common people.

Conclusion

The significance of symbols and symbolic representations in transmitting ideologies and galvanizing collective action within traditional societies is well-established. In the Indian context, symbols played a pivotal role in fostering mass consciousness regarding cultural values and practices. Notably, regional leaders such as Sidhu-Kanhu and Ganga Narayan effectively mobilized individuals through symbolic means during the Indian freedom movement. Furthermore,

Mahatma Gandhi's strategically-designed symbols resonated with the broader populace and garnered widespread acceptance, both during and after his lifetime.

The enduring relevance of symbols Is evident in contemporary India, as exemplified by the Ashokan pillar, Sengol, and the nation's new Parliament. Consequently, examining symbols offers a valuable framework for understanding the complexities of history, society, religion, and culture.

Reference:

1. Anderson, B. (1983). Imagined communities: Reflections on the origin and spread of nationalism. Verso.
2. Erikson, T. H. & Nielsen, F. S. (2013). The power of symbols. In A history of anthropology (pp. 120-137). Pluto Press.
3. Gandhi, M. (1997). Hind swaraj and other writings. Cambridge University Press.
4. Gupta, C. (2012). "Fashioning" swadeshi: Clothing women in colonial North India. Economic and Political Weekly, 47(42), 76-84.
5. Habib, I. (1995). Gandhi and the national movement. Social Scientist, 23(4/6), 3-15.
6. Habib, I. (2017). Nationalism in India: Past and present. Social Scientist, 45(3/4), 3-8.
7. Hobsbawm, E. & Ranger, T. (1983). The invention of tradition. Cambridge University Press.
8. Kishwar, M. (1985). Gandhi on women. Economic and Political Weekly, 20(40), 1691-1702.
9. Prayer, M. (2001). The "Gandhians" of Bengal: Nationalism, social reconstruction and cultural orientations 1920-1942. Rivista Degli Studi Orientali, 74, 1-363.

10. Rana, L. N. (1999). Gandhi's constructive programme in Jharkhand (1924-1929). Proceedings of the Indian History Congress, 60, 737-751.
11. Singh, U. & Pearson. (2013). A history of ancient and early medieval India: From the Stone Age to the 12th century (3rd ed.). Pearson.

Mahatma Gandhi and Panchayatii Raj System

Dr. Sachin Verma
Assistant Professor,
Department of Sociology
Government College, Hasanpur, Amroha
Email: vermasachin469@gmail.com

Abstract

Panchayati Raj in India has its origins in the Vedic period (1700 BC). Since the Vedic period, the village (gram) has been considered the basic unit for regional self-governance in the country. Panchayati Raj Day is celebrated every year on 24 April in India as the foundation of democracy. An overview of the Panchayati Raj system reveals that the reason for celebrating Panchayati Raj Day on 24 April is the 73rd Constitutional Amendment Act, 1992, which came into effect from 24 April 1993. India is the largest democracy in the world and any country, state or institution can be considered truly democratic only when there is appropriate decentralization of powers and the flow of development is from lower to upper level instead of from upper to lower level. In order to make the flow of development from lower to upper level in the Panchayati Raj system, Panchayati Raj was given the status of a separate ministry in the year 2004. The concept of formation and empowerment of Panchayati Raj in India is based on the philosophy of Mahatma Gandhi. In the words of Gandhiji-

"True democracy does not run the state by sitting at the centre, but it runs with the cooperation of every person in the village."

Mahatma Gandhi advocated panchayati raj as the foundation of India's political system, as a decentralized form of government in which each village would be responsible for its own affairs. The term for such an approach was gram swaraj ("village self-rule"). Instead, India developed a highly centralized form of government. However, this has been tempered by the delegation of many administrative functions to the local level, empowering elected village panchayatis. There are significant differences between the traditional panchayati raj system, which Gandhi envisioned, and the system formally adopted in India in 1992. Households associated with the panchayati raj system have seen increased participation in local affairs. The reservation policy for women in panchayati councils has also substantially increased women's participation and shaped the focus of development to include more domestic issues.

Keywords: Panchayati raj overview, 73rd Constitutional Amendment, Decentralization, Village Self-Rule, Reservation Policy, Democracy etc.

Introduction

Panchayati Raj (Council of Five Officials) is the local self-government system of villages in rural India, as opposed to urban and suburban municipalities.

It consists of Panchayati Raj Institutions (PRIs) through which the self-governance of villages is realised. They are entrusted with the task of "strengthening economic development, social justice and implementation of Central and State Government schemes including 29 subjects listed in the Eleventh Schedule".

Part IX of the Indian Constitution is the section of the Constitution dealing with Panchayatis. It stipulates that in states or union territories with more than two million inhabitants there are three levels of PRIs:

• Gram Panchayati at the village level
• Panchayati Samiti (Block Samiti, Mandal Parishad) at the block level
• Zilla Panchayati (Zilla Parishad) at the district level

States or union territories with less than two million inhabitants have only two levels of PRIs. The Gram

Panchayati consists of all registered voters residing within the area of the Gram Panchayati and is the organisation through which the residents of the village participate directly in local government. Elections for members of panchayatis at all levels are held every five years. According to federal law, panchayatis must include members of scheduled castes (SCs) and scheduled tribes (STs) in the same proportion as the general population and at least one-third of all seats and chairperson positions must be reserved for women. Some states have increased the minimum proportion required for women to half.

Jawaharlal Nehru inaugurated Panchayati Raj in Nagaur on 2 October 1959. The day was chosen on the occasion of Mahatma Gandhi's birthday. Gandhi wanted Gram Swaraj through Panchayati Raj. Rajasthan was the first state to implement it. Nehru inaugurated Panchayati Raj in Andhra Pradesh on 11 October 1959 on the occasion of Dussehra. This system gradually became established all over India. This system was revised in 1992 with the 73rd Constitutional Amendment.

Balwant Rai Mehta Committee, headed by Member of Parliament Balwant Rai Mehta, was a committee appointed by the Government of India in January 1957 to examine the work of the Community Development Programme (1952) and the National Extension Service (1953) and to suggest measures to improve their work. The recommendation of the committee was implemented by the NDC in January 1958, and this set the stage for introducing Panchayati Raj institutions all over the country. The committee recommended the establishment of a scheme of 'democratic decentralisation', which eventually came to be known as Panchayatii Raj. This resulted in the establishment of a three-tier Panchayati Raj system: Gram Panchayati at the village level, Panchayati Samiti at the block level and Zila Parishad at the district level.

The Constitution (73rd Amendment) Act 1992 came into force on 24 April 1993 to provide constitutional status to Panchayati Raj institutions in India. With effect from 24 December 1996, this amendment was extended to panchayatis in tribal areas of eight states: Andhra Pradesh, Gujarat, Himachal Pradesh, Maharashtra, Madhya Pradesh, Odisha and Rajasthan. This amendment includes provisions for the transfer of powers and responsibilities to the Panchayatis for preparation of economic development plans and social justice as well as for implementation in respect of 29 subjects listed in the Eleventh Schedule of the Constitution, and also includes the capacity to levy and collect appropriate taxes, fees, tolls and charges. The aim of the Act is to provide for a three-tier system of Panchayati Raj for all States having a population of more than two million, to hold regular Panchayati elections every five years, to reserve seats for Scheduled Castes, Scheduled Tribes and women, to appoint a State Finance Commission to make recommend-dations regarding the financial powers of Panchayatis and to constitute a District Planning Committee. Elections

Members are directly elected at all levels of Panchayati Raj, while at the intermediate and district levels, the chairperson/chairman are indirectly elected from among the elected members. At the village level, the chairperson/chairman is elected in a manner prescribed by the state government. Some states use direct elections to elect the chairperson of the village panchayati, while others use indirect elections (elected from among the members).

For the purpose of representation, the village panchayati, block panchayati and district panchayati are divided into constituencies/wards, each of which is represented by an elected member. These members constitute the Panchayati Council. In some states, there are ex-officio members at the block or district levels that are not elected members, such as MLAs, MPs, etc.

Tenure

The term of Panchayati Raj Institutions at all levels is 5 years and elections are conducted by the respective State Election Commission.

Reservation of seats

Reservation of seats in Panchayati Raj Institutions is a mechanism to ensure representation of marginalized and disadvantaged sections of society. These reservations usually include seats for Scheduled Castes (SC), Scheduled Tribes (ST) and women. The percentage of reserved seats varies from state to state depending on demographic factors and social considerations.

The system in practice

Over the years, Panchayatis have been dependent on federal and state grants to sustain themselves financially. The absence of compulsory elections to the Panchayati Council and irregular meetings of the Sarpanch have reduced the dissemination of information to villagers, leading to greater state regulation. Many Panchayatis have been successful in achieving their goals through collaboration between various bodies and political mobilization of previously under-represented groups in India. Many Panchayatis face the barrier of literacy for the participation of villagers, with most development plans being on paper. However, households connected to the Panchayati Raj system have seen increased participation in local affairs. The reservation policy for women in panchayati councils has also substantially increased women's participation and shaped the focus of development to include more domestic issues.

Conclusion

In 1992, the 73rd Amendment was passed, which changed the role of women in Panchayati Raj. The 73rd Amendment established the reservation of one-third of the seats for women in basic village councils. This reservation has led to a significant increase in women's participation in local governance. Women are now serving as elected representatives in various positions, including Sarpanch (village head) and Panchayati members. Women also demonstrated their positive and enlightened thinking in the Panchayati to respond to the government's expectations from women. The supportive actions of their families are encouraging women to attend every PRI (Panchayati Raj in India) meeting. Even though the bureaucracy was completely male-dominated, Gandhiji hoped that Panchayati Raj could be the framework for an independent Indian political system. The 73rd Amendment was also opposed because the reservation of seats meant that upper caste people had to accept marginalized caste women in the political empower-rment system. Indirectly, this leads to corruption when the government dedicates funds to grassroots panchayatis where the resources and money are exploited by bureaucratic channels.

References:

1. Renukadevi Nagashetty (2015). "IV. Structure and Organisational Aspects of Panchayatii Raj Institutions in Karnataka and Gulbarga District". Problems and Challenges in the Functioning of Panchayatii Raj Institutions in India. A Case Study of Gulbarga District Panchayati (PhD). p. 93. hdl:10603/36516
2. Sharma, Shakuntala (1994). Grass Root Politics and Panchayatii Raj. Deep & Deep Publications. p. 131.
3. Singh, Surat (2004). Decentralised Governance in India: Myths and Realities. Deep & Deep Publications. p. 74. ISBN 978-81-7629-577-2.
4. Singh, Vijendra (2003). "Chapter 5: Panchayatii Raj and Gandhi". Panchayatii Raj and Rural Development: Volume 3, Perspectives on Panchayatii Raj Administration. Studies in Public Administration. New

Delhi: Sarup & Sons. pp. 84-90. ISBN 978-81-7625-392-5.

5. Sisodia, R. S. (1971). "Gandhiji's Vision of Panchayatii Raj". Panchayati Aur Insaan. 3 (2): 9-10.

6. Sharma, Manohar Lal (1987). Gandhi and Democratic Decentralisation in India. New Delhi: Deep & Deep Publications.

7. Sitaram, Mukkavilli (1990). Citizen Participation in Rural Development. Mittal Publications. p. 34. ISBN 9788170992271OCLC 23346237.

8. Dwivedi, Ritesh; Poddar, Krishna (1 December 2013). "Functioning of Panchayatii Raj Institutions in India: A Status Paper". Studies. 3 (2). doi: 10.21567/study.v3i2.10183

9. Singhal, Vipin (17 November 2015). "Dynamics of Panchayatii Raj Institutions - Problems and Prospects". Rochester, NY. SSRN 2692119

10. Kaul, Shashi; Sahni, Shraddha (1 July 2009). "Study on Women's Participation in Panchayatii Raj Institution". Studies on Home and Community Sciences. 3 (1): 29–38. doi: 10.1080/09737189.2009.11885273. ISSN 0973-7189.

11. Kaushik, Anupama; Shaktawat, Gayatri (December 2010). "Women in Panchayatii Raj Institutions: A Case Study of Chittaurgarh Zila Parishad". Journal of Developing Societies. 26 (4): 473–483. doi: 10.1177/0169796X1002600404. ISSN 0169-796X.

12. Tiwari, Nupur (January 2008). "Women in Panchayatii Raj". Indian Journal of Public Administration. 54 (1): 34–47. doi:10.1177/0019556120080103. ISSN 0019-5561.

13. Shourie, Arun (1990). Individuals, Institutions, Processes: How One Can Strengthen the Other in India Today. New Delhi, India: Viking. ISBN 978-0-670-83787-8.